PRAISE FOR THE NOVELS OF HOLLY ROBINSON

Haven Lake

"Family, secrets, and how to love each other. No one does it better than Holly Robinson."

—Susan Straight, National Book Award finalist and author of *Between Heaven and Here*

"*Haven Lake* is an emotionally charged novel about love, loss, and the intricacies of modern family. Robinson weaves a plot so poignant you won't be able to put it down."

—Emily Liebert, author of *When We Fall*

"Holly Robinson's spicy yet tender *Haven Lake* will have you crushing on Hannah, cheering for Dylan, and keeping your fingers crossed for Sydney. It's an absorbing read about trust and taking chances that will keep you up well past your bedtime."

—Kristin Bair O'Keeffe, author of *The Art of Floating*

"In *Haven Lake*, a troubled boy forces a mother and daughter to reexamine the past and the tragedies that drove them apart. Robinson expertly depicts the ways in which we hurt the ones we love most and our propensity for forgiveness. Real and raw, the characters stayed with me long after the last page was turned."

—Lorrie Thomson, author of *What's Left Behind*

continued . . .

Written by today's freshest new talents and selected by New American Library, NAL Accent novels touch on subjects close to a woman's heart, from friendship to family to finding our place in the world. The Conversation Guides included in each book are intended to enrich the individual reading experience, as well as encourage us to explore these topics together—because books, and life, are meant for sharing.

Visit us online at penguin.com.

Beach Plum Island

"Robinson masterfully paints the portrait of a damaged family in the quake of a tragedy . . . a thoughtful exploration of the fragility, and the tenacity, of the ties that bind." —T. Greenwood, author of *Bodies of Water*

"[An] absorbing, bighearted novel."

—Elizabeth Graver, author of *The End of the Point*

"Holly Robinson is a natural-born storyteller, and her tale of three mismatched sisters and the lost brother they search for will keep you turning those pages as she quietly but deftly breaks your heart. I loved every single one of her characters, and you will too; here is a novel to savor and share."

—Yona Zeldis McDonough, author of *You Were Meant for Me*

[A] triumphant family saga filled with heart and hope. I couldn't put it down!" —Amy Sue Nathan, author of *The Glass Wives*

The Wishing Hill

A *Ladies' Home Journal* Great Summer Read

"One of the deep pleasures of *The Wishing Hill* is Holly Robinson's keen sense of story. Another is her willingness to give all her characters, young and old, second chances. Many readers will surely glimpse themselves in this vivid, compassionate novel."

—Margot Livesey, author of *The Flight of Gemma Hardy*

"Who and what make us who we really are? In Robinson's luminous novel of buried secrets, she explores how the past can jump-start the future, how motherhood can be more than genetics, and why finding yourself sometimes depends on discovering the truth in others."

—Caroline Leavitt, *New York Times* bestselling author of *Is This Tomorrow*

"A novel that sings: of love for a child, loss and regret for a life, and the quiet triumphs of survival and finding each other again."

—Susan Straight, National Book Award finalist and author of *Between Heaven and Here*

"A story about love, loss, secrets, and finding out where we're really supposed to be in our lives. As Juliet navigates the terrain of divorce, pregnancy, and exploring new love, her greatest gift comes from a place she never expected to find it: revisiting her unsettled past. I loved this book."

—Maddie Dawson, author of *The Opposite of Maybe*

"Sparkles with warmth and wit while tackling the prickly sides of a mother-daughter relationship. . . . With deeply emotional passages tempered by humor and some surprising romance, Robinson's portrayal of family members striving to forge deeper connections after self-imposed absences is compelling. Fans of Martha Southgate and Heidi W. Durrow will enjoy this tender, full-hearted tale of quiet triumphs, mended fences, and new connections."

—*Booklist*

"There are relationship twists aplenty. . . . Robinson's fiction debut is a good beach read for those who like to reflect on the complexity and messiness of family relationships."

—*Kirkus Reviews*

"So appealing and addictive."

—Novel Escapes (4½ stars)

"An . . . engaging read, *The Wishing Hill* is an excellent choice for book lovers who can relate to the sometimes thorny aspects of family life."

—*Merrimack Valley Magazine*

ALSO BY HOLLY ROBINSON

The Wishing Hill

Beach Plum Island

Haven Lake

Holly Robinson

NAL Accent
Published by the Penguin Group
Penguin Group (USA) LLC, 375 Hudson Street,
New York, New York 10014

USA | Canada | UK | Ireland | Australia | New Zealand | India | South Africa | China
penguin.com
A Penguin Random House Company

First published by NAL Accent, an imprint of New American Library,
a division of Penguin Group (USA) LLC

First Printing, April 2015

Copyright © Holly Robinson, 2015
Conversation Guide copyright © Penguin Group (USA) LLC, 2015
Penguin supports copyright. Copyright fuels creativity, encourages diverse voices, promotes free speech, and creates a vibrant culture. Thank you for buying an authorized edition of this book and for complying with copyright laws by not reproducing, scanning, or distributing any part of it in any form without permission. You are supporting writers and allowing Penguin to continue to publish books for every reader.

REGISTERED TRADEMARK—MARCA REGISTRADA

LIBRARY OF CONGRESS CATALOGING-IN-PUBLICATION DATA:

Robinson, Holly, 1955–
Haven lake/Holly Robinson.
p. cm.
ISBN 978-0-451-47149-9 (softcover)
1. Family secrets—Fiction. 2. Dysfunctional families—Fiction.
3. Mothers and daughters—Fiction. 4. Domestic fiction. I. Title.
PS3618.O3258H39 2015
813'.6—dc23 2014033335

Printed in the United States of America
1 3 5 7 9 10 8 6 4 2

Set in Adobe Caslon Pro • *Designed by Elke Sigal*

PUBLISHER'S NOTE
This is a work of fiction. Names, characters, places, and incidents either are the product of the author's imagination or are used fictitiously, and any resemblance to actual persons, living or dead, business establishments, events, or locales is entirely coincidental.

For my husband, Dan, the keeper of my heart.
And for our children, Drew, Blaise, Taylor, Maya, and Aidan:
you make everything I do matter more.

Haven Lake

CHAPTER ONE

Her cell phone buzzed, angry as a wasp in her pocket. Sydney debated whether to answer it. She'd forgotten her headset and Route 1 was crawling with cops. Still, what if it was something urgent?

She'd scheduled only two appointments on Wednesday, because the first was a school visit in Quincy and she knew she'd hit a nightmare of snarled traffic through Boston in both directions. It had been a good visit—the teacher was creative, even compassionate toward Sydney's third-grade client—but now her nerves were on edge. She hated missing calls. You never knew when a client was going to be in crisis.

The phone stopped, but just as Sydney's shoulders relaxed, it started vibrating again. That did it. She pulled into the parking lot of the Agawam Diner and glanced at the incoming number. Dylan's school. Various scenarios played out in her mind: sixteen-year-old Dylan mouthing off in class, an unpaid tuition bill, Dylan throwing up in the nurse's office.

She wasn't Dylan's stepmother yet, but she and Gary had been seeing each other for two years and planned to marry in October. She'd grown fond of Dylan, trying to spend time with him without pushing too hard. Since Gary was a surgeon and couldn't take calls in the OR, she was listed as Dylan's alternate emergency contact.

Outside, the May morning was chilly and the gray sky was spitting raindrops that pelted her windshield, making Sydney wince even though she wasn't getting wet. "Hello, this is Dr. Bishop."

"Ah, Dr. Bishop," Gloria said. "I'm just calling to check on Dylan."

"Yes? What's the problem?" Sydney had met the school secretary a few times. She'd hate to be on the woman's bad side. Gloria had a gladiator's shoulders and an accountant's passion for details. Every school should be lucky enough to have someone like that in the front office.

"I don't know." Gloria sounded peevish. "That's why I'm calling. Is Dylan sick again? Is that why he went home after first period? You do realize, I hope, that this is his seventh absence in a month. It's his junior year and he's in two AP classes. He can't afford more absences."

Sydney was confused. "Wait a second. I dropped Dylan off myself this morning. Are you saying he's not in school? He *left*?"

"Yes. No one has seen him since first period and he never signed out. I did try to call his father," Gloria added. "Dr. Katz is extremely difficult to reach."

Sydney felt her face burn at the rebuke. "I'm sorry. Gary's probably in surgery." She hated feeling so defensive, but she was new at this parenting thing and, despite her profession as an educational psychologist, always felt like she was getting it wrong. "I'm sure Dylan's at home. Let me check. Did you try his cell phone?"

"We don't keep student cell phone numbers on record," Gloria said. "Students aren't allowed to use cell phones during the school day."

Right, Sydney thought, thinking of every kid who came into her office texting with the urgency of bomb technicians defusing explosives. "I'm sure that's a very good policy on paper," she said before she could stop herself, then rang off.

Dylan's cell phone went straight to voice mail, so Sydney called the house. No answer. She tried Gary's cell next; of course it went straight to voice mail, too.

What if something was really wrong with Dylan? She left a message and decided to wait a few minutes to see if Gary would return the call. That would at least give her a chance to grab some lunch in the diner to go; her hands were shaking, though whether from nerves or hunger, she couldn't tell.

Her office was in a historic brick mill building on the Merrimack River that had once housed a family of famous New England silversmiths and was now a beehive of medical specialists. There were five practitioners with Sydney in the Children's Mental Health practice—a psychiatrist, two other psychologists, and two social workers. And Ella, of course, the secretary who mothered them all. Right now, for instance, Ella was tirelessly helping Sydney plan her wedding.

At her desk, Sydney wolfed down the turkey club, chips, cookie, and soda she'd hastily picked up at the Agawam—bad, *bad* girl, inhaling carbs and sweets instead of slimming with salads—then paced her office. Five more minutes. Then she'd phone Gary's secretary and ask her to page him in the OR.

From the window of her second-floor office, the Merrimack River looked oddly flattened out, like a sheet of metal beneath the heavy gray sky. She loved working here because the view made her remember the history of this area, and how manufactured goods had once been transported from factories in Lowell and Haverhill up this river to Newburyport. Everything from combs to carriages had then sailed across the ocean to Europe on clipper ships built right here.

The magnolia trees along the riverbank were in bloom. The pink blossoms reminded Sydney of how her mother once convinced her as a child that fairies used them as teacups. This wasn't an entirely happy memory, so Sydney shook it off as tension pushed like a fist against the back of her neck. She was having trouble taking a full breath.

Sydney recognized the onset of a panic attack and began talking herself down from the proverbial ledge. She'd learned to do this in therapy years ago: *You're happy,* she reminded herself. *What's past is past. You're beyond all that now.*

This positive self-talk helped ease her breathing, but Sydney couldn't banish her immediate worries. Why had Dylan left school without telling anyone? Some of the other kids at school had cars, licenses. What if he'd gone off in somebody's car, and even now the car was nose-first in a tree?

Another possibility: Dylan could really be sick. Feverish. Even unconscious. There had been a meningitis outbreak at one of the universities recently.

A more likely explanation: Dylan was just ditching classes. But that idea led her down a dark mental corridor to her fear that Dylan's increasing disinterest in school, his lack of engagement in anything beyond computer games, was related to Gary marrying her.

She had a client coming at two o'clock. It was nearly one now. Did she have time to drive home to check on Dylan?

Whatever she did, she'd better let Gary know what was going on. Maybe he'd take charge. Dylan was his son, after all. That's the way it should be. Sydney had vowed she wasn't going to be one of those stepmothers who took over. She'd seen too many of those in her practice.

She phoned Gary's office again. To her relief, the receptionist said Gary was out of the OR and put him on the phone.

"Hey, sweetie. I was just about to call you back," Gary said. "What's up?"

The sound of his deep voice, slow and with a hint of Virginia, calmed her. Gary would know what to do. She heard him chewing and smiled. Probably wolfing down one of his cardboard-tasting fiber bars for lunch. There was a reason Gary still weighed the same at forty-six that he had in college.

Sydney wished she could say the same, but no. She was ten years younger than he was, but her curves kept getting curvier. "Sorry to bother you," she said, "but Dylan's school called and he's not there. Have you heard anything from him?"

"I don't think so. Hang on." Gary put her on hold, then came back on the line. "Nope. No missed calls on my cell, and Amber says he hasn't tried the office. When did he leave school?"

"After first period. He's not picking up his phone. I think one of us should go home and look for him."

"He's probably just playing hooky. It's a perfect rainy day for computer games, right?"

"I don't know. It does seem like he's been sick a lot lately. And you know he's not eating enough."

"Yeah, well, if he'd play sports and get off the damn computer, he'd have a better appetite and a healthier immune system."

An old argument. Gary could be right. At the same time, Sydney secretly sympathized with Dylan, who was clearly irritated whenever his father brought up his own stellar sports records. Gary had been a Division I pitcher and had a trophy case in the den to prove it. He'd been drafted by a major-league team senior year, but had chosen to go to medical school instead.

"Do you want to check on him, or should I?" she asked.

Sydney could hear Gary tapping something into his computer, probably checking his schedule. He was the king of multitasking. She admired this quality, though less when she was only one of his many tasks.

"I hate to ask, but could you possibly do it?" he said. "I've got two more surgeries this afternoon and the patients are already prepped and waiting."

"Sure, no problem."

They exchanged a quick note about dinner—salmon, Gary's turn to cook, thank God—and hung up. Sydney glanced at her watch. She'd drive home, have a quick word with Dylan, then call the school on her way back to the office, reassuring them that everything was under control.

Tonight, though, they'd have to sit down for a family meeting, find out what was really going on. Gloria was right: this was junior year. Dylan couldn't afford to blow his final exams.

She went out to the reception area, where Marco Baez was talking with Ella and flipping through his mail, making Ella laugh. Sydney had joined the practice eight years ago after earning her doctorate in educational psychology; her specialty was assessing school performance problems and evaluating children for learning disabilities. Marco was the clinical psychologist in the group. He had joined the practice last year; she had already referred several of her most troubled clients to him with positive results.

She had also seen the effect he had on women. Marco—with his soccer player's wiry build and curly black hair—turned heads whenever mothers were in the waiting room. Even the older teachers sat up straighter to adjust their sweaters during school meetings he attended.

Sydney was amused by him, but nothing more. Marco was fun to have around and good eye candy, but he was a player socially as well as on the soccer field, judging by the various attractive women she saw accompanying him to office parties. She'd been there and done that. She didn't need any more players in her life.

"Hey, Ella, I've got to run home," she said, "but I should be back before my two o'clock."

"Okay," Ella said. "Want an umbrella? It's nasty out there."

"No, I'm fine. The car's close."

"All right. See you later."

Annoyingly, Marco dogged her out of the office and into the hallway, where he stood too close as she waited for the elevator. "You okay?" he asked.

Sydney sighed. It was often a drag working with other mental health professionals. Nothing went unnoticed and they were always checking in with one another. It was like being screened at an airport, only this was an empathy check; she'd prefer a quick X-ray anytime. She'd gone into educational testing precisely because it was the most analytical field of psychology.

"I'm fine," she said. "It's just Gary's son, Dylan. He left school and we don't know where he is. I'm going home to see if he's there."

"I'm sure he is," Marco said.

"You don't know one thing about him."

He surprised her with a grin. "You're right. I apologize. I only said that because I want it to be true for your sake."

"Me, too."

"Nobody could be a better friend to him than you are, Sydney."

"I'm not trying to be his friend. I'm trying to be his stepmother."

"To a teenager grieving his mom like Dylan is, a good friend might be more important."

Sydney jabbed at the elevator button. "Gary says I baby him." She hadn't meant to confide this to Marco, or to anyone, but the hallway was empty and here he was, Dr. Sympathy with his spaniel eyes. "He says Dylan needs to man up and play sports, get off the computer."

"Depends on what he's doing on the computer," Marco suggested. "For some kids, that's a social lifeline. Or a future career. I'm sure Bill Gates spent plenty of time on the computer in high school."

Interesting. Sydney would have pegged Marco as one of those ban-the-computer types, with all of his big talk around the office about building good family communication skills. But there was no time to get into that now. The elevator arrived and Sydney stepped into it, ready to face whatever waited for her at home.

He hadn't expected it to be such a freakin' drag to hitchhike. Dylan had caught a ride with one of the seniors from his school in Hamilton to the center of Newburyport. From there he'd walked up Route 1 to Route 110 in Amesbury, where he'd stood for two hours in the rain by the on-ramp to Route 495 with his cardboard sign reading "Seattle" in dripping Magic Marker. Finally a guy in a battered pickup truck pulled over.

Dylan hesitated before getting into the truck. He'd seen plenty of those movies where the idiot kids get sliced and diced by some masked guy with a chain saw. But the driver of this truck wasn't evil looking. Just some old dude with paint-spattered work boots.

"Don't see many hitchhikers these days," the guy said as they rattled up the highway ramp.

"Yeah, well, school's out for summer and I'm headed out west to see my girlfriend."

Lies and more lies today. But Dylan liked the vague sound of "out west" and the old guy didn't seem to care. He just nodded like *of course* that's what a sixteen-year-old kid would be doing on a Wednesday morning in May, then merged onto the highway without bothering to glance at the oncoming traffic.

The truck lurched as the old man shifted the clutch, but Dylan wouldn't let himself cling to the dashboard like some pussy as they took the corner on two wheels. He wouldn't let himself worry about the stink of booze on the guy's breath, either. How drunk could somebody be at eleven in the morning?

"So what about you?" Dylan asked. He'd read somewhere that you should make conversation with potential sociopaths so they'd bond with you and not want to slit your throat. "What are you doing with all that stuff in the back?"

"Selling shit for scrap."

Dylan glanced over his shoulder at the truck bed. It was piled high with enough metal parts to build a submarine. Maybe this was a line of work he could check out once he got to Seattle, if Typhoon Entertainment wouldn't hire him as a beta tester. That was his dream: to test video games for a living and design them himself one day. He had a couple of apps he was working on now.

The driver talked about his own hitchhiking experiences as they rattled west. Dylan could hardly make out the words over the bum muffler, but most of the stories involved bloody bar fights or getting "some great pussy like you wouldn't believe." Dylan mostly tuned him out, nodding and saying, "Wow, cool," or whatever, to keep him talking. The farther west they drove, the more distance there was between Dylan and his so-called life.

He wouldn't let himself turn on his phone. He was done with phones. Nobody could track him down and that was exactly the way he wanted it.

The driver—who at some point said his name was "Mack," like that was a real name—eventually dumped Dylan off in Fitchburg, where Mack said he needed to gas up before heading north to New Hampshire, to whoever in the universe bought scrap metal and probably paid Mack in beer.

Mack pointed toward the entrance ramp to 495. "You're gonna want to wait there, like you did for me. Don't hitch on the actual highway or the cops will snatch you up."

Like Dylan didn't know that already. But he thanked the guy and even offered him money for gas. Mack waved him off. "You need it more than I do, kid," he said. "Seattle's far. Might as well fly to the moon."

If there was a way to leave the planet entirely, Dylan would do that. Instead, he hefted his backpack onto his shoulders and started walking slowly up the road in the rain, wondering if he looked as pathetic as he felt: a skinny, no-ass kid in a *Doctor Who* T-shirt and expensive soggy sneakers traveling alone to a destination that really did seem as far as the moon.

It was raining hard enough that Dylan wished he'd brought that stupid raincoat Sydney was always nagging him to carry to school "just in case." It was a North Face jacket—she knew most of the kids at his prep school wore that brand—but Dylan refused to wear it for exactly that reason, even though he did feel kind of bad about her spending all that money for nothing.

Having Sydney around was okay most of the time, but Dylan didn't need her nosy questions. She couldn't fool him. That mom act she put on was totally for Dad's benefit. Other women had tried getting on Dad's good side, too, hoping to trap him. Who didn't want a rich surgeon for a husband?

Besides, with Sydney around, he could feel the memories of his mother wavering, like some kind of fading hologram. He didn't want that. Especially since Dad showed no signs of wanting to remember Mom at all.

Even before Sydney, Dad had trashed Mom's clothes and stuff. Pictures, too. Or maybe he'd burned them. What did Dylan know? Anyway, every family photo except the one Dylan kept hidden in his dresser drawer was gone. That one was of Dylan sitting on Mom's lap and blowing out the candle on his first birthday cake. You could tell from the picture that she was going to help him blow out the candle and get his wish.

Not that he did. Whatever wishes he'd made as a one-year-old couldn't have included a dead mother splattered on the highway the month he turned twelve. Happy birthday to him: a mother mangled in a car that looked like an accordion after it flipped over in a ditch.

Dad tried to keep Dylan from seeing the pictures in the newspaper, but of course they were all around the Web. His mom had been driving her friend's cheap shitbox Kia; her friend hadn't died, only Mom at the wheel. Dad hadn't let Mom take her BMW. He'd hidden her keys because he didn't want her driving home drunk. Irony alert: Mom would have probably lived if she'd been driving her own car.

An hour later, he finally caught his second ride. A boxy Subaru. Parental hand-me-down, Dylan guessed, since the driver was in his twenties and wore a striped skater hat and jeans. A skateboard was belted into place in the backseat like a kid. Next to it sat a duffel bag, unzipped and vomiting clothes. The car reeked of pot and the kid was smiling and shaggy. If this guy were a dog, he'd be jumping on Dylan and wagging his feathery tail.

"Hey, bro, I can take you to Greenfield," he said. "Not far, but it'll get you out of the rain for an hour."

"Cool." Dylan dropped his backpack on the floor and climbed in, hoping the guy wouldn't mind a puddle on his passenger seat.

The driver, Brooks, seemed oblivious. "Seattle, huh? From Greenfield you should go south on Ninety-one and hit the Pike. If I were you, I'd stop in Amherst and sleep at UMass. Somebody there would let you into one of the dorms. You could sleep in a lounge, start again in the morning. Trust me. You do *not* want to be thumbing rides in the dark, man. Nobody will pick you up. Or, if they do, it won't be the kind of person you want to ride with."

So far, Dylan had avoided toll highways, not wanting cameras to capture his image on film. But he pretended to go along. He could figure out an alternate route later. Right now he just needed to dry off.

Brooks was a senior at Worcester Polytech studying chemical engineering. He was on his way to visit his girlfriend at UVM, he said. "You should totally head north with me and see Vermont before you hit Seattle. Vermont's got it all going on: mountains, green pastures, waterfalls. It's a fucking paradise."

"Sounds sick." Dylan didn't want to admit that his father had a ski chalet in Vermont and was always bugging Dylan to go up there. Skiing was the very last thing Dylan was good at, right after any sport involving a ball or a stick. "But I've got business to take care of in Seattle, you know? I'm applying for jobs in the gaming industry." He hoped he sounded older than he looked.

It didn't matter. Brooks was all over *that* answer. He slapped the steering wheel. "Good for you, dude! Fucking too true! That's what all the great ones did: Dell, Zuckerberg, Gates. They didn't bother slogging through pointless college classes, did they? They just fucking dropped out and made their fortunes. That takes *cojones*."

Brooks lit a blunt, offered it to Dylan, who shook his head. "My girlfriend, man, she'd skin me if I didn't finish my degree," Brooks said. "She already thinks I'm a slacker. Women, man. You know what I'm talking about, right?"

Dylan nodded. He didn't understand much about girls, but he knew this: Brooks was right. If you were stupid enough to fall in love, that girl had you by the balls.

He would have done anything for Kelly. *Any fucking thing.* But it hadn't mattered. Whatever he'd done, or wanted to do, wasn't enough. Kelly hadn't just broken his heart. She'd shredded him, chewed him up, spit him out, and stomped on him with her spike shoes before setting fire to his head.

Brooks left him off at the Route 2 rotary in Greenfield, where headlights and taillights blurred in the rain like streaky yellow and red ribbons. From above, Dylan imagined the rotary would look like a giant dizzying pinwheel, like the one his mom had bought for him at the Topsfield Fair a month before she died. It was still hanging from the curtain rod in his room.

Dylan had left the pinwheel behind, proof he was done with grief. He could miss his mom, fine. But he wasn't going to be the sort of dumb ass who cried—actually *cried*—like he had in front of Kelly. Never again.

Kelly had tweeted his pathetic whimpering to the whole world: "Skeleton Boy is leaking in front of me right here on the sidewalk! Ew!"

It wasn't just raining, now. It was bucketing. Brooks had given Dylan a trash bag to put over his head and backpack to keep him dry. Wearing it made Dylan feel like a homeless meth addict, so he took it off as soon as the Subaru joined the kaleidoscope of lights, leaving its own trail of red and making Dylan wish he'd gone to Vermont after all.

Somehow, the lambs had squeezed through the wrong gate instead of following their mothers. Now they were in the upper pasture, separated from the ewes happily grazing in the lower fields and bleating as if their little hearts were broken. Meanwhile, their mothers were enjoying their uninterrupted gorging on tender new green grass.

The noise was shattering Hannah's concentration. To make matters worse, it was raining hard, the water needling the surface of the pond below the barn that Allen had dubbed "Haven Lake" when they first bought the farm. The rain had already filled the tractor ruts with icy puddles.

Hannah suddenly had an idea based on something she'd read in a book: she could try tricking the lambs to follow her through the gate into the lower pasture.

She shed her yellow oilskin jacket, shivering a little as she got down on her hands and knees in the mud in her white T-shirt and jeans, feeling cold and stupid as she began baaing like a sheep. Never mind. Nobody was here to see her. She only needed to fool one lamb into following her through the gap in the fence and the rest would follow.

Hannah baaed again, feeling perfectly *sheepish*, and suddenly thought of Rory. Her brother-in-law had loved animals. Rory would have helped her find humor and grace in this moment, as he had in everything. Well, almost everything.

"Forget your perfect offering," Rory used to say. "There's a crack in everything. That's how the light gets in."

It was a quote from one of the folk songs Rory used to sing in high school. Funny how often she'd been thinking about him today. And Allen, too. Then again, it was a rainy day in May. Even after twenty years, Hannah still felt a piercing grief when spring brought the rain like this, when everything reminded her about Theo and Allen being gone. After Theo died, everything fell apart, as if the boy had been holding their community together.

The cops—the whole town, really—had blamed the adults on the farm for Theo's death. Not only Lucy, Theo's mom, but Hannah and Allen, too. "With ownership comes responsibility," one cop said. As if she didn't know that already. Life on Haven Lake was one chore after another, until every night she went to bed and was afraid to let herself lie flat, knowing the ache would crawl up the sore muscles of her back and shoulders like a live, gnawing animal.

A lot of outsiders viewed the farm as a commune where drifters and druggies congregated. "It's because those people are heathens," Hannah had heard one woman say in Shelburne Falls a few days after Theo died. "They had it coming, living the way they did. Nobody was watching those children."

That was untrue, especially where her own daughter was concerned. Hannah had carried Sydney in a cloth sling for months, like she was still part of her own body instead of a separate creature, the baby's white-blond curls tickling Hannah's chin as she cupped Sydney's hard, hot head in her hand to protect it as she worked, pulling weeds or taking bread out of the oven. She'd taught Sydney how to read and write, how to swim and ride a horse. She'd watched Sydney fall in love with Theo and then nearly die of grief.

Her daughter's decision to leave the farm after Theo and Allen were gone still set off a noisy, percussive symphony of sorrow, anger, and hurt. Once triggered, those emotions reverberated up Hannah's spine like an orchestra out of tune.

She gave herself a mental shake. *No sense living a life of regrets.* She'd done enough of that already. Besides, the sheep needed her now.

That was the thing about farming: you had to focus on the weather, the plants, and the livestock and forget about your own pitiful, small self.

One of the lambs was finally approaching her. She'd named this one "Casper" because he was one of the few snowy white ones in this year's crop. Too bad he was a little ram. She'd had to castrate him. There wasn't much call for rams these days. Another couple of weeks and she'd have to truck him up to the broker who sold the rams as meat. Sad, but one of the practical aspects of raising sheep.

Hannah kept up her steady baaing. Finally Casper nosed through the gap. The other lambs were soon jostling around him, piteously bawling for their mothers until the ewes called back. Soon mothers and babies were reunited and happily grazing, a picture-perfect postcard despite the steady rain. Beyond the sheep, the foothills of the Berkshires rose in an undulating silhouette above the pond like a woman lying on her side, the water reflecting the curves of the land. She'd always loved this place and loved it still, despite everything.

Hannah stood up, flicking her thick braid over one shoulder and rubbing her knees. At fifty-nine, she was definitely getting too old to be role-playing with sheep. But this was the life she'd chosen. The only work that kept her moving forward, day after day, instead of always looking over her shoulder to mourn the people she'd lost.

CHAPTER TWO

Sydney knew the house was empty even before she searched the rooms. Gary's Victorian—a tall, narrow-shouldered blue house on Newburyport's prestigious Federal Street—felt chilly and still, as if its occupants weren't just out for the day, but dead and buried.

She shivered as she went from one high-ceilinged room to another, dutifully calling Dylan's name. A small, shameful part of herself longed to be in her own small cottage on the river instead of here, dealing with this. The problem with marrying someone was that you married his problems, too.

"Dylan?" Sydney called. "Hello? Honey, are you here?"

Stupid, but that's what people did: "Hello, hello? Anyone here?" even when the answer was obvious: nobody was home. Nobody at all.

She circled back downstairs into the pale yellow kitchen with its cherry cupboards and gleaming granite counters. Gary liked a clean house; he went on a tear every weekend and had cleaners come in twice a week besides.

She was reaching for her phone to text Gary when she saw the note, printed on a scrap of envelope and trapped in place by the silver pepper mill:

Dear Dad and Sydney,

I'm done with school, this puke-cute dinky-ass town and you. It's time I emancipated myself. Don't try to find me. I'll write when I land.

Chill,

Dylan

P.S. Sorry.

It was the "sorry" that broke her heart. *Jesus.* The poor kid. What was going on that Dylan thought running away would solve his problems? And why hadn't she and Gary seen it coming?

Sydney sank onto one of the counter stools in the kitchen and stared out at the rain. She started to cry, slow, lazy tears that she realized were there only when she tasted salt on her lips.

Just last Sunday, she'd gotten up early to make tea and read the Sunday paper. She had been sitting right here on this stool, excitedly waiting for the kettle to boil and planning how to tell Gary she was pregnant.

Knowing how much Sydney wanted a family, Gary had eagerly agreed to start trying for a baby soon after their engagement. Sydney was sure that having a baby would help them feel more like a complete family. Dylan was reserved, a loner, but she'd felt confident from the start that she could eventually connect with him. She'd devoted her career to helping children. Why not this one?

She had done everything she possibly could to let Dylan know that he didn't have to accept her as a mother—too soon for that—but he could trust her as a friend: school shopping, movies, the skateboard park. She'd enjoyed watching him grow from an undersized boy of fourteen to a young man of sixteen who had to shave and take pills for acne.

Recently, she'd been rewarded during one of their movie outings when Dylan confided in her about his desire to design video games—something he'd never shared with his father. She knew this was because, as much as Gary loved Dylan, he was hard on him. Gary thought computer games were more than just a waste of time; they were "the downfall of civilization."

She hoped the children she and Gary had together—she had always envisioned having two babies before her fortieth birthday—would create a bridge not only between herself and Gary and Dylan, but between the past and present. Gary and Dylan could heal their grief, and Sydney would be the sort of reliable mother—and stepmother—who loved her children unconditionally. The sort of mother who was as unlike her own mother as possible.

"We're going to have a wonderful adventure," Gary had murmured into her hair as they made love the night he agreed to start trying for a baby. "You're going to be an amazing mom."

Sydney had been silently, giddily excited when her last period was late and the home pregnancy test was positive. She'd decided to wait and tell Gary last Sunday because he wouldn't have to go to work and they could celebrate properly.

Then, between the time the kettle boiled and her tea had fully steeped, her fantasy popped like a rainbow-tinted soap bubble. She'd stood up to reach for a teacup in the cupboard and felt the unmistakable trickle of liquid on her thigh. She twisted her nightgown around, and at the sight of the bright bloom of red on the pale cotton, she had wept, thinking, *What if I missed my last chance to be a real mom?*

Irritated now by her pointless self-wallowing, Sydney hastily texted Gary. When he didn't answer, she called his office and told his receptionist to page him.

He was still in surgery; she had to wait ten minutes for him to return the call. When he did, Gary sounded terse and tired.

"Don't call the cops," he said after she told him about the note and said she wanted to contact the police. "It's time we took the tough-love approach. I've given that kid everything from a huge allowance to private school, never mind thousands in therapy. I'm sick of how ungrateful and entitled he acts. Let Dylan see for himself what it's like out in the real world. Did he take his computer?"

"He has his laptop for school, I imagine, but his PC is here on his desk," Sydney said. "Why? What does that matter? We can't just let him run away! It's not safe. I don't even think that's legal. Plus, what if he doesn't have any money?"

"Dylan always has money," Gary said. "And if he has a laptop and a cell phone, he can reach us whenever he wants. Look, Sydney. Dylan's not stupid. I know my son. He won't take any real risks. He's probably holed up with a friend, licking his wounds over some teen drama. I'm betting he'll be back by tonight. If he's not, we'll call the cops then. Sorry. I've got to go. They're paging me. I'll call you in a few hours when I'm out of the OR."

Gary hung up. Sydney sat with the phone in her hand, feeling frantic and useless. She glanced at the stove clock. She'd be late for her next client if she didn't leave now. What to do?

She headed out the door, dialing the police as she went. Calling them might make Gary mad, but she couldn't sit by and do nothing. She explained her situation to an officer, then asked, "Can I file a missing person report for a child who isn't mine?"

The cop who took her call was kind, but didn't seem any more concerned than Gary. "Anybody can submit a missing person report," he said, "but you have to come into the station and file the report in person. We'll need a photograph to get the process started, and then we'll keep an eye out for your boyfriend's son on the streets."

"But you wouldn't actually start an official search?" Sydney pressed.

"He's sixteen, you said? No, probably not yet. Not unless you have good reason to believe the boy is in immediate danger, ma'am," the officer said. "The thing is, until a few hours pass, he's really not a missing person, right? Just a teenager who's not in school when he should be. For now, I'd suggest checking with the boy's friends. If you don't make any headway, come see us at the station tonight and we'll get right on it."

Frustrated, Sydney drove the rest of the way to her office, pulled into the parking lot behind the medical building, and bolted up the stairs. She reached the waiting room just as another woman approached it, a redhead with hair worn the way Sydney wished she could wear hers, in a sleek, no-nonsense bob.

Instead, Sydney's shoulder-length blond hair usually looked as if she'd been hanging upside down and just turned herself right side up. Every morning she grimly waged a hair war, taming her thick waves into a ponytail or jamming pins into a French twist, then spraying her hair in place.

"Mrs. Golding?" Sydney extended her hand. "I'm Dr. Bishop. Nice to meet you." She invited the other woman to sit down and have a cup of coffee in the waiting room. "I'll be with you in a minute. Let me set things up."

The next hour went by in a blur as Sydney focused on Mrs. Golding's account of her eight-year-old son's problems in school. A typical menu: impulsive behavior, trouble sitting still in the classroom, bullying, anxiety. Sydney's mind wandered to Dylan again. How could she trust herself to help other parents when she hadn't noticed that Dylan, a teenager she practically lived with, was unhappy enough to run away?

At the end of the intake session, she gave the mother questionnaires for the teachers, plus one for her to complete about family history and behaviors at home. "I'll use these questionnaires as part of my evaluation," Sydney explained. "I'll also do some testing when you bring him in next week to identify any learning difficulties. After that, I'll write a report for you to share with his teachers, outlining what kind of specialized instructional approach he might need."

"What Quinn *needs* is for his damn teacher to stop holding him in from recess as a punishment for acting out in class," Mrs. Golding said.

"I beg your pardon?" Sydney asked. "Did you say he's being punished by being denied recess?"

"Yes." The other woman drummed her fingers on the desk and bounced her foot. "Then they don't get why Quinn has more trouble sitting in the afternoon than the morning."

Mother may have attention issues herself, Sydney scribbled in her notes. But Mrs. Golding was right. If anything, a child described as "impulsive," "anxious," and "unfocused" could benefit from an *extra* recess to help him blow off steam and relax.

"Thank you for sharing that," she said. "Let's gather our information, and then I'll make some recommendations. Don't worry. We'll get your son the help he needs."

By the end of the session, Sydney's head was throbbing. She wanted nothing more than to go to her own house and sink into her favorite armchair with a good book and a glass of wine. But Gary would be home tonight to make dinner, and there was Dylan to worry about. She'd have to spend the night in Newburyport.

She would normally write up her intake report before leaving the office, but she couldn't face doing anything else today. Sydney stood up from her desk, stretched, and went to the couch, where she curled up against one arm of it. Bliss. Her headache began to recede.

She was sound asleep when Ella woke her. "You planning to camp here all night?" Ella asked in her honeyed Southern voice.

Ella was from South Carolina, from a small town in a place she called "low country." The way Ella said it, "low country" sounded like a land of velvet and silk, a place where you'd exist on fried chicken and biscuits. Sydney wanted to go there. Right now, if possible.

"No, I'm about to leave," Sydney said. "I was just thinking and I must have dozed off."

"Thinking about what? Wedding plans? Your *honeymoon*?" Ella cocked a hip and twirled her string of silver beads, making Sydney laugh.

Ella could always make her feel better. She was nearly sixty years old and long divorced, but magnificent to look at: six feet tall and well built, Ella was of mixed French-black-Mexican parentage and usually wore her lustrous black hair coiled in an intricate knot at the base of her neck. She was never without eyelash extensions and a gel manicure. She was also the only woman Sydney had ever met who was a size sixteen and didn't care who knew it.

"More to love," was Ella's view.

Sydney patted the couch beside her and Ella accepted the invitation, pulling Sydney's head down on her shoulder. "Tell me."

"Dylan," Sydney began. She described the phone call from the school, the empty house, the reactions by Gary and the police. "I'm so worried."

"Well, of course you are! I think Gary's right and Dylan's probably safe—he's a smart one, that kid—but you have to ask yourself why he did it."

"I'm afraid it's because of me." Sydney's stomach clenched at the thought.

"Nonsense! His mama was dead and gone for two years before you showed up, bless her heart. No, there's got to be something else going on. You talk to his friends yet?"

"No. I don't really know who they are." God, Sydney hated admitting this. What kind of stepmother was she going to be, that she still knew so little about Dylan after two years?

On the other hand, Dylan was a teenager and most teenagers were, by definition, difficult to know. His entire social life seemed to be conducted online. Occasionally she'd hear a crowd of men shouting in Dylan's room via Skype as he was gaming. It always shocked her to realize that those men could be anywhere from Korea to Spain, teaming up to play Call of Duty. She'd once asked Dylan to teach her the game, thinking this would be something they could do together, but she was terrified as her screen self rounded every corner, expecting a sniper to gun her down from a rooftop.

Marco appeared and asked if they wanted coffee. "Still some left in the pot," he said. "I'll have to toss it if we don't drink it."

Ella shook her head. "Not for me, sweetie. It's after five. Anyone want to join me for a bucket of wine and a plate of wings at the Grog? It's comedy night."

"No," Sydney said. "I'd better stay sober until Dylan comes home."

"What for? Honey, if anybody needs a bucket of wine tonight, it's you," Ella said, making her laugh.

"Did you talk to Dylan's friends?" Marco asked.

His brown eyes were so intent on Sydney's face that she felt herself flush and had to look away as she repeated what she'd told Ella. "He must socialize a little at school, but he's never brought anyone home since I've known him."

Marco frowned. "Does he have a job?"

"Yes. He bags groceries at Shaw's."

"How about talking to people there?"

"That's a good idea. I should have thought of that." Sydney glanced at the clock on her desk. "This would be his shift. I'll stop by Shaw's on my way home."

It was nearly six o'clock by the time Sydney pulled into the Port Plaza parking lot. There were two plazas beside each other in Newburyport; this one had a Shaw's and the other a Market Basket. Each grocery store had a pharmacy and a liquor store beside it. Driving here reminded Sydney of Dylan's Grand Theft Auto game as she maneuvered through the parking lot and dodged distracted drivers, shoppers, and boys retrieving long trains of shopping carts.

Sydney parked on the outer edges of the lot. A walk would do her good. (Really, why didn't she just join that cheap gym? No more excuses! Her wedding was in less than four months!) She immediately regretted the distance between her car and the store, though, as the rain sent rivulets of cold water down the collar of her blouse.

Only two of the baggers looked around Dylan's age. She approached the one closest to the door, a stocky kid with a stained purple necktie, and asked if he knew Dylan. He didn't, but the second boy—older, with a shock of red hair and alarming blue braces on his teeth—nodded when Sydney mentioned Dylan's name.

"Have you seen him lately?" she asked, trying not to wince at the way the boy was dropping cans on top of bananas in a bag while the poor shopper had her back turned, wrestling her toddler back into the cart.

"Yeah, he worked Saturday with me," he said.

"Have you seen him since?"

The boy shook his head and plunked the bag into the woman's cart, then started heaping items into another one. "No. We don't go to the same school. Why?" The boy's eyes were alight with curiosity.

"He left school early today and his dad and I haven't heard from him," she said, choosing her words carefully. It would be better if this boy thought she was Dylan's mother. "If you can think of anybody who might know where Dylan is, I'd love to talk to that person. We just want to know he's safe."

The boy's eyes flickered toward the door, then back to Sydney's face. "You could try his girlfriend, I guess."

"Girlfriend?" Sydney hoped she didn't sound as shocked as she felt. She'd had no idea Dylan was seeing anyone. That could explain his recent erratic behavior. *Let it be love,* she prayed silently, *that's making Dylan act like such an idiot.* "What's her name?"

"No clue." The boy dropped the second bag of groceries into the woman's cart. "We call her 'Rite Aid Girl' because that's where she works."

"Thanks." Sydney headed for the drugstore, hoping to find answers there.

Really, what was the point of Seattle? He only had seven hundred and thirty-two dollars, all of his birthday money plus the shit money he'd earned this year for bagging groceries. How long would that last? And who would really hire him?

You have skills, Dylan reminded himself as he pulled his collar higher against the steady rain. If Typhoon Entertainment didn't want him, he'd earn his GED and go to community college. He'd work as a dishwasher or something, establish residency, then get a computer science degree at the University of Washington. One thing he was good at was school. Lots of people stupider than he was made a living. The important thing was to put as many miles as possible between him and home.

Dylan just wished it weren't such crap weather. He'd finally turned his phone on just to check the time, then shut it down before he could be tempted to read the texts or listen to the messages. It was almost seven o'clock and darker than dark. Why hadn't anybody picked him up? Did he really look that sketchy?

He supposed all of those school shootings and bombings in the past few years had pretty much stripped people of any trust they had for guys his age. Especially guys with backpacks. Who could blame them? If they wanted to spare the country more deaths-by-guys-going-postal, they should have laws keeping guns out of the hands of dudes between the ages of fourteen and thirty.

Brooks was right. He should forget about trying to go on tonight. He'd hitch to Amherst and spend the night. He didn't want to stand out here anymore.

Was there a bus from Greenfield to Amherst? Dylan looked around, but the rotary was disorienting. No sign of an actual town, just roads spiraling in different directions.

Then Dylan had an idea that pierced the wet night like a lightning bolt: Hannah, his grandmother, lived near here. She wasn't his actual grandmother—she was Sydney's mom—but the few times he'd met her, she'd seemed pretty cool. Weird that she and Sydney were related. Hannah was all laid-back, while Sydney was always nagging him about homework or eating breakfast or didn't he want to read a book for a change. Just like Dad. No wonder they fell in love.

The thought of love led Dylan, for a brief, sickening moment, to remember his mother: his beautiful giggling mother, setting out stuffed animals in a laundry basket in the living room so they could pretend they were adrift on the sea after the *Titanic* hit the iceberg. She and Dylan had rowed another laundry hamper over to rescue the animals, using all of the Band-Aids in the house to mend them. The house was always a mess when his mom was alive, but at least she knew how to have fun.

Dad probably fell in love with Sydney because she was quiet and sweet and pretty. Not model fine like Mom, who was all angles and sharp edges and magazine clothes, but comforting pretty the way a milkmaid is or something. Sydney would be even better-looking if she lost a few pounds.

Dylan knew he probably focused on weight more than he should, but it grossed him out, this whole food obsession thing in this country. At the same time, he hated his own judgmental nature. Too much like

Dad's. Dad was some kind of fitness fiend, still running marathons and going on cleansing fasts even though he was almost fifty.

Dylan hated it when Dad criticized what Sydney ate. He always said stuff like, "Really, Sydney? You're having dessert? I thought we were off desserts." Or, "Sitting is the new smoking, you know." It wasn't right for one person to judge another like that, at least not out loud.

Hannah didn't look at all like Sydney. She was built like a greyhound, all long face and bony arms, long legs. At least Dylan *thought* so. Kind of hard to tell, since the few times he'd met her, Hannah was wearing sweaters big enough to keep an Eskimo warm.

She definitely looked too young to be anybody's grandmother. Hannah had long hair, dark and wavy with one silver streak in front, and an aging rock star sexy vibe. Like Steven Tyler or maybe Mick Jagger, only not that old. She didn't look much older than his dad, really, so Hannah must have had Sydney when she was pretty young.

Something weird happened with Sydney's father. Dylan didn't know what. He only knew the guy wasn't in the picture. Dad teased Sydney about her "hippie, tofu-eating past," saying that's why she didn't eat more vegetables now. Dylan could tell Sydney didn't like the teasing, but she never told Dad that.

Anyway, Hannah was cool. She and Dylan both liked to talk about geeky nature facts, and she had one of those loud belly laughs you usually only heard guys do. He was almost sure she'd come pick him up and let him spend the night at her house.

But how to reach her? Duh: she must have a landline way out here in the Berkshires. Dylan pulled out his iPhone and Googled her number.

Hannah had meant to bring the hay down earlier today, but she'd gone with her friend Liz to a poultry auction after dinner. They'd driven home with thirty pullets and a dozen Indian Runner ducks. One of the farmers had fished the chickens out of a pen with a long wire hook, then unceremoniously stuffed the squawking, indignant birds into big wire cages. The ducks were in a separate, smaller wire cage.

"Why runner ducks? What will you do with them?" Hannah asked on the way home, turning around and laughing at the way the ducks stood upright in their cage, craning their skinny necks forward like subway commuters watching for a train.

Liz had waved a hand. "God, I don't know. At our age, why do you and I do anything? Because we can, right? I just *liked* them. Maybe you can train that hyper dog of yours to herd them."

Hannah was now up in the hayloft after dark, never her favorite place to be at night. Especially when it was raining, as it was today, as it had been the night she burned down the barn—the smaller barn, where Allen had died. Put a match to it herself after the funeral, saying a prayer. She wasn't just burning the site of his death. She was burning everything they'd built together. Allen, of all people, would have understood that. She'd had sense enough to do it in the rain to ensure that the fire trucks would arrive in time to save the rest of the farm.

Hannah forced herself to move quickly through the maze of towers formed by the hay bales, maneuvering her way partly by headlamp, partly by feel as she slid bales across the wooden floor and shoved them through the trapdoor and down the chute. The hay plunked onto the cement floor and set the ewes and lambs baaing impatiently.

"Easy, girls, dinner's coming," Hannah called. She could hear her border collie, Billy, circling down there, too. The dog was restless because he liked to go everywhere with her. He hadn't yet figured out how to climb ladders, thank God.

She pushed the last bale down the chute and descended the ladder. Back in the house, she stripped off her rubber boots and wet jeans in the hallway to avoid tracking mud through the kitchen. She ran a bath upstairs and longed for a shot of whiskey. Or maybe a whole bottle.

People said alcohol kills you, shutting down brain cells and your liver. Hannah had discovered that was a lie. Alcohol actually lets you survive things you never thought possible. It was only the things you did while using alcohol that might kill you. Or, when you stopped drinking, the things you felt without it.

Sheep knew what to do to survive: they flocked together. If a coyote or another predator approached, sheep formed a white wall to protect themselves. Every predator was born knowing that the surest way to feast on mutton or lamb is to cut a sheep away from its herd. A lone sheep is vulnerable.

After Hannah was left alone on the farm, she felt her vulnerability. She didn't become an alcoholic, but she did drink. She drank so things wouldn't hurt so much.

Booze had led her down some dark roads. But, oh, how she used to treasure that sweet moment in the evening when she finally had a glass in her hand and the day was behind her. She'd loved how whiskey turned her spine to liquid and quieted the noise in her head.

She should probably have left Haven Lake and her ghosts behind, but she couldn't do it. She was in no financial or emotional condition to undertake that transition. Even now, Hannah still hated having to walk past the upstairs bedrooms, empty and silent, the white curtains lifting and falling as if the house were breathing with her, waiting, but she couldn't abandon the farm. She was tied to it now.

Booze, along with the ghosts, grief, and loneliness, had caused her to seek out men in bars, online, at university lectures and country fairs. Hannah never had trouble finding companionship even here, in the sparsely populated Berkshire hill towns. She tried not to choose married men, but occasionally one slipped through the net. She'd had fun. Been distracted.

Then one day she'd met Les Phillips, a chemistry professor, in an Amherst coffee shop. They were both standing behind a coed who gave such an absurd order for a mocha-soy-double-shot-decaf-no-whip something or other that she and Les started laughing.

"I remember when it was just coffee, black or regular," he said. "The most complicated thing was how many sugars."

He was a good-looking man, going soft around the middle, but with a bulldog's determined profile and a full head of kinky brown hair. They'd gone out for a drink a few days later, which had turned into several drinks while Les cried over his new divorce and losing custody of his kids.

She'd vowed not to see him after that—she had enough baggage of her own without shouldering this guy's troubles, too. But Les wouldn't let up. He'd called every day until she finally agreed to have dinner with him. That date had turned into the sort of nightmare that Hannah banished from her thoughts whenever the memory threatened to surface.

That was two years ago. She hadn't dated since; she hadn't gotten drunk, and she'd mostly avoided going into Amherst. She'd seen Les a few times anyway. He had even cruised her street with the windows down in his truck. Once, she was outside in the kitchen garden when she spotted him, and fear caused her to flatten against the side of the house so hard that the clapboards scraped her back through her shirt. After that she started sleeping with an unloaded shotgun under her bed. But she hadn't told anyone, even Liz, what had happened.

Hannah slid down to her shoulders in the hot water and closed her eyes. She was nearly asleep when her phone rang.

Who the hell could be calling her at this hour?

Hannah climbed out of the tub, wrapped herself in a towel, and ran down the hall to answer the phone in her bedroom, nearly falling on the slippery wooden floor in the process. It would serve her right, too. Why should she answer? This wasn't even a number she recognized.

Wait. That was the area code for the North Shore. *Sydney,* she thought, with equal parts panic and hope.

"Hello?" Hannah barked into the phone.

There was a small silence, during which Hannah heard the unmistakable rush of traffic in the background. A prank call or a wrong number, probably. "Hello?" she said again. "If you don't identify yourself immediately, I will hang up and call the police."

"Hannah?" an uncertain male voice said. "It's Dylan."

Even before he said his name, Hannah recognized the voice as belonging to that teenage kid of Gary's, the doctor Sydney was planning to marry in the fall. She also knew, by something tightly wound in the boy's voice, that he was in trouble.

"Are you okay? Where are you?" she asked, again thinking *Sydney*, stomach heaving. "Has there been an accident?"

Another brief hesitation. Then Dylan spoke again, raising his voice to be heard over a siren shrieking behind him. "I'm fine. It's just that I'm a little bit stuck. I'm hitchhiking—"

"You're *what*?" Hannah asked. She couldn't have heard him right. Dylan was a nerdy straw of a boy who went to some tony private school and rarely, if ever, emerged from behind a computer screen to make conversation when Hannah was visiting. (Whenever Sydney *allowed* her to visit.)

"Hitchhiking." Dylan sounded defiant.

Hannah had to smile. Good for him. Nice to know not all teenagers were coloring inside the lines these days. "That must be an adventure." She had returned to the tub while they were talking. Now she settled back down in the water, warming her shoulders. "Where are you headed?"

"Seattle," he said. "Only now it's dark and I haven't made it very far. I was wondering if maybe I could, you know, sleep at your house or something and start again in the morning."

Hannah nearly asked whether his father and Sydney knew about this plan, but caught herself in time. Of course those two probably didn't have a clue what this child was up to; parents rarely did. "Does this mean I would have to pick you up?" she asked. "Or are you planning to get a ride here? Do you even know where I live?"

"Not exactly," Dylan said. "It would be great if you came and got me. I mean, if it's not too much trouble. I'm in Greenfield."

Hannah glanced down at her body—her slim, muscled, but definitely older body—no longer relaxed but thrumming with tension. It was nearly eight o'clock. She'd gotten through another long day. She'd done her chores and earned her reward. Was it too much trouble to drive half an hour to pick up a mopey teenage boy who was running away from home?

Of course it was, damn it.

"I'll be right there," she said. "Tell me exactly where you are."

As promised, Gary came home in time to make dinner. He had grilled salmon and steamed spinach on the table by seven. They each drank two glasses of white wine while talking about Dylan and trying not to argue. Gary was nervous and irritable during dinner, getting up several times to refill his water glass and talking too fast. He still believed Dylan would reappear on his own.

Now they were sitting on the couch, exhausted by their emotional wrangling. They rarely fought. Maybe that's why Sydney felt so emotionally bruised now: she'd never seen Gary this short-tempered.

"I really thought he'd text by now," she said. "If we don't hear from him soon, we should file a missing person report." She didn't mention her earlier call to the police station, counting on a different detective being on duty by now.

"It's too soon. Think about it, Sydney," Gary said. "Dylan's almost seventeen. Practically old enough to go away to college. And if what that girl at the drugstore said is true, it probably means Dylan was deluding himself about having a relationship with her. Now he's upset and holed up somewhere."

"I didn't trust that girl," Sydney said. "She was definitely hiding something."

Gary laughed and pulled her closer to him on the couch, kissing her swiftly. "I love how fierce you are," he said, "especially when it involves my son. Come on. Finish your wine. Try to relax. If Dylan hasn't called by midnight, I promise to go to the cops. Give it two more hours, okay?"

When she nodded, Gary turned on the television and played a recorded episode from one of his BBC dramas. Sydney settled against his shoulder, but instead of seeing the screen, she pictured the girl at Rite Aid: Kelly, with her too-pink lipstick and her blue eyes lined in black, her impossibly tall shoes. A music video girl, the kind of background vocalist who'd make any lame lyric sound sexy.

After leaving the grocery store, she'd found Kelly furtively texting behind the counter at Rite Aid and asked the manager if she could have a word with her. Kelly followed Sydney outside, where they huddled against the windows to keep out of the blowing rain.

"Thank you for taking a minute to speak with me," Sydney had said. "A boy at the grocery store says you know Dylan Katz."

"His last name is *Katz*?" Kelly shook her head. "Okay, whatever. What about him?"

"The boy I talked to says you're his girlfriend."

Kelly snorted. "Yeah? He told you wrong."

Sydney had frowned at the girl. Something was off. Her defensive answer had come too quickly. "But you do know him."

"Yeah, sure. But I know *lots* of people." Kelly shifted from one foot to the other. Her shoes were expensive sandals with four-inch wedge heels and straps that wrapped around her ankles.

Sydney had felt furious in the face of the girl's gum-chewing nonchalance. She hoped those shoes hurt, then immediately felt petty and mean. Kelly was just a child, too. "Dylan is missing. Do you have any idea where he might be?"

"No. Why would I?"

"Because that boy said you were Dylan's girlfriend!"

Kelly gave her a pitying look. "Listen, we hooked up this one time. That's it. Dylan knows I have another boyfriend. I can't help it if he got the wrong idea and thinks I like him or whatever."

"How would he get that idea?" Sydney asked, forcing a smile. "I mean, other than the fact that you slept together?"

"I let Dylan give me a ride home one day after work. We went to my place and hooked up. I mean, it's not like we *dated* or anything. And we definitely didn't go *out*."

Sydney knew from working with teenagers that, on Planet Teen, *going out* was more serious than *dating*, which meant more than *hooking up*, but she still had trouble applying this adolescent code to Dylan. Dylan had never expressed an interest in girls. He was home every night for dinner and spent weekends on the computer unless they dragged him off on some family outing. He didn't even have a driver's license yet.

"What do you mean, he gave you a ride home?" she asked. "What car was he driving?"

"A sweet blue BMW." The girl smiled. It was a pretty smile, expensive like her shoes, the teeth lined up and stark white. "Dylan came back here yesterday to pick me up after work, too, but my boyfriend was waiting in the parking lot and I thought it might be, you know, awkward."

"I'm sure you were right," Sydney said, wanting to slap her. "Well, if you hear from Dylan again, could you please let me know?" She had handed Kelly one of her business cards.

She hadn't told Gary most of these details. Not one word about Dylan hooking up or driving his mother's car. Gary would blow up if he knew Dylan had been driving the BMW without permission. There *should* be consequences, of course. But they could deal with that after Dylan was home safely.

Sydney had only told Gary about the girl because she hoped he'd understand Dylan's heartbreak and sympathize. Surely that was possible, since Gary had been so hurt and betrayed by Amanda. She glanced at his strong profile and couldn't help smiling. It was such a treat, always, to look up and see Gary beside her. He was handsome, the kind of silver-haired man with unflinching blue eyes you saw in ads for life insurance or retirement funds. A doctor who was both intelligent and compassionate, a problem solver with a big heart.

His only blind spot seemed to be Amanda, whose very name had the power to enrage him. "Absolutely thoughtless every day of her life," he had explained to Sydney. "No wonder Dylan's such a selfish kid."

Sydney knew Gary's anger at Amanda would ease over time. About Dylan, she didn't think the boy was selfish, only lost and grieving. She knew how that felt; she'd lost a parent when she was around Dylan's age and understood all too well about adolescent acts of self-preservation.

Gary was still watching television, jiggling his knee and setting Sydney's teeth on edge. He made occasional comments about the characters, but to Sydney the actors in their elaborate period costumes might as well have been puppets. She watched the clock, waiting for Gary to set things in motion.

At last the credits began to roll. Sydney sprang up from the couch. "Let's go to the police."

Gary sighed and ran a hand through his hair. "All right. It's not like we're going to be able to sleep anyway."

Suddenly, her cell phone rang. "Wait," Sydney said. "Maybe that's Dylan." She lurched across the coffee table, nearly knocking their wineglasses to the floor, and rooted around in her purse. The phone showed a number both familiar and undesirable. "God, it's my mother."

"Shouldn't you answer?" Gary asked. "It must be important. She never calls."

Sydney looked up at him, panicked. "What do I say?"

"How about 'hello'?"

Gary was right. Her mother went to bed early and rose with the roosters. She wouldn't be calling this late unless it was an emergency—cancer, a fall, a fire? Sydney pressed the talk button. "Mom. Are you okay?"

"I'm fine, but I have something that belongs to you."

"What do you mean?"

"I have your boyfriend's kid."

"*What?* How could Dylan be with you? Is he all right?" Sydney sank down onto the couch next to Gary, who watched her intently.

"He's fine," Hannah said. "He called me from Greenfield a while ago and said he was hitchhiking to Seattle and needed a place to crash. I went and picked him up."

"Seattle? Jesus, Mom," Sydney said, furious now. "Wasn't it obvious he was running away? Why the hell didn't you call us before? We've been worried sick!"

"It was obvious, yes. Of course it was. But Dylan was adamant about not wanting me to tell you where he was. I waited until he went to bed so he wouldn't hear me calling you. I was afraid it might spook him and make him take off if he heard me."

"Did he say anything about why he ran away from school?" Sydney couldn't bring herself to say "home."

"No. What's going on?"

"I have no idea. Is he okay, Mom?"

There was a brief, heavy silence, but Hannah's unspoken thoughts were clear to Sydney: *This is what it's like to have a child reject you.* Then Hannah said, "I'm not sure. He's extremely skittish. I tried to feed him, but he wasn't hungry. He was drenched to the bone, of course, and exhausted. I made him take a shower and gave him some dry clothes. He's in your old room. I just checked and he's fast asleep. Look, Sydney, you must have some clue about why he ran away. Did something happen at school? With a friend, maybe?"

Sydney wanted to hurl the phone across the room. How *dare* her mother make veiled accusations about Sydney not knowing Dylan? Not taking care of him?

This is about Dylan, Sydney reminded herself sternly. *Not you.* "All I know is that Dylan's seeing some girl, or thought he was, and she ended things. He might be upset about that." Then, before she could stop herself from blurting it out, Sydney added, "I'm hoping it doesn't have anything to do with me marrying Gary."

She waited—unreasonably, childishly—for Hannah to reassure her, to say, "Don't be silly. You'll be a wonderful stepmother. The boy loves you."

But Hannah had never been one to sugarcoat the truth. Instead, her mother said, "Of course he's going to resent you. That's to be expected. I'm not sure you can do much about it. The only thing Dylan has told me is that he doesn't feel like he belongs at home or at school and needs to live somewhere else."

What had propelled Dylan to seek out Hannah for refuge, of all people? And why would he confide those feelings to *her*, a stranger, when Sydney had been here at home, asking Dylan all the right questions?

Of course, Hannah always did have a way with children. Even Sydney had thought her mother was magical, once upon a time. Every child on the farm did.

She remembered Hannah leading them down to Haven Lake at night, a line of little children. Her mother taught them how to pull a knotted rope across a rock, then hop off the rock and swing out into the middle of the black star-studded pond and let go.

"Hear that, kids?" Hannah had whispered as they stood shivering on the rock, daring one another to be the first to try the rope. "The frogs are calling you! They want you to turn into a frog tonight and swim with them, just for one night!"

They had all jumped into the pond, Theo first, of course, shrieking into the blackness. They'd been young enough that Sydney imagined her skin turning slick and green, had expected her fingers and toes to become webbed as she frog-kicked her skinny legs through the water.

"What do you want to do?" Hannah was asking now. "Do you and Gary want to get Dylan tonight? Or tomorrow? His plan is to leave for Seattle in the morning, so you'd have to get here early to catch him. Unless the two of you want to let him try his wings."

"Don't be ridiculous, Mom. He can't go to Seattle alone. And he certainly shouldn't be hitchhiking. He's sixteen!"

Gary raised his eyebrows at this. "What the hell's going on? Is Dylan all right?"

She nodded. If it were up to her, she would get in the car immediately and drive the two hours to the Berkshires to bring Dylan home. But this was Gary's child. "Let me talk things over with Gary. I'll call you back."

Gary shook his head and grabbed the phone, nearly jerking it out of Sydney's grip. She was too surprised to protest. "If it's okay with you, Hannah, we'd like to leave Dylan at your place for now," Gary said. "I'm calling his bluff. Please let him know we'll pick him up Saturday, because that's the only day that's convenient for us. Otherwise he can take a bus home. Dylan should have plenty of money for that. Please don't use your own funds. And if he does, by some stroke of idiocy, decide to keep hitchhiking, that's up to him. Just remind him that colleges don't like dropouts and he'll be throwing away his education."

He mouthed "sorry" and handed the phone back to Sydney, who couldn't believe Gary had sounded so harsh. Obviously Dylan was in a crisis. He needed them to come to his aid, not lay down the law!

But what could she possibly say? This was Gary's son, not hers. Dylan was safe at the moment. Plus, she wanted to present a united front to both Dylan and her mother.

"Mom?" Sydney said. "I'm sorry you got caught in the middle of this, but I agree with Gary. Dylan should be held accountable for his actions. I hope this isn't too much of an imposition. Tell Dylan we love him and we'll pick him up Saturday."

"That's it?" Hannah demanded. "You're going to stick me with this mopey kid and expect me to look after him? Well, all right. Apparently I have no say in the matter. I'll try to make him stay until then. But no promises, understand?"

Sydney fumed after they hung up. Of *course* Hannah wouldn't do one thing to stop Dylan. She'd never been the sort of mother to give children boundaries. That was the trouble with her parents: no rules. "If it feels good, do it": that tired refrain from the sixties and seventies had somehow permeated Haven Lake right through the eighties.

"Sorry, honey," Gary said. "I shouldn't have hijacked the phone like that. But we need to send a strong message to Dylan that he can't manipulate us."

"I know you love him," was all Sydney could think to say.

"I do," Gary said. "And I love you for standing by me on this."

He gathered her into his arms and rested his chin on top of her head. Sydney closed her eyes and pressed her face to his chest, trying to find comfort in his heartbeat, strong and steady. But she was having trouble swallowing. She knew they'd made the wrong decision.

CHAPTER THREE

Dylan opened his eyes and freaked. He had no idea where he was.

He sat up so abruptly that the room spun. He had to lie back again and prop himself up on his elbows. From this angle, he could see sky—bright blue, thank God, not a wet fucking gray blanket like yesterday—but not much else.

Hannah's house. Dylan stared up at the ceiling. It wasn't white, like an ordinary ceiling, but pale blue. The walls were dark red and the trim was white.

He was lying under a quilt made out of so many fabrics and colors that looking at it made him have to keep blinking. The walls were hung with abstract paintings in the same vivid colors. A bright green pottery mug filled with colored pencils sat on the bedside table next to him, and a wind sock—orange, green, red, and white—dangled from the curtain rod above his head.

Whose room was this? Sydney's? It was cool looking, like being inside one of those bright box kites Mom used to fly with him on weekends.

It was quiet enough here to imagine he was the last survivor of a zombie apocalypse. His room in Newburyport faced the street. Even at night you could hear cars, sirens, people talking, dogs barking. Between the noise outside and the noise inside his room at home from the humming computer and his phone alerts, Dylan always felt both claustrophobic and lonely. Here, all he heard were the birds chatting one another up.

The smell of coffee got him out of bed and into his clothes, which Hannah must have hung up, because here they were on the chair by the window, dry and clean-enough smelling: shorts, a T-shirt, and a hoodie he didn't really need because the air today was warm and soft. He dressed, wrapped the sweatshirt around his waist, and pulled on his socks. His shoes must be downstairs. Probably still had a bucket of water in them.

What time was it? Dylan dug around in his pockets for his phone, then remembered leaving it in his backpack downstairs. He didn't even know if he'd brought the charger. Not that it mattered: he'd given up his phone for a reason.

He'd have something to eat, say thank you, hit the road. Dylan went downstairs, made a few wrong turns before finding the kitchen. He must have been really out of it last night. He didn't remember anything about this house.

He was scanning the black-and-white squares of the kitchen floor for his shoes when some kind of animal, brown and round and furry, skittered beneath the four-legged stove, making him jump. Definitely not a dog. Couldn't be a cat, either. Right size, wrong shape. Did Hannah have, like, really big rats? Possible, out here in the middle of nowhere. Did rats bite your feet?

Dylan inched his way over to the stove, watching every step. He reached the counter, breathed a sigh of relief, and poured coffee into a fat blue mug sitting beside the pot. Then he finally picked up his head and studied the room.

The sunny kitchen was painted light blue with green trim. Every windowsill was a tiny forest, jammed with potted plants. There were more plants in long boxes on metal shelves along one wall. The rug by the sink looked like a craft project his Montessori teachers used to have the kids make in his elementary school: an oval of bright cotton rags braided and sewn together.

There was no microwave, just a black stove on curved legs. No dishwasher, either, only a double metal sink. It was like he'd dropped through a time portal to *Little House on the Prairie*. The counters were clean and clear of clutter, except for a note scrawled on the back of a receipt:

Help yourself to food. Sneakers and backpack in pantry. See me before you go.

H

Okay, that was good. Hannah didn't expect him to hang around. Though Dylan had to admit, if only to himself, that it was strange she wasn't trying to stop him. Nobody was, apparently. He'd half expected the cops to pick him up by now. His dad was a smart guy. He'd know how to search for him, use GPS or some kind of app that tracked lost iPhones.

But maybe Dad didn't want to find him? With him out of the way, Dad could just start his new, perfect family with Sydney.

Fuck the pity party. Pathetic. Move on. That was going to be Dylan's motto now: *Move on.*

He scanned the counters, light-headed with hunger but not wanting to be lured into eating much. Yesterday he'd had a breakfast bar and a handful of almonds, nothing else. That was ideal. Hannah tried to make him a sandwich last night, but Dylan had told her he was too tired to chew. He had to be careful to eat just the right amount of food every day to keep him going without having that brick in his stomach weighing him down.

These muffins were going to be a serious problem, though. Hannah must have baked them this morning; she'd left the pan on the stove and the muffins were still warm. Dylan knifed just a corner of muffin free—banana nut—and ate it off his fingertips, licking up every crumb. Amazing.

Soon he'd wolfed down three muffins without even sitting down. He drank a glass of milk on top of that, the milk colder and better and thicker than any he'd ever tasted. It was in a glass bottle with no label. What the hell? Was it sheep's milk or something? How much fat was in this?

Whatever. It was fuel. That's how he had to see it. He might not eat again on the road.

The sudden infusion of calories and caffeine led him to crash. Dylan groaned and finally sat down on one of the chairs, closed his eyes. He willed himself to feel sick enough to upchuck the food, but couldn't make himself throw up. No matter how desperate he was, he'd never managed to do that, even after that girl in his English class, Tiffany, a dancer who could recite all of Sylvia Plath's poetry by heart, tried to show him how.

"Just stick your fingers down your throat," she'd urged as they huddled together behind the gym after lunch, but he'd been frightened by her bad teeth and the fact that she was so skinny you couldn't tell where her neck ended and her face began.

He must have fallen asleep in the chair, because the next thing he knew, Dylan was startled awake by a weird sensation on his foot. He glanced down, too terrified to move. There was that furry beast again, sitting on his foot and chewing on the raggedy end of his sock.

"Get off!" he yelled, shaking his leg furiously and sending the animal scurrying back under the stove with a weird little whistling sound.

Hannah started laughing. She had silently materialized in the doorway behind him. "You've met Oscar, I see," she said.

"What the hell?" Dylan asked. "Is that thing a *pet*? I thought it was a rat!"

"Well, he didn't start out as a pet," Hannah said. "Oscar's a woodchuck. He's the kind of pest most farmers would shoot on sight, but nobody ever told *him* that."

She clucked in the direction of the stove. The creature waddled back in their direction, its sleek brown head peeping out first from beneath the stove, then the rest of its body emerging, plump and furry and caramel-colored.

Oscar stopped when he saw Dylan and sat up on his hind legs, chattering away at him, his little hands or paws or whatever clasped like a monk's over his round belly. It was like having a cartoon come alive in front of him.

Dylan felt the corner of his mouth twitch. "Sorry I scared him."

"Oh, don't be. I'm always shooing Oscar away. He was probably trying to nibble crumbs off your foot." Hannah gestured at the floor, where Dylan was embarrassed to see a handful of muffin crumbs scattered like confetti.

"I ate three of your muffins," he said, horrified by his own gluttony. "Sorry."

Hannah grinned. "Good. Wouldn't be much point in making muffins if nobody ate them."

She was dressed like a man, in a green plaid flannel shirt over a pale blue T-shirt and jeans, her feet tucked into knee-high green rubber boots. But Hannah's silvery black hair was coming loose from her braid and there was something cool about her. How to describe it? *Free.*

Last night, Dylan had been startled by a black pickup truck roaring toward him around the rotary. The truck's bumper was papered with feminist stickers: "Well-behaved women seldom make history." "Just say no to sex with pro-lifers." "Think outside the boxers." *Wow,* he'd thought, *way to wear your politics on your sleeve. Probably some hippie chick from UMass.*

Then the truck slid to a stop in front of him and Hannah had rolled down the window, shouting at him over the rain and the traffic to get into the truck.

"Want to hold Oscar?" Hannah was asking now.

"I don't know," Dylan said, alarmed. "Probably not."

"Suit yourself. But you'd be missing out. How many chances in life will you get to cuddle a woodchuck?" She clucked again.

Oscar came running over to her, wriggling his fat body and bristly tail. Hannah scooped him up and kissed his round head. "I found him under the porch all by himself. Later I found his mother on the road, run over."

Dylan's breath caught in his throat. Everybody at school knew death was an off-limits topic around him. Especially dead mothers. Somehow, though, the sight of Hannah holding Oscar was so weirdly funny that Dylan didn't feel the usual punch to the gut he got when he heard something on the news about a mom dying or watched a Disney movie about yet another orphan.

"I guess I could try holding him," he said finally.

Hannah smiled and handed him the woodchuck. Oscar felt like a wriggling warm pillow. Dylan rested the animal on his knee and studied its glassy brown eyes and knobby head. Hannah gave him a bit of muffin and he fed it to Oscar. The woodchuck's appreciative squeaking noises made Dylan laugh.

"So what's your plan?" Hannah poured herself a cup of coffee and gestured at Dylan's cup.

He shook his head at the coffee. The stuff in Hannah's pot was so strong, it felt like it had burned the skin right off his tongue. "Guess I'd better hit the road soon," he said without enthusiasm. Maybe it was the muffins, or the feel of the warm animal against his chest. He didn't want to leave. What had he been thinking, going to Seattle with no plan, no money?

He'd been thinking he needed to get away from Kelly, that's what. Kelly and her insane boyfriend.

Hannah was studying him with those unnerving eyes of hers, so like Sydney's, but even more intense: green and gold like a dappled pond. Weird how a mom and daughter could look nothing alike except around the eyes. He wondered if people ever thought that about him and Dad, both skinny, both blue-eyed, but otherwise nothing in common.

Dylan thought of that last *Hobbit* movie he'd gone to with Sydney. With her long braid and fierce eyes, Hannah could be one of the woodland elves, maybe the one the filmmakers created to be head of the Mirkwood Elven Guard, pissing off Tolkien fans around the world. Dylan could picture Hannah shooting a bow and arrow.

"Did you call my dad?" he asked, sure that Hannah had, even after he'd asked her not to before going to bed last night. Dylan was also certain she'd lie about it. All adults lied.

To his surprise, though, Hannah shrugged and said, "Of course. I couldn't let him think you were dead on the highway."

Shit. This woman really knew how to pick the right words to hurt him. Then again, maybe not. Sydney didn't meet Dad until two years ago, and they hardly saw Hannah. Maybe Hannah had no idea how Mom died.

Either way, it wasn't worth getting pissed off. Hannah had picked him up and let him stay the night. And he supposed all adults must have some kind of pact about checking up on kids.

"So what did Dad say? Is he on his way here now?"

"I don't think so."

"*What?* You're kidding me." Dylan felt his face and neck go hot with anger. Embarrassment, too. How could his father and Sydney let him run away? Didn't they care what happened to him? Runaway kids were murdered every day, or became drug addicts and the victims of sex traffickers!

"No, I'm not." Hannah pulled another kitchen chair out from the table with a scraping sound that startled Oscar into clawing his way down Dylan's leg and racing back under the stove. "Your father wanted me to remind you that if you keep hitchhiking, you'll be throwing away your education. You can take a bus home, or he'll pick you up on Saturday, when it's convenient for them."

Convenient. "Yeah, that sounds like Dad," Dylan said, his throat thick with resentment.

Hannah raised a dark eyebrow. "Can you blame him? He's a busy man."

Dylan shrugged. "Not really, I guess." How could he blame his father for anything, when Dad worked like a zillion hours a week putting broken people back together?

Dad was one of the good guys. Too bad he had such a piece-of-crap kid. Dylan was about to say something pitiful to Hannah about how he might as well keep going to Seattle, since nobody cared enough to pick him up, when he became aware of a faint whimpering sound outside.

Hannah stood up and opened the door. A tornado of black-and-white fur whirled into the kitchen. "Sit!" she yelled, her voice whip-sharp.

The dog screeched to a halt at her feet, grinning up at Hannah, long pink tongue lolling, then rolled its eyes slyly backward to look at Dylan.

Dylan couldn't help himself: he grinned back at the animal. "Great dog."

"This is Billy. He's cute, but he's a pain in the butt." Hannah pointed to the rug in front of the stove. "Lie down and act civilized, Billy, or you're out the door." Billy raced to the rug like it was a magnet, circled twice, and plopped down with a sigh, head on his paws, his eyes never leaving Hannah. "Good boy," she said, and resumed her seat at the table.

"Wow. He really understands you," Dylan said.

"Billy is part human, and like any human, he can be a sneaky bastard." Hannah folded her hands in her lap. "So, what now? Do you want to stick with your plan and head west? Or do you want to go home?"

He was amazed that she was actually giving him a choice. Too bad he didn't really know what he wanted to do. "I didn't actually have much of a plan, other than to get away from things and think for a while," he admitted.

"You've succeeded, then," Hannah said. "Here you are. Away."

"Yeah. Here I am."

She cocked her head at him. "Why did you leave?"

"Too many reasons to pick just one."

"Want to tell me about them?"

Dylan froze. "No."

Again, Hannah surprised him by letting it go. "That's fine," she said. "I'm not much of a navel gazer, either. Let me know when you've made up your mind about what you're doing. I can always give you a ride to the bus station." She turned toward the door, carrying the coffeepot and whistling for the dog as she tossed the coffee grounds outside. Billy was at her side in a flash.

If this dog were something else, Dylan thought, he'd be an arrow. "Wait," he said.

Hannah paused in the doorway and glanced at him over her shoulder. "Okay, but make it quick," she said. "A farm doesn't run itself. I've got work to do."

"I just wanted to ask if I could stay with you until Saturday."

"So you're not going west?"

"I don't know. I have to think about it," he said. "I might need a better plan. And more money. Plus, there's only four weeks left of school. Maybe I should just go back. I'll screw over my college applications if I quit now."

"That sounds sensible," Hannah said, folding her arms and narrowing her eyes at him. "Is that what you really want, though? To be sensible?"

He'd expected Hannah to applaud him, not question him. Then Dylan remembered something Dad had said about her. "Is it true you were a wild, drugged-out hippie in the old days?"

Hannah tipped her head back and laughed. "A *wild, drugged-out hippie*? Huh. I don't know. Maybe. Is that what Sydney told you? I kind of like that description." She laughed again. It wasn't a ladylike giggle, either, but that belly laugh he remembered from last Christmas. Dylan snorted. Even the dog grinned and wagged his tail.

"Come on," Hannah said when she'd caught her breath. "I'll take you to meet my girls."

"You have more daughters?" he asked, confused.

She rolled her eyes. "The sheep," she said. "They're my family now."

Sydney was up before the alarm went off on Thursday morning. She rolled onto her side and studied Gary's profile. Even in sleep, he looked intelligent, a slight frown between his silver brows. She leaned over to kiss his neck and chin.

Gary opened his eyes and smiled. "What time is it? Did I sleep through the alarm?"

"No. I woke early. I was just remembering how we always used to deliberately set the alarm early so we could have sex in the morning before you went to the hospital. Maybe it's time to renew our tradition, since we've both been so tired at night."

"Hmm. Let me take that suggestion under consideration." Gary rolled on top of her and slid her nightgown up around her hips.

Their lovemaking was gentle and quick. Not urgent, but deeply satisfying. Sydney always knew what to expect: Gary liked being on top, where he'd thrust rhythmically, his eyes closed, his forehead wrinkled in concentration, until she either came or faked it, depending on whether she could get out of her head enough to focus on her own pleasure instead of his. Then he'd come with a stifled moan that always made her shiver with joy, because it made him seem so open and vulnerable. So not in control. Rare for him.

In the shower afterward, Sydney thought about the first awkward times Gary had invited her to sleep in this house. She'd been so nervous about Dylan hearing their lovemaking that she'd been stiff and unyielding in bed, until Gary reminded her that his son slept on the third floor and wouldn't even know she was there. Even then, she'd made sure to leave before daylight, not wanting to upset Dylan by taking his mother's place.

Now, as Sydney dressed and went downstairs, her anxiety came roaring back. What if Dylan took off from her mother's this morning? She ate a slice of toast and paced the kitchen. Somehow, she had to convince Gary to cancel his surgeries so they could drive out west to pick up Dylan today. It was too risky to wait until Saturday. If Dylan left the farm, they might never find him again.

She hadn't been back to Haven Lake in twenty years. With Gary, though, it seemed a little less daunting. Gary had spoken to her mother in that deliberate, no-nonsense tone he used to deliver surgical outcomes and treatment plans to patients: respectful, calm, decisive. Gary could sound sure of himself even when the world was falling down around his ears. They'd volunteered together on medical missions twice, once in the

Philippines and once in Mexico; both times, Gary had easily adopted a leadership role, sorting out medical teams and supplies, and operating on patients with minimal medical facilities. He always knew what to do in a crisis.

Except now. Sydney was certain Gary was floundering when it came to his son. Dylan had never tested them like this. He'd always been an easy kid, quiet and polite, bringing home report cards with high grades and praise from teachers who inevitably remarked on how bright he was, especially in science.

When she heard Gary coming downstairs, Sydney poured him a cup of coffee. Part of her hoped Gary would say he wanted to drive up to Haven Lake today, but alone. She hated the idea of returning to the farm, yet it was almost as if she'd already started on that journey. Knowing Dylan was with Hannah had unlocked some door in her mind to admit memories that crowded her head like children who refuse to stay outside and play: some were sweet enough, but others were demanding and exhausting.

As she was trying to get to sleep last night, for instance, she'd been thinking about playing in the vegetable gardens of Haven Lake. She and the other children who came and went with their parents, who worked on the farm in exchange for room and board, were naked and barefoot whenever weather allowed, and sometimes even when it didn't. They'd play hide-and-seek in the cornfield, get yelled at for squatting to pee among the carrots and cucumbers, and be periodically shooed away by musky-smelling women bending over the soil, planting or weeding or harvesting.

The men worked with the machinery in the fields, did the heavy digging and building, and occasionally went into town to barter goods or do a day's labor for cash when the farm needed actual money. Meanwhile, the women were left at Haven Lake to tend the crops and children, working in rows like peasants despite the fact that most had been to college until they dropped out to play in the dirt. So ironic, the way the work fell along traditional gender lines, in that post–Golden Age of feminists like her mother making so much noise for equal this and that.

God, what a childhood. Gary didn't know much about how she'd grown up, and Sydney hoped to keep it that way. He'd had one emotionally damaged wife already. He didn't need to worry about marrying a second.

"Here you are." Gary came into the kitchen with his briefcase in one hand, his phone in the other, necktie still dangling loose around his neck. "You got out of bed so fast, I hardly knew what hit me. It was like I dreamed you." He kissed her, then took a step back, studying her face. "What's wrong?"

How could he even ask? "I'm panicking about Dylan."

"Don't. What good will that do?" Gary set his briefcase and phone down on the table. He ignored the coffee she held out to him and wrapped his arms around her instead.

"Aren't you freaking out? Just a little?" She waited, hoping Gary would say he was worried enough to change his mind and drive out to the Berkshires.

But Gary had no such thoughts. When Sydney made the suggestion, Gary sighed and said, "Sydney, please. Let it go. We'll pick Dylan up Saturday. That's what we told Hannah, and we should stick to the plan."

"I don't understand why we're waiting." Sydney's coffee had grown cold; she tossed it down the sink.

"Because Dylan needs to learn that the world doesn't revolve around him." Gary knotted his tie and gathered his things. "He'll be fine. Think about it. What did Dylan do when he couldn't hitch a ride?"

"He called my unreliable mother, and amazingly, she went and got him."

"Oh, come on," Gary said. "Hannah's obviously somewhat responsible, or she wouldn't have driven out to Greenfield to pick him up and called us later. In some ways, this is a good thing. Dylan should get to know her, right? Hannah's going to be his grandmother. Anyway, the point is, he didn't end up with some meth addict or pimp. He found a safe place to crash. Dylan has a strong sense of self-preservation. You can bet he'll be right there at Hannah's house Saturday morning, waiting for us to ferry him home like the prince he believes himself to be."

"Boy, you really don't let up on the poor kid, do you?" she said.

"Poor kid?" Gary grimaced and fixed his tie. "I've given Dylan every break I can think of since his mother died. I'm done coddling him. It's time my son stood on his own two feet. If he makes a mistake, he'll have to live with it. You need to back me up on this, though, or it won't work."

Gary's eyes were bloodshot, the irises slightly yellow, and his hands were jittery. He looked so exhausted that Sydney softened. His cheeks were hollow and his eyelids were a bruised violet. He must not have slept any better than she did. He was probably more worried about Dylan than he was letting on.

"All right," she said. "But you have to promise we'll drive out there early on Saturday."

"You got it. A dawn departure." Gary kissed her good-bye after taking one of his fiber bars out of the cupboard and shoving it into his pants pocket for the short drive to the hospital. "We'll get him back, Sydney. I promise."

Sydney waved to him from the front door, wishing she felt as confident as he did.

CHAPTER FOUR

May meant the end of the school year and parents panicking about placements for September. This particular morning, Sydney saw three new clients. Two of the mothers were so tearful that she felt emotionally drained. Sometimes it seemed like there were no more happy children left in the world. No more kids who willingly got up in the morning, went to school, played at recess, and came home to do their homework in front of the TV. Maybe this morning seemed harder than most because she was becoming one of those anxious, frantic parents wondering where they'd gone wrong.

She snatched a quick lunch in the café on the first floor, managing to stick to salad. This afternoon she had an evaluation scheduled with Quinn, the boy whose redheaded mother had described him during their intake session as "climbing right out of his skin."

She suspected that Quinn's mother was hoping for an ADHD diagnosis that would lead to a psychiatric referral and medication that could help her son focus well enough for him to perform at grade level and curb his impulsive behavior so he could make friends.

"My kid is a social pariah," Mrs. Golding had said about Quinn.

The problem, of course, was that there was no perfect pill. If drugs weren't properly prescribed and carefully monitored, the medications available posed nearly as many problems for children as they solved. Sydney usually chose to refer clients for medication as a last resort, trying other interventions first.

She went out to the reception area to pour a cup of coffee. She liked to greet families out here, then ease the child into conversation so he'd willingly come alone with her into the office. If a child was too anxious, she'd let a parent come in for the evaluation, but that always made the testing more difficult. Most parents couldn't keep their mouths shut.

Ella looked up from her desk. "Every time you come into the reception area, it's like the sun rising all over again, Miss Sydney."

Sydney laughed. "I can never tell if you're pouring on that sweet Southern drawl because you want something."

"Oh, I always *want* something, sugar," Ella said, ramping up her twang.

Today Ella was wearing a snug, violet cap-sleeved dress that showed off her copper skin. Her hair was in its usual complicated braid and she wore high-heeled nude sandals. Sydney—in practical black ballet flats, beige tunic top, and elastic-waist black slacks—felt dowdy and boring next to Ella, as usual.

"So what do you want from me today?" Sydney dumped two packets of Splenda and nondairy creamer into her coffee. God help her, she was going to lose ten pounds before the wedding even if it meant ingesting chemicals and diet drinks that tasted like cleaning fluids.

"I want you to come to Carrie's birthday party with me tomorrow night," Ella said. "And I want you to dress like you're going to do something other than garden."

"Ha-ha." Sydney felt her face flush. She did, in fact, garden in these pants sometimes. "You know I can't."

"Why not?" Ella was pouting now. On her, the pout looked menacing rather than little-girl cute. "You haven't been yourself. And you certainly haven't been acting like an excited bride-to-be."

Sydney sighed. "I'm *not* an excited bride-to-be. I'm a worried stepmother-to-be. Gary wouldn't go get Dylan this morning. I don't even know whether he's still at Hannah's."

"Have you called to ask?"

A reasonable question, if they were talking about anyone other than Hannah. "No. I'm afraid if I challenge her, Hannah will do the opposite of whatever I want her to do. Dealing with my mother is like dealing with a cranky, nap-deprived toddler. Anyway, you know I can't go to Carrie's party. Gary's always too tired to go out on Fridays."

Ella waved a hand. "Did I invite Gary? I did not. This is a dance party, and I know for a fact how much that man hates to dance. But Carrie's feelings will be hurt if you and I don't show. She's turning forty, and if I can remember back that far, forty is a big deal! I'm asking *you* to come with *me*. And I want you to let me help you find something other than those bag lady clothes to wear. You are too young and good-looking to cover up your assets."

"Assets." Sydney snorted. "I've got about twenty pounds of assets more than I need."

"Probably twenty pounds of clothes on you right now," Ella said. "Maybe you should try weighing yourself naked."

"Ew. I'm beyond naked." Sydney held both hands up in surrender before Ella could protest. "All right, I'll go. But only because you're looking at wedding dresses with me next weekend."

Linda Golding showed up a few minutes later, wearing jeans and a T-shirt, her feet tucked into bright pink plastic Crocs a child might wear at the beach. Eight-year-old Quinn was dressed just like his mother, right down to the pink shoes. Sydney suppressed a sigh. No wonder his mother had said Quinn was a social pariah.

Quinn was red-haired like his mom, with an impish freckled face and round brown eyes. He clutched Linda's leg when Sydney approached him in the waiting room and said, "Hi, Quinn. I'm Dr. Bishop. Your mom tells me you're great at building with Legos. I have a kit in my office. Think you could help me with it?"

"Yeah." The boy popped out from behind his mother's leg. "I can do anything with Legos!"

Quinn poured himself into the office ahead of her, talking nonstop and touching every object within reach. That impulsive touching might be another reason his classmates didn't want to socialize with him; Sydney made a mental note to ask the boy's teacher if there were social skills classes available.

They sat at the small table by the window, where Sydney had put the "Battle of Smallville" Lego set, still in its box. She observed him quietly while Quinn concentrated on sorting the pieces before he began building. Most ADHD kids were bright and capable of this sort of hyperfocus for tasks that interested them; the problem was that public schools required a lot of sitting still and repetitive tasks, like work sheets. Bright, hyperactive kids weren't about to sit and quietly color after finishing an assignment—*if* they finished it—so they acted out instead.

"Do you know why your mom brought you here today?" Sydney asked.

Quinn shook his head. "No. Probably something dumb."

She smiled. "Well, it might sound dumb, but it's important stuff. You know how you go to the doctor every year to see if you're growing right?"

"Yeah. He gives me shots." Quinn gave an elaborate shudder.

"I can promise that I won't give you any shots, okay?" Sydney said. "Never. That's not my deal. But I am going to give you a checkup. This is a learning checkup to see how you're doing in school. We're just going to do a little reading and writing and math, and you can show me what you know."

The boy nodded, busily clicking Lego pieces into place. "I know a lot," he warned.

Sydney laughed. "I'm sure you do," she said, and prepared to begin the testing, feeling refreshed by the boy's energy and confidence, and happy to be away from the complications of her own life.

Hannah toured Dylan around the farm while she did her usual roundup of spring chores, which included filling water buckets and collecting samples of poop to analyze under the microscope later. Thank God lambing season was over.

She'd been furious with Gary and Sydney last night. How dare they stick her with this depressed boy, no relation to her, just a pale, wet bundle of bones in two-hundred-dollar sneakers—sneakers he'd probably ruined in the rain—when Sydney could barely bring herself to talk to her on the phone?

Even after twenty years, it ate away at Hannah that Sydney had chosen to live with Allen's parents after he died instead of here with her at Haven Lake. Things were bad for a while, but Hannah had checked herself into the nuthouse and gone through so much therapy it was like a part-time *job*. Still, Sydney wouldn't have anything to do with Haven Lake after Theo drowned. Or anything to do with *her*.

She knew Sydney was brokenhearted when she lost Theo. Those two had always been so close. But living with Allen's parents had ruined Sydney. She'd immediately drunk the Kool-Aid and claimed to love life in the "Big House," as Hannah had always called the yellow Colonial in Ipswich where Allen and Rory spent their want-for-nothing childhoods.

"I just want an *ordinary* high school," Sydney had told Hannah in that flouncy way of teenage girls when Hannah tried to force her to come back. Sydney wanted to be a cheerleader, of all things, and take college placement classes. "I'm too old to be homeschooled anyway," she'd said. "Besides, Grandma and Grandpa need me. They're sad about Dad dying, too. He was their *son*."

Like Hannah didn't know that. Like attorney Ron Bishop and his wife, the insufferable Georgia Bishop, hadn't let Hannah know from day one that she wasn't good enough. Especially for Allen, their oldest, whom they had expected to follow in his father's footsteps to law school. They blamed Hannah for what had happened to both their boys. Vietnam didn't even enter into it.

"What do you do with all these sheep?" Dylan asked.

They had walked down from the barn and stopped by the lower pasture to watch the lambs, bounding over tufts of new green grass, one another, and sometimes even onto the back of her resigned-looking llama, Larry. Dylan stood next to her, hands shoved into the pockets of his jeans, grinning. That's why she'd brought him down here: the lambs had that effect on everyone. Better than any antidepressant she'd ever tried.

So odd to have a boy on the farm again. The boys who'd come and gone from Haven Lake over the years were, like Dylan, all knobby knees and long arms, awkward as colts, not knowing where their bodies began and ended. Dylan's rangy build reminded her of Theo's, but where Dylan was internalizing whatever was going on in his life, Theo had expressed everything, his energy and joy and light. Until that final disastrous spring, that is, when Theo had gone dark.

Hannah pushed that thought away and focused on Dylan. He was so pale, it was like looking at a cave-dwelling creature. And that crew cut was a travesty, though Hannah knew from seeing teenagers around town that short hair was apparently in now. She missed the shaggy hair and dreadlocks, the Afros and muttonchops of her youth. She hated thinking the nation was raising a generation of skinheads and baby-faced soldiers who practiced killing things on computers.

"I shear the ewes," she said. "The fleeces are spun into wool and then sent back here, where I sell the wool to spinners and fiber artists. People buy from me ahead of time. It's a yarn shares program, like a CSA, community-supported agriculture. I keep some of the lambs and sell the rest to breeders or to a local butcher."

Dylan looked like he wanted to gag. "How can you watch the lambs playing out here, all happy and everything, and then *slaughter* them?"

"Don't you eat meat?"

"Sometimes," he admitted. "Not red meat, though."

If ever a kid needed red meat, it was this one. But Hannah wasn't going to say that. Not her kid, and definitely not her job to fix whatever ailed him. "Well," she said, "would you rather eat meat from an animal that's been penned up in knee-deep shit all its life, maybe pumped up with hormones along the way, or from an animal that was respected, well cared for, and happily grazing outside until its last day of life?"

"Yeah, yeah. I get the argument. But I still don't see how you do it *personally*."

Hannah shrugged. "It was difficult at first. I used to be a vegetarian. But to be human is to be an omnivore by nature. The important thing is to respect the things we kill for food and be kind to them."

They continued walking the fence lines, Hannah occasionally yanking out a burdock or nettle plant. She explained to Dylan how she used rolls of portable poly-twine fencing and electrified wire to stake out the grazing pastures in the spring, moving the lines whenever a certain section had been grazed down. "Sheep are eating machines," she said. "You don't want to overgraze a pasture. You have to keep rotating them through the land."

"What are you doing with the poop?" he asked as she squatted down to put another sample in a jar.

"I look at it under a microscope. All sheep have parasites—just like we do—but you want to make sure the worm load in their guts isn't too high."

Dylan looked a little green again. She changed the subject, telling him how her llama served as a lamb nanny. "A coyote could easily snatch one of my lambs if Larry wasn't here to protect them," she said. "Llamas know how to stand their ground."

"Have you always had sheep?"

Hannah wondered how much Dylan knew about the farm and its history. Probably nothing. "No. At first we only raised organic vegetables."

Dylan glanced at her, shading his eyes against the sun. "Who's 'we'?"

"Sydney's dad and I bought the farm when we got married. It was a wreck back then."

"When was that?"

She bent down to take another sample of poop, labeled the jar, and tucked it into her jeans pocket. "In 1978. Allen tried going to college after he came home from Vietnam, but it wasn't for him. We both decided to drop out and travel for a while instead of getting our degrees. Then we bought this farm."

"That's cool," Dylan said approvingly. "Where did you go?"

She glanced at him, surprised by the barrage of questions. The few times she'd visited Sydney in Newburyport, Dylan had struck her as a closemouthed kid. He wasn't faking interest to be polite, either; he was looking at her attentively.

"India, and all over Europe."

Suddenly, Hannah felt her face freeze as she was seized by an almost physical pain. *A memory shard*, that's what Liz called these sudden sharp reminders. This particular glittering, jagged fragment was a memory of the Taj Mahal, of the view she and Allen had of that majestic temple from the rooftop of their hostel. Allen, bearded and with a ponytail longer than hers, turned to her as the bright orange sun seemed to float above the city of Agra like one of the flowers the Hindi women sold in the markets.

"The Taj is a monument to a love as great as ours," Allen had said, gesturing toward the temple. "You know that when we get back, you and I are getting married, right?"

It was always that way with Allen: either he was flying high and taking her with him for the ride, snatching the air from her lungs, or he was digging himself into one of his dark corners, a scary place where she couldn't follow.

"What's wrong?" Dylan's blue eyes were dark with curiosity.

"Just difficult, sometimes, remembering my husband, even though he's been dead twenty years," she said. "Pain is a funny animal. It can bite you when you least expect it."

Dylan nodded. From the way he fixed his eyes on the ground, this boy knew pain. His mother had died in a car accident, she remembered suddenly.

But Hannah didn't want to think about this boy's grief. Her own pockets were already full of grief, leaking pebbles of it wherever she went. So she kept talking, telling Dylan about how when she and Allen were finished traveling, they'd returned to the Berkshires to "live off the grid," as Allen put it, "falling out of step with mainstream capitalist America."

She stopped, took a breath. No need to get into Allen's rants about wanting to be surrounded by green, after having been in the scarred fields and charred villages of Vietnam. "A month in the bush and you stop being anything but the lowest kind of animal," Allen had told her feverishly, his dark eyes shiny as damp stones. "You're living in filth, bodies gone black from the sun, flies everywhere. Feet and hands and even the heads missing. I made the world a worse place. Now I want to make it better by healing the earth and feeding people."

To Dylan, Hannah said, "My husband and I learned a lot about sustainable agriculture while we were traveling, and we wanted to try it ourselves. After we bought this farm, we joined the WWOOFing movement. Allen called the farm 'Haven Lake' because of that big pond in the middle of our fields. We dug it out to make it even bigger. The name was a joke, but we were serious about this being our peaceful haven, a sort of Utopian community in a world gone mad."

"What's WWOOFing?"

"World Wide Opportunities on Organic Farms," she translated. "It's a global network of organic farms hosting volunteers from around the world. People came from everywhere to work the land with us: Japan, Spain, Norway, Israel, England, you name it. We gave them room and board in exchange for labor. It was a cheap way to go—the only way we could afford to start the farm, really. And we hoped some of the people we taught would love the lifestyle and start their own farms."

"But you don't have any vegetables now. Or any people."

"I do have vegetables, but just a kitchen garden," Hannah said. "Oh, and a lavender field. Nothing's better than lavender sachets to keep moths out of wool. But you're right. No people." She shrugged. "Now I work with sheep instead."

"And you really like it way out here by yourself?"

She laughed. "You do realize we're only two hours from Boston, right?"

"If you say so."

"I do. And, yes, I like it." Hannah took a deep breath, exhausted by the sound of her own voice. It had been a long time since she'd had anyone walk these fields with her.

They had reached the crest of the hill, the highest point above Haven Lake. Below, they could see the sheep grazing, sixty-eight brown and white and black puffs, the lambs like smaller tufts floating across the grass. She'd chosen to raise Icelandic sheep not only because she loved the luxurious feel of their wool, but because they were once raised by the Vikings and were hardy enough to handle New England winters, she explained to Dylan.

"This is the only livestock you have? Just sheep?"

"And chickens, of course. I wanted to be a shepherd because it's different from raising cows and pigs. Sheep are prey animals, so they need our help. We protect them, help care for them, deliver their babies. They all have distinct personalities, too. Never believe anyone who tells you sheep are dumb. They just have a different intelligence than ours, one based on instinct. Sheep can teach you a lot about life."

"It's cool that they come in all colors."

She nodded. "A white ewe can have one black lamb and one spotted one, or a gray ewe might have a white lamb and a brown one. The surprises during lambing *almost* make you forget about how tiring it is to tend births at three a.m."

They stood on the hill for a few minutes in silence. Below, the pond reflected the midday sun like a giant coin tossed into the valley between green hills. The house was just beyond it, a solid brick Georgian Colonial with a hipped roof and twin chimneys.

Hannah had come to think of the house as an extension of herself, her second skin. It had sheltered her through pain, joy, loss, and now peace. She had few complaints, other than the dull ache she felt for those she'd lost along the way: Theo. Allen. Rory. Sometimes their names were words that no longer fit in her mouth, the grief just a whisper. Other days, she missed them so much that she imagined their ghostly figures climbing the cool dark staircase ahead of her to bed at night.

"Okay, my turn to ask questions," she said. "What's your story? I mean, other than your dead mother."

Dylan gave her a startled look. "What do you know about my mom?"

"Only that she died in a car accident. Tell me about her."

"My mom was beautiful. She used to be a model. She was a lot of fun, too, but in the end she loved to drink more than she loved us," Dylan said flatly.

"Do you really believe that?" Hannah noticed how the boy had clenched his fists.

"Yes. My mom never could say no to booze."

"Was she a good mother when she wasn't drinking?"

"Mostly, yeah. I guess." Dylan turned away, wiped his nose on his arm. "Can we go back now? I need to figure out if I'm leaving before my dad gets here. I might still do that, you know."

"You might," Hannah agreed. "Just remember that somebody—Hemingway, I think—said it's always a mistake to confuse movement with action."

"I hated reading Hemingway in school."

"I don't blame you. He was a dick to his wives, and I never liked all that repetition in his descriptions. Too self-conscious."

Dylan granted her a small smile. "Do you want me to leave tonight?"

"I don't know. Do you want me to kick you out?"

He shook his head.

"Fine. Then stay," she said. "I can survive anything for another night or two. Even a pissy teenager."

"What if I wanted to go right now? What would you do?"

The boy was pushing her, she realized, issuing a challenge. Well, she wasn't playing that game. He wasn't her responsibility. "I'd give you a ride to Amherst," she said. "They have a ride-sharing board at the university. Or I could let you use my computer to check Craigslist for rides west. You might get lucky and find somebody who's not a serial killer."

"You have a computer?"

"Welcome to the twenty-first-century world of farming," she said.

"How else would I sell my sheep and wool? Plus, Web sites like sheepandgoat.com are my lifeline when I want to read up on parasites."

"Gross," Dylan said.

"Oh, don't be such a wimp."

By the time Dylan had helped Hannah finish watering and feeding the sheep, his arms and back ached and his hands were on fire from grabbing the rough twine around the hay bales and heaving the hay down the chute from the barn loft. He didn't know how Hannah did these chores day after day. She was smaller than he was and even older than his dad.

Tomorrow was only Friday. That gave him some options. He could get an early start in the morning or even leave early Saturday. The other, riskier option: go home. Endure his father's stupid punishments and Sydney's lame questions. Finish junior year and face up to the whole thing with Kelly.

He couldn't make up his mind without knowing if Kelly had said anything more about him online. Dylan had sworn not to check Kelly's Twitter feed, an easy enough promise to keep when his phone was dead, but once Hannah said he could use her computer, he couldn't stop himself. He tried using his laptop first—he'd brought his school laptop in his backpack—but Hannah didn't have Wi-Fi and he'd forgotten his charger anyway. Her computer was already set up, an ancient desktop beast with a giant monitor, so Dylan used that instead.

He glanced over his shoulder to make sure Hannah hadn't somehow sneaked into the office—she had a way of soundlessly appearing—then logged on to Twitter. Lots of tweets and selfies on Kelly's stream, most of the pics designed to make any guy shoot his wad. Those tits. Shit. What he wouldn't give to hold *those* again.

Not that he'd really known what to do with them when he had the chance.

They'd met for the first time outside Rite Aid. Kelly was smoking in front of the drugstore when Dylan was leaving his job at Shaw's in his mom's blue BMW. He didn't have his license yet, but he'd driven the car to work because otherwise he would've been seriously late. His father and Sydney had no idea he ever drove it, but his shifts only lasted until six and they were never home before seven o'clock.

The Beemer still smelled like Mom. Sometimes Dylan would imagine his mother sitting in the car with him, tipping her head back to laugh, tossing her sleek brown hair and looking like a knockout magazine model instead of a mom. She had blue eyes like his and she was taller than his dad. She was an actual model in New York City—no lie—before Dad scooped her up at a party and made her a doctor's wife.

"It's what my parents wanted for me, this country-club life," she'd say whenever Dylan asked how she fell in love with Dad. "And I'm glad for it, really I am. Otherwise I wouldn't have you."

Mom was all about parties and nice clothes. And Dad, well, he still had the same T-shirts he'd worn in college and just *knew* there was another plague or terrorist strike or hurricane around the corner. "Come out and play with me, Dr. Downer," Mom used to tease him.

Mom could have saved her breath. Dad would never change. Even in his spare time, Dad went out to find miserable suffering homeless bleeding people and help them.

Dylan loved driving Mom's BMW, navigating corners carefully even on his bad days, when some little voice in his head was screaming, *You could drive into a tree, too, just like her! Try it!*

On the day he met Kelly, Dylan had made it to work under the wire. Afterward, he'd stripped off his tie and walked to the car as fast as he could.

Kelly had just finished her shift at the drugstore and taken off her apron; the apron was dangling from her finger like a red flag as she stood on the sidewalk, watching him with those black-lined eyes. Well, okay, to be exact, Kelly was watching the car. She'd nearly creamed herself over the BMW. Racewalked to stand next to the driver's side before he could pull out of his parking space.

"Sweet car," Kelly said, bending to peer inside it, her breath an intoxicating mix of smoke, mint, and girl. "Want to drive me home? It's not far."

He'd never seen her before, even though Kelly was only a year older. She went to Newburyport High School, while Dylan went to private school. But Kelly sometimes hung out with Bethany, his lab partner in AP chemistry, a girl less obnoxious than most of the others at his school. "She's so ratchet," Kelly said.

Dylan had no idea what that meant, but nodded. As Kelly directed him to a street of nearly identical supersized faceless houses in a neighborhood by the state park, he remembered visiting Bethany here when she asked for his help on the midterm. None of the trees in this neighborhood were taller than he was. He could see Bethany's house just down the street from Kelly's; Kelly's house had a black door and Bethany's was red. That was pretty much the only difference.

"Nobody's home," Kelly said. "Come in and have a beer or whatever."

Dylan didn't like beer. Once, Mom had given him a sip of hers, and it had tasted like warm piss. But of course he manned up and said, "Sure," tossing the car key up in the air and, miraculously, catching it before it hit the driveway, which was sparkling a little in the sunlight. He said something then about the sparkle matching Kelly's nail polish, "like you have stars on your fingers."

"Aren't you the poet?" Kelly said, and giggled all the way through the front door and into the kitchen, where she uncapped a couple of beers.

The kitchen was separated by a counter from a living room with a weird-ass fireplace, a hearth built in the middle of the room and encased in glass. The furniture was white and the circular rug had a red-and-black pattern that made his eyes hurt. No newspapers or books, forgotten sunglasses or coffee cups. Dad would love it.

"How long have you lived here?" he asked.

"Just a year. It's my aunt's house, but she's at work," Kelly said. "My parents are divorced and, you know." She shrugged. "Want to see the rest of this dump?"

She led him straight to her bedroom. A poster of a psycho-looking kitten in a tree hung above a dresser where lipstick tubes were lined up like little missiles. The bed had a canopy over it made out of white lace. A princess bed.

"I'm always so totally exhausted after work," Kelly said, dropping onto the bed. "Must be sweet just bagging groceries and not having to talk to anybody."

"People talk," Dylan said.

Kelly raised her eyebrows. "Yeah? Do *you* talk?"

Dylan laughed. He was feeling the beer now, the alcohol a soft, warm hand stroking his spine. "Not much," he admitted.

"Well, come over here, then, and don't talk to me," Kelly said.

He didn't know how it all happened, exactly. Not at the time, and not later, even though he replayed it in his mind a million times. But Kelly had pulled him down, not onto the bed, but onto *her*, like it was totally natural for some hot girl to want *him*, Dylan Katz, the top scorer on the school's math team, to put his tongue in her mouth and his hands on her incredible body, *all over her body*, until they were both undressed and she was moaning, "Come inside me now, you've got protection, right? I've got something in the drawer if you don't. Come on, oh baby, hurry up!"

He'd thought he would know what to do when the time came for him to be with a girl. He'd seen plenty of stuff online: this body part went here, that one went there, you could do it this way or that way, in a bathroom stall or under the bleachers, and girls would *love* it and beg for more.

But actually touching a girl, a real flesh-and-blood, warm, soft girl, was so much hotter than anything he could have prepared for in a *lifetime* of Internet porn that Dylan couldn't handle it. It was like fireworks were exploding in his head, blinding him with colors and loud popping sounds.

Only it wasn't a firework going off. It was him! Then Kelly was glaring at him with black-lined eyes like she was an assassin and he was her assignment.

"Ew," she said. "Did you *come* already?"

"Um. I guess," he said.

She shoved him off her. "Dude, you're supposed to *ask* whether I'm ready! Girls have to come first! *Then* the guy does it!"

"Sorry. I'm really sorry. It was an accident." Dylan stared into her eyes, but his gaze kept dropping to Kelly's miraculous round, bouncy, naked boobs with their brown nipples like eyes staring back at him. He felt himself getting hard again. "Look, that was just, you know. Foreplay. We could do it again."

She eyed him suspiciously. "For real?"

"Of course, for real," he said, and this time he took his time, making sure to kiss her and put his hands here and there, any place that made Kelly Lanscomb moan, especially that secret dark tunnel where . . . and then it was over again, a hot puddle of shame on his own thigh before he could even enter her. Jesus. He was pathetic.

This time Kelly wasn't having any apologies or second tries. She nearly shoved Dylan off the bed and went to her lipstick-covered dresser, where she yanked open the top drawer and fished around until she pulled out something purple and plastic and penis-shaped. "Looks like I need a slower ride, little dude. Want to watch?"

And, God help him, he both did want to watch and didn't, but what could he do? He stayed on the bed with his pants around his ankles and watched Kelly get herself off—he was sure the neighbors could hear that squeal—then cleaned himself off with a handful of tissues out of a pink flowered box on her bedside table and went home. Miraculously, he arrived just minutes before Dad did, bellowing, "Hey, big guy, how was school today?"

"Fine," Dylan said, as he always did.

The next day, Dylan had arrived at work determined to give the whole sex thing another try. He had jerked off in the morning and again right when he got home from school, just to be sure. He didn't care if he came with Kelly. He just wanted to give her the kind of pleasure face he saw women making online when guys did things right.

Dylan had been so sure things would work out, he'd even told another kid at Shaw's he was "You know, hooking up with this girl at Rite Aid" after work.

Big mistake. The guy was relentless after that, saying things like, "Hey, Dylan, tell Rite Aid Girl I've got a boner for Axe coupons!"

After his shift, Dylan rushed to the BMW and drove it to the fire lane, where he let the engine idle. He plugged his iPhone in, put on some glitch hop, and rested his head against the seat, hoping no cop would show and tell him to move along.

Pretty soon Kelly came out in her tall shoes. She looked around like she was waiting for him. God, she was hot. He was already hard.

"Down, boy," he commanded his eager dick.

But it didn't matter. Nothing he did or didn't do would matter, it turned out, because Kelly already had a boyfriend, Tyler Fantini, a kid he remembered from elementary school, a whirling top at Cub Scout meetings. Now Tyler was in the *Daily News* every season, an MVP lacrosse player with the arms of a gorilla, a guy who could toss a car through a brick wall.

Kelly waved to Tyler across the parking lot. At first Dylan had convinced himself she was only waving at Tyler to be friendly. Why would she want to get with Tyler in his battered Honda Civic, a moron who'd had multiple concussions last year, and not with Dylan in a BMW? Dylan was definitely going to college. Girls liked guys with a future.

Dylan drove the BMW over to Kelly before she could cross the parking lot to Tyler, who didn't even have the manners to go pick her up by the sidewalk so she didn't have to walk across the parking lot in those dumb but seriously hot shoes.

"Hey," Dylan said through the open window. "I thought you might want a ride home."

Kelly raised an eyebrow at him. "A ride like yesterday? No, thanks, little dude. I'm set."

Dylan got out of the car and opened the door for her. "Come on. I can do better, I promise. That was my first time."

Now she was staring at him like he had two heads. "The first time? How old are you, anyway? And who owns that friggin' car?"

"Doesn't matter," he said. He could feel his throat tighten. He didn't want to say "My mom" in any kind of sentence. Especially not in a sentence to Kelly. "What matters is *us*. I'm in love with you, Kelly." He was suddenly tearful, open, ready to pull this girl into his arms and commit to love.

But then Kelly waved her red Rite Aid apron like a flag for a bull and Tyler came charging over in his Honda. The ape threw himself out of the car like he was carrying a lacrosse stick instead of car keys and made like he wanted to check Dylan into the drugstore wall. Dylan scrambled back into the BMW and took off, blinded by tears.

And later? Later, his shame was out there for everyone to see, his shredded heart and pathetic virginity set on fire in the public square, Twitter. Kelly's 3,402 followers included Bethany and her friends, too. Friends at his school and their friends. Dylan got a headache just picturing the Venn diagrams overlapping: Bethany's friends, who had other friends at his school, who surely had friends at whatever schools they were from, and so forth. That was the thing about social media. There was no way to build a dam that would hold unless you quit it entirely. Even then he had his doubts.

Kelly's last tweet had said, "Skeleton Boy's dribbling from his peepee and his eyes. Don't slip on the slick."

Nothing about him today, though. Radio silence.

Dylan looked over his shoulder to see if Hannah had managed to sneak in behind him again, then checked his phone, which he'd juiced after finding the missing charger stuffed into the bottom of his backpack.

And there they were, more reasons to erase his own life and start a new one: three texts from Tyler, who must have gotten his number from Kelly, each more ominous than the last:

Don't show your face or I will F you up

I know where u live

Die 2day so I don't have to kill you 2morrow

Hannah was calling him from the kitchen. "Dylan? Want some dinner?"

"I'm not hungry, thanks." Dylan powered off her computer and shut down his phone. "Guess I'll leave tomorrow if it's still okay for me to stay tonight."

There was a brief but potent silence, one Dylan recognized as the thick air around an adult trying to stop herself from arguing. Would Hannah try to stop him?

No. Apparently Dad was right about Sydney's mom being a free spirit, because Hannah said, "Sure, if that's what you really want."

Dylan didn't really know what he wanted, other than to climb out of his own skin and into somebody else's life.

CHAPTER FIVE

Friday afternoon, Ella insisted on meeting Sydney at her cottage after work. "I am *not* having you ditch me," she said.

Sydney stopped by the hospital on her way home, intent on talking Gary into coming with them to Carrie's party. She found him in his office, still in his scrubs and finishing up paperwork, his eyes red-rimmed and tired. The receptionist and both his partners were gone for the day.

"Hi," he said with a smile. "This is a nice surprise. I thought you were going out."

"I'm just on my way home to change. You look done in," she said, feeling a pang of sympathy. He'd left the house at five to get to the gym before work.

"I was, but I'm suddenly awake, seeing you." He opened his arms. "Close the door."

Sydney did, then went over to sit on his lap. As they caught up on the day, she rested her head on his shoulder. Despite Gary's relaxed posture, she knew he was anxious by the tension in his shoulders and his constant foot tapping. If only there were some way she could help him relax.

Every partner in a couple should provide sanctuary for the other, and she'd found hers in Gary. They'd first met at a hospital gala two years ago, a fund-raiser for a children's psychiatric unit, where they had talked about area hikes. Sydney was bluffing. Her idea of a hike was the rail trail in Newburyport, one flat mile with a coffee shop on the Merrimack River as her ultimate destination.

After the party, Gary had called to invite her on a group hike sponsored by the Appalachian Mountain Club. She'd had to admit she wasn't an experienced hiker, but he reassured her. "It's with the over-forty crowd," he said. "A great group of people. You'll be fine."

The other hikers were cheerful professionals in smartly cut, multi-pocketed shorts; floppy-brimmed hats; and expensive, lightweight walking shoes with bright woolen socks. They looked so much like a bunch of Swiss children hiking the Alps that she kept expecting them to yodel. Gary had to help her up the tougher, rockier paths—she had stupidly worn sandals and jeans—never seeming to mind that Sydney, despite being younger than everyone else, needed to rest more than the others, even the seventy-year-old woman with the umbrella contraption attached to her hat as a sunshade.

From that day on, she and Gary had nurtured an intimate connection based partly on their relief at having found each other after previous unreliable partners. Gary's marriage to a flighty, flirtatious former model had ended in tragedy. Sydney hadn't suffered anything nearly as awful, but her dating history bordered on embarrassing.

Just before meeting Gary, for instance, she'd broken off a three-year relationship with a filmmaker who rented a loft apartment in Gloucester. The apartment was crammed with props—mannequins, a carousel horse, costumes, Victorian furniture—from various short films he'd made. It was like making love in a circus tent.

Ben was in his early thirties, but saw himself as "just getting started." Meanwhile, Sydney felt increasingly settled in her profession and ready to "put down roots," as she'd explained to Ben when he expressed doubts about the wisdom of her buying a house. She had ignored him and bought her riverside cottage anyway, feeling extremely grown-up.

She then happily went shopping in secondhand stores to furnish her new home, fantasizing about Ben sharing the house with her. Meanwhile, Ben occasionally spent the night with Sydney in the cottage, but for the most part he still slept on a futon on the floor of his loft, saying it was better for his back and allowed him to wake up alone in the mornings, "when I have the most creative energy to write."

Sydney didn't mind. She appreciated Ben's dedication to film and knew he was working on a screenplay. Ben was clever and decent in bed, despite being built more like a slope-shouldered academic than the French filmmaker she guessed he aspired to resemble, given his beret and addiction to clove cigarettes. By the time Sydney had furnished her cottage, she was finished with her doctorate and willing to put up with Ben's smoking and strange schedule if it meant a future where they married. He could stay home with the children, maybe, while she brought home the steady paychecks.

However, one day Sydney was driving into Gloucester to surprise Ben with a gift for his birthday—an expensive new camera, which, thankfully, she'd kept the receipt for—and she was the one who was surprised.

Ben was a passenger in the car right in front of her. His beret and sharp goatee made him easy to spot in profile, even in a stranger's car, a squat Mini Cooper in an unfortunate lemon yellow. Sydney recognized Ben as he turned to speak to the driver. She smiled, enjoying this unexpected glimpse of her lover's life.

As the miles and minutes ticked by, Sydney realized that the driver was an older woman she had met at Ben's parties several times, another filmmaker. A woman who dyed her hair the color of purple pansies and wore blue contacts and black capes. A woman named Marla who might, or might not, have a British accent, but whom everyone in Ben's circle described as "fascinating."

Just as Sydney finished processing these thoughts, the light ahead of them turned red. Marla stopped at the light and Ben leaned over to kiss her. Not a peck on the cheek, either, but one of those full-blown movie kisses where the hero can't contain himself any longer and has to pull the woman to him in a crushing, lifesaving embrace to put his mouth full on hers for sustenance.

As Ben drew Marla to him, what distressed Sydney most was that he had never kissed her like that in the entire three years of their relationship. So she put her hand on the car horn and held it there, blaring noise at them as if this was a life-threatening emergency. It felt like that: an urgent life-or-death situation.

There was hell to pay, of course. Ben broke up with her, calling her a "psycho stalker," and Sydney never did get her possessions back from his apartment. She especially missed her little makeup bag, the floral one her grandmother had given her for college.

Sydney thought about all of this in the few minutes she sat on Gary's lap. Then she kissed him and asked him to change his mind about the party. As expected, he sighed and said he had more work to do.

"I'll wait for you to finish," she said. "It doesn't matter what time we get to Carrie's party. It'll go late, I'm sure. Carrie booked a private room, a live band, dancing, the whole bit. Come on! It'll be good for us to get out. We haven't done anything fun in ages."

Gary's thighs tensed beneath her, his foot still jiggling. She was clearly annoying him, pleading like that. Sydney forced herself to stop talking. Gary was under enough stress; he didn't need her whining about something as stupid as parties. Besides, Ella was right: Gary hated to dance. The one time she'd talked him into going to a club, Gary had danced like a trained seal twirling a ball on his nose, self-consciously clapping his hands to the music.

Gary gently moved her off his lap, then stood up and stretched. "A party sounds like a little circle in hell to me right now," he admitted. "You go. Have fun with Ella. I just want to go home, take a shower, and collapse in front of the TV. Sorry, sweetie. I'm showing my age, aren't I? But I just don't have it in me."

Sydney stroked his cheek, feeling the rough stubble. "I get it. You're exhausted and Dylan's on your mind."

At this, Gary pulled away so quickly that she nearly lost her balance, as if she'd been leaning on him instead of just standing in front of him. "Don't remind me," he said grimly.

"Let's go get him right now," Sydney said impulsively. "I don't care about the party. Let's get in the car and drive to the farm tonight instead of tomorrow morning."

Gary shook his head. "No. That would be letting him manipulate us," he said. "I can't let this kid keep calling the shots. I've been doing that too long, and where has it gotten me?"

Sydney knew from Gary's tone that arguing would be pointless, so she kissed him and said good-bye. His eyes were already drifting back to the paperwork on his desk as she was leaving. In this respect, she and Gary were alike: work was their most reliable sanctuary of all.

She pulled into her driveway a little after six. So odd that she owned a house but was so rarely in it anymore. Especially *this* house, the cottage she'd fallen in love with at first sight. Even now, a month after the For Sale sign had gone up, she had to turn her head to avoid looking at it because seeing it made her feel melancholy and displaced.

She hated the idea of anyone else owning her house, but Gary's Victorian was far more suitable for a family. Besides, he'd promised she could redecorate his place after the wedding. "Do whatever you want," he said. "It'll be a fresh start for both of us." He'd then named a budget that made her gasp.

Sydney had no budget at all for decorating when she bought this cottage nine years ago. But one of the best things about growing up on Haven Lake was that she'd learned it was possible to do almost anything yourself, from refinishing floors to making your own pillows.

The cottage was a two-bedroom shingled bungalow with a screened porch overlooking an expanse of salt marshes. Beyond the marshes lay the Parker River. It was easy to imagine getting on a boat from the tiny marina here—the one with the giant stone marker declaring this as "The first landing place in Newbury, 1635"—and traveling along the river and straight across the ocean to England, home to those brave original settlers.

The cottage had been empty for years, abandoned after the old woman who owned it went into a nursing home and died. Sydney first spotted it while aimlessly driving the coastal roads one Sunday during her last year of graduate school, when she'd come up to visit her grandparents. The house was a wreck. The shingles were stained, many so rotten you could poke your finger right through them. Ivy hung like tangled horsehair from the porch roof and the spirea bushes on either side of the front door had grown to Dr. Seuss proportions.

Still, Sydney knew at once that she had to have this house. Despite being in a densely populated little neighborhood, the cottage had an air of privacy because of the tall pines shielding the front yard and the fact that nobody could build on the protected wetlands around it. She'd first seen the house in the spring, when great blue herons were standing along the marshes. Pausing on the porch after the Realtor let her in, Sydney had felt the kind of serenity that comes from standing beneath a vast sky and realizing that your problems, no matter how large they might seem, are only petty human ones.

She'd been able to buy the house only because her mother's father, Grandpa Leo, had sold his auto shop in Ipswich that same year and given her the down payment as a graduation present when she earned her doctorate. "Your mom's got the farm and Grandma Jenn is long gone," he'd said. "Take the money. You're starting your life. I'm winding mine down. There's not one thing to stop me from fishing all year in Florida if I want."

It was the only time Leo had ever been able to help her financially, and Sydney knew it was important to him that she accept his offer. She had taken the gift after making him promise to visit every year.

"You'll always have a bed here, Grandpa," she'd said, but both of them knew he probably wouldn't make the trip. So far, he hadn't; she'd had to fly down to see him. Grandpa Leo now had a house in Key West and a girlfriend, too. "I'm in hog heaven," he always said when she visited. "No more of that shit snow to shovel."

After shoring up the basement and having the house rewired and insulated by a motley crew of Leo's Ipswich pals with dubious credentials, Sydney had replaced most of the shingles and stained the house a warm gold, then painted the trim a seafoam green. She'd planted an English garden in front and an herb garden around the back patio.

Sydney sighed, dreading the heartache she'd experience when she gave up her private sanctuary. But Gary and Dylan were worth the sacrifice.

She began stripping off her clothes in the bedroom, where the windows faced the marsh. She'd painted the walls a deep plum and the trim soft cream. The four-poster maple bed was a remnant from grad school—she'd found the frame at a yard sale for twenty-five dollars and refinished it—and she'd made the quilt out of natural linen, embroidering it with red poppies.

Sewing and embroidery were her favorite ways to relax. She hadn't done enough of either lately. Sydney decided to bring her sewing machine to Gary's next weekend. She'd set it up in the spare bedroom and keep the door open when she was sewing; that room was right across from Dylan's. Maybe if she sat upstairs every night, it would be easier for him to talk to her. The thought cheered her.

She showered and towel-dried her hair, then slicked it back into its usual tight French twist. After discarding several outfits, she settled on the same wide-legged black slacks she'd worn to work, a white tunic with cap sleeves, a strand of red beads, and her go-to black ballet flats. At least she'd be comfortable. She was too tired and worried to be anything else.

Sydney slicked on a little lip gloss, then stood in front of the open bedroom windows, breathing in the salt air and watching a white boat motor along the river. It was cloudy, the last silver light of day illuminating a strip of water ahead of the boat like a mirror. Seagulls tailed the boat and dove for fish in its wake.

She wished Gary could see this view right now, maybe have a glass of wine with her. They could make love and then go to the party together, forget the stress that seemed to be swallowing them up.

Sydney glanced at her cell phone on the dresser. Should she call her mother, find out if Dylan was still there?

She picked up the phone, but was interrupted by Ella's noisy arrival before she could dial. Ella breezed in as she always did, with a knock and a Southern-style "Yoo-hoo, y'all!" that made Sydney smile. She didn't care if Ella exaggerated her accent for effect. She loved it.

"I'm in the bedroom," Sydney called back. "Hang on."

She hastily stuffed her lip gloss, wallet, and phone into a black clutch as Ella came through to the bedroom in a scarlet sleeveless dress that hugged her hips. With her shiny black hair coiled in a knot low on her neck and her gold hoop earrings, she looked like a Spanish dancer. Her lipstick matched her dress.

"You look like Flamenco Barbie," Sydney said, smiling.

Ella snorted. "And you look like Skipper, Barbie's dorky little sister. You're not really wearing *that*, are you?"

Sydney glanced down at her outfit. "Why not? It's practical. I wanted to be comfortable at the party."

"Oh, no, sweetie. 'Party,' 'comfortable,' and 'practical' are three words that should never be used in the same sentence," Ella reprimanded. "Parties are for being *seen*. You can get comfortable later, after you finish strutting your stuff."

"I'm engaged! There won't be any stuff strutting unless you're the one doing it."

"You're engaged, not *dead*," Ella pointed out. "And every woman should strut her stuff."

"I have to lose weight first," Sydney mumbled.

Ella put one hand on her hip and stared at her. "Honey, it doesn't matter how much you weigh. It's who you are that counts. Didn't you get that memo the feminists put out? I would think your crazy mother would have taught you that much on the farm. Anyway, let me tell you this from experience: no matter how much you weigh, this is the youngest and sexiest you will ever look. This moment! Ten, twenty years from now, you'll be looking back at photos of yourself and wishing you'd showed yourself off a little more."

"I doubt I'll have any photos of myself," Sydney said. "You know I'm camera shy."

"I know you're hopeless. Enough! Show me your damn closet."

Sydney sputtered a protest, but Ella tugged open the closet doors. "I should have known you'd be the type who organizes your closet by color," Ella said grimly as she began pushing through the hangers.

"It makes it easier to find things," Sydney said.

"I don't know why you bother, since everything in here is either black or white."

"Taupe," Sydney said, feeling a smile tug at her lips. "I have lots of cream and taupe, too."

Ella turned and rolled her eyes. "Taupe is the color I like my coffee," she said, "not my party dresses." She peered into the closet. "Don't you have a red section anywhere?"

Dylan couldn't help himself: he had to check his phone. He was immediately sorry. His stomach roiled as he read another stream of texts from Tyler:

I will end you

stay away from her

I will fuck u up

u r 2 dumb to live

answer me bro show some respect or else

I know where you live

That last message caused Dylan to picture Tyler stalking him at home when Dad and Sydney were at work, pounding him, then putting the video up on YouTube. He threw the phone as hard as he could against the wall.

He left the phone in pieces and stormed over to Hannah's computer. On her Twitter feed, Kelly had posted a picture of an earthworm. She'd added a digital penis and written a caption: "Watch out, ladies! The Dylan worm will slither his juices on you but leave you high and dry!"

Dylan shut his eyes and forced himself to breathe like it was a new skill. Then he Skyped Mark. His only friend, really. They'd met in elementary school and bonded over Pokémon, Nintendo, Magic cards, *Lord of the Rings*. Even learned to speak Elvish in middle school. Then Dylan's dad insisted on private school and Mark went to Newburyport High.

School ate up the week—shuffling from class to class, trying to pretend any of it mattered—and jobs chopped up the weekends. They hardly saw each other but still played Call of Duty and League of Legends online. Sharing music was their thing, too: dubstep, trap, glitch hop, trance.

"Dude, where you been?" Mark said.

On the screen, Mark's eyes were barely visible beneath the brim of his Red Sox hat. As if Mark was any more likely to play ball than Dylan. They'd learned to memorize the sports headlines of the newspaper in middle school to keep up with the chatter about the World Series or the Super Bowl or whatever, but they never fooled the kids who mattered. *Dweebs, pussies, losers.* "Our middle names," Mark used to joke.

"Not around. Sorry, man," Dylan said. "How's it going?"

He knew people mostly avoided him because he was weird and silent and had that dead-mother vibe. Mark was weird, too, and had an absentee dad, but it was his noise that pushed most people away. He told the whole world what he was thinking and how he was feeling, a running commentary on life, emoting like a smoking volcano. You knew where you stood with Mark.

"Okay. I've been online all night," Mark said. "Fuck, what's that hellish background?"

Dylan glanced over his shoulder and noticed, for the first time, an oil painting of a ram's head hanging on the wall behind him. "I'm at somebody else's house," he said. "Obviously."

He wanted to tell Mark where he was, to explain how surreal it was to be in a place where fuzzy cartoon animals lived under the stove and you could pat actual sheep. Then he remembered the text threats and decided it was better if Mark didn't know, in case Tyler found out they were friends. The world was too small. Even way out here at Haven Lake, Dylan felt freaked out by the woods, by how easy it would be for Tyler to hide in there. What was to stop Tyler from tracking him down and beating his head in? He had a car. He'd made it clear that Dylan was dead meat.

"You getting on now?" Mark said. "I might be able to play one more before Mom's head spins around."

"Sorry. Can't," Dylan said. "Look, I just wanted to tell you I might not be around for a while. Online or in person, either."

"What the hell?" Mark leaned forward toward the webcam, making his brown eyes look like mud puddles.

"Yeah, man, sorry. Guess you haven't been on Twitter."

"You know I left that fucking snake pit last year."

"Right. Well, just so you know, this girl is streaming stuff about me. So I left school and now I'm here."

"What? You and a *girl*? What the fuck? Who? And where's *here*? What the hell happened?"

"I can't tell you."

"Thanks a lot, dude."

"No, I mean it. I really can't," Dylan said. "Her boyfriend's pissed at me and I'm in hiding. I don't want him coming after you."

Mark sat back and pulled his hat brim lower. "Does this dickwad go to your school?"

"Nope. Yours."

"Shit."

"No worries. You probably don't even know him," Dylan said hastily. "I didn't. Not until all this."

"What do you mean, 'all this'?"

But then Dylan heard Hannah's footsteps in the hall and realized she was probably listening, so he cut the connection.

. . .

"So what's he going to do?" Liz asked as she poured the last of the mint tea into Hannah's cup.

"I don't know," Hannah said. "Dylan's a grown man. If he decides to hit the road, that's up to him."

Liz handed the cup to Hannah. "Sixteen is not a grown-up. Especially not for boys. Teenaged guys are like ten steps behind girls on the puberty ladder. You've got to keep him here until his father picks him up tomorrow."

"Yes, well, I *know* that's a good idea," Hannah said. "But how?"

She stared into her teacup and couldn't help smiling at the design of blue violets in the white bowl. Liz was gay and had a shaved head and so many tattoos on her arms that Hannah had thought she was wearing a patterned long-sleeved shirt when they first met. Yet Liz insisted on serving tea out of delicate china cups she'd inherited from her mother. Hannah used to think this was ridiculous until she'd realized how much calmer she felt, drinking out of china. You couldn't make sudden decisions or move quickly with a china teacup in your hand.

"I was hoping Dylan would realize it was a good idea to go home," she said. "It seemed like he might. A little while ago, though, he told me he was still thinking things over and might go back to his original plan."

"He doesn't want to be roped into anything," Liz guessed. "What made him run away in the first place?"

"No clue. But I've never seen a jumpier kid. I'm afraid if I tell him he can't leave, he might just bolt."

"He might," Liz said, adding, "He *is* a teenager," as if that explained everything.

Maybe it did. Liz should know: she taught math at the local high school. She also raised Scottish Highland cattle, chickens, and now those silly runner ducks on the farm she'd bought with her partner, Susan, shortly before Allen died. For the past twenty years, Liz had been the steadiest among Hannah's friends. They shared tractors, snowblowers, a haying contract with another local farmer, and holiday dinners.

Five years ago, it had been Hannah's turn to help Liz through grief when Susan died of breast cancer.

Today, Hannah had let Dylan sleep late, then gave him a list of chores to prevent him from leaving. Not for her sake, and certainly not for Sydney's or Gary's—she was still fuming over those two—but for the boy's. He seemed too poorly equipped to deal with life on the road, for sure.

Dylan had worked hard, doing the watering and weed-whacking along the fence lines. He'd even mowed the front lawn while she made stir-fried chicken and rice for lunch. She didn't tell him the chicken was from one of her own hens, but even so, the kid had only picked at his food.

The boy was surprisingly good company. He shared her enthusiasm for bizarre nature shows like *Meerkat Manor*, which still aired occasionally. Finally Hannah had offered him a ride to Amherst—but only when the afternoon light was fading, the sky an uncertain gray over the green hills, fat rain clouds gathering.

"Maybe you should wait and leave in the morning," she'd suggested, pointing them out.

To her relief, Dylan had agreed. "Is it okay if I use your computer again to check some things?"

Hannah wanted to ask what things, but didn't. She'd logged in to her computer for him earlier that afternoon, partly out of habit—she never trusted anyone with her password, couldn't be too careful about hackers—and partly because she was embarrassed to have the boy know her password was "sheepgal."

When she caught him on the computer later—some other boy's acne-pitted face on the screen—Hannah had chosen to walk by the office without saying anything, equal parts galled and impressed that Dylan was able to get online. How? Was he able to figure out her password by watching her fingers on the keys? That was probably it: for kids these days, watching fingers on a keyboard was probably like lipreading.

She'd left him to it—God knew, the kid needed friends—and walked the half mile to Liz's rambling farmhouse to give Dylan privacy.

Sydney and Gary were idiots, not coming to get him right away. She didn't know enough about Gary to say what he was really like. But he was the last man on earth she would have expected any daughter of hers to marry: a Republican with a pedometer, pager, and cell phone attached to his belt, like he was 007 and the only man standing between the planet and mass destruction. Sydney could talk all she wanted to about Gary's tireless service to patients and families, but Hannah still didn't like him. Too self-righteous and dull.

"Do you think Dylan running away has anything to do with Sydney and Gary getting married, like Sydney said?" Liz asked.

"No idea," Hannah said. "For all I know, it's drugs. The kid is twitchy as hell and doesn't eat."

"So what are you going to do?"

"What *can* I do? He's too big for me to hog-tie. Anyway, you know I'm no expert on kids. The only child I have won't even come home to see me."

Liz reached across the table to rest her weathered hand on Hannah's. "Not your fault," she said. "Extenuating circumstances. If anything, blame Allen."

"If anything, I blame Vietnam," Hannah said, furiously blinking away the unexpected sudden sting of tears as she stared at the numbers tattooed on Liz's wrist: the draft number for Liz's brother, who died at nineteen in Vietnam.

Hannah thought of Allen, of how he'd been at twenty-one, when he'd arrived at UMass after the war. No longer the beefy high school jock, he was lean, almost stringy, his army haircut grown into a dark fringe over his eyes. He'd looked haunted, his brown eyes glittering, fingers drumming on the table at the student union, where he'd arranged to meet her. Rory, who was studying classical guitar at Berklee College of Music, had told him that she was at UMass, too.

During that first meal together—and here, Hannah pictured herself at eighteen, a skinny freshman in braids and patched bell-bottom jeans, her favorite Frye boots—Allen had told her that people spit at him when he came back in uniform. "To them, I was a baby killer," he'd said.

Hannah stood up abruptly and rinsed out her cup at Liz's sink. "I'd better get back," she said. "Who knows? Maybe Dylan's already gone." She wished she could feel relieved by that idea instead of anxious.

Liz stood up to hug her, smelling of mint and chocolate. "What if you offered to let Dylan stay with you for the rest of the school year?"

"Oh, sure. That would go over well with everybody."

"Why not?" Liz insisted. "I could talk to the principal. If Dylan claims your house as his residence, the school would be legally required to admit him. He could finish junior year, get a break from what's eating him."

"But maybe running away isn't the answer. Maybe this is something he needs to work out. Besides, even if the school did say yes, what the hell would I do with a teenager hanging around?"

"He could help around the farm. You said he was a hard worker, right?"

Hannah frowned. "Sydney wouldn't like it. She doesn't trust me. She thinks I'm a negligent parent whose life is all free love, drugs, and drama."

"Don't be absurd. You, of all people, have never been about free love, drugs, and drama," Liz said. "No more than the rest of us who came of age in the seventies. Besides, Dylan ran away from her house, not yours. Obviously things aren't perfect in paradise, either."

"What do you mean, 'either'?" Hannah jabbed Liz in the ribs. "Speak for yourself."

"Oh, I was," Liz said. "My life is full of cracks and potholes."

"And crackpots," Hannah said. "Don't forget that. I'm standing right here."

Liz laughed. "Good night. Let me know if you need me."

Hannah walked slowly up the road, enjoying the smell of new grass and the deep blue evening sky. Her eyes soon adjusted to the light cast by the yellow moon made milky by clouds. In the moonlight, the gravel road nearly glowed, the forsythia blossoms gleaming like thousands of miniature yellow lanterns. Bats wheeled overhead, swooping and soaring like black kites on strings.

At the house, Billy lurched off the porch and greeted her as if she'd been gone a year. The dog circled her legs, whomping her with his tail and herding her safely inside. She hadn't let him come to Liz's because Billy had a thing for Liz's old calico cat. He didn't understand why the cat wasn't ever pleased to see him.

The dog settled on the rug by the kitchen stove with a sigh, resting his head on his paws, his eyes tracking her movements. Oscar poked his head out from beneath the stove, but disappeared again when no food was forthcoming. Dylan must have fed him something or the woodchuck would be begging.

Hannah watered the herbs on the windowsill and listened for signs of the boy in the house. Already she'd gotten used to someone else being present. Not good: she supposed the ghosts would return when Dylan was gone again.

But what if she tried Liz's suggestion? Could she convince Dylan to stay? Would that ruin her relationship with Sydney?

What relationship? she reminded herself. *Your daughter wrote you off years ago.*

Besides, if Sydney was allowing this sixteen-year-old boy to hitchhike across the country alone, Liz was right: Sydney was hardly in a position to criticize. Liz was also right about Hannah needing help around the farm this summer. Maybe it could work out for both of them: she'd save her back and Dylan could escape whatever demons he was fighting.

Unless the demons came with him. There was that possibility, too. Hannah knew that from experience. And she didn't have it in her to battle anybody else's demons. Her own kept her too busy.

Hannah's pulse throbbed in her temple like someone pushing a finger there, in and out. She scanned the counters but saw no sign of a note.

She edged into the living room. Empty, though the pillows were arranged differently. He must have been sitting here. Doing what? How long had she been at Liz's? Hannah glanced at her watch: only an hour.

Something glimmered on the floor. Shiny, metallic, blue—she walked over to peer at it, but it was only when she squatted to pick up the metal rectangle that she recognized it as the back of a cell phone. Where was the rest of it? She scanned the floor from her crouched position and spotted the battery near the couch leg, the front face of the phone several feet away on the hardwood floor near the edge of the rug. It had to be Dylan's.

Hannah collected the pieces and snapped them back together. The phone booted up. She wondered if he'd thrown it, or whether the phone had fallen out of Dylan's pocket.

Threw it, she decided. Otherwise the phone wouldn't have flown apart like this. But why? Because he hadn't liked whatever message or call had come through on it?

Hannah tried reading the messages, even knowing she shouldn't, but the phone was password-protected. She pocketed the device in her jeans, frustrated, and continued through the house, peering into the mudroom and downstairs bathroom.

Finally she made her way toward the office off the dining room, a room she hadn't used in years for anything other than knitting projects. Several of those were scattered about the table in various stages of completion. Beginning a knitting project was easy. Finishing it was hard. Like anything else in life, she supposed.

There was no light on in the office, but Hannah's shoulders relaxed when she saw Dylan was there, headphones on. Text on the screen. Not porn. Thank God for small mercies. She would imagine porn was unavoidable for kids today. She wondered what it did to the male psyche, growing up and having that kind of access, thinking that's what sex was.

She shuddered, thinking of Les Phillips. Bastard.

Hannah retreated silently to the dining room, where she turned on the light, sat down, and picked up a sweater she'd started earlier in the month. The yarn was from one of her favorite ewes, brown and white, and the pattern was a simple one. It called for knitting downward from the neck on circular needles, so there would be no side seams to sew. Unfortunately, she'd done something wrong when she divided for the sleeves. Now she'd have to pull out half her work.

Story of her life: making a mess of things, starting over. As always, knitting gave her the metaphors she needed. Even a beginner's garter-stitch scarf contained twelve thousand stitches. When Sydney was young, maybe ten years old, Hannah had tried to teach her to knit. Sydney had gotten so frustrated, she'd thrown the scarf she was working on right into the woodstove.

"How can you knit?" she'd screamed when Hannah tried to reprimand her. "I'm never going to be patient enough to do that!"

Hannah had shaken her head at the wild fever in Sydney's eyes. "You don't have to be patient to knit," she'd tried to explain. "You learn patience by knitting."

She didn't tell Sydney that she'd set fire to a sweater once, too, after realizing she'd knitted a back and a front with sleeve holes that wouldn't line up no matter what she did.

Hannah had pulled out most of the stitches by the time Dylan emerged from the office, blinking in the dining room's strong light. "I didn't hear you come in," he said.

"Doesn't matter." Hannah kept her head down, concentrating on the yarn. She wasn't going to ask about his plans again, she decided. No use in making the poor kid feel cornered. She decided not to say anything about the computer, either.

She finished winding the loose yarn onto the ball and looked up. Dylan's appearance—putty-faced and hunched, like a wizened middle-aged man instead of a sixteen-year-old boy—alarmed her. What the hell was going on?

Whatever it was, there was no way she could let this boy go off alone tomorrow. "Listen, you were a big help to me around the farm today," she said. "Thank you."

"Least I could do," he said listlessly as he dropped into the chair across from hers.

Honest to God, Hannah thought. How could any kid be this lifeless at sixteen? Was he chemically depressed, maybe even bipolar? She was too old and tired for this caretaker crap.

She took a few deep breaths and started knitting again from the point where she'd finished pulling out the stitches. "Do you know how to knit?"

"No. Why would I? No offense, but it seems kind of lame." Dylan picked at a cuticle. "I mean, what is that, a sweater? You can buy a sweater at Target for twenty bucks. I'm guessing you make more than twenty bucks an hour. How many hours does it take to make a sweater? The numbers don't add up."

Hannah smiled. She'd made the same calculations herself countless times. "True. But there are lots of reasons to make things yourself, if you forget about money."

"Yeah? Like what? Because the world's going to end and only the survivalists will be prepared?"

Smart-ass. Probably just like his father. Hannah pitied Sydney. Then again, Sydney was a smart-ass, too. No gray in that girl's life. Only black-and-white extremes.

"It's good to know how to be self-sufficient," Hannah said. "It's also important to understand the rhythms of life. Sydney's father and I started the Haven Lake community because we wanted to make everything we needed ourselves, live with a lighter footprint on the planet, and use the rest of our time for creative pursuits."

"Did it work?" Dylan's eyes were a grayish blue against his pale skin. He looked rinsed of color.

"Not always." Hannah took another deep breath and held it a minute, literally swallowing memories that otherwise might churn upward from her gut. "But I did learn that it's profoundly satisfying to know how things are made."

Dylan frowned. "Only if you have a shitload of time. What if we had to lug water from a well or make our own clothes? Then we couldn't have jobs and make money."

Money again. He'd missed the point entirely. And why wouldn't he? Dylan had been raised indoors on a computer. Now he'd come to Haven Lake, where the natives spoke a different language and the customs were primitive.

"If I were your age, I'd be tempted to go to college, get a job, and earn lots of money, too," she said. "But money for what? A big house? A brand-new car? And then what? Where does it stop? If I have to make something myself, I develop a deeper appreciation for whatever the end product might be, whether that product is a sweater or a loaf of bread. And that makes me take better care of what I own and need less."

Hannah gave him a ball of yarn—her favorite natural white—and rummaged around in her knitting bag for a pair of needles. She chose the biggest pair, wooden needles size 10.5, and said, "Watch me." She began casting on stitches, then handed the needles to Dylan. "Okay. You do it. Cast on sixty stitches," she said. "You're going to make a scarf."

"But I don't need a scarf," he said, staring at the needles, practically slack-jawed in shock.

"Not now, you don't. But in winter you might. Or you can give it to someone as a present."

"I don't do presents," he mumbled.

"Then you should learn," she said. "Come on. Let's see if you were watching."

Dylan struggled with the first few cast-on stitches, then mastered the technique. She continued to knit, watching him out of the corner of her eye and reminding him to count, her throat tightening at the memory of Rory teaching her to knit.

Rory had long, thin fingers like Dylan's and that same way of biting his lower lip when he concentrated. So strange to think of herself and Rory at Dylan's age, when she was now old enough to be his grandmother. She *was* practically his grandmother.

Rory had learned to knit by watching *his* grandmother and in eleventh grade taught Hannah. They'd made matching six-foot scarves from yarn in bright neon colors.

"Fucking queer faggoty faggot's at it again," Allen would say whenever he saw Rory knitting, but Rory always shrugged.

Hannah had met Rory freshman year of high school. One afternoon she'd left her job in the school office, where she filed and typed letters to earn extra money, and heard piano music coming from the auditorium. She'd gone to the door and seen a boy with copper hair tied in a ponytail, a boy in a T-shirt and faded Levi's who looked like he lived in his own universe.

Rory's universe, she discovered that day, was filled with music: anything from Chopin to Pink Floyd, from Santana to Bach. Hannah was so stunned by the sounds coming out of the piano—tracks off Chick Corea's *Now He Sings, Now He Sobs* album, she discovered later—that she had to lie down between the last two aisles in the auditorium while Rory played, feeling the music in her backbone.

"I know you're there," he'd announced suddenly. "Come sit with me. I'm lost and alone up here, Gypsy Girl."

She'd laughed and joined him, brushing off the seat of her jeans. "Gypsy Girl" was Rory's immediate nickname for her, and it suited her back then, with her black hair falling in waves to the middle of her back, her sandals and bracelets and beads.

Rory wasn't lost. She had never met anyone so content in the moment. His fingers never faltered on the keys. But she'd joined him at the piano, turning the pages of sheet music when he nodded. That had become their afternoon ritual and the start of their friendship.

They were best friends after that: Rory'n'Hannah, Hannah'n'Rory. Everyone at school said their names like one word because one was so rarely without the other. It didn't matter to either of them that Rory Bishop—"a name like a millionaire in one of those racy books you read," her father teased—lived in one of the biggest houses in Ipswich, or that Hannah's father owned the gas station in town, her mother was Greek, and she lived in a tiny red Cape behind the garage.

She'd go to Rory's house on weekends, where Hannah loved sitting on his broad front porch, knitting and not talking about school—they both knew school was beside the point—but about the world beyond: the Kent State shootings, the invasion of Cambodia. Or sometimes Rory would play his guitar and sing, his voice surprisingly deep for a boy with such a slender frame. He played anything with strings: banjo, cello, fiddle. He even had a harp, handed down to him from a grandmother who trained as a singer in Paris.

She never would have met Allen if she hadn't been on that porch. Allen was two years older, a popular varsity athlete. He'd arrive home dripping wet after football or basketball or baseball practice, depending on the season, a towel draped over his muscular neck, and sit on the porch with them, swilling orange juice or milk straight out of the carton and making Mrs. Bishop yell but not do anything about it.

"You gonna make yourself some culottes to go with that scarf, little fairy?" Allen would ask Rory. "A nice little pair of hot pants, maybe?"

Rory never rose to the bait. And, to be fair, Allen never said these things with malice: he was playing a part. Even Hannah understood that. And he didn't tease *her*; he'd even nod hello to her in the school hallway.

Summer weekends, Allen would occasionally take them down the Ipswich River in his canoe. He'd bring beer; Rory brought his guitar. Hannah never wondered at the time why Allen didn't invite his teammates or other friends. Looking back, she realized that even then Allen had been capable of compartmentalizing himself, of separating his body from his mind, his intellect from his heart. Only much later would she find out why.

Once, after admiring a drawing she gave Rory, Allen asked her to paint him something. She had surprised him with a watercolor of his canoe, and of Allen in it, alone, his broad shoulders bare and brown and rippling with muscle. After his death, she'd found the painting in a box he kept in the attic of the farm, along with a Bible he'd carried in Vietnam.

That summer on the Ipswich River was electric with tension, the two brothers vying for her attention, diving off the bridge in too-shallow water—once Rory, skinnier but more agile than Allen, had to pull Allen out of the muck because he'd literally gotten stuck headfirst in the muddy bottom. He'd come up laughing, and said, "There's mud in my eye, but a song in my heart."

Allen chided Rory and Hannah about their long hair, their jeans and beads, the protests they talked about joining against the war when they were old enough to drive. "You really want the Commies to take over the world?" Allen demanded any time their conversation turned to Vietnam. "You think life would be so much better if they were in charge of things?"

He'd enlisted at the end of senior year, saying, "What does the world need with another college boy, if there's not going to be a world like we know it?"

Allen's decision to join the army upset Mrs. Bishop so much, she'd gone to stay with her sister in Connecticut for two weeks. His father, on the other hand, approved. "There's always time to get your degree and practice law, son," he told Allen. "Nothing makes a man out of a boy like war."

Rory had cried, huddled in Sydney's arms in the shade of the maple tree in her backyard. "What if he doesn't come back?" he said. "It should be me who goes. My parents won't survive if Allen dies."

Hannah had shaken him hard by the shoulders. "Don't be an idiot. Nobody asked Allen to go," she said. "He wasn't even drafted! He's only trying to get out of going to college because he hates school. You just have to hope your number won't come up."

It didn't. Allen left for Vietnam; meanwhile, Rory and Hannah graduated and Rory went to Berklee College of Music while she went to the state university, because that's all her father could afford.

Before they left for college, she'd tried to kiss Rory for the first time, suggesting that they lose their virginity to each other. "At least we can laugh about it together even if it's awful," she said.

They were in a cornfield, lying on the thick soft dirt between the rustling stalks. Rory had cupped Hannah's face between his long musician's fingers and pressed his forehead to hers. "Not like this," he whispered. "I want you to love me, Hannah. I've always wanted that. Not like a friend, but like you're in love with me. Then we can make love."

She had reared back so fast that his nails scratched her cheek. "We're friends," she'd said desperately. "How can I fall in love with you if you're my best friend?"

"That's the question you have to ask yourself, I guess," Rory said. "Think about it when we're apart."

She did, but not much. UMass, it turned out, was a hotbed of excitement: concerts on the lawn, dorms teeming with hormonal students whose main purpose seemed to be to get drunk and screw, in that order.

The first night she was there, Hannah drank cocktails of Grand Marnier and Scotch and vomited on the new orange Indian print bedspread she'd bought with babysitting money; that same night, four basketball players had come reeling through the dorm rooms on her floor, ripping the doors off the rooms and fencing with the coatracks they yanked out of the closets. It was like trying to stay out of the way of a herd of angry giraffes.

She and Rory exchanged letters, but there was a divide, now, of ninety miles, college classes, and new people to meet. Then, her first October on campus, Allen had come to find her, seeking her out in a way Rory never had, his eyes brimming with need, his voice hoarse with desire and the experience, she discovered much later, of Vietnamese prostitutes who opened their legs and mouths to stay alive. Sex was survival for those girls, and it had come to mean the same to Allen: if you were having sex, he'd told her once, you couldn't be dead.

She never made love with Rory because you didn't have sex with your best friend. You didn't let him take you to an apple orchard on the hill above the university on a crisp fall day and push your jeans down around your ankles, whispering your name as he touched you and then entered you, arching his back scarred from shrapnel and coming up like a swimmer gulping air, gasping as his tanned shoulders gleamed in the sunlight, as he threw his shoulders back so far that Hannah could imagine wings there, as if Allen were a bird of prey and he'd taken her in the field, his great wings rising behind him and pinning her in place on the fragrant dirt, sun-warmed and a little bruised, breathless and in love for the first time with a man she almost didn't recognize, a stranger so damaged from war that his eyes were the bright, desperate black eyes of an injured animal that will fight for what it needs, or else drag itself into a corner and die alone.

Hannah shivered a little and forced herself to focus on Dylan again, on the yarn, breathing in rhythm with the peaceful sounds of knitting needles ticking together, making something out of nothing, one stitch at a time. Her salvation.

When he'd finished casting on, Hannah showed Dylan how to knit. He caught on quickly, but shrugged when she complimented his stitches. "Good thing nobody's here to Snapchat me. They'd think I was gay for sure."

"Are you?" Hannah asked.

The boy nearly dropped his needles. "What? No! I'm not gay!"

"You sure?"

Dylan rolled his eyes. "Yes. I think I would know, right?"

"I don't care if you are. I was only asking."

"I'm not!" Dylan said fiercely. "I like *girls*, okay?" He was knitting faster now.

"Any girl in particular?"

"One. Sort of. But that's over, apparently," he mumbled.

So Sydney was right. "I'm sorry," she said. "That sounds difficult."

"Sucks, yeah." Dylan was silent for a minute, reaching the end of the row. "Now what?"

"Now you purl." Hannah showed him how to turn the scarf over and start purling, watching closely until he'd mastered the stitch. "Good," she said. "When you reach the end of that row, you turn the scarf over and knit the next row. And so forth. That's called the stockinette stitch."

"Still sounds gay," Dylan said, but he continued to work the yarn.

"Only if you've got a one-track mind," Hannah said. "You know, men have always been knitters. In Japan, samurai soldiers used to knit their own socks and gloves. A lot of military men have been knitters. The actor Russell Crowe is a knitter. You're in good company."

The boy's face was more relaxed, but he was still supernaturally pale.

Hannah got up and went to the kitchen, where she toasted two slices of the oatmeal bread she'd made that morning, lathered them with butter and some of her own strawberry jam, and brought them to the table with a glass of milk. She put the food on the table without saying anything and resumed her own knitting.

At last Dylan took a break, eyed the toast, and picked up a piece. He nibbled at it, then devoured the two slices as if eating for him was like someone else gasping air after a long swim. "Huh," he said after finishing the milk in three swallows. "You made this bread?"

"Yes. Early today," she said. "You were still sleeping."

"Good thing. Otherwise I would've eaten the whole loaf."

Hannah decided not to push things by asking if Dylan wanted more, but she was pleased. She would just keep putting food on the table and ignoring him. If he ate, fine. If not, well, what was she supposed to do about it?

At the same time, she felt compelled to tell Dylan about her conversation with Liz. He would say no, and that was for the best. But he would like to be asked. Hannah felt sure of that. "What would you think about staying here through the summer?" she said. "I could pay you to help me around the farm. If you wanted to take classes at the local school, you could probably still finish junior year. You could go home after the summer, or keep going west. That way you'd have more money if you still want to go to Seattle. September is probably a better time to look for a job out there anyway."

"I doubt my dad would go for that plan."

"Why not? He was going to let you hitchhike across the country. How would this idea be worse, in his eyes?"

"Dad thinks any idea I have is shit, basically. Anyway, what would I do here?"

"Well, besides finish whatever classes you're taking, you could help me with the animals, and with maintaining the fencing and the pastures." Hannah was warming to the idea, surprising herself. "There's haying as soon as we get a dry week in mid-June. You could help with the kitchen garden and canning, odd jobs around the house and barn. I can teach you whatever you need to know."

"I'm not sure," Dylan said.

Hannah was surprised to feel a little sting of rejection. What the hell? Here she'd practically offered the kid the moon, and he was turning her down?

Fine. No skin off her nose. Dylan wasn't *her* problem. "Fine," she said. "I'm not sure it would work out, either. I'm used to living alone."

"I wasn't saying no," Dylan said.

Hannah eyed him warily. "Okay," she said slowly. "Maybe we should do a test run. One week. See how it works out for both of us. No hard feelings on either side if it doesn't."

"That might be okay. I could do a week."

"Me, too," Hannah said, thinking maybe teenagers were like sheep: they felt threatened if you looked them directly in the eyes. You needed to let them approach you, not corner them.

If only she'd known that years ago with Sydney, would things have turned out differently?

The party was in full swing by the time Sydney and Ella arrived. Carrie had rented out the back room of the restaurant and hired a blues band. The lead singer was a rotund black man in a porkpie hat and black shirt; he was wailing about careless love making him want to weep and moan.

Amen to that, Sydney thought. No more careless love for her.

She wobbled across the room behind Ella on the black peep-toe heels she'd bought for a friend's wedding years ago and forgotten until Ella dug them out of her closet. If only she'd thought to tuck a sweater into her purse. Not because the room was chilly—the room was too warm, if anything—but because of the way the dress clung to her body.

The dress was a gift from her grandfather Leo's new girlfriend. She'd never worn it. It was an odd color but a "timeless design," according to Ella, a green jersey wrap dress that Ella also insisted brought out the color of Sydney's eyes and "makes you look like you got a whole lot going on."

By this, Sydney assumed Ella meant the dress showed off the cleavage she usually tried to hide. Sydney hated her big boobs, plain and simple, more than any other part of her. At age twelve, her breasts had seemed to arrive overnight, as if delivered by some malicious little breast fairy who'd wanted to give Sydney a reason to hunch her shoulders and feel self-conscious.

Not that she'd needed to worry about her body on Haven Lake, where she was homeschooled, and where so many of the women around the farm went braless, or even shirtless in hot weather. Nobody much noticed Sydney's breasts on the farm until Theo did. The memory of his hands on her breasts, even mixed as it was with grief, could still make her shiver with pleasure.

She supposed the one positive thing about natural living was that you were expected to have mammary glands, just like cows. The women who came and went from Haven Lake with their infants seemed proud to be giving milk like cows, too. You were supposed to enjoy the fact that your body was healthy. The motto on the farm was that any natural act that made you feel good must be good for you, even sex. Maybe especially sex, judging from the way the so-called "adults" of Haven Lake swapped partners.

However, when Sydney moved in with her grandparents, she'd started at a traditional high school and discovered that breasts were a nuisance around boys who were less enlightened. More than one guy had groped her in the hallway, until she started wearing oversized tops with sports bras beneath them to keep the jiggle to a minimum.

College and graduate school were better—a well-cut bra and loose blouse could disguise almost any figure flaw, and she'd found plenty of men who were attracted to her for reasons other than her breasts—but there were still some days when Sydney wished she could just remove these ancillary parts of herself and be done with them.

Fortunately, Gary was a leg man. He commented often on her slim legs, and when they made love, he caressed her thighs and buttocks, ran his hands down her calves, was tender with every part of her, his mouth soft on her mouth and neck. She felt protected and cherished.

Now, in this clingy low-cut dress and with the glittering silver choker Ella had found while rummaging through a box of forgotten jewelry in her dresser drawer, Sydney felt as though she might as well be announcing, “Boobs coming! Make way for boobs!” Men turned to stare as she crossed the room. Even worse, Ella had made her leave her hair down, and it was everywhere, streaked gold from her hours of gardening.

She’d brought a gift for Carrie, a white cardigan she’d bought and then hand-embroidered with violets in a plum silk thread along the border. She spotted Carrie now, standing at the table closest to the band, and cringed a little. Carrie was Sydney’s least favorite person in the office. She disliked the way Carrie was always trumpeting about “making a difference in the world, one child at a time” and doing that social worker thing, asking, “How are you feeling, *really*?” even if you were just choosing vanilla yogurt out of the fridge instead of strawberry.

Most of the other women here were dressed like Sydney, or how Sydney would have been dressed if Ella hadn’t intervened: in dark pants and loose tops, with the occasional elastic-waist skirt. And beads, lots and lots of beads: beaded earrings, beaded necklaces, beaded bracelets. Social workers and psychologists all loved beads, it seemed.

In this crowd, Carrie stood out as much as Ella and Sydney. She was tall and rangy, with that slinky catwalk stride only extremely tall women managed without looking ridiculous. Tonight, as usual, Carrie was dressed as if she were headed into a corporate boardroom: in a straight black sleeveless shift that showed off her toned arms, and pearls that sat like smooth baby teeth around her neck. Carrie looked classy, not trashy like Sydney. What had she been thinking, letting Ella dress her?

The truth was that Sydney hadn’t been thinking at all. She was too worried about Dylan and about having to go back to Haven Lake tomorrow.

As she and Ella threaded through the crowded room to wish Carrie a happy birthday, she decided Carrie was attractive mostly because she was so unusual looking, with high, flattened cheekbones, white-blond straight hair, and bright blue eyes inherited from her Finnish parents. It was easy to imagine her skiing cross-country, or even herding reindeer.

The only personal thing Sydney really knew about Carrie was that she was fluent in Spanish and had a thing for Latin men, whom she described in avid detail whenever she returned to the office after one of her jaunts to Mexico or Spain. Given her propensity for "hot tamales," as she called these lovers, Carrie was likely to fall into a near swoon around Marco.

Like right now, for instance. Marco was standing with the small knot of people gathered around Carrie at the bar, handing her a cosmopolitan and saying something that made Carrie dip her head and smile, her bright blond hair swinging forward across her bony collarbone.

"That girl's skinny enough to snap like a twig," Ella said close to Sydney's ear. "Wouldn't take more than one good gust of wind to blow her across the parking lot."

"Oh sure, now you try to make me feel good," Sydney hissed back. "Why didn't you let me wear the damn Spanx, at least?"

"Because no man wants to feel a cement block waist instead of real woman flesh when you dance with him," Ella replied.

"News flash: I'm not dancing," Sydney said.

Carrie had spotted them by now. "Oh, good, you made it!" she cried. "Fantastic! I was so afraid nobody would come to my little soiree."

She was lying, Sydney knew. Carrie's confidence in any situation was what made her so valuable a colleague, but otherwise annoying. Sydney wasn't above lying right back.

"Oh, come on. Nobody would want to miss your *birthday*," she said, kissing Carrie's cheek and ignoring the eyebrow Ella raised in her direction. "Where do you want us to put the presents?"

"Over there on the table against the wall is fine." Carrie touched Sydney's dress. "This is pretty. Vintage? Your hair looks great, too." She cocked her head at Sydney. "You don't even look like you." This sounded vaguely accusatory.

"I don't feel like me, either," Sydney said. "Ella dressed me."

"She was going to wear her *gardening* pants," Ella clarified.

"I'm glad you had your way with her, Ella," Marco said. "She looks like a cross between Pink and Scarlett Johansson."

Sydney flushed. "I'll be right back," she announced, mumbling something about putting Carrie's gift on the table.

Halfway across the room, she tripped in the unfamiliar high heels and went sailing forward, falling to her hands and knees onto the carpet. Sydney gathered her legs under her, shaking and humiliated, and felt a hand on her back.

"You okay?" It was Marco, somehow still beside her even though she'd ditched him at the bar.

His sympathetic voice and the warmth of his hand uncorked the emotions she thought she'd successfully stoppered for the night. Tears pricked her eyelids. "Obviously not," Sydney muttered, still sitting on the floor. "I feel like an idiot."

"Here. Take my hand. Nobody saw, you know." Marco pulled her to her feet, his grip strong, then leaned close and said, "Sorry if I embarrassed you. I think you look gorgeous."

"Ha. If you like sausages wrapped in jersey casing."

"Stop it." Marco pulled her closer. Now she could smell him, musky, a slight overtone of whiskey. "Nobody here comes close to how beautiful you are." He gestured around the room without letting go of her.

Sydney shook her head, furious now. "Save the Latin lover talk for Carrie," she said. "It's her birthday. I'm engaged. Besides, I know my butt is twice the size of Montana. Don't bother lying to me." She tried to pull away, but he wouldn't let go of her hand.

"I don't lie," Marco said in a low voice, his lips almost, but not quite, touching her ear. "And I know you're engaged. But dance with me, Sydney. They're playing our song."

"What the hell are you talking about? What song?" She scowled as Marco led her by the hand to the dance floor.

Sydney thought about resisting, then relented and danced with him.

What the hell. She knew what he was like. Everybody did. He was teasing her. And the last thing she wanted to do was make a scene and draw attention to herself.

After a few surprising minutes of moving with Marco on the dance floor, it felt oddly wonderful to just give up and let the music take over her body. All through her childhood there had been musicians on the farm. Uncle Rory was always in the kitchen or on the porch with his acoustic guitar and banjo. He was mostly a folk musician—all the oldies, like James Taylor, Jim Croce, Cat Stevens—but he could go heavy metal or rock, too. Other musicians had come and gone, fiddlers and flutists and even a guy with bagpipes. When there were too many musicians for the porch or kitchen, they held impromptu jams in the bigger barn, where they cleared the floor for dancing and set up hay bales as tables and chairs.

Sydney had been dancing from the time she could walk, and once she let herself go, she was surprised by how pleasurable it felt to move to the music. Marco guided her around the floor with skill, and after a few minutes she found herself easily following his hips and feet. She finally let him take her in his arms to twirl and dip, forgetting where she was, everything fading away but this moment and the mysterious, nearly forgotten, unmistakable joy of being in motion to music.

CHAPTER SIX

The rooster woke him, a Cartoon Network bird with a smoker's cough.

Dylan sat up and immediately felt for his phone. Not there. He'd trashed it last night. He wanted to throw up, remembering Tyler's texts:

answer me bro show some respect or else

I know where you live

What if Tyler had tracked him to Haven Lake, and was planning to ambush him down by the barns today? That thought had made it difficult to fall asleep last night and Dylan woke this morning feeling dry-mouthed with fear.

Then there were Kelly's tweets. After the worm with the penis and the hat, she'd posted a YouTube video of a dancing skeleton and captioned it with his name.

Dylan watched the sky lighten through the window and wished he were playing Call of Duty. He wanted a virtual gun in his hands. Stalk and shoot. Scope and splatter.

Parents had it all wrong: video games didn't make kids violent. A lot more kids would be out there offing people for real if they didn't have computers.

Dad tried to control his screen time, freaking out about him spending too much time inside. "You didn't do anything today, pal," he'd say. "You've got to get outside, enjoy nature."

Dylan argued that it wasn't like nature was outside and we were inside. "Your skin is a zoo, Dad. You're a doctor. You should know our bodies are microbiomes crammed with organisms. You know how many bacterial cells are on our bodies? Like, a hundred trillion just in our stomachs, right? I don't *have* to go outside to be in nature. I *am* nature. I'm like one giant walking planet of viruses and bacteria."

Without a phone, Dylan had no clue what time it was. Just the rooster, hollering about the excitement of a new day even though the sky was still inky purple and Dylan could barely see his hand in front of him.

He could get up now and leave. There was nothing to stop him from putting on his shoes and walking down the road. Dylan looked out the window. The barn was still dark. Hannah wouldn't even know he'd gone.

Except she would, though. Hannah had some kind of spooky Spidey sense. She was probably listening for his footsteps right now. Or Billy would bark and wake her if Dylan tried to sneak downstairs, maybe herd Dylan up against the wall the way he bunched the sheep up and got them going in a certain direction when Hannah whistled. Or that woodchuck Oscar would trip him and bite his ankles. And Tyler could be waiting for him behind the stone wall.

This entire freakin' house was booby-trapped.

Dylan turned on the light beside his bed, suddenly creeped out in the darkness. What if Hannah forced him to go home with his dad this morning? He couldn't do that. Not now. Maybe not ever. Tyler had it in for him. Even if that weren't true, how could he show his face around Newburyport? Kelly knew people from his Cub Scout troop, from elementary school, even from his high school. His chem partner, for fuck's sake. Thank you, Social Fucking Media.

Dylan's heart was like a live animal clawing at his chest. His throat was clogged, like somebody had rubbed his tongue and tonsils with a glue stick. Maybe he was having a heart attack. He opened and closed his hands, thinking about his destroyed phone on the living room floor. Had Tyler texted him again? Had Hannah found the phone?

He was such an idiot, breaking the stupid phone. No way would that keep Tyler off his ass. Tyler had said to answer him and show some respect. He'd be even more pissed off if Dylan didn't text back.

His eyes scanned the bedroom for weapons. All he saw were the stupid knitting needles stuck in the ball of white yarn like chopsticks in rice. Better than nothing. Dylan got out of bed and picked them up. At least you could stab somebody in the eyes with knitting needles.

Then his gaze landed on his puny two inches of scarf. He felt the square of knitted cloth, stroking it between his thumb and forefinger. The yarn was soft and not white-white, more like cream. He thought of Casper, the lamb that had bounced around in the grass while he walked with Hannah through the soggy field yesterday. Patting the wool was like putting his hand on that lamb's soft head.

Dylan sat down on the edge of the bed and inserted the needle. Yarn over, pull through, needle in, yarn over, pull through.

Once he started knitting, his chest loosened. Soon he was breathing, his heart rate slowing. His mind cleared. The fog of red fear lifted as he finished knitting the row and flipped it over. He fingered the ridges and valleys, thinking of samurai soldiers and sheep, how those two things he'd never have put together in his mind were together now. Then he began purling, keeping his eyes on the stitches as the sun rose, trying not to think about anything but the wool in his hands.

They left Newburyport before dawn, armed with travel cups of coffee, bananas, and granola bars. Sydney drank her coffee too fast and burned her mouth. The banana was green, but she ate it anyway to counter the sudden caffeine rush.

It hadn't been a good year for bananas. For a lot of crops, actually, due to the polar vortex in the Midwest, the unexpected freezing temperatures in the South, and that protracted drought in California. Gary read three newspapers a day and kept her so informed that Sydney felt guilty each time she ate fruit out of season.

He'd been asleep when she came home last night. They were only now talking about Carrie's party. She'd told him Carrie seemed surprisingly okay about turning forty and had a live band, but she didn't tell Gary about dancing. Or about how, when Carrie came to claim Marco after that first breathless number, saying, "Hey, babe, you owe me a birthday dance," Sydney had felt a sinking sensation as unexpected as the joyful abandon she'd experienced while moving to music with Marco's hands on her waist and hips.

"How was the food?" Gary asked.

Sydney glanced at him, startled. He never asked about food. If meals were left up to Gary, he'd eat like an astronaut or a soldier: freeze-dried meals out of pouches. The kind of high-protein food that could be airlifted thousands of miles and dropped from helicopters. She admired this about him, especially when they were on aid missions together, like that trip to Mexico after the last earthquake and to the Philippines post-typhoon. Sydney, on the other hand, had craved bread and chocolate, wine and good cheese on those trips. She didn't have it in her heart to marvel at the quality of freeze-dried spaghetti.

"Not great," she said. "Ella said if the chicken had been an exit on the highway, we would have missed it two stops ago."

Gary didn't laugh. Sydney didn't blame him. She was never any good at repeating jokes. Though maybe Gary wouldn't have laughed anyway. He seemed nervous this morning, his fingers tapping on the steering wheel, a twitch in his temple.

Sydney was worried about him. She wanted to slide closer, put her hand on Gary's leg to reassure him that things would be all right once they brought Dylan home, but he always snapped at her whenever she distracted him while driving. Besides, how could she say that when she didn't fully believe it herself?

Gary had been the one to call Hannah this morning to tell her they were leaving. "How was Mom on the phone?" she asked now, setting her coffee back in the holder to let it cool.

"Chilly but collected. Her usual."

Sydney nodded, though having her mother described as "collected" and "chilly" startled her. When she was young, Hannah had been the sort of impulsive, energetic mother whose laughter filled the air like music. She could do anything: make dresses out of burlap grain sacks and turn empty yogurt containers and old car parts into toys for kids. She'd taught Sydney other, handier skills, too, like how to bake bread so that it was crusty on the outside and the perfect texture on the inside, and how to jump a car with a dead battery and change the spark plugs.

"You don't ever want to be helpless," Hannah had often reminded her. "That's how people get themselves in trouble. Women, especially."

Hannah had been her protector, too, whenever Dad went into one of his rages. Dad was a quiet man, never singing or joking around like Uncle Rory, and definitely not a friendly pothead like most of the other men passing through. Despite Dad's tangle of wild brown hair and ragged jeans, he was the undisputed leader on the farm. You didn't sow a seed or collect an egg unless Dad said it was okay. Maybe his authority was derived from his stint in Vietnam—a time he never talked about, unless something set him off and he turned red-eyed and muttering.

She remembered a particular July Fourth when someone new had arrived at Haven Lake and thoughtlessly set off fireworks over the pond. Her father had thrown himself flat on the ground and covered his head, screaming, "Incoming! Green star cluster!"

Later, Dad trembled in her mother's arms in the kitchen after everyone went to bed, while Sydney sat on the bottom stairs and listened. "Every shadow's a gook," he'd whispered. "Every night, you're waiting to kill or be killed. The whole black night is your enemy. You don't know, Hannah. You just don't know."

Gary took the exit off 495 for Route 2 west. They were halfway to the Berkshires. She wondered if the farmhouse would look the same, and thought about how they'd gathered for meals outside on rough handmade tables in warm weather. Every meal included chapatis the women made by hand, mixing flour with water and salt, then cooked on a skillet and filled with sprouts and tomatoes they grew themselves, honey from their own bees, cheese and coconut peanut butter from the People's Co-op in Amherst.

During meals, Dad dispensed work orders. Everyone reported back to him in the evenings before going off to smoke dope and make music. If he was satisfied, Dad would give the workers a small smile and say, "That's okay, then," his equivalent of a cartwheel.

Most of the time, he was like that: perfunctory and polite. But every now and then Dad would go off as suddenly as those matches you could strike on anything. Boom! He'd start yelling and cursing the stupidity of whoever had displeased him. Only Mom—magical Mom—could calm him. She'd stand in front of him and place her slim, callused hands on either side of Dad's narrow skull as if she were holding him in place.

Soon after she moved to her grandparents' house, Sydney had broken a lightbulb when she was sweeping the kitchen too carelessly and the end of her broom handle whacked the overhead light. She'd frozen in place, as she had learned to do on Haven Lake to make herself invisible whenever she did something that might set off Dad. What an astonishing relief it was to know that he was gone.

Then guilt washed over her: How could she not mourn her own father?

Sydney finished her coffee even though her stomach was churning. Did Dylan experience the same conflicted emotions about his mother that she did about her father? She hoped not. Maybe Dylan was able to feel a purer kind of sorrow because Gary carried enough anger at Amanda for them both.

She glanced at Gary. "What are you thinking?" she asked as a way of climbing out of her own head.

He smiled and reached for her hand. "That it's a shame we don't come out and hike in the Berkshires. It's so beautiful here."

She was surprised he hadn't said anything yet about Dylan. Then again, maybe not. Gary had once told her that he compartmentalized things during surgery so he could focus on the tasks his hands had to do. "If I think about the life of the actual person whose body I'm trying to mend, I'm all thumbs," he'd confessed. "I have to think about the human body like it's a machine while I'm in the OR."

Maybe that's what he was doing now, setting aside the problems with Dylan as if his son were a riddle to be solved during a quiet hour alone. But they should have a plan in place before then.

"We should talk about Dylan," she said.

"What's there to talk about?"

"Well, for starters, what if he's not there? Or what if we get there and he won't come home?"

"Neither of those things is going to happen. He isn't stupid, Sydney."

"No, but he might be desperate. Unpredictable."

"Desperate about what?" Gary glanced at her. "I still can't understand his behavior. Can you?"

"No," Sydney admitted. "We don't really know much about his life. He does well in school, so we assume everything is going smoothly, but we never see his friends. I don't even know if he *has* friends. We have no idea what he's doing at home alone while we're working."

Gary snorted. "Yes, we do. He's wasting his time gaming. Worst decision ever, me letting him have a computer in his room."

"Maybe. But he was gaming before, and he didn't run away. So this has to be something else—don't you think?"

"Whatever it is, we'll get to the bottom of it. Don't worry," Gary said, his voice grim.

They'd reached the foothills of the Berkshires, the sunrise igniting them bright green. As they turned off Route 2 and descended into the village of Shelburne Falls, Sydney said, "We used to come to this town in the summer, back when they let you swim in the glacial potholes. It was such a rush, being in that cold, cold water on a hot day and then sunning yourself at the base of Salmon Falls."

Gary squeezed her hand. "Were you skinny-dippers? I mean, being hippies and all."

Sydney laughed. "Of course not. It wasn't the sixties. Out here in the big city, we had to act like regular people or we'd get arrested."

"What about at the farm?"

"At Haven Lake we never bothered with suits. There were so many European backpackers coming and going from the farm, and most people in Europe enjoy nude beaches. If people got hot working, they'd strip down and jump right into the pond."

"Sounds like you got quite the eyeful. And an education."

"I did," she said, smiling. "And I'm happy to share what I know any time."

It was a running joke between them, the fact that Gary had led a buttoned-up, traditional childhood, while hers was free-range. Gary had gone to a huge regional high school and she'd been homeschooled; his father worked in a bank and hers ran an organic farm; his mother's kitchen was filled with cans and packaged food, while the shelves at Haven Lake were crowded with preserves, pickled vegetables, dried grains, and wooden crates filled with seasonal fresh fruit and vegetables.

Sydney knew that Gary was attracted to what he called her "Bohemian past," but was also uncomfortable with it. Somehow he couldn't seem to stop equating nudity with sexuality, for example, and didn't believe she was still a virgin until college.

As they turned onto Red River Road, Sydney's breath caught at the sight of the fields. The dew glistened on the new grass, sparking in the sun, and the mountains cast purple shadows on the green fields. Sheep dotted the upper pastures.

As they drew closer to the house, familiar landmarks greeted her like long-lost relatives: the stone walls spotted with green and white lichen, the enormous copper beech with its silver-lined leaves, the rough pine lean-to where they set up a farm stand. She was both anxious and excited to be here, a knot in her throat making it hard to swallow.

The old brick farmhouse looked like it had leaped off the pages of a storybook, the ancient bricks glowing pink in the morning light, the trim white and clean. You couldn't see the pond from the road, but Sydney imagined it glinting blue against the green fields and shaded black on the side near the woods.

She had been expecting—maybe because of her own unhappy memories of Haven Lake—that the farm would look dreary and morose, a Gothic pile of a house surrounded by spooky trees and a maze of fields. Instead she saw a place that was lush and full of life, with forsythia bushes blazing yellow along the upper pastures. Crocuses grew in purple and white clumps by the stone pillars marking the entrance to Haven Lake's long driveway. The oak trees weren't yet in full leaf, but when they were, they would form a canopy above it.

"We used to race our horses bareback down this driveway," she said as Gary turned the car down the long lane.

Gary kept both hands on the wheel, avoiding potholes. "Who's 'we'?"

"Usually me racing against Uncle Rory—my dad's brother—and my friends Theo and Valerie." Sydney smiled. "Valerie was always too scared to go fast, so she always lost."

"How many horses did you have on the farm?"

"Maybe three or four at a time. We never bought any horses. Just rescued them or took them in trade." Sydney thought for a minute. "I was about five or six when they gave me Lord, this ancient gray gelding, a draft horse with hooves as big as pancakes. That horse tossed his head like a stallion even though he must have been ninety in people years. It was more like riding a couch than a horse."

Gary laughed. "Sounds ideal for a kid."

"He was. Then I got Foxy, a chestnut Thoroughbred that had foundered at Suffolk Downs racetrack. They were going to put her down, but somebody gave her to us in exchange for a pickup truck full of vegetables at the Boston farmers' market. Mom worked some miracle cure so Foxy could run again."

Sydney fell silent, remembering how Foxy's gallop was so smooth it was like floating. She would lie flat against her neck and give Foxy her head as she raced Theo on that bay colt someone had given her parents because they said it couldn't be tamed. Maybe not, but Theo had ridden him. Neck and neck, the horses had raced, Sydney and Theo nearly lying across their withers, eyes tearing as the horses' manes whipped their faces, using their legs to urge the horses on.

In hot weather they'd take the horses down to the pond, ride them into the water on the shady wooded side away from the small kids and sunbathing women from France or Denmark with their freckled breasts and strong backpackers' legs. The horses snorted as they swam with Theo and Sydney clinging to their necks, their legs floating out across the backs of their mounts as if they were one with these powerful creatures. Pure joy.

They sold the horses when Dad died. The small barn burned down about a month later. Mom said the fire was an accident, but Sydney had never believed it. What could cause a barn to burst into flames on a rainy June night?

By the time Gary pulled up to the house a few minutes later, Sydney's chest was tight with anxiety again. She clung to the door, unable to force herself to open it. Then Gary was standing in front of the car, giving her a curious look, eyebrows raised. He looked so capable and solid in his black polo shirt and khakis that she unfolded her legs, took a deep breath, and joined him. This was for Dylan, she reminded herself.

"You never told me how big this place was," Gary said, stretching his back and taking in the scenery with a smile. "Does all of this land around the house belong to your mother?"

"Oh yes."

"How many acres?"

"About a hundred, I think."

"She's got quite a garden over there."

Sydney glanced at the kitchen garden edged in its picket fence. It had been tilled and fertilized, and Mom had probably already planted her peas. Too soon for anything else. Later there would be tomatoes, runner beans, cukes, and squash, with cardboard boxes flattened between the rows, straw scattered on top to keep down the weeds. Mom would plant marigolds around the edges to deter insects.

"Mom always did have a green thumb," she said.

How bizarre to approach the house as strangers about to knock. Only they didn't have to knock, because Hannah opened the door before they reached the steps. A dog flew out to greet them, barking like a maniac and whirling around their legs until Hannah called the animal back with a sharp word.

Her mother was dressed in jeans, a T-shirt, and a sweater against the early morning chill. The sweater was another of her enviable handmade creations, a fisherman's cream-colored cabled cardigan with brown leather buttons. Hannah's long hair was in a single braid down her back, her hips slim as a boy's, her jeans tucked into knee-high green rubber boots. Immediately Sydney felt fat, too put together in her khakis and white blouse, her sensible but expensive loafers. Even without makeup, Hannah reminded Sydney of those middle-aged but well-toned models you saw wearing improbable tapestry jackets and long turquoise earrings in catalogs meant for people with ski chalets in Aspen.

But Sydney saw the tightness around Hannah's eyes—her smile didn't quite reach them—and noticed how her mother had hitched her shoulders too high. From this, she understood that Hannah was irritated, but determined to be polite.

Her father had ruled Haven Lake's farm and fields by direct command, but Hannah had directed the women and children, the house and the livestock, through some kind of shadow dynasty, making her wishes known without actually expressing them aloud. Her power was born of an internal core of confidence that radiated heat even in the face of a husband whose temper once caused him to toss his wife to the floor like she was nothing more than a chair to tip over.

Hannah had calmly picked herself up and brushed herself off afterward, saying, "There, Allen, I do hope you feel better. Now come take a walk with me."

Which was what she said to them now, an eerie echo of Sydney's thoughts: "Walk with me. We'll have some privacy for a few minutes. Dylan's still upstairs. I'm not sure if he's even awake yet."

Sydney and Gary followed her down to the barn, the dog trotting ahead while Hannah talked about Dylan, telling them what a nice kid he was, how hardworking and polite. "You've done a good job with him," she said, addressing Gary and avoiding Sydney's eyes.

"I've done what I can," Gary said. "It hasn't been easy since his mother died. Especially given the circumstances. Sydney has told you, I imagine."

Sydney hadn't told Hannah anything, really. Only that there had been a car accident when Dylan was twelve.

Gary easily matched Hannah's long stride. Sydney hung back a little, shocked to the core by familiar sights: the wisteria, so much bigger now, but still climbing the trellis she'd helped her father build; the hayloft where she and Theo used to go for privacy that last spring, pressing their clothed bodies together, wanting each other but afraid.

"I'm sure it must have been difficult," Hannah was saying to Gary. She glanced over her shoulder at Sydney, her expression coolly appraising. "At least Sydney can relate to your son, having lost her own father as a teenager."

"Yes, Sydney's great with Dylan," Gary said. "It helps that she's had so much experience with troubled kids in her work."

Sydney was about to make a snide remark about not talking about her in the third person when Gary turned around to look at her as well. Unlike Hannah, he waited, hand outstretched, until Sydney caught up with him. He took her hand, kissed it, and said, "Sydney's made my life not only bearable, but enjoyable again."

Gary kissed Sydney's cheek then. These were such rare displays of affection, this kiss and the hand holding, that she wondered if he was doing it for her mother's benefit.

"You never wanted to marry again?" Gary asked Hannah, tugging Sydney forward so all three of them were walking abreast.

"Never saw the point," Hannah said. "Been there and done that." She waved a hand, dismissive. "Besides, I'm married to the farm now."

"Must be a lot of work to keep it going," Gary acknowledged.

"You have no idea," Hannah said. "Of course, I didn't, either, until I was up to my knees in muck and wool. Happily, I might add."

Sydney couldn't stand it anymore, this endless stream of small talk, Hannah pretending to be the gracious hostess. She was impatient to see Dylan and make sure he was all right, then get back on the road, sort things out at home. "We really appreciate you looking after Dylan, Mom," she said. "How does he seem?"

"Miserable and jumpy. I was wondering about drugs. Does he do any?" Hannah bent down and yanked a thistle out of the ground by her feet.

The weeding was a ruse, Sydney thought, so they wouldn't think she was accusing them, when clearly her mother was doing just that: if Dylan did drugs and they didn't know it, they must be terrible parents. Hannah could say they were neglectful and self-absorbed, too taken up by work and each other to see what was right in front of them.

"Of course not," Sydney said, more sharply than she'd intended. Her hands were fluttering. Nerves, she thought, then realized, no, it was anger: her whole body was shaking, seized by an impotent fury at her mother's smug demeanor. "I would know if Dylan was smoking," she went on. "I'm certainly familiar with the smell of pot, as well as with the effects of alcohol, mushrooms, acid, uppers, downers, whatever. You made sure of that, didn't you, Mom?"

Hannah straightened abruptly and looked straight into Sydney's eyes. Sydney was satisfied to see a glimmer of shock before her mother's green eyes went flat and unreadable again.

"I wasn't suggesting that you were ignorant about drugs, Sydney," she said. "But all teenagers can get themselves into risky situations. It's in their nature to experiment."

"Dylan's never been much of a risk taker, though," Gary said, pressing Sydney's arm against his side, though whether to warn her to back off or comfort her, she wasn't sure. "He's a good student and a good kid. I guess that's why we were so shocked when he pulled this stunt. I'm sorry we didn't come get him right away, but I wanted to send him a clear message: he's not the one who calls the shots."

"I see," Hannah said. "And how's your son's physical health? Any concerns there?" She turned and led them deeper into the barn, where the sweet scents of new grass and spring flowers they'd been inhaling outside were overlaid by the more complicated smells of hay, acrid sheep urine, manure, and lanolin.

"He'd be healthier if he didn't play so many computer games," Gary said. "I've done everything I can to encourage Dylan to take up a sport. Signed him up for hockey, baseball, tennis, you name it. Nothing took. He'd rather sit on his rear and shoot cartoon villains."

"Computers have certainly transformed the very fabric of childhood, haven't they?" Hannah was checking the thick rubber water buckets in the barn now, occasionally reaching in to pull hay out of the buckets with her bare hands. "We used to worry that TV would be the end of civilization. I suppose that's not even on the radar screen of important parental concerns these days."

The big doors were open at the far end of the barn, and below Sydney could see the pond: glimmering blue, the rickety wooden dock fish-scale silver, edged on one side by the narrow beach with its line of greenish flat stones like oversized turtles leading into the water. As children, they'd sunned themselves on those stones, or leaped from one to the other. She and Theo and Valerie would keep jumping until they hit the water, trying to propel themselves through the pond that way even after they were in over their heads, leaping from toe to toe, struggling to keep their chins above water.

A wonder more of them didn't drown. Who had kept watch over the kids at Haven Lake? Everyone and nobody, Sydney thought.

On the right side of the pond were the woods, mostly pines. Sydney couldn't see if the rope they once swung on was still dangling from the biggest tree limb over the water. She wondered, too, if Uncle Rory's cabin was still in the woods, along with the yurts and tent platforms built by the temporary residents of Haven Lake. The detritus of an optimistic age. Had they really thought they were closer to nature, sleeping out there? Felt in tune with the "rhythms of the planet," as they were always claiming? And where were all those idealists living now?

Sydney turned away, shivering. The air here was like a truth serum, making it impossible to ignore her memories or avoid what was right in front of her. “Dylan hardly eats at home,” she blurted. “Did he eat much while he was here? I’m starting to worry that he might be anorexic.”

Hannah frowned. “Really? It’s true that he doesn’t have much of an appetite, unless I put out something sweet.”

“No.” Gary hastily dropped Sydney’s hand, his expression a frowning mixture of disbelief and betrayal. “There’s nothing pathological about Dylan’s eating habits,” he said. “I know you deal with psychologically impaired children and their families, Sydney, but my son doesn’t suffer from anything worse than his own tendency to be a couch surfer. If he’d just get some exercise, he’d be fine.”

“You can’t just keep saying that to make it true,” Sydney shot back.

Gary turned to Hannah. “Dylan has a healthy diet. You’ve seen him! Not an ounce of fat on his body. He just needs to build up some muscle.”

Hannah turned off the hose and hung it up. “I see,” she said. “Well, I’m all set here. Let’s go inside and see if Dylan’s awake.”

Sydney walked beside Gary. This time he was the one who hung back from Hannah. “There’s nothing wrong with Dylan,” he said to her in a low voice. “You, of all people, should understand that he’s controlling his food intake as a power play.”

She didn’t want to argue with Gary where her mother could see them fight, so she nodded and said, “I’m sorry, honey. I’m just worried about him.”

“I know you are.” He sighed. “I am, too, of course. Sorry. I shouldn’t have snapped at you.”

“It’s all right,” she said, but it wasn’t.

Dylan wasn’t in the kitchen or living room. Sydney’s heart lurched. What if he’d left while they were in the barn? What if he was on Route 2 right now, his thumb out for some trucker?

She forced herself to sit at the kitchen table while Hannah went upstairs to check the bedroom. Gary sat down beside her. “You know, it doesn’t help anything if you go off on your mother,” he said. “She did us a favor, taking Dylan in and keeping him safe.” He smiled and added, “Besides, one day that hippie shepherdess will be my mother-in-law. I have to stay on her good side.”

"I know. I just can't stand being here," Sydney said. "It brings it all back, you know?" She longed to close her eyes against the memory-saturated kitchen, with its plant-laden shelves and wide pine floors that could never be scrubbed completely clean because of the cracks between the boards.

Gary took her hand. "I understand. It's the same reason I had to get rid of Amanda's things. I thought it would be easier for Dylan and me to move on without triggers."

"It probably was," Sydney said, though hearing him say this made her feel sorry for Dylan.

There was a scuttling noise beneath the stove. A brown head popped out, then disappeared again. "What the hell?" Gary said, startled into laughing. "Was that a hedgehog?"

Sydney rolled her eyes. "Don't you remember? When Mom came for dinner last time, she was telling us about a baby woodchuck she rescued. That must be it."

"Haven Lake is certainly a palace of wonders," Gary said, making her smile.

Then Dylan came downstairs, smiling a little, but giving them a wary glance. The circles were gone from under his eyes and his face was pink from the sun. He looked healthier than Sydney had ever seen him. Maybe Gary was right and all the boy needed was more time outside and less time on the computer.

"Hi, Dad. Hey, Sydney," Dylan said. "Sorry about all the hassle."

The apology surprised Sydney into standing up to hug him. She couldn't believe how glad she was to see him. "That's okay, sweetie. You scared us a little, but whatever reasons you had for leaving, I'm sure they were important. I'm glad to see you and happy you're okay," she added quickly, sensing Gary gathering a head of steam behind her. Where was Hannah? She hadn't come down with Dylan.

Gary stood up, too, but didn't approach his son. His face had reddened and he crossed his arms. "Sydney's wrong, buddy," he said. "What you did was definitely *not* okay. Your decision to take off like that was completely irresponsible. You owe us a damn good explanation."

"Maybe later, right?" Sydney said, feeling suddenly claustrophobic. Gary sounded just like her father. Once, Dad had slapped her across the face because she forgot to close the gate and the cows got loose. He was about to hit her again, but her mother had gotten between them and shouted at Sydney to run for Uncle Rory.

She had, barefoot through the woods, feeling sticks pierce her feet and branches scrape at her face and arms as if beasts were chasing her across a bed of nails. Uncle Rory was in his cabin, sprawled on his bed and reading, but he'd bolted out of the door, so fast and sure-footed as he ran toward the house that he left Sydney far behind. His bare chest gleamed in the moonlight; it was like watching a stag moving through the forest ahead of her.

"No," Gary was saying. "Dylan has to understand there will be consequences to his actions."

"Honey, please. Let's just get on the road," Sydney begged.

"Actually, that's the thing. I was going to call you early this morning, but my phone died," Dylan said.

"Why?" Gary demanded. "To make sure your chariot was on its way to ferry you home?"

"Stop it, Gary!" Sydney said. "Sarcasm won't help anything."

"I wanted to tell you guys not to bother coming," Dylan said. "I'm not going back with you. I can't." Now he was standing with his arms crossed, too, facing his father, his expression mirroring Gary's: the blue eyes steely, the mouth set in a thin line.

However rebellious and determined the boy was trying to look, Sydney felt sorry for him. Dylan had none of Gary's bulk, his arms too thin even in the sleeves of his favorite gray hoodie.

"What do you mean you can't go back with us?" Gary's voice had risen a notch. "Of course you can. And you will."

"No, Dad. I won't." Dylan's brush cut stood on end, his light hair looking as determined as the rest of him. "Hannah said I can stay here for a week. Just a trial. I'll help her around the farm, and if it works out, she says I can finish junior year at the local high school. Then, when I get to Seattle, I'll find a job, maybe get my GED."

"What the hell are you talking about?" Gary said. "Are you insane? You don't have any choice in this matter. You're coming home with us *today*. You can't just throw away three years at that private school. Don't be an idiot! You can't stay here and be some kind of, some . . ." He sputtered for a minute, then exploded, *"Shepherd!"*

"Dad, calm down," Dylan said. "I'm not going to raise sheep, if that's what you're so worried about. Jesus. Did you hear a word I said? I told you I'll keep going to school. I just want to do it here while I sort things out. Hannah said I could."

Now Sydney, who up to this point had been feeling sorry for Dylan, felt her anger percolating along with Gary's, though for a different reason: How *dare* her mother intervene and make this absurd offer, without even discussing things with them first?

"Dylan, your dad's right," she said. "You need to come home and work things out. I know things are bad with that girl, but it's not the end of the world. Everybody gets their hearts broken in high school. I know I did."

"Wait a minute. That girl at the drugstore?" Gary said. "Is that what all this is really about? Why you're willing to throw away your whole *life*?"

Dylan spun on Sydney, his face contorted with anger. "How do you know about Kelly? Have you been *spying* on me?"

"No, of course not." Sydney reached out to touch his arm, trying to soothe him, though inwardly she was panicked by the fury on Dylan's face. Fury directed at *her*. "It's just that, when we didn't know where you were, we asked some of your friends and I went to see her."

"Fuck." Dylan jerked out of reach.

"Don't you dare swear at us, buddy," Gary said.

Dylan remained focused on Sydney. "You mean you actually *talked* to Kelly?"

"Just for a minute," Sydney said. "I was trying to find you. Kelly told me you gave her a ride home once, but that she has another boyfriend. Is that why you ran away?"

Now Gary turned on Sydney as well. "Dylan *gave her a ride home*? How? He doesn't even have his license yet!"

"I'm sorry," Sydney said, looking at Dylan, who was tight-lipped, silent, drumming his bony hands on his blue-jeaned thighs. She was, too. She hadn't meant to tell Gary anything about the car.

"Did you drive illegally, young man?" Gary stepped toward Dylan, his face thrust forward, cornering Dylan against the sink. "You've only got a learner's permit. I hope to hell you weren't driving unsupervised. That kind of stupid move could cost you another year before you get your license, if some cop happens to stop you. Only that's not going to happen, because I'm taking your permit now and you're grounded. How could you be that irresponsible? You're as bad as your mother. Don't you ever *think* before you act?"

Gary was shouting by now and Dylan was shrinking in front of him, tucking his head down protectively in a way that made Sydney's own back ache with tension. She crossed the room and put a hand on Gary's shoulder. "There's no need to yell," she said. "You're scaring him."

"I hope to God I *am* scaring him!" Gary yelled, his eyes fixed on Dylan, who was staring at the floor. "For Christ's sake, Sydney. This kid has no business on the road. He could kill somebody! I knew I should have sold Amanda's car. Really, what possessed you to pull a stunt like that, Dylan?"

"So sue me," Dylan muttered, lifting his head. "How else am I supposed to get to my job on time, when you're both at work all day?"

"You should have talked to us about that, honey," Sydney said gently. "We could have helped you find rides."

Dylan gave her a look that told her what he thought of that solution.

"Oh, no, Dylan," Gary bellowed. "This is not going to be Guilt Trip Lane. Not after everything I've done for you. You're too smart not to know right from wrong. I want to hear what else you're keeping from us." He glanced at Sydney with a look that terrified her. "*Both* of you lied to me! How serious are things with this girl?"

"Serious. At least for me," Dylan said to his shoes.

Gary grabbed Dylan's shoulder and shook him a little. "Look at me when you talk to me, buddy. Show some respect! And I don't believe you. How can you be serious with a girl who denies ever going out with you?"

"I don't care what she says. I *slept* with her, okay, Dad? We had *sex*!" Dylan said, a catch in his voice. "I slept with her and I love her. I *still* love her!" His blue eyes had gone dark with anger despite the fact that Gary had pinned him against the sink with one powerful arm.

Behind Sydney, Hannah spoke sharply. "Gary, let go of the boy at once."

To Sydney's amazement, Gary obeyed. Why would he listen to Hannah, but not to her?

Dylan took the opportunity to duck around Gary and run from the house, the dog barking hysterically at his heels, the screen door slamming behind them.

"Mom, what the hell? You can't just tell Dylan he can stay here!"

"I certainly can, and I did," Hannah said. "Coffee?"

"No, thanks," Gary said tersely. "We can't stay."

"Oh? What a shame," Hannah said. "You just got here. But I suppose it is a long ride back."

Sydney stared at her mother in disbelief as Hannah filled her own mug, then leaned against the counter and sipped it, her expression amused. Did she think this whole thing was *funny*?

"Sydney's right," Gary said. "You have no business inviting my son to live with you, Hannah."

"I have every right to invite whomever I like to stay at the farm," Hannah countered. "This is my home. It's not my problem if your son doesn't want to live with you. In fact, it's not your problem, either. This is Dylan's life and something he has to resolve."

"You still had no right, Mom," Sydney said, but she heard the defeat in her own voice.

Hannah blew across the top of her mug, then took another sip of coffee. "Dylan and I have discussed this. We'll have a trial period of one week. He can check out the local school during that time, and we'll see how we get along. I do expect him to follow certain rules at my home just as he does at yours."

"Rules?" Gary sputtered. "Hannah, this kid has broken every rule in the book! And from what Sydney says, you don't exactly observe normal conventions. I doubt we'd see eye to eye on what kind of standards my son should adhere to if he's going to grow up to be a responsible, civilized adult."

"You think I couldn't do as well with him as you do?" Hannah seemed to genuinely want to know.

Sydney felt suddenly sorry for Gary. She could tell by the rigid set of his shoulders that he felt helpless. This wasn't a feeling Gary knew well. He was a widely renowned surgeon. A fixer. A healer. A problem solver on a global level.

She edged close enough to press her shoulder against his to show her support. His skin felt hot through his shirt. "Gary's right, Mom," she said. "You've never believed in respecting normal boundaries. Why would you start doing that now? Dylan will just curb your style."

Hannah tipped her head back and laughed. "Oh, Sydney. Listen to yourself! You keep trying to make this conversation about you—about us—but what matters is Dylan. This is a kid who's too miserable, for whatever reason, to stay in his school or live in your house. He needs a change. You, of all people, should understand that."

"That's not true. I work with kids so they won't *have* to run away from their problems." Sydney dug her hands into the pockets of her khakis. The awful thing was that her mother was right. She and Gary really didn't know what kind of situation Dylan had landed in; he might actually be better off somewhere else if things were as bad as they seemed. If they brought him home against his wishes, what would keep him from running away again?

Gary's voice was strained. "Thank you again, Hannah, for all you've done to keep Dylan safe during a time when he is obviously making some questionable choices," he said. "But it's time my son came home. Sydney and I will help him sort out whatever trouble he's in. He's in an excellent school and has a bright future. College, maybe a career in engineering or medicine. I'm sure his teachers will reach out to him as well. Having him stay with you is simply not an option."

To Sydney's horror, Hannah continued to look amused. Her green eyes danced between Gary and Sydney. "I'm sorry. I thought we were discussing Dylan's best interests here."

"We are, Mom," Sydney said.

"Really? Because just now it sounded like Gary was talking about the things that were important to him, not to Dylan," Hannah said.

Sydney bit her lip, because every answer she could think of amounted to the same petty sentiment: she hated her mother at this moment, because Hannah had reduced her to being sixteen and furious again.

"I beg to differ, Hannah," Gary said. "Dylan getting a good education *is* in his best interest. It's my duty as a parent to see that he finishes high school, gets into a good college, and prepares for a career that doesn't involve raising livestock in the middle of nowhere."

Sydney saw that her mother's expression had shifted to one of pity. She actually felt sorry for Gary! Well, it was pointless trying to reason with her, as always. "Gary," Sydney said, touching his arm, "can we please talk outside?"

Gary shook her off. "This isn't the time. I'm going to find Dylan and make him get in the car."

He set off through the kitchen door, shutting it gently behind him.

After a moment of silence, Hannah said, "I've got chores to do. If you want to say good-bye before you go, I'll be in the barn."

Then her mother was gone, too, leaving Sydney alone in the silent kitchen and staring at the round yellow clock on the kitchen wall, its ticking like a series of small bombs, one more reminder that everything at Haven Lake was always beyond her control.

CHAPTER SEVEN

Hannah stood on the sunny brick patio by the back door. Below the house, Gary raced around the barn, calling for Dylan. There was something off about that guy, but she couldn't put a finger on it. He was so changeable, alternately chill and manic. Even his eyes were jittery. What in the world did Sydney see in him?

The sheep had gathered in the far corner of the pasture, heads raised in alarm, circled around the lambs. The llama stood tall beside them to watch these foolish human antics. Gary finally ducked inside the barn.

She sighed. This was all so pointless. Dylan would never hide in the barn. He was a feral creature, escaping from predators. It would be against his instincts to be cornered like that. Her guess was that either he'd run down the driveway to hitch a ride on the road, or he was hiding in the woods by the pond.

Such a shame. If Sydney and Gary had been calmer, had talked to Dylan instead of shouting, he might have gone home with them. Now everything was a mess.

Well, Dylan would either find another bolt-hole—he had relatives in Connecticut, an aunt and uncle, she remembered—or show up at the farm after Gary and Sydney were gone.

But what would she do if Dylan did show up, and said he wanted to stay here? If she defied Gary and let Dylan stay, she'd ruin any possible relationship she might have forged with Gary—a relationship she had fleetingly hoped might be a bridge to mending things with Sydney.

Should she go back to the kitchen, talk to her daughter? Seeing Sydney's evident distress during all that shouting had made Hannah want to put her arms around her. She could still do that, but anxiety about how Sydney would respond kept her feet rooted to this spot. Sydney didn't seem to want her anywhere nearby.

How had their lives reached this point, Hannah wondered, where the thought of trying to comfort her own child in her own kitchen left her feeling so paralyzed by regret and fear?

When Sydney was a baby—such a beautiful baby, with yellow curls and a rosebud mouth, like a baby in a princess fairy tale—and other people started flocking to Haven Lake, the kitchen had been Hannah's prison and her sanctuary, too. She had spent countless hours in that room boiling cloth diapers, canning and pickling vegetables to store in the root cellar, putting up preserves, making butter and cheese, cooking meals, and even braiding garlic to hang from the ceiling alongside her mint, rosemary, thyme, and basil drying in bundles. She thought she might sink under the weight of all that labor.

At the end of the day, when the others gathered to play music, Hannah would sometimes sneak out to the kitchen garden with Sydney sleeping in a basket she'd woven herself so she could carry the baby with her everywhere. She'd set her daughter's basket down next to her while she stretched out between her carefully tended herb beds, feeling the bricks still warm from the sun like hands on her shoulders and buttocks, only the rustling sparrows in the bushes for company. The house was filled with strangers, but this backyard was her private domain, a room of her own. Hers and Sydney's.

Hannah was startled out of this reverie when the kitchen door opened and a very grown-up Sydney came outside to stand on the back stoop. Sydney's arms were folded tight against her body, her expression pinched and severe.

With her mouth set like that, and dressed as she was in those khakis and that white blouse, Sydney looked nothing at all like a princess, but like a lighter-haired replica of Allen's bosomy, bossy mother. A woman who lived to play tennis and bridge. A woman who had said to Allen, on the day he married Hannah, "It wasn't enough to throw away your dreams and sign up for Vietnam instead of going to college. You had to marry beneath you. A mechanic's daughter! A Greek! How could you, Allen? How could you do this to me? You've broken my heart, and your father's, too!"

Of course, Mrs. Bishop had to have known Hannah was in the downstairs bathroom just off the kitchen and listening to every word.

Now Gary was coming up the hill. He crossed the yard, ignoring Hannah and shaking his head at Sydney. "He's not down in the barn," he said, squinting in the sunlight and running a hand across his face.

Gary was a decade older than Sydney—almost halfway between her age and her daughter's, Hannah realized—and today he looked his age, with deep worry lines creasing his forehead and mouth. But he was also handsome, muscular, and trim. An ex-athlete, she guessed. Maybe that's what Sydney saw in him: her father had once been a gifted athlete, too. Like Allen, Gary was a powerful man confused by his own mercurial emotions—a compelling combination for a caretaker like Sydney.

"He hasn't come back inside," Sydney said. "I went upstairs to see if I could spot him in the fields from any of the windows, but there wasn't any sign of him. Maybe he ran down the driveway and he's on the road, thumbing a ride."

"Come on," Gary said. "Let's go look for him in the car."

Sydney hesitated and looked at Hannah. "What do you think, Mom?"

Hannah was touched; she sensed Sydney's need for reassurance beneath the cool tone. But she couldn't lie to her. "I don't know how much good it'll do. If Dylan wants to hide from you, he will. We might be better off waiting for him to come back here."

"He's not going to do that," Gary said. "I've already told him he can't stay on the farm."

In her solitary existence, Hannah had forgotten how stubborn some people could be. "Gary, I know you mean well," she said, "but Dylan's a teenager. When he was little, you could force him into his car seat or threaten him until he ate his vegetables, but that tactic won't get you anywhere now. He'll just fight you harder. You're going to have to treat him like an adult if you expect him to act like one."

Hannah's face flushed as she felt Sydney staring at her. She was afraid to turn and look at her daughter's expression. What would she see there? Nothing pleasant—she'd bet on that.

"I will treat Dylan like an adult when he behaves like one," Gary said. "Right now, I'm going to look for him on the road. I'll make a pass with the car in both directions. I'll check the highway ramps, too. And, if I don't see him, I'm going straight home."

"But won't that send the wrong message, too?" Sydney came down the steps. "What if he's just down in the woods or something, and you're not here when he comes back? Dylan will think you don't care whether he comes home or not. We need to talk to him. Let's wait a while."

Sydney was standing close enough that Hannah could smell her shampoo: something with mint. She wished Sydney wouldn't keep her hair pinned up like that, sprayed in place and shiny, like fruit varnished for a model kitchen.

"No. He doesn't get to call the shots." Gary's voice was firm as he turned to Hannah. "On the off chance he does show up, can I trust you to call and let me know?"

"Of course," Hannah said.

"And will you please put him on a bus home?" Gary said.

"That I can't promise," Hannah said.

Gary gave her a curt nod. "Fine, then. I'm off. Come on, Sydney."

He headed for the car, a new Lexus sedan, silver and sharklike. Sydney, after a moment of shocked silence, ran to catch up with him, saying something Hannah couldn't hear. Gary shrugged away from her.

Hannah couldn't stand watching them argue. "Listen, I'm going to do a few chores," she called. "Good luck!"

Neither of them answered. *Fine*, Hannah thought, and circled around the house toward the barn.

She was collecting eggs from the henhouse when she heard the car engine start. She caught the flash of silver between the oak trees as Gary peeled out, going much too fast for that potholed driveway. He could kiss his struts good-bye, driving like that.

She was sorry to see her daughter go, but Hannah could breathe more easily now. She set the basket of eggs down on the table in the old tack room and made her way quickly down the barn's dusty center aisle and out the back door, where she stopped and squinted at the pond below. There was enough breeze to ruffle the water's surface.

One side of the pond was darker where the water lapped the shoreline at the edge of the woods. It was an idyllic place, but Hannah hadn't been in that water since Theo died.

She kept walking along the sunny side of the pond toward the woods. When she passed the beach—just a strip of open grassy shoreline, with a line of big flat rocks leading into the water—she glanced at the rotting dock, silver with age, and the old rowboat tipped upside down to one side of it. No footprints or other signs of disturbance.

Finally, in the shade cast by the forest, she whistled three times. A few seconds drummed by while Hannah held her breath. Then there was a flash of black and white and Billy came running toward her from the woods, the border collie's belly low to the ground.

Hannah smiled. Her hunch had been right.

She walked down to meet the dog. Billy was so beside himself to see her that he began barking and whirling in circles, spinning around her legs and nearly tripping her as she kept walking toward the woods. "Good dog! You're a good, good boy," she murmured, stopping to pat him.

At this, Billy gave her an ecstatic look and waved his tail, falling into step beside her.

"You know where Dylan is, right?" Hannah said, smiling down at the dog's bright eyes. "Where's Dylan, Billy? Take me."

Billy paused midstep to stare up at her, his brown eyes glittering with excitement—there was no game this dog loved better than deciphering human code—then trotted ahead of her, his tail carried like a fluttering parade flag.

They crossed the beach and entered the hushed woods. Hannah hadn't been in the woods for ages, either. She was shocked by the height of the trees. The people who'd owned the farm for decades before she and Allen bought it had planned to turn this part of their property into a Christmas tree farm. The pine trees towered and grew in straight rows, making it easy to walk beneath them because the trees shaded out any undergrowth and left a soft carpet of needles that was probably a hundred years deep. Sydney and Hannah had read *The Lion, the Witch and the Wardrobe* together, and afterward Sydney had always called these woods "Narnia."

Sydney and the other children who came and went from Haven Lake used to play here. They built fairy houses out of twigs while the adults constructed their own shelters, tent platforms and yurts and tepees. Like the yurt Rory had built for Lucy; she'd stayed here every summer, returning to her big house in Rhode Island during the school year so Theo and Valerie could attend private school, courtesy of her on-again, off-again husband.

Until that last winter, when Lucy had arrived unexpectedly one frigid January afternoon, weeping. There had been an ice storm and the trees were still encased and glittering, the crust on the snow hard and blue as new milk. Hannah had been tempted to tell Lucy she couldn't stay, but she felt sorry for the children, who stood wide-eyed in alarm at their mother's tears.

Lucy's yurt wasn't here anymore. Hannah had burned it down, the same night she burned down the little barn where Allen shot himself.

Now these tall trees hid the evidence of the abandoned good intentions of people who were always sitting cross-legged and sleeping on the floor or right on the ground, trying to be one with the planet's rhythms. Hannah would take her bed, thank you very much. She didn't mind simplicity, but there was no need to torture yourself.

She shivered in the cooler air as she walked deep enough into the woods to be invisible to anyone outside the perimeter of trees. Another memory shard was waiting to puncture her skin here in the deep shade: Rory, sitting on a stump in front of his cabin and playing his banjo, grinning up at her from beneath a shock of auburn hair, the freckles pronounced across his nose, the sleeves of his flannel shirt rolled up to reveal strong forearms.

What if he had agreed to make love with her when they were teenagers, as Hannah had wanted to, during one of those many breathless nights spent pressed together in the sleeping bag Rory borrowed from an uncle—a bag with a flannel lining with duck-hunting scenes and infused with cigar smoke? Even now the smell of cigars made Hannah ache with desire, remembering her bare breasts against Rory's chest, his soft mouth, their limbs entangled, her jeans damp. She had tried so hard to get him to agree, but Rory had held fast for true love and said no.

If she and Rory had been lovers, surely her story—their story—would be different. She wouldn't have gone off to the University of Massachusetts with no plans to see him until Christmas. Allen wouldn't have sought her out, thinking she could fill his bottomless urgency for connection after returning from a place where nearly every one of his relationships had ended in death. And maybe she wouldn't have believed Allen when he said that she, alone, could heal him after the war.

There was the difference: Rory loved her. Allen needed her. She and Rory both knew that. And so Rory had stepped aside, because he loved his brother. And Hannah, to her shame and regret, had let him. Had never said—didn't yet know, really—that Rory might be the one *she* needed.

She and Allen had been on Haven Lake for five years when Rory came to live with them. He'd graduated from college and gone off for a few years to play guitar and fiddle and banjo for movie scores in Hollywood. Then he'd returned to Massachusetts. "I found out I'm not one of the beautiful people," he'd told Hannah. "And I couldn't get used to grass being brown. I had to come home to New England."

She'd never been so happy to see anyone in her life. She could see that Allen was glad, too, by the way he cuffed Rory's head and said, "About time you came to your senses, man. Together we can make this farming thing work."

Rory played in two bluegrass bands in bars around Northampton and Greenfield. Sometimes Hannah and Allen and the others would pile into one of their rusty vehicles to go hear them. Hannah didn't do drugs—she coughed when she inhaled, even with a bong—so she always drove. Allen had learned to rely on pot to relax him, on uppers whenever there was a harvest to get in before the rain, and on dropping acid to let him escape his own head.

Once, on their way to see Rory's band, Allen had yanked the truck's steering wheel out of her hands, shouting, "Snakes in the road! Snakes in the road!" He'd nearly killed them. Hannah had no idea what he'd taken that night. After that, she always made him sit in the backseat.

Hannah could see Rory's cabin now. She hesitated, but Billy was still weaving through the trees ahead of her. This must be where Dylan was holed up: a surprising sanctuary he stumbled upon when he ran. She hadn't been in there, either, since Theo died.

Hannah squared her shoulders and kept moving, keeping her eye on the little house as if the building might pick up its skirts and run from her. Rory had built the cabin out of fallen pine trees. No more than ten by fifteen feet, it was the same size as Thoreau's cabin at Walden Pond, which Rory had used as a model.

This little shack had a cockeyed look, though, because Rory had collected abandoned windows of different sizes along the roadside in his cranky Volkswagen van. He'd made a rope bed and found a simple pine table and chair by the curb near the university.

The door to the cabin was closed. Billy stood in front of it and wagged his tail, alternately glancing at Hannah over his shoulder and staring at the door as if he could force it open with the power of his gaze. If any dog could, it was this one, Hannah thought, smiling as she reached the door and gave Billy another solid pat.

Then she knocked. "Dylan? It's me, Hannah."

No reply. Had she gotten it wrong?

Not a chance. She could have been mistaken, maybe, but not the dog. She turned the knob and went inside. "Dylan?"

It took a minute for her eyes to adjust to the light, even dimmer in here than it was in the shady woods. Once they did, she made out Dylan's thin body stretched out on the rope bed. He was lying with one arm over his eyes, so still that at first Hannah wondered if he was asleep. Maybe he hadn't even heard his father calling him.

But then Dylan's shoulders trembled, and Hannah realized the boy was crying. Oh, Christ. She was so not prepared for this. She nearly turned and left. Why not give the boy his solitude, when he'd worked so hard for it?

He must have sensed her temptation to leave, because Dylan lowered his arm and spoke. "I should have known that damn dog would sniff me out."

"Not much gets past Billy."

"Is my dad gone?"

"I think so."

"So he's royally pissed off at me now."

"More frustrated than angry, I think. He loves you. You know that, right?" Hannah sat down on the ladder-back chair by the window, wincing as her back touched the chilly slats of wood.

"If you say so," Dylan mumbled. His eyes were red-rimmed, his face a pale oval against the dark pine wall. "Mostly he thinks I'm a fuckup."

"He doesn't understand how upset you are over this girl," Hannah said.

Dylan made an exasperated sound. "Yeah, well, how could he get it, when Dad is always so rational?" He wiped his face on one arm. "It's not like the love I feel makes sense. I know she doesn't feel me like I feel her."

Hannah sighed. "It's awful when it happens that way, I know. But, believe it or not, it happens a lot. Many people fall in love with the wrong partners. Sometimes you just can't help it. Love is the product of chemistry, or circumstances, or a moment of wild abandon. Then you're in too deep and your heart gets broken no matter how many fences you put up."

Dylan sat up, long legs over the edge of the bed now, his shoulders pressed against the wooden wall. "Did that ever happen to you?"

Hannah gave Dylan a long look. Maybe he needed to know that everyone makes mistakes. Even grandmothers. "Sure. Only I didn't know I was with the wrong person until it was too late to make things right."

"Are you talking about Sydney's dad?"

This was uncomfortable. Hannah hadn't talked about Allen in years, not even with Liz. Somehow, though, in this small dark space, it seemed like the right thing to do. Maybe because Dylan had no filters. He wore his hurt like a second skin.

"Yes," she said. "I loved Allen. Or thought I did. But he was too damaged by war to really know how to love without hurting people. I'm afraid it was hard on Sydney, growing up with him."

"Hell for you, too, right?"

She nodded. "But I was responsible for my own choices. Sydney just happened to be born into our family." Hannah crossed her legs. "The war did something to Allen. He was never the same again after he came back. I should have known better than to marry him."

"Did you still love him when he died?"

"Yes, but not the way a woman should love her husband. I felt sorry for Allen by the end. I thought I could help him heal. Turns out I was wrong. That's part of the reason Sydney's so mad at me. She thought I could do more to help her father. But the truth is that I didn't know what else I could do. I was just trying to survive my marriage one day at a time."

How straightforward the trajectory of her marriage sounded when she described it like this, when in reality her relationship with Allen was a boggy, thorny mess from the start. Part of its magnetic appeal, she supposed. "Anyway, you don't have to make the mistakes I did. Your job is to think about things, to understand what went wrong with you and this girl. Once you do, maybe you can find somebody who's a better match for you next time."

Dylan sighed. "Maybe. But one reason I can't go back is because I'm not sure I can stay away from her, you know?"

Obsession, Hannah thought. She knew what that felt like: an oddly pleasurable addiction. You just had to hope it didn't kill you in the end. "Then maybe you're doing the right thing to stay away," she said. "My offer still stands. You can stay with me here."

He smiled and looked relieved, then glanced around the cabin. "This is a pretty cool place. What's it for?"

She laughed. "What do you mean? It's a house. Somebody lived here."

"Who?"

"Sydney's uncle built it and lived here for a long time."

"Is he your brother or Allen's?"

"Allen's," Hannah said.

"Did he work on the farm, too?"

"Oh yes. He did that and played music professionally. He was with us for many years."

"Where is he now?"

Hannah swallowed hard, but forced herself to answer. "Nobody knows. Rory disappeared not long after Sydney's father died. They found his car in San Francisco, abandoned by some cliffs."

"Wow. That sucks. What do you think happened?"

Hannah shrugged. A long time since she'd thought about any of this, but it wasn't true that time heals all wounds. Given enough time, the wind blew dirt over the place where you buried your memories. But if you poked around, the memories were still there, just as sharp and maybe even more dangerous, because they could slice you up when you least expected to find them.

To Dylan, she said, "I don't really know. The cops concluded he'd either gone for a swim in the bay or else fallen from one of the cliffs, since they found Rory's wallet in the car. Between the tides and the sharks, there wasn't any hope of recovering a body."

Her voice stuttered to a halt as another memory surfaced. The summer Rory showed up at the farm, she and Allen had gone swimming with him in the pond one night. It was hot, so it was surprising that they had the little beach to themselves; this was the night Allen had finished the dock and they wanted to christen it. Everyone else must have been up on the porch playing music or already asleep after a sweaty day of harvesting vegetables.

The three of them were sweaty and dirty, too. They shed their clothes and jumped off the dock holding hands, yelling, *"Uno, dos, tres, amigos in your face!"* the same senseless cry they'd uttered as teenagers jumping off the floating dock at Hood's Pond in Topsfield. The water was inky velvet, warm on the surface but frigid below, where natural springs fed the pond.

Hannah had swum toward the island, doing a hard crawl that made her lungs burn, laughing as Rory and Allen tried to catch her. Swimming was the one physical thing she did better than they did. It was a cloudy night, no stars or moon, the air so sultry and humid that Hannah could scarcely tell when she surfaced for her first gulp of air. She felt a leg beneath her, or was it an arm? She reached out and grabbed the limb, laughing, knowing she had to strike first or be dunked.

Then he pulled her close. Her legs scissored around his waist. She felt dizzy as her breasts touched his chest, realizing with a shocking thrill that it was Rory, not Allen, who'd embraced her with a burning desire that cut through the cold water like a lightning bolt through the black night.

Rory pushed her away and swam fast to shore, running back up to the farmhouse, his buttocks gleaming white in the darkness while Hannah marveled at how electric a body could feel while submerged in water.

"Hey! Hannah! You okay?" Dylan was giving her a concerned look.

"Sure. Fine," she said. "What were you saying?"

"Rory was a musician, huh?"

She nodded. "Give him something with strings, and he could play it: banjo, fiddle, guitar. He was an incredible pianist, too. He played with an orchestra in California for a while, doing movie soundtracks, and traveled around with a few local bands while he lived at Haven Lake. He always had somebody to jam with here at night, because lots of people traveled with their instruments."

"So this must be his, then, right?"

"What must be?" Hannah had been so busy talking, she'd lost focus again. Now her eyes followed Dylan's hands as he reached down to pull something out from under the bed. When she saw what it was, she had to press her lips together to keep the sound inside: a screech of disbelief.

"This guitar."

"Don't!" she said sharply, but it was too late. Dylan had unlatched the lid of the dusty black case and taken out the guitar.

For an instant, time stood still. The fly that had been buzzing at the window might as well have been trapped in amber, and the dust motes caught in the cobwebs sparked in the sunlight. Hannah had to force herself to take a breath.

How could Rory have left his original guitar here in the cabin? This was his most precious possession, a blond Martin acoustic guitar he'd begged his parents to buy him for his eighteenth birthday because it was the sort of guitar Bob Dylan and Neil Young had played when they first started out. Rory owned many instruments, three or four guitars at least, but the Martin had been with him through college and his life in California. He said he used it for songwriting because there was something special about the sound and feel of it.

Dylan plucked a few chords. "Cool," he said, despite the strings being so out of tune.

He started to tune it, twisting the knobs, his long fingers mesmerizing Hannah even as she wanted to beg him to stop because it was as if his fingers were reaching inside her chest and squeezing her heart, the sensation dull and painful at the same time. She took another long, slow breath and the fly buzzed in the window again. She was about to speak when a piece of yellow lined paper folded into a small square fell out of the guitar's hole.

Again, Dylan was too quick for her, unfolding the paper and reading it before she could say anything. She might as well have turned to wood, her arms fused to the chair arms, the heels of her boots tacked to the chair's rungs.

"It's a note to somebody named 'Gypsy Girl,'" he said, squinting to make out the handwriting.

Even from this distance, she could see that the handwriting was Rory's: loopy and generous, the letters sprawled across the page the way he had been sprawling across the bed the night Theo died, nursing the gashes in his arm Theo had made with Rory's knife.

"Let me see it." She managed to pry one arm off the chair and reached for the paper.

Dylan handed her the note and continued tuning the guitar while she read it.

Gypsy Girl,

If you find this note, it means I've gone for good and left you my guitar as a souvenir. Burn it or play it. I don't care. The music was all for you, every song I sang, every word I wrote. We always said we couldn't be together unless the unimaginable happened, and then we couldn't be together because it would be the worst time of our lives. Both things are true. Now all I can do is keep you and Sydney safe from the truth. What happened that night was nobody's fault and nothing can change it now anyway. I don't trust myself not to speak the truth to you, because you have always been the keeper of my heart. So this is my gift to you: my absence.

Be well. Love those who love you. Most of all, be happy when you can. The blame is mine. You are innocent. Forgive me, Gypsy Girl, but most of all, forgive yourself, and know that I'm with you wherever I am.

Love,

R

Dylan had put the guitar away and was watching her. "So who's the note to? His girlfriend?"

"Must be," Hannah said, tucking the note into her back pocket with a trembling hand.

He was watching her closely. "I bet it was hard staying at Haven Lake after your husband died."

"Sometimes."

"Why did you?"

"I don't know." Hannah spread her hands, as if she could gather all of Haven Lake and pick up the pieces. "I thought about leaving. But I wanted to keep the farm alive. You can't always run from your feelings."

Dylan stood up. "So I guess that's your way of telling me I should have gone home with Dad and Sydney to deal with shit."

"No," Hannah said. "When you get to know me better, you'll know that I always say what I think."

"Yeah? And what's that? About me, I mean."

"I actually think that you probably did the right thing, not going home. You seem like the kind of person who wouldn't just run away without a good reason. And I know you're not deliberately trying to hurt your dad or Sydney."

"Thanks." Dylan glanced out the door, where the sound of the wind in the pines made a whistling sound and a woodpecker had started drumming. "This place is kind of creepy."

"Only until you know what the noises are." Hannah cocked her head at him, wondering. "Or do you have a real reason to be scared?"

Dylan looked away from her and swallowed hard. "The whole point of me being gone is so I won't be found," he said.

"I can do a better job of keeping you safe if you tell me what you're afraid will happen."

He shook his head. "Not your problem. And there's probably nothing to worry about anyway." He gave her an unconvincing smile. "Did other people live out here in the woods, too?"

"Sure. There's one other cabin, but most workers stayed in tents or yurts, or sometimes slept on the ground. People stayed in our house when there was room, too, or slept in the hayloft."

"Wow," Dylan said. "It must have been nice but crazy, living with so many people."

"It was." Again Hannah thought of Lucy, who arrived at the farm the summer after Rory did. Lucy had brought her kids back every summer after that. Theo and Valerie were both quiet at first, small enough to cling to their mother, a nymph in gauzy cotton clothing, black hair cropped close to her head, her voice breathless and shy. Lucy wore her vulnerability like a damp overcoat, so that people wanted to take it from her, help her dry off and get warm. Her overcoat's pockets were filled with Lucy's psychic maladies: her memories of childhood abuse, her troubled marriage, a passion for pills that made her frantic and thin.

Hannah wrapped her arms around her torso. Why had Rory disappeared when she needed him most? He had left her this note, probably never imagining it would take her so long to find it. What had he meant by keeping her and Sydney safe from the truth? She had to assume the note was about Theo's death. What was it that Rory wanted to tell her about that night, but couldn't?

If only she could pinpoint when things had started to unravel, maybe she could absolve herself of guilt, or at least understand the chain of events leading to Theo's mysterious death and Allen taking his own life. Was it when they bought the farm? When she and Allen decided to invite people to live here? When Lucy had arrived with her children, with her story of a marriage turned sour and her helplessness?

So pointless to keep asking those questions. Knowing where you'd gone wrong in the past was like pulling apart a sweater one stitch at a time, trying to find the place where you'd made your first mistake, only to realize that the only way to fix it was to start all over again.

Dylan interrupted her thoughts, pulling her back to the present. "I never realized until I came down here how big that pond is. It's more like a lake."

"That's what Allen thought, too. That's why he called it Haven Lake."

"Is that your boat?"

"Yes. Though I never take it out anymore."

"What about swimming? Can you swim in the pond?"

"We used to, a long time ago. I don't anymore. You shouldn't, either." She stood up, so claustrophobic suddenly that her skin prickled. The note in her back pocket burned like a coal. "Want to help me do a few chores? I need to get another load of hay from down the road. I could use a hand."

Dylan's gaze shifted to the door again. "You sure my dad's gone?"

"Positive," Hannah said. "Come on. Let's get to work."

The farm was ten minutes away, bigger than Hannah's, a white house with black trim. Four barns with red metal roofs and a ton of activity in the yard, a couple of guys on tractors and a kid racing around on a dirt bike, a German shepherd running alongside and barking.

The kid on the dirt bike rode across the dirt yard to greet them, kicking up dust. It wasn't until the rider took off the helmet that Dylan realized she was a girl his own age, with satiny dark brown hair that fell to her waist.

She flicked her dark eyes over at Dylan, then addressed Hannah. "You here for hay?"

"Yes," Hannah said. "Your dad knows I'm coming."

"Okay. I can help load it. He's got the doors open around back."

"Thanks, sweetie," Hannah said.

The girl stuffed her hair back into the helmet and took off on the bike.

"That's Sloan. She's a fun little devil," Hannah said as they followed the dirt bike around to the back of one of the barns.

Dylan stared at the girl's gleaming black helmet and strong blue-jeaned legs. He remembered his weeping earlier in the cabin and felt ashamed.

Sloan threw the hay bales down from the loft and Hannah and Dylan stacked them in the truck bed. Hannah had slotted plywood panels around the truck bed so they could stack the bales eight feet high. It took Dylan a few minutes to learn how to grab the rectangular bales by the twine and line them up the right way to fit in the truck, but after a while he enjoyed the feel of swinging them into position. He felt the girl's eyes on him but didn't let himself meet her gaze.

Afterward, Hannah dug around in her pocket, brought out a wad of bills, and handed them to a guy who looked enough like Sloan that Dylan decided it had to be one of her brothers: short and compactly built, dark hair, sharp cheekbones. He actually had a hay straw clamped between his teeth, something Dylan thought only movie cowboys did.

"That wasn't so bad," Dylan said as they drove away.

Hannah glanced at him and smiled. "You did a good job. You're stronger than you look."

"Aw, shucks, ma'am," he said, and pulled a hay straw off his shirt to stick between his teeth, making her laugh. "Why don't you grow your own hay?"

"I do. Up on the other side of the hill from the sheep pastures. If you stick around, you'll be helping me bale it in June. But my ewes almost all birthed twins this year, so I have more mouths to feed than I'd planned on. Luckily, the grass is almost good enough now in the pastures for me to quit giving them hay soon."

Hannah had another errand to run in Greenfield, something to pick up at the farmers' co-op, so they drove there next. Seeing the town by daylight, Dylan could admire the neat farms along the road. He recognized one of the intersections and realized she must have driven him this way from the Route 2 rotary the night he arrived. It was good he hadn't tried to hitch to her house; they passed only one other car. Not exactly a superhighway.

Greenfield center reminded him of cowboys and the Wild West, too, with its main street of flat-faced, low brick buildings. The people on the streets were a mix of farmers, hippies, and students.

The co-op was in a big warehouse on the outskirts of town. Hannah said he could wait in the truck, but Dylan came in and was stunned by being in a place that actually sold things like saddles and halters, muck boots and flannel shirts, birdseed, giant bags of feed, and barrel-sized plastic bottles of animal vitamins. The building smelled like molasses. Hannah had a special order in, she said, a new roll of portable fencing. She paid at the cash register and was given a pink slip so they could drive the truck around to the loading dock.

A big guy in a denim work shirt was coming up the steps of the co-op as they were leaving. He paused to tip his baseball cap at Hannah, then gave her a squint-eyed grin.

"Hannah! Haven't seen you in a dog's age." He opened his arms. "Come say hello."

To Dylan's shock, Hannah flattened against the railing and hissed, "Don't you dare touch me, Les Phillips."

Les put on a wounded look—Dylan could tell it was fake—and crossed his arms. "Why, Hannah, is this any way to greet an old friend?"

"You're old, but you're no friend of mine," Hannah said.

She tried to pass the man on the steps, keeping her back against the railing, but Les closed in on her, tipping his head back to laugh as he cornered her. "Come on, babe. Play nice. We had ourselves a nice little time, didn't we?"

Hannah's face was frozen in shock. For a heady, ferocious moment, Dylan imagined himself stepping between them and shoving the guy off the steps. But what if the man fell and hit his head? Or—and this was even easier to picture—what if that big guy knocked Dylan out or shot him, then grabbed Hannah and dragged her into a car?

These thoughts filled his mind with an oil slick of panic. Dylan was rooted to the spot. Then Hannah reached for his hand and yanked him past Les toward the parking lot at a half run, both of them breathing hard.

Dylan felt his face go hot with embarrassment. Why hadn't he acted, instead of freezing up like that? No wonder Kelly thought he was such a loser.

"Who was that?" he asked once they were in the truck and driving around to the loading dock.

"Oh, just a guy I dated a long time ago who still likes to give me a hard time. The King of the Assholes."

Dylan wanted to ask more, but by Hannah's set expression, he knew the subject was closed.

Back at Haven Lake, they drove the truck down to the barn, jouncing on the ruts in the dirt drive hard enough that Dylan bit his tongue. He swallowed the metallic taste of blood but forgot about the pain when he started loading the hay on the creaky conveyor belt that carried it up to the hayloft. This was a cool contraption, something else he'd never seen.

Hay had to be stored inside to keep it dry, Hannah explained. "Wet hay molds and rots, and then it heats up and can spontaneously ignite in your barn," she said. "Plus, if a pregnant sheep eats moldy hay, she might abort."

They worked steadily, Hannah lifting bales faster than Dylan. "Now what?" Dylan asked once they'd finished, wiping his brow with one arm. His eyes were stinging with sweat and his muscles burned.

"That's it, until we bring the sheep in for the evening. Want something to eat?"

He hadn't had breakfast because his dad had arrived too early, but he could last a few more hours. "I'm fine," he said.

"Come in for a glass of cold water, anyway. It's important to stay hydrated when you're working."

Dylan nodded and climbed back into the truck for the short bumpy ride back up to the house. He wondered where Billy was. Odd, he thought, that the dog hadn't come with them, since he went everywhere with Hannah. Why wasn't Billy here in the yard, at least, barking a greeting?

As they entered the kitchen, Dylan felt his chest heave in shock: Sydney was seated at the table and flipping through a magazine, Billy sitting beside her with his head in her lap.

CHAPTER EIGHT

Dylan tried to back out of the door unseen, in a silent panic, but Hannah grabbed his shirtfront and tugged him into the kitchen. "So what happened?" she asked. "Where's Gary?"

"He went home." Sydney glanced up. Her green eyes widened in surprise when she saw Dylan and she jumped to her feet. "Oh, thank God!" she said. "I was picturing you being chopped up by some madman at a rest stop."

"Nope," he said. "Sorry to disappoint you."

"Not funny," she said.

He felt bad then because Sydney looked like she'd been crying. Hannah went to the sink and poured them each a glass of water, then started rummaging in the fridge. "So what happened?" she repeated, her voice muffled by the refrigerator door.

Sydney's eyes were still on Dylan. "Your dad looked everywhere for you. When he didn't see you here, he figured he'd drive along the highway and look. After that, he was going home to see if you'd show up there."

His dad must be royally pissed off. Well, so what? That wasn't anything new. Still, Dylan's stomach clenched with guilt. "Can you text him and let him know I'm okay?" he asked, quickly adding, "But tell him I'm staying here. I can't go home, Sydney."

When Sydney hesitated, he was afraid she might refuse. But then she nodded and pulled out her phone.

Hannah, meanwhile, made a stack of sandwiches out of wheat bread, cheese, lettuce, and tomatoes. Dylan wasn't going to have one, but as he watched Sydney and Hannah eat—neither of them suggesting that he take a sandwich—he tentatively picked one up, promising himself he wouldn't eat more than half. In the end, though, he ate three halves and drank the lemonade Hannah put in front of him, too.

The women were busy being polite to each other, making occasional brief remarks about the weather, the dog, the house. Dylan thought about the things Hannah had told him about Allen and Rory, and he suddenly wished she and Sydney would quit this crap and make up. They should know how good they had it, that they still had each other, a mother and daughter together.

He missed his own mother suddenly with a lumpy, undefined sadness that rose, thick and doughy, to fill his throat and nostrils. Even here, Mom was with him. He didn't know if that was good or bad. What if he felt this way all his life?

Then he was doomed to be the Dribbler, leaking all over.

Gary called back half an hour later to say he had arrived home. Sydney went outside, not wanting to talk with him in front of Dylan and Hannah, who were feeding bits of food to the woodchuck Hannah kept as a pet despite the fact that there were surely laws against domesticating wild animals.

Behind the house, she could see sheep grazing the fields and rocks made white by lichen peeping through the grass at the ridgeline, like a patch of scalp showing through tufts of hair. The quiet was so profound that she was tempted to walk on her toes.

"I can't believe you just drove home without me!" She paced the back patio, the phone pressed so hard to her ear that it hurt. "Why didn't you come back to pick me up?"

"I'm sorry. I thought you'd made it pretty clear you wanted to wait for

Dylan." Gary sighed. "As it turns out, I guess you were right to stay. I'm the one who blew it. Christ. I still can't believe Dylan came back to the farm."

Sydney heard the hurt in his voice. "He didn't exactly come back on his own," she reassured him. "Mom found him in the woods down by the pond."

"If she thought he was hiding in the woods, why didn't she tell me to look there?"

"I think Mom had her own agenda, as usual." Sydney thought about the way her mother had literally towed Dylan into the kitchen with one hand on his shirtfront. Sydney had never touched Dylan like that, so naturally, and with so much authority. Like a mother.

"What do you think we should do now?" Gary was saying. "Do you want to bring Dylan home with you on the bus? Or do I need to drive back and pick you both up?" Then he added, "I'm afraid that I'd just set Dylan off again. You might do better with him on your own."

Sydney bit her lower lip. It pleased her that Gary thought she could talk Dylan into coming back with her, but she knew he wouldn't. "Maybe we should let him stay here," she said. "I know you think it'll screw up his junior year, but what if he just hangs out here for a week to think things through? We can talk to his teachers about having him make up missed work."

"I hate that you're trying to undermine my authority."

That felt like a slap across the face. "I'm not! How can you think that? I just want what's best for Dylan. What's best for us as a family," she added, though in truth she'd never felt less like they were a family.

"What's best is for you to bring Dylan home."

"And if I don't?" Sydney felt her temper rise. Why was this suddenly her job, managing his kid?

"You will," Gary said. "I have faith in you. Call me when you're on your way." He said good-bye and hung up before she could keep arguing.

Sydney wanted to throw the phone across the garden. She shoved it into her pocket and stomped through the grass. How could Gary have left her here to deal with everything?

She walked to the edge of the vegetable garden, where the tidy furrows reminded her of "ruby hunting" with Theo and Valerie; that's what they had called their search for cherry tomatoes. Her dad made that up, she remembered, tipping her face up to the sun to more fully imagine the pleasure of that sudden burst of warm sweetness, the juice running down her chin as she popped a tomato into her mouth straight off the vine. Dad could be as clever and fun as Mom if you caught him at the right time, and even more charismatic. She'd adored him as much as she feared him.

She was standing like that when Hannah found her. Hannah approached warily, as if Sydney were some sort of wild animal loose in her garden. Sydney didn't blame her. She could easily imagine whirling around and baring her teeth at her mother. That's how out of control her emotions felt at the moment.

"What did Gary say?" Hannah's hair was coming loose from its braid.

"He's home. He said he'd come back and get us, or we can take a bus."

Hannah shook her head. "Dylan won't go home with you."

It was that kind of certainty that made her mother so infuriating. It was one thing for Sydney to think this, but Hannah had no business interfering. "You don't know what Dylan will do, Mom. You don't know one thing about Dylan's situation or about us. You're clueless as usual."

Her mother only shrugged. "Probably."

Sydney dug her nails into her palms. She had never been any good at arguing with her mother. Whatever she said, Hannah would manage to deflect the remark in some clever way.

The late May sun was surprisingly strong. Hannah's face glistened with sweat. She moved away from Sydney to sit on the shady stone bench beneath the horse chestnut tree. The tree was just starting to bloom, the white candelabra blossoms about to unfurl. "So how are you going to convince Dylan to go with you?"

Sydney's back prickled with heat. She moved into the shade, too. "I don't know. You made things impossible for us by telling Dylan he can stay here."

"I was only trying to help him. I'm sure you and Gary are, too."

A peace offering. Sydney was suddenly exhausted. She dropped to the grass. From this vantage point, she could see splashes of color beginning to show in the flower gardens bordering the brick paths leading from this side of the house around to the front door: tulip shoots nosing their way out of rotted leaves, purple crocuses and grape hyacinths, pale yellow narcissus blossoms rolled tight as cigarettes.

"I'll tell Dylan he can come back with me on the bus, but I'm not going to force him," Sydney said. "Do you happen to know how often buses run between Amherst and Boston on Saturdays?"

"No. But you can check online. I'm sure the schedule's there." Her mother gazed off in the distance, at the land falling gently behind the house into a bowl, sloping to the edge of the pond. "I was hoping you'd spend the night."

"You know I can't."

"Why not?"

"I wouldn't be able to sleep here."

Her mother studied Sydney's face until Sydney turned away. Then she said, "How much longer are you planning to punish me?"

"I'm not." Sydney furiously pulled at the grass beside her, yanking it up by the roots. "Has it ever occurred to you that I'm just trying to protect myself?"

"Because I didn't? That's what you're saying, isn't it? But not everything was my fault. You're old enough to realize that now."

Sydney looked up. "No?" She had to squint; her mother's back was to the sun, creating a halo of silver around her wild black hair. "Which part wasn't your fault, Mom? The part where you let Dad keep on being depressed and crazy? The part where you invited all of those wanderers and potheads and free love dropouts to live here and buy into Dad as their leader, doing drugs and having sex with him, like he was some kind of feudal lord? Or the part where you never once tried to bring me back from Ipswich after I left?"

"I tried to bring you back. You wouldn't come with me!"

"You tried once, Mom. *Once.*"

"That isn't true," Hannah said. "You know it isn't true."

Sydney didn't have time for this bullshit. She knew her mother was lying. "You were always the strong one, Mom. Not Dad! If you'd only put your foot down like a normal wife and mother, Theo never would have drowned!"

Her mother slid off the bench to sit cross-legged in front of Sydney, too close. "What are you saying, Sydney? How did anything I do cause Theo to drown?"

"You let everybody do what they wanted! You created a community without rules. Theo was upset that night because Lucy was sleeping around. That's why he went swimming alone." Sydney felt her face contort as she held back tears. She'd never said any of this to her mother, or to anyone else. "But it's also my fault that he drowned. I'm the one who told Theo that his mom was with Rory."

"Lucy slept with everyone," Hannah said. "You're not to blame for Theo swimming in the pond that night, Sydney. We always hope we can control the people we love, but it isn't true. You, of all people, should know that by now."

Sydney felt a roaring in her ears. "Jesus, Mom. How could you stand living with Dad when he was so unstable, and having all of those crazy people coming and going with their own baggage? Why did you *stay*? And why are you still here now?"

Hannah stood up and brushed off the seat of her jeans. Her face was a blotchy mask. "Let me know when you're ready, and I'll drive you to the bus station," she said.

Sydney remained on the ground for a few more minutes, trying to ease the tightness in her chest, feeling rejected, but relieved that her mother had stopped the conversation before either of them said anything unforgivable.

Back in the house, she collected her purse and found Dylan in her old bedroom, sitting at the desk and drawing with colored pencils. It was a picture of Billy, running low to the ground the way she'd seen him this morning, ears back, mouth in a grin.

"Not bad," she said, her heart twisting at the sight of the patchwork quilt her mother had made. She used to love that quilt. As a child, it had made her feel safe, as if her mother were in the room with her. "I didn't know you liked to draw."

"Sometimes. Usually I draw on the computer. I have a couple of different apps for that."

"Oh," was all she could think of to say. Her brain seemed to have retreated to some tight, cold corner of her skull.

Sydney perched on the bed, smoothing the quilt beneath her. She recognized swatches of her father's shirts, her mother's jeans, and some of her old T-shirts and dresses. She'd helped her mother cut up the fabric and piece the swatches together, one of many projects meant to teach her math at home. She kept wanting the pieces to all be the same size and shape, because rectangles would be easier to line up and sew, but her mother would have none of that.

"It wouldn't be a family quilt then," Hannah had said. "It takes all shapes and sizes to make a family."

Dylan swiveled in the desk chair to look at her. "I guess now is when you give me the big lecture about how I have to go home and resolve my 'issues.'"

"No," she said. "I'm done trying to talk you into anything you don't want to do, Dylan. Mom's taking me to the bus station in a few minutes. You can come with me if you want. Otherwise, I'll say good-bye."

"Oh. I thought you might stay overnight, at least. It's the weekend." The boy twisted the pencil between his fingers, twirling it until he dropped it and had to pick it up again. "You shouldn't have told my dad all that stuff about the car and Kelly."

Sydney's eyes burned with the effort not to cry. She hated thinking that she'd ruined whatever trust had started to build between herself and Dylan. "I know you feel like I was snooping and ratted you out, but I didn't have a choice," she said. "I was asking people questions about you because I was worried. And parents have to tell each other things about their children." There: she'd laid claim to him in a small way, at least.

She was going to be his stepmother and she wanted him to know she wouldn't give up loving him, no matter what he did.

"I guess. But I wish he didn't know. I wish nobody did," Dylan added abruptly. "Now Dad will hate me."

Sometimes Sydney forgot, looking at Dylan—thin, but so much taller than she was now, and with a man's broad shoulders—that he was still a child. "No, he won't. He's concerned about you, that's all."

"He just wants to make sure I go to some fancy college so I can find a job and get out of his hair."

"God, don't be so simplistic," she snapped, losing patience. "It doesn't suit you. Yes, of course your father wants you to succeed in school and have a good life. Can you blame him for that?"

"But maybe my idea of a good life is different from his," Dylan muttered. "I want a life that isn't all about working around the clock and making money."

Her mother was already casting her spell, Sydney thought, no doubt filling Dylan's head with rants about sustainability and simplicity.

She sighed. "Look, it's your life. You get to live it, not us. But think about it: at least if you go to college, you'll have more choices. Meanwhile, it's natural for you to feel rebellious around your father. Totally normal."

His mouth twitched. "You're such a friggin' therapist."

She smiled back. "I am what I am. You'll have to accept that."

"I guess. But why are you as pissed off at your mom as I am at my dad, if you know so much about psychology and that shit?" Dylan started twirling the pencil between his fingers again. "Do you think Dad and I will still be fighting in twenty years, like you and Hannah? Seems like a shitty waste of time and energy."

"I don't know. That's up to you."

"What about you?"

"What about me?"

"Why haven't you used all that voodoo therapy so you and your mom can, you know, *resolve your issues and reconnect*?" Dylan's tone was biting.

"I don't know." Sydney stood up and looked out the window. "Too much happened to us, I guess."

"Like what? Your dad dying?"

"He didn't just die. He committed suicide."

"Oh. I didn't know that. I'm sorry. That sucks."

"Yeah, it does."

"How?"

Sydney turned around and found the boy looking at her with so much sympathy in his blue eyes that she had to turn back to the window. Even so, she felt the warmth of his gaze on her shoulders. "Dad shot himself in the small barn. He used the same shotgun he used for killing rats."

"What small barn?"

"It's not there anymore. It burned down." She barely stopped herself from adding, "My mother set it on fire." She didn't really know that. It could have been spontaneous combustion from damp hay, as her mother had always claimed.

"Why?"

"Why, what?"

"Why did your dad off himself?"

"That's a terrible way to put it," Sydney said. "But I guess he did it because he was depressed and had given up thinking he'd ever feel better. Death probably seemed like a happier alternative."

"If you ask me, that's pretty psycho, putting a rat gun in your mouth and blowing a hole in your head. I mean, I think life sucks, but I wouldn't do that."

Thank God for that, Sydney thought. "Vietnam left my dad pretty traumatized," she said. "After he came home, he had nightmares, insomnia, rages. All classic signs of post-traumatic stress disorder—I'm sure you've heard of PTSD, right?—though of course I didn't know it back then. I just learned pretty early on that when Dad was in one of his black moods, I should stay out of his way. Then there was a drowning in our pond," Sydney added, the words tumbling out before she could stop them. "That upset him, too. I imagine he felt responsible."

"What pond? This one here? Haven Lake?"

She nodded.

"Who drowned?"

Sydney sat down on the bed again, her legs wobbling beneath her. "One of the kids who used to come work on the farm with his mom and sister every summer. My friend Theo. He was fifteen."

"That's horrible. How did he drown?"

Sydney felt suddenly exasperated. Not with Dylan, but with the fact that this story was part of her history and always would be. Why had she even brought it up?

"It was an accident," she said. "Theo went swimming alone at night. It was rainy and cold. It was May—too soon to be swimming—and nobody even noticed Theo was missing until the next morning. It's easy to drown if something happens and you're alone."

She stopped talking, abruptly. Who was responsible for Theo that night? Who was watching the kids, while the adults played? Why didn't anybody sound the alarm that a child was missing? Though they were hardly children at that point.

Somebody must have known where Theo was. There were so many adults around that spring, it seemed like somebody was always telling them to do this or that, even if it was only to keep the smaller kids out from underfoot. There were people everywhere around the farm. Haven Lake was its own bustling village.

Sydney had been especially fond of Millie, an Englishwoman in her sixties. Millie loved to take the rowboat across the pond and back every morning, her birding glasses around her neck. Sydney had done it with her once, marveling at how Millie's wattled arms flashed bluish white like fish bellies as she powered the oars through the dark green water.

Millie was the one who'd found Theo: she'd taken the boat out and discovered Theo's body floating in the weeds by the tiny island. Her screams brought them all running down to the pond; the men rowed the boat back out and ferried Theo's body to the beach, where Lucy keened and had to be dragged away so the medical examiner and cops could do their thing.

Naturally the police said they'd compromised the investigation by moving the body, but who could have left Theo there, floating in that cold water by himself? The farm was all about love and togetherness. They all stayed with Lucy and Theo by the water until the police sent them back to the house with threats and even, in one instance, a gun fired overhead.

Sydney stood up again, feeling nauseated. "I need to go," she said.

Dylan nodded. "Don't take any shit from my dad because I'm staying, okay?"

"Okay." Sydney reached out and rested her hand on the boy's head. She didn't want to leave him here for more reasons than she could name. Dylan's scalp was warm, almost hot, the light brown hair soft as feathers between her fingers. "I'm on your side. Remember that."

Dylan looked up at her, his blue eyes dark with pain. "I know," he said, and stood up to give her an awkward hug.

The hug sustained Sydney as she rode, mostly in tense silence, with Hannah to the bus station in Amherst, rehearsing what she could say to Gary to make him understand why she had come home alone. Hannah didn't get out of the car to say good-bye.

Sydney was grateful for the bus, where she could be pleasantly anonymous. She settled into a seat beside a middle-aged man who immediately fell asleep with his head lodged against the window. She enjoyed the quiet hum of noise and her view of the cars on the highway, hurtling to unknown destinations, then let herself rest her head against the seat.

Millie's screams. That's what had awakened her the morning after Theo died.

She had first met Theo when they were both eight years old. His sister, Valerie, was nine. Their parents, Lucy and Sam, arrived that summer with the kids in a blue Volvo.

"Trust fund babies," Sydney heard one of the women in the kitchen mutter. She hadn't known what that meant at the time.

Lucy was a pretty, doll-like woman with enormous brown eyes and elfin features. She wore gauzy cotton clothing that wrapped in complicated ways around her slight body and played a wooden flute, often with her legs crossed and her eyes closed, the way Sydney imagined people summoning fairies in the woods. Sometimes she played the flute while sitting in a tree. She didn't seem like anybody's mother.

Sam, Lucy's husband, was much older, a silent man shaped like a bullet. Bald except for a monk's fringe of brown, tufted hair. He was a lawyer, brooding and critical of everything on the farm: Why didn't they have solar power to heat water for showers? Had they thought about composting human waste as well as vegetable matter? He walked the property like he owned it and argued constantly with Dad.

Sam left the farm after two weeks, much to everyone's relief. "Back to his job," Hannah explained when Sydney asked. "Most people with jobs only get two weeks of vacation in the summer."

"Oh." Sydney didn't understand this—her parents worked around the clock, yet somehow took time off when they wanted, too—but it didn't matter. She didn't care about Sam or Lucy. She only cared that Theo and Valerie were staying.

Valerie, a timid girl with a habit of chewing the ends of her lank, toast-colored hair, was quiet but slyly clever. She and Sydney read the same books and, as children, fully believed in mermaids, talking animals, tiny people living under the floorboards, time travel, and mind reading. Theo was Valerie's opposite in every way. He was a year younger than his sister, but already taller. He was dark-haired and fierce, intense and loud, often hotheaded.

In the beginning, Sydney wished she had a brother like Theo, who was protective of his mother. He brought Lucy cups of tea in the morning when she was still in bed, hovering over her if Lucy said, in her little girl's whisper, that she might have a headache.

Sydney, who knew every path through the pines and every rock in the fields, delighted in showing Theo and Valerie around. The adults on the farm called Valerie "the Wait-for-Me Kitten" after a story Hannah used to read them, because Valerie was always slower and shyer than the other children.

The three of them looked after the younger children or did field chores alongside the adults. When they were bored—as Theo often was—they created their own projects, constructing forts and tree houses out of scrap lumber, building dams across the streams in the woods, spying on the antics of the adults and comparing notes on who did what drugs, who was sleeping with whom, who seemed craziest. The adults left them alone. Hannah's theory—which she no doubt still clung to now, given how she was treating Dylan—was that children needed to map out their own journeys, just like adults.

In their case, Theo, Valerie, and Sydney weren't only mapping out individual journeys. They were making their own world.

Theo and Valerie disappeared every September to go back to school. Sydney would suffer through withdrawal, feeling bereft without them. Valerie wrote to her, but Theo never did. Haven Lake had no phone, television, or computer while she lived there.

And no friends, other than a boringly straight, red-haired girl up the road whose parents didn't like her visiting the farm and "being polluted by those dirty hippies," as Sydney overheard the girl's mother say once. Sydney did her studies in the kitchen with Hannah and worked on the farm. She was callused and muscled and stayed brown-skinned all year, her hair in crazy wild tangles.

This rhythm went on for seven years. Then, the year Sydney and Theo turned fifteen, Lucy showed up in the winter, telling Hannah, "I need to clear my head, man. My husband is toxic. Even that house is poisoning me." She'd pulled Theo and Valerie out of their prep school, figuring Hannah could homeschool them along with Sydney.

Sydney knew her mother was opposed to Lucy moving in with them full-time—she'd witnessed a hissing argument between her parents—but her father never turned anyone away, not even crazy-eyed Charlie Bentley, another Vietnam vet who was out of his mind after too many acid trips and thought the trees came alive and danced at night.

Sydney was delighted, thinking she'd have a brother and sister year-round now, but her giddy joy at seeing her friends again was dimmed by the change in Valerie, who was sixteen and held herself apart. Valerie had grown taller and thinner than Sydney. She bit her nails down to the skin and plucked her eyebrows to thin threads with her fingers. Despite this odd behavior, Valerie was beautiful, her wavy brown hair falling like water down her back, a new sway to her hips.

Finally, Valerie told her what was different: she had discovered sex. An older boy with a car. She was pining for him and didn't want to be at the farm.

"You kids go play," she told Theo and Sydney over and over, dismissing them. "I'm too old to run around in the woods. I'm going to listen to music."

Sydney felt both jealous and betrayed. Valerie seemed to have donned an impenetrable, musty adult cloak that set her apart from Sydney and the silly antics of children.

"She's a little vixen, that one," one of the men staying on the farm that year said about Valerie. Which one? Josh, in his denim skirt and with a paintbrush beard? Lukas from Norway? Isaac from New York, who'd come to the farm directly from a kibbutz in Israel? Her own father or uncle?

Sydney couldn't remember. But whoever it was had expressed what every man at Haven Lake must have been thinking, as Valerie swayed about the house in her faded jeans, her hair winding around her brown shoulders like ribbons, blue shadow on her eyelids.

It wasn't the same without Valerie to hang out with, but in some ways, it was better. When Theo took Sydney's hand as they scrambled up their favorite pine tree overlooking the pond, Sydney suddenly experienced an electric charge, a new kind of excitement. She felt breathless and even bolder around him.

She and Theo were both strong and athletic, eager to test themselves and each other. They went snowshoeing in the woods, following the lacy tracks of mice and birds, losing themselves in the hills. They built a hut on the iced-over pond despite the booming cracks of ice beneath them, and followed the creek that fed the pond deep into the woods, where they discovered a shallower pond with a fox frozen beneath its surface, its sharp snout curled in a grimace. They built bonfires and got high. By now they knew where every resident of Haven Lake kept a stash. Not that they had to look far: Allen had bins of pot on the kitchen shelf, stuff he'd grown himself in the greenhouse attached to the small barn, and baskets of mushrooms that weren't for cooking.

One night, Sydney dared Theo to follow her out of the hayloft window of the big barn and onto its metal roof. The moonlight glinted on the metal so that it was like climbing up a silver waterfall. It was only May, but the roof was still warm. The stars blinked overhead and the mountains humped like a giant black beast against the lighter sky, the pine trees standing in sharp quills along the ridges.

Theo produced a bottle of apple wine he'd stolen from Allen's cache in the basement. They drank it, though the wine was sweet enough to make Sydney feel sick. Then they lay back on the warm metal, feet pressed firmly against the gutter to keep themselves from sliding off, the danger of doing so making Sydney's heart drum like a trip-hammer against her ribs.

It started to rain, a sudden downpour, deafening on the metal roof. They climbed back into the hayloft, terrified about slipping off but laughing to show they weren't scared. Theo made it into the loft first and reached out to take Sydney's hand to pull her inside.

And then he kissed her.

His mouth was sweet from the wine. Their T-shirts were wet and stuck to their skin, but Sydney wasn't cold at all. She was burning up. Feverish and trembling.

They kept kissing, touching each other tentatively at first, then with more urgency. Their bodies recognized what was happening even before Sydney's mind grasped the fact that a feeling low in the pit of her stomach caused her to want to press her pelvis against his.

She pushed him against the hay bales. At some point the hay bales toppled and she was on top of him, moving frantically, reaching her hand inside his jeans to take hold of him, wanting him but not knowing what to do next. She'd seen Theo naked, of course—they all swam naked at Haven Lake—but touching him like this was different, his hot rubbery cock rigid in her hand, terrifying, but her own power even greater, because she knew she could take his cock inside her and hold it there, make him cry out the way she'd heard the adults moan in pleasure. She wanted that for him. For her.

But Theo stopped her, a hand on her wrist. "If you keep doing that, we won't be able to stop," he whispered against her neck.

"I don't care. I want to do it." Sydney could hardly breathe.

"Well, I care," Theo said, pulling Sydney's hand out of his jeans. He brushed the hair out of her face, placed a palm on her cheek. "We need to take precautions."

"Oh," Sydney said, sounding so dismal that Theo laughed.

"I only mean let's wait until tomorrow," he said. "I'll get something. And either of us has permission to change our minds, right? You're my best friend, Sydney. I'd say you're like a sister except that sounds sick. I want us to *stay* friends. That matters more to me than anything."

Sydney felt ashamed then, that Theo had thought through things so carefully, when all she'd been thinking about was pleasure.

The next night Theo came to her room. This time the kissing was still urgent, but softer and sweeter, both of them asking: "Here? Like this? Do you want me to do that?"

Then there was a sharp knock on the door. Her mother. "Honey? Have you seen Uncle Rory?" A rattle of the knob. "Why is this door locked?"

"I'm busy, Mom," Sydney said. "Uncle Rory's with Lucy. I saw them going back to his cabin."

"Oh." A moment's hesitation. Sydney knew her mother was wondering whether to tell them to open the door, because they had rules at Haven Lake: *Every door is an open door.* Sydney had never broken that rule.

Then Hannah's footsteps receded. Later, Sydney would ask herself why Hannah, that night of all nights, had let her keep the door locked, when any other night she might have forced her to open it. If only, if only, if only it had been otherwise, Theo might still be alive.

"What's my mom doing with your uncle?" Theo asked, sitting up so suddenly that Sydney, who had been on top of him, was nearly bucked off the single bed.

She shrugged. "I don't know. Probably sleeping with him."

"No she isn't."

If only, if only, if only. But here, again, another mistake: Sydney had laughed. "Yes she is," she said. "I've seen her coming out of his house in the morning."

What she'd seen was Lucy coming out of Rory's cabin early one morning, wearing nothing but one of his flannel shirts, her black hair a nest of tangles, her thin legs so pale they nearly glowed against the deep red pine needle path.

"She can't do that!" Theo jumped out of bed, pulling on his jeans. "Dad's expecting her back. She promised! She came here to get her head together. My parents are working things out." His face contorted. "Don't freak me out with that stupid shit."

"I'm sorry." Sydney reached out a hand to touch him, but he jerked away. "Why do you even care? I thought they were getting divorced," she said, puzzled, because that's what she'd heard. Besides, after those first two weeks, Sam had never come to the farm with Lucy, not for seven summers, and Sydney had seen Lucy with other men, too. Even with Crazy Charlie, though she suspected that was because Charlie always had some mind-altering treasure to barter for blow jobs or more. Lots of women had been with Charlie.

"My parents are getting back together," Theo said, yanking on his T-shirt. "Dad told me. I've got to find her and stop her! You don't get it, Syd. My mom's a crazy person without Dad!"

And then he was gone, banging the door open behind him and leaving Sydney alone in her bed. Naked, exposed, abandoned.

She had cried herself to sleep. This was supposed to be her special night. She'd woven a bracelet for Theo to give him afterward, so that neither of them could forget being the other's first. No matter what happened in their lives, they would always have this love between them. This one night.

Millie's screams from the pond woke her the next morning.

Now Sydney pressed a hand to her eyes and turned her face to the bus window. If only, if only, if only.

If only she hadn't gone back to Haven Lake, she wouldn't have had to relive this again.

Gary was waiting for her at South Station, craning his neck as he watched the passengers descend the steps of the bus behind her. "Where's Dylan?"

"He's staying with Mom."

She'd been nervous that Gary would get angry. Instead, he looked genuinely distressed. "I've never seen a kid this bent out of shape over some *girl*."

"I don't think it's just that."

"That's not very helpful," Gary said as she followed him to the car.

She fell asleep once they were in motion and woke abruptly in the driveway like a toddler with drool on her chin. Gary had made her favorite Italian wedding soup. They had salad with it and a bottle of chardonnay. Then Gary went to his desk to catch up on paperwork while Sydney did the dishes, the two of them painfully polite. Sydney longed to escape to her own little cottage on the river, but that would be cowardly. When they were married, there could be no such thing as a full retreat. She'd better get used to that idea.

In bed later, Gary lay on his back, eyes fixed on the ceiling. "I'm sorry I'm not handling things better, Sydney." He sounded miserable. "I should have stayed with you. I think I left because I'm afraid something is seriously wrong with Dylan."

"What makes you think that?"

"Why else would he run away?" Gary turned on his side to face her, propping himself up on one arm. "I can't face it if somehow Amanda and

I screwed up our kid. I really can't. We had all the privileges two people could have, but we fucked up. His mother's death has permanently damaged him, and I must not be doing the right things to help him. He's never going to recover, is he?"

"I don't think that's true." She reached over to stroke the hollow below Gary's throat, where his pulse felt hummingbird fast. "I don't even know how much of what he's going through right now has to do with Amanda. Teenagers are emotional by definition."

"Most don't run away."

"I did."

Gary blinked rapidly in surprise. His blue eyes were bloodshot, the lids purple and creased. "You didn't run away. You made a decision to stay with your grandparents because your mom was going haywire after your dad's suicide."

She nodded. "That's a pretty accurate description." She moved over and kissed him. When he responded, Sydney pressed herself against his body, pulling one of his thighs between hers. "But my mom still saw it as running away, and I guess now, looking back, I have to say she was right. I left Haven Lake for good. She was alone after that."

"The circumstances are completely different," Gary said. "You had reason to leave home if your mother wasn't taking care of you. What have we done to make Dylan leave?"

"Nothing." Sydney was beginning to believe that now. "I think he left because of whatever's going on with him socially. But my point was that I turned out all right, didn't I, even if I lost a parent when I was Dylan's age?"

"Better than all right." Gary stroked her thigh beneath her nightgown. "What really happened the night your dad died? You've never really told me the details."

"I don't like to talk about it."

"But maybe it would help me understand you better."

She had promised herself that if Gary ever asked about the farm, she would tell him the truth. She spoke slowly, sorting through her words carefully. This was always the difficult part when recalling the past: knowing the difference between what was true and what you imagined to be the truth, as you continually took a certain memory out to examine.

"I was asleep when Dad died," she said. "The sound of the gun woke me up. The farm is so quiet—you know that now, you've been there—that the gun sounded like a bomb going off. I didn't know what it was. I looked out my window and saw my mom running to the barns. There was a full moon and she had on a white nightgown. It was like watching a ghost. I knew right away something bad must have happened." Sydney pressed her lips together to stop the trembling.

"When was this?"

"A month before my sixteenth birthday."

"Did your father leave a note?"

"No. Not that I know of, anyway." Hannah could have destroyed it, Sydney thought, not for the first time. The same way she'd probably burned down the barn where it happened. "A boy had drowned on the farm a week before, though, and I think my dad blamed himself for the boy's death."

"Why?"

"I'm not sure. Maybe because it was his farm, so he felt responsible? Plus, it was his brother who'd kind of been the cause of the drowning. The boy, Theo, was upset that night because he thought my uncle Rory was sleeping with his mom." Sydney couldn't bring herself to tell Gary the rest of it: that she and Theo were in bed together that night, and that she'd been the one to tell Theo about Lucy. Even now, she couldn't believe that Theo had so naively believed that his mother would be loyal to his dad, when Lucy had always been the one to stir things up between the men at Haven Lake.

"Was it true? Was Theo's mom sleeping with your uncle?"

Sydney shrugged. "I don't know. Rory denied it, but he could have been lying. Anyway, even if Lucy and Rory were sleeping together, I'm sure it wasn't serious. Everyone slept with everyone else at the farm."

"Did you?"

Back to that old song. Sydney felt irritated that Gary's insecurity about her sexual past was once again superseding the real story. Why should he even care? She was here with him now. Shouldn't that be what mattered most?

Unless he knows you're not completely satisfied with him in bed, a small voice in her head whispered.

She smothered the voice, literally sitting up and flipping the pillow over, patting it down as if she could trap those words beneath it. She *was* satisfied with Gary. He was tender in bed and she knew what to expect; she could "take charge" of her own pleasure, as women's magazines always instructed, and have her orgasms with or without him. Orgasms couldn't be the cornerstone of a marriage. Every couple grew old, even physically infirm. What mattered was your deeper, emotional connection. Right?

To Gary, she said, "I wish you'd stop worrying about that. You know I was a virgin until sophomore year of college."

"I'm glad. Though I still wish you'd waited for me."

"That would have been a long wait."

"I know. I'm kidding. Sort of." Gary raised her hand to kiss it. "I'm an idiot."

"That's the thing about being human, right?" Sydney said, moving to put her head on his shoulder. "We're all idiots half the time, driven by impulses we don't understand."

"How did you get to be so wise? Oh, wait. You're a psychologist! You read people's minds!" Gary smiled and pulled her on top of him, moving his hands over her ass and thighs. "As pleasant as it is to talk about traumas past and present," he murmured, "let's both shut up and escape for a few minutes."

She smiled. "Best idea I've heard all night."

He kissed her neck, slid his mouth slowly down to her breasts, tonguing her nipples. Then Gary shifted her onto the bed and moved on top of her.

There was something wrong, though. Gary wasn't making love as he usually did, but too fast. As he entered her, he pinned her wrists to the bed and flattened himself against her body in a way that crushed her breasts and hip bones. He must still be upset about Dylan, Sydney thought, about his own helplessness. Maybe he was trying to feel powerful with her.

Sydney closed her eyes and moved a little, though with his weight distributed like that, it wasn't easy. Still, she tried to excite herself as well as make the right noises so Gary would know she wanted to be there, with him, and nowhere else. She hoped her body could convince him that her mind and heart were engaged in these actions, instead of feeling like they were trapped in separate little wire cages.

It worked. For him, anyway. Gary came with a groan. "My God, you're sexy," he said.

Afterward, Sydney lay with her eyes squeezed shut, trying to figure out what had just happened. It was as if some kind of switch had flipped inside her: one minute she was on, the next off. She had always enjoyed their lovemaking. Typically she was the one who initiated it, in fact. What had happened tonight? Was Gary really behaving differently? Or was she just exhausted?

There was one other possibility as well: maybe being at the farm had triggered so many emotions that she was momentarily mired in the past. Haven Lake had pulled her back in as if she'd never escaped.

Gary sat up with his back to her, felt for his slippers under the bed. "Sorry. I'm too agitated to sleep," he said. "I might as well get up for a while. Otherwise, I'll keep you awake."

"I'm not sleepy, either," she said, but it was too late. He'd already left the bedroom.

Sydney lay in the dark, nearly choking in the thick air, as if she'd held her breath for too long underwater.

Hannah woke Dylan early the next morning. "If you're going to live here, there won't be any lollygagging," she explained over breakfast, pressing her lips together to avoid nagging him about not eating his eggs. She hadn't forgotten Sydney's worry about the boy being anorexic, but what could she do about it, besides keep putting food in front of him?

"That's a weird word," he said, groggily pushing his scrambled eggs around. "Lollygagging?"

"Look it up later. Right now we need to move the sheep to a new pasture."

They walked down to the barn, where Hannah explained the basics about sheep behavior. "You can't approach a sheep too directly, or it will run away. Sheep have a flight zone—that's like the sheep's personal space—and it will face you as long as you don't enter that flight zone. Once you do, the sheep will try to run. When we're moving sheep, it's best if we stay out of their flight zone and lead them rather than have to chase them."

"Damn," Dylan said, eyeing the sheep milling around in the pen.

"It's fine. You'll see. I'm going to funnel them toward you into the new fenced area. Your job is to lead them with a bucket of corn."

It almost worked. But then the ewes realized the corn was in Dylan's hand and rushed him all at once, chasing him as he panicked and ran away, not realizing that he still carried the bucket and was leaking corn as he went. Hannah would have laughed if the upper pasture hadn't been precisely where she didn't want the sheep, because it was all grazed out.

They went through the exercise again. This time, Dylan managed to hang on to the bucket and scatter enough corn on the ground to distract the ewes while Hannah closed up the fence behind them. Now the sheep were effectively penned in place and they could set up the new electric fencing in the lower pasture.

"How did you end up wanting to raise sheep in the first place?" Dylan asked as they began unrolling the fence. "I mean, why not cows or goats?"

"Back when we first got together, Allen and I traveled through England, Ireland, and Wales. That's where I fell in love with sheep. In the

UK, you can walk forever in the windy wet weather and feel *unencumbered*. That's something people in this country rarely feel."

"Who taught you what to do?"

"The sheep did," Hannah said. "I made a lot of mistakes in the beginning. Like, the first winter, it never occurred to me that an electric fence is useless if you've got three feet of snow on the ground. I never could have imagined myself pushing my hand into a ewe's cervix to feel around for a lamb's hooves and nose to help with a difficult birth, giving shots of penicillin for mastitis, or cleaning fleeces. But the sheep teach you to rise to the job."

Even as competent as she usually felt around her flock, Hannah couldn't believe how much easier it was to put up the fencing with Dylan. He caught onto things quickly. Soon the sheep were happily grazing in tall grass, the lambs leaping about the llama like he was their private playground. Dylan and Hannah headed back to the barn then, where Hannah asked Dylan to clean the manure off the barn floor and spread fresh straw.

They worked hard throughout the morning, mostly in silence. That suited Hannah. Putting her energy into chores meant she'd have less to spend on fretting over Sydney.

She baked after lunch while Dylan was out with the rototiller. She'd noticed that Dylan could resist just about anything but sweets, so she made a lemon pound cake and a batch of molasses spice cookies. She left these out on the counter and went about her business, grooming Billy, throwing in a load of laundry, cleaning the upstairs bathroom, and putting fresh towels on Dylan's bed. It felt good to have someone to do things for, she realized. She'd missed that.

There were parts about being married that she'd thoroughly enjoyed. Just having someone to get up with in the morning, a partner to share your days, your worries and hopes, was a blessing. She and Allen had done well at marriage in the beginning, despite their hasty wedding. Hannah hadn't cared about making it official, but when she told Allen she was pregnant, he'd surprised her by insisting, saying, "A kid needs a father, and no kid of mine is going to be a bastard."

They'd gotten married by a justice of the peace in Amherst. His parents had attended the bare-bones ceremony, his mother weeping audibly and definitely not with joy. Hannah's father had shown up at the last minute, scrubbed clean of auto grease, in a too-tight suit frayed at the cuffs. Hannah's own mother had died long before that; her friend Deb helped her find a dress, choose a bouquet, make a cake to have with a bottle of champagne in the kitchen garden at Haven Lake.

Hannah had hoped the baby would bring Georgia Bishop around to accepting her, but Allen's mother stayed only a few minutes after the ceremony, exclaiming loudly at one point that Hannah had used her pregnancy to entrap their son.

"Do we even have any proof that this child is Allen's?" Georgia had wailed during the pathetic little reception, weeping into her silent husband's handkerchief.

She made such a scene that Hannah's father told Mr. Bishop to take his wife home "before I say or do something to that wife of yours that we'll all regret." Attorney Bishop looked all too glad to make his escape. Allen, instead of being upset, grinned at the departing car bearing his parents away.

"Guess we showed them," he said.

Hannah had no idea what he had meant at the time. It was only over the next few years that she realized Allen had gone to Vietnam and married her, in part, to escape whatever life his parents had tried to shoehorn him into. Allen had insisted on buying the farm with a trust left to him by his grandparents because he wanted Sydney to grow up in the Berkshires. "I don't care if she never sees Ipswich and the North Shore," he declared. "I want to raise our family as far away from my toxic parents as possible."

Hannah was content to comply, though she did sneak off every now and then to bring Sydney to visit her own father, who adored her and always gave Hannah a twenty-dollar bill "to put away for yourself," he'd beg, touching Hannah's frayed shirts and braids. "Go back to school if you can. Your mother would want that."

As more and more people came and went from Haven Lake over the sixteen years of their marriage, Hannah would wake up sometimes to find Allen gone from their bed. After a moment of confusion, she'd go back to sleep. She never went looking for her husband after those first few times, knowing he'd be with someone else.

It was actually more difficult when he came back to her at night, smelling of another woman's shampoo or Lucy's patchouli oil—a scent she learned to detest. Thank God Sydney had no idea that Lucy had been with Allen. No matter who he was with, Allen always insisted he still loved Hannah, that she was the one he'd chosen to spend his life with, and Hannah had believed him.

"You should explore relationships with other people," Allen had often urged. "I don't want us getting bored. We have to keep growing and surprising each other to keep our love alive."

"I don't need that," Hannah said. She wasn't bored with Allen. She was just tired.

And another truth, one she'd never shared with anyone: Hannah was glad, sometimes, to have the bed to herself, to know that another woman was the vessel for Allen's emotions, which burned like red embers beneath his skin, occasionally surfacing to scald anyone in his path.

Occasionally, too, she dreaded their lovemaking because it could be physically painful. Allen's need for intimacy and physical release was so desperate that her muscles ached from holding herself still as he drove himself into her. She was sometimes left with bruises from the pressure of his fingers on her skin.

"I would die without you," Allen said every time they made love, and the awful thing was that Hannah believed him.

"Why didn't you ever leave him?" Liz asked years after Allen was gone, when Hannah finally told her how it really was.

"Because I still loved him," she said. "And Allen was never just an angry man. He was silly at times, or tender, or thoughtful. He was clever and complicated. He could be noble. And he was Sydney's dad."

"Why didn't you sleep with anyone else, at least?"

"I could never do that to him," Hannah said, though she didn't explain why: because the only man she wanted was Allen's own brother.

Rory still loved her. He had been with other women, but Rory stayed on the farm to be near her. He'd never said so. She just knew it. They had always understood each other. If Allen was in a mood, Rory was always the one she called to help her. They could manage him together.

"Walk it off, brother, come with me, let's walk it off," Rory would say, leading a raging or sobbing Allen outside to the woods, the pond, the paths through the hills beyond the farm. Sometimes Rory would throw food into a backpack and Hannah wouldn't see them for days. She didn't know where they went. She only knew Rory would keep Allen safe when she couldn't do it anymore.

When she came back downstairs now, Hannah was pleased to see that Dylan had eaten three slices of cake and a handful of cookies. Not exactly a well-balanced meal, but at least the boy had something in his stomach.

She heard the sound of a car in the driveway and remembered Liz was coming. The other woman entered the kitchen wearing her usual overalls, her short gray hair spiked straight up.

"Brought your milk," Liz said, handing her a glass bottle. "What smells like heaven in here?"

"Help yourself." Hannah pointed to the counter.

"Oh my God. You angel. I'm running on empty." Liz took a plate out of the cupboard, loaded it with cookies and a slice of pound cake, and poured herself a glass of milk. She dropped into a chair with a groan. "Feels good to sit."

"Why? What have you been doing?"

"Three of my heifers got out and I had to chase them all over creation. Then my dog went after those damn ducks and I had to chain him up and catch them, too. Those little bastards are like roadrunners." Liz bit into the cake and made ecstatic noises.

Dylan came into the kitchen just then. He hesitated when he saw Liz, but Hannah urged him forward. "Dylan, this is my friend Liz. She teaches math at the high school."

"Hey," Dylan said, giving Liz a quick chin nod.

Liz smiled at him. "Any chance you'll be joining us? We could use new blood on the math team."

"Maybe." Dylan hovered uncertainly near the refrigerator.

Hannah realized he'd probably come in for more food, but didn't want to eat in front of them. "Sit with us," she said.

"That's okay. I don't want to interrupt." Dylan hastily backed out of the kitchen.

Liz took another cookie. "Man of few words, huh?"

"He's pretty chatty when you get him alone. And he was a big help this morning. Makes me wish I'd started hosting runaway teens years ago."

Liz eyed her thoughtfully as she sipped her milk, then put the glass down. "I thought Sydney was coming yesterday to get him."

"She did." Hannah didn't want to go into everything. "She had to leave again."

"Big nasty scene?"

"A medium nasty scene," Hannah admitted.

Liz brought her dishes to the sink and jerked her head in the direction of the doorway. "So what happens now?"

"Your guess is as good as mine."

After Liz left, Hannah found Dylan hunched forward over her desk in the office, shoulders as bony as bird wings. She could see from the doorway that he was on the computer; she could just make out a girl's profile picture, a blonde with black-rimmed eyes. She was surprised to see that he was looking at a Twitter account. She supposed Facebook wasn't cool anymore, now that it had been infiltrated by parents and teachers.

Hannah cleared her throat, making Dylan jump and swivel around with a guilty look. Good. He *should* look guilty. "Listen," she said. "We need to establish a few ground rules about my computer. First of all, you need to ask permission before you use it. I'm a little peeved that you jacked my password."

She held up a hand as Dylan began to sputter an explanation. "I don't care how you got online," she said. "I'm sure you're clever. Kudos to you. But I *do* care that you took advantage of me. I also care about you wasting time, especially on social media, since that's bound to make you feel worse, not better. Let's say half an hour a day online, and no screen time during daylight hours. Otherwise you can go home. Or wherever."

Dylan's face had turned red. "Fine. What do you want me to do now? Shovel more shit?"

"Nope. We're going out to the garden. I've got vegetables that need planting."

Hannah directed Dylan to carry the seed trays she'd started in the kitchen. Outside, she pointed out the different rows, indicating what should go where: cucumbers, squash, carrots, beans, cabbage, and onions she'd started in the greenhouse attached to the barn. They worked silently for an hour.

"Seems like a ton of vegetables for just one person," Dylan said when the tension had gone from his shoulders.

"My goal is to feed myself for a year. I can or pickle whatever I can't eat during the season, or barter it for other things. Liz gives me milk, for instance, and she's crazy about my tomatoes." Hannah grinned. "I have a special ingredient to make my garden grow."

Dylan raised an eyebrow. "Sheep shit?"

"Wow. You're catching on fast."

His phone wasn't anywhere in the living room. Hannah must have picked it up and stashed it someplace. Now he was determined to find it.

Dylan didn't know whether Hannah was keeping him from the computer for her own reasons or because his dad had said some shit like

Dylan was a computer addict, but he wasn't going to live like a Luddite and never go online. Refusing to use his phone was a stupid idea, too. The only way to find out whether Tyler had quit his *Game of Thrones* power rampage or whether Kelly gave a crap about him was to get online.

He was relieved to see that Kelly hadn't posted anything about him lately. Only Tyler. Kelly had put up a ton of screenshots of Tyler in plaid boxers. She probably took the screenshots from Instagram. Dylan wondered whether Tyler knew Kelly had posted these. Probably. What guy wouldn't want the whole world seeing him in boxers, if he was jacked like that?

The phone had to be in Hannah's office; Dylan had searched everywhere else. He'd waited until he heard her come upstairs after dinner and go to bed, and then he waited another hour until he was sure she had to be asleep. Afterward he felt his way back downstairs from his bedroom with one hand on the wall and made his way into the office.

He closed the door, but kept the light off anyway as he fumbled over to the computer and turned it on. Shit! The noise of that dinosaur booting up sounded like the Batmobile at full throttle. What if he woke Hannah? No doubt she'd toss him onto the street even in the middle of the night if he broke her rules. Ironic, considering his dad and Sydney thought Hannah was such a shitty parent.

Next Dylan used the flashlight he'd found in his bedroom to search the closet shelves and file cabinets. Who even had file cabinets anymore? Hannah should switch to online record keeping. Maybe he could help her with that.

He pulled out one file folder because it was bulging like it could have a phone inside, but found only photographs. He flipped through them and saw a history of the farm in pictures: the house before the kitchen garden and front path were in place, two barns instead of one, acres of vegetables with lines of people bent over them.

There were several photos of Hannah, looking hardly older than he was now, skinny and beautiful with black hair falling to her waist. Which one was her husband? he wondered. Two different guys showed up in most of the pictures. Finally he decided the one holding baby Sydney—had to be Sydney, with that cloud of white-blond curls and that same freckled nose—must be Allen, because he wore an army tag around his neck.

Allen was a skinny guy with squared-off shoulders, shaggy dark hair that nearly covered his eyes, and a foxy face with a pointy nose. He stood like a marine. Or a prisoner. This was a dude you would definitely not want to mess with.

So the other guy had to be Rory. He was skinny like Allen, but his shoulders were wider and he had a softer face. His hair was lighter than Allen's and pulled back in a ponytail except in one shot, where it was wet and hung nearly as long as Hannah's. Rory wore his jeans low and held an instrument in almost every shot: a guitar, a banjo, a fiddle.

Shit. They really were hippies, just like that movie about Woodstock they'd watched in American Studies class. If he hadn't seen these pictures, Dylan never could have imagined Sydney having these people for parents. How did she turn out the way she did? Maybe Sydney had some kind of inner hippie inside. Wouldn't Dad be surprised.

There were a lot of photographs of baby Sydney, but only a few of her as an older kid, like whoever was taking the pictures lost interest or got too busy. He only found one of Sydney as a teenager. She wore faded baggy jeans and a T-shirt that showed off her boobs. Her face was smudged with something and her blond hair was flying everywhere, so knotted it was practically in dreadlocks. Next to her stood a skinny kid with dark curly hair. He wasn't much taller than Sydney and had a big grin. To the other side of Sydney was a shorter girl with straight hair pressed tight to her head with a bandanna. She looked pissed off at something but she was still hot.

This wasn't getting him anywhere. Dylan shoved the folder back into the cabinet and went to the desk. He started with the top drawer and then searched the shelves.

Finally, on the open bottom shelf, he found his phone. He pulled it out, nearly groaning with relief—really, what had he been imagining, thinking he could go without a phone?—and booted it up. It had been turned off, so it still had juice.

The texts popped up immediately, the same stupid shit. The last one was sent half an hour ago: *I got firepower and know how 2 use it.*

After his initial spike of panic, Dylan got pissed. This kid must be mega bored. Shouldn't he be busy with lacrosse? Wasn't lacrosse a spring sport?

Wait. What if Tyler really did have a gun? And what if he found out where Dylan was, somehow, and just drove right out here and used it? He could pose as one of Dylan's friends, maybe call Sydney up and pretend he wanted to hang out with him or something. She'd tell Tyler where he was and that would be the end of him.

Dylan stared at the phone. If he answered Tyler's texts with something groveling, maybe that would satisfy him. What else could he do? Realistically, he wouldn't win this fight. Kelly had already made her choice. Dylan texted, *Hey, man. You won. She's all yours. Congrats.*

Then he shut down the phone, fear like a stabbing pain in his chest, as if he'd swallowed something sharp. After a minute, he turned off the computer, too, and just sat there in the darkness, his head buzzing like an alarm was going off in his brain.

The next morning, Hannah acted distant. Dylan began worrying that maybe she suspected he'd gone on her computer again. She never said anything about it, though, so he forced himself to choke down the eggs she put in front of him and said they were great, even though the texture of the scrambled eggs was like cobwebs and he couldn't stop picturing chickens pooping them out.

He helped Hannah move the sheep into the lower pasture. That took his mind off stuff for a while. He was beginning to know one ewe from another. The one with the big pink nose was Brandy, and Cheddar had the dark ears and was always wagging her tail. Dylan also had a soft spot for Daisy Chain, a big lumbering brown ewe with sweet gold-brown eyes.

He liked working outdoors, especially in weather like this, beneath a blue sky with white clouds racing across it like sailboats. The apple trees on the hill above the farm were in bloom and buzzing with bees.

When Hannah said she was going to catch up on some accounts and told him he was free for the afternoon, Dylan hiked to the top of the highest hill above the pastures and threw himself onto the ground, trying not to be freaked out by the noisy sound of bees in the pink flowers of the tree over his head. He thought about how he'd learned in biology class that bees could see colors and used spatial relationships to help them decide which flowers to feed from. So much cool stuff in the world. Why weren't humans ever satisfied?

He sat up with his back against the tree and gazed down at the sheep, searching for Casper. That was still his favorite lamb, because of the way Casper always ran over to Dylan and butted his leg whenever he thought Dylan was carrying grain.

"You won't like it so much when Casper's a sixty-pound ram," Hannah warned, but Dylan had just laughed and grabbed the lamb's soft ears and rubbed his knobby head.

Out of the corner of his eye, Dylan detected movement. He turned and squinted down at the pond. There was so little wind that the water was flat and solid looking, like you could just go down there and walk across its surface. The movement wasn't from the pond, though. It was in the woods. Dylan shuddered a little, looking at the creepy dark shadows beneath those big trees, and kept his eyes fixed on the black spaces between the trunks.

There it was again. A swatch of bright red among the trees. He couldn't be imagining it. Could it be a cardinal, one of those birds Mom used to always make him come see at the feeder?

Dylan stared so hard into the woods that his eyes began to water. Finally, the color appeared again. It was a man in a red shirt, walking in the pines near that funky cabin, just hidden enough in the woods that his features were blurred and Dylan had only a vague impression of someone as tall as he was. Or maybe bigger.

What the hell? Was it a hunter? Who would be in Hannah's woods? He hoped it wasn't that weird guy they'd met at the co-op.

He stood up and brushed off his jeans, intending to run down the hill to tell Hannah. Then he thought better of it. What if that man in the red shirt was Tyler? Could Tyler be so friggin' serious about stalking him that he'd figured out where Dylan was and come after him?

Fear was a heavy-booted foot holding Dylan in place. He stretched flat on the grass again and lay low, holding his breath until the man disappeared again. Then he bolted for the house.

CHAPTER NINE

The week before going to Haven Lake, Sydney had met with the Carlsons for an initial intake appointment about their seventh grader, Brianna. Jack Carlson and his wife had explained that they wanted her to evaluate their daughter because they were displeased by Brianna's middling grades.

"Look, we know she's not the sharpest tool in the shed," Mr. Carlson had said. "She's got a disability. Those lazy turds at her school just haven't bothered to find it." He spread his big hands across the knees of his gray slacks, the green stone in his class ring glinting like a dragon's eye in the gold setting. "We need to get this kid into a top college. She'll never do that from her public school at this rate." He leaned forward, adding, "But between you, me, and the wallpaper, we can't afford to put her anywhere private without assistance."

Sydney hated clients like this, who were so obviously trying to con the school districts out of money. This man—a real estate lawyer in three-hundred-dollar shoes—could easily afford to send his daughter anywhere. She had turned her attention to his wife, a round woman with gray hair whose looks and demeanor suggested a pigeon huddled on the icy ledge of a tall building.

"And what do you think, Mrs. Carlson?" she asked.

The woman had twisted the straps of her black leather handbag without meeting her eyes. "Private school, yes," she had said, then fell silent, her eyes on the floor.

Today, Brianna's mother was bringing the girl in for her initial evaluation. They arrived early and Mrs. Carlson shooed the girl into the office with Sydney. "You know what to say," Mrs. Carlson reminded her daughter.

What did she mean by that? Sydney wondered as she welcomed Brianna, a sweet-faced brunette, even rounder than her mother, into the office and closed the door. The girl was dressed in flowered leggings and a form-hugging minidress silk-screened with a portrait of Mozart. When Sydney asked about school, the girl insisted she was happy.

"I don't want to change schools," Brianna pleaded. "I love my friends, and my music teacher is really cool. I'd stay at school all day if I could." Her voice dropped to a whisper and she cast a panicked look at the closed office door. "It's my parents I hate."

"Why?" Sydney asked gently.

"They just don't get me. My dad—" she began, then stopped herself by shoving her thumb into her mouth and gnawing at her cuticle. No amount of prodding would get her to finish the sentence.

It wasn't unusual for a teenager to say she hated her parents, but clearly this child was holding something back. She was speaking out of desperation, not anger.

Sydney needed to see Mrs. Carlson alone. That would have to wait; she didn't want to give Brianna any reason to mistrust her. After she'd run a battery of tests on Brianna, she said good-bye to mother and daughter in the waiting room and gave Mrs. Carlson a card. Mrs. Carlson tried to avoid taking it, but Sydney pressed it into her hand.

"We'll just need a quick follow-up appointment," she said. "You and me. No need to bother your husband and have him miss work. Take a look at your calendar and give me a call."

As she wrote up her reports that afternoon, Sydney's mind drifted back to Dylan. She wondered how he was faring on the farm. Gary refused to call him and had instructed her not to do so, either.

"He made his bed," Gary had said over a rushed breakfast this morning. "Let him lie in it. Don't worry, Sydney. He'll miss his computer and having his own bathroom. Pretty soon we'll get some urgent call to come get him *now*. And you know what? I'm going to tell him to take the damn bus home after that little stunt he pulled on Saturday."

Sydney had called Dylan anyway. Twice this morning, in fact. Dylan didn't pick up his cell. She would try him one more time tonight. Then she'd resort to calling Hannah, even though her mother was the last person Sydney wanted to talk to about Dylan.

After work, she and Ella drove to Boston in Ella's ancient but dignified black Lincoln, which made Sydney feel like she was riding in a sofa bed. This was their first attempt to shop for a wedding dress, despite the fact that Ella had been nagging her for weeks. The whole idea of a wedding dress made Sydney nervous.

"I still don't know what I'm looking for," she finally admitted after they'd visited three different shops downtown.

"You must have *some* idea," Ella said.

"No, I really don't. I only know what I *don't* want: nothing white, nothing with ruffles, nothing strapless, no sequins. Oh, and no train. *Definitely* no train, veil, hat, or any other princesslike accessory."

Ella snorted. "Might as well get married in your black pants."

"Ha-ha."

They ate dinner at an Italian bistro on Newbury Street after wearing themselves out in two more boutiques. With chilled glasses of Pinot Grigio to calm their nerves, they sat outside at a tile-topped table and reviewed the wedding menu and flowers. Should there be a DJ? Or a live band, maybe even the one Carrie had at her birthday? Ella was full of suggestions. It was all too much to think about. Especially now, when all Sydney wanted to focus on was Dylan.

She didn't realize she'd tuned out until Ella prodded her foot under the table. "Bad weekend?"

"Not exactly."

"What happened after you went out there to get Dylan?"

"I told you."

"Not really. All you said was he's staying at your mom's for a bit."

"All hell broke loose. That's what happened."

"How so?"

Sydney picked up her wineglass, then put it down again without drinking. "Dylan refused to come home and ran away from the house when Gary tried to insist. He came back to my mom's house only after Gary left. Gary wasn't too happy about that, as you can imagine. He also went ballistic when he found out Dylan's been driving his mother's car and had sex with that girl I told you about. Neither of us had any idea he'd been driving illegally. Though I think I was actually more shocked to hear Dylan was sexually active."

"Sounds like your boy is growing up."

"Hardly. He's been lying to us!"

"Exactly. What teenager doesn't lie to his parents?"

"I never did!"

"You didn't have to," Ella said. "Your parents were hippies. You had to rebel in a different way."

"What do you mean?" Sydney was startled by this idea. She'd never rebelled against anything in high school or college. Always well-mannered, always earning honors, and she had the transcripts to prove it.

"Look at yourself! You're doing the opposite of what your parents wanted you to do. I mean, here you are, a professional carrying a briefcase and wearing sensible shoes. Hardly living off the land and sticking it to the man, right?"

Sydney laughed. "You sound like you understand what it was like to drink the Haven Lake Kool-Aid."

"Huh. If I'd been a rich white girl with a trust fund, maybe. Remember, honey, the seventies was my time, too. I'm even older than your mom. And you know what? Even though I didn't march against Vietnam or the U.S. involvement in El Salvador or Nicaragua, or even for school desegregation in Boston, I admired people who did. I was too chickenshit to be political. I knew I'd be more likely to end up in jail than the white kids if I got up to anything."

Sydney was stunned. She'd never given much thought to how Ella must have grown up in the sixties and seventies like her parents. "I never pictured what you were like as a teenager."

"Good thing. Believe me, I'm a lot happier now than I was back then. Those were not the best of times for black girls. We didn't have Beyoncé showing us how to be Queen Bee, no ma'am." Ella sipped her wine, then said, "Anyway, back to Dylan. I'd say you should count your blessings that he's not out stealing or dealing."

"How can I do that, when I still have no idea what Dylan's really doing when he's out of the house?" Sydney countered. "Plus, this whole thing makes me realize that Gary and I have totally different parenting styles. We've got to resolve that before we have kids of our own."

"Why? I don't know many moms and dads who agree on everything."

"I know, but this is extreme. Gary wants us to hold firm and not help Dylan in any way, but I think Dylan's behavior is a cry for help. Gary's so upset, he isn't sleeping at all—he gets up after he thinks I'm out—and he keeps losing his temper. His anger at Dylan seems all out of proportion, too."

The waiter delivered their salads. "Does Dylan look like Amanda?" Ella speared a shrimp on her fork.

Sydney frowned, feeling derailed. What did that matter? "I don't know."

"How can you *not* know? You've seen pictures, right?"

Sydney shook her head. She hated to admit, even to Ella, that there weren't any photographs of Amanda in Gary's house, so she'd trolled through every news article about Amanda's car accident to find pictures; she'd only seen the same photo over and over again. From that, she knew Amanda was a striking brunette with almond-shaped blue eyes and a cleft in her chin. Dylan did look a lot like her, now that she thought about it.

"Gary has pretty much purged the house of her," Sydney said. "No photographs or clothes, nothing personal. I don't even think he kept the same furniture after she died."

"Uh-oh."

"What's that supposed to mean?"

"Your boyfriend isn't over her yet. Sounds to me like he's trying to literally keep her in a box. A box with the lid nailed shut."

Sydney had taken a bite of salad; now her throat felt like it was filled with cotton. She forced herself to choke down the lettuce and tomato, then said, "I know it'll take time for him to get over her."

Ella's dark eyes were sympathetic. "Sure. But, honey? Until your man is over his dead ex and forgives her for dying on him, there won't be much room for you in his life. Or for Dylan. Sounds like Gary's nursing a grudge."

"Gary's not like that!"

"Hey, whatever you say. You're the doc." Ella signaled the waiter for two more glasses of wine. "How did Gary and your mom get along?"

"She pissed him off the way she does everybody."

Ella laughed. "By doing what?"

"By saying Dylan could stay with her even after Gary made it clear we wanted him to come home." Sydney felt a familiar swell of anger. "I mean, who does she think she is, butting into our family like that?"

"She didn't butt in, exactly," Ella reminded her. "Dylan showed up on her doorstep, right? Sounds like she just wants to help him."

"Or get back at me. She's never forgiven me for choosing to live with my dad's parents after he died."

"Now why would your mama be mad at you for that? She has to know what she did, drinking and curling up in her room and leaving you on your own to cope."

"On some level, I guess." Sydney folded and refolded her napkin. The truth was that she and her mother had never talked about any of this. "She had to know I was looking for a safe place to land."

"And what happened after that? Did she try to bring you home?"

"Once. It was a disaster."

"Why?"

Sydney shrugged. "I refused to go back to Haven Lake. Finally my grandparents threatened to call the cops if she didn't leave the house. My grandfather was pals with the police chief, so Mom had no choice but to leave without me."

"Sounds like she really wanted you to come home."

"Why, because she asked me *once*?" Sydney felt a flush of familiar anger. "After that, she dropped off the planet as far as I was concerned. Mom never went to my art shows, or the plays I was in, or even my high school graduation. The weird thing is? I looked for her every time, during all of those big moments."

Ella nodded, her dark eyes sympathetic. "We never stop wanting our mamas. So maybe Hannah's trying to make up for letting you down by taking care of Dylan now."

"Maybe."

As the waiter deposited their new glasses of Pinot Grigio, Ella asked, "So how was it for you, finally going home?"

"Haven Lake isn't my home." Sydney gulped her wine. "I couldn't wait to leave again. So much baggage there."

"Baggage you carry with you," Ella reminded her. "Gary's not the only one with some serious sorting and tossing to do."

Thankfully, the entrées arrived before Sydney could protest. What would she have said anyway? Ella was right. Being at the farm had brought everything up again. Only instead of feeling distraught and furious and grief-stricken, as she'd expected, Sydney had also felt the first stirrings of another powerful emotion: curiosity. Seeing the farm as an adult made her realize how much she still didn't know about what actually happened the night Theo died.

She pushed her food around. The police had questioned everyone at Haven Lake and eventually ruled the death an accidental drowning, but many questions lingered. Nobody could understand why Theo had chosen to swim alone in the pond on a cold spring night, especially when he'd never done anything like that before and it was one of the few activities strictly forbidden on the farm.

Sydney had been questioned along with everyone else. "What kind of mental state was your friend in when you saw him that night?" one cop had asked when she told him Theo was with her. "Were you kids high? Was he drinking? Tripping?"

The attitude of the uniforms was plain. The police, along with many residents in the surrounding area, didn't see Haven Lake as an organic farming collective, a place where people were trying to heal the planet by growing food and creating a kinder community lifestyle, but as a bunch of drug addicts, drifters, and dropouts. Sydney remembered how rough the cops were, physically pushing the residents—even hysterical Lucy and poor, trembling Millie—as they ordered them into bedrooms for questioning.

The autopsy showed that Theo had suffered blunt-force trauma to his head and cuts on his arms, but proved little about the circumstances of his death beyond the fact that he had water in his lungs. Apparently, it was common for bodies to drift in water and get banged up. One theory was that Theo had tried to dive off the pier and hit his head. But how, then, had his body floated halfway across the pond? That had never made any sense to Sydney.

Her father was brought to the station for questioning several times, and even held overnight after Josh, a bearded ex–Hare Krishna who still wore a scrap of his orange robe over denim shorts slit up the sides so they flared out around his skinny legs like a skirt, told the police that he'd heard Theo and Allen arguing in the woods the night before. Rory was questioned at the station, too, when someone else told the police they'd heard a shouting match between *him* and Theo.

Sydney didn't know any other details. She hadn't wanted to know more. The only thing that had mattered was that it was her fault Theo was dead. She was the one who'd told him Rory was sleeping with Lucy, causing Theo to bolt from her room. But she hadn't shared that with a soul at the time, not even with her mother.

Later, of course—much later—she wondered why she hadn't told the police. She was horrified by her own omission. What was she thinking, holding back details like that, when the police were trying to investigate a suspicious death?

Every time she asked herself that question, though, the answer was the same: the cops were on one side of the law and the people of Haven Lake were on the other. That was what she'd been raised to believe.

"Pigs," her father always called cops. "High on power," he said. Her parents had both been teargassed and arrested at peace demonstrations many times. The cops at Haven Lake had done little to make Sydney believe that her father was wrong about them. She didn't like any of the big, burly, red-faced men in uniforms rampaging through their house and property, their black boots tracking mud on the stairs and floors, terrorizing everyone who had come to the farm to live in harmony.

A week after Theo drowned, Dad shot himself. His shocking suicide had whipped up the gossip, already swirling through the local towns after Theo's death, into frenzied, tsunami-sized rumors: that Theo was upset when he saw his mother with Rory, or that Rory had been molesting Theo and had killed him when Theo threatened to tell. Others were certain that Rory and Allen had fought over Lucy, and that Theo had tried to stop them, getting killed in the process. But most believed Theo was just a reckless teenager, high as a kite, who couldn't tell the difference between up and down when he dove into the pond, and that the adults were to blame for failing to protect all the children at Haven Lake. The Op-Ed pages and letters to the editor were full of rants about how the Haven Lake "commune" had defiled children, gotten them addicted to drugs, and brought shame on the town.

People began leaving the farm. "Bad vibes here, man," Josh declared solemnly, stroking his beard. "Time to dissipate the negative energy."

Her father's suicide hadn't shocked Sydney nearly as much as Theo's death. Perhaps she was already numb with grief, but it was also true that her father had been depressed for years. She figured Theo's death had finally pushed him over the edge. Sydney pictured this literally sometimes: her father clutching the edge of a building with his callused fingertips and slipping into the abyss when he couldn't hold on any longer.

Dad might have killed himself because Haven Lake was no longer the sanctuary he'd created and he couldn't stand the loss, Sydney thought. Or maybe Theo's death simply highlighted every wrong turn he'd taken in his life: enlisting for Vietnam instead of going to college; disappointing his parents by marrying Hannah instead of a more suitable match; starting the farm and a family instead of remaining a footloose political activist.

In any case, after Dad died, resurrecting the community was impossible. Haven Lake was just a shell of a house with fields that would never be planted with vegetables again; the ashes of a small barn; and small, roughshod buildings left to rot in the woods. Lucy took Valerie back to Rhode Island. Rory drove to California in his rusted van full of stringed instruments and disappeared in either a suicide or an accident off the cliffs in San Francisco, where they'd found his abandoned vehicle and everything still inside it.

Ella was right. Instead of resolving any of those past questions, Sydney had chosen to do exactly what Gary had done and remove any reminders of a past life. It had been a survival strategy, because the memories always seemed powerful enough to suffocate her present existence.

After dinner, Ella dropped Sydney off at the medical building to pick up her car. Sydney remembered some files she'd wanted to bring home but forgot in her rush to leave for Boston, so she waved good-bye to Ella, then went up to her office to retrieve them.

Her heart thudded in the elevator on her way back down. So weird to be alone here at night, when it was quiet enough to hear the Merrimack River lapping against the shore by the edges of the parking lot.

Except she wasn't alone. As Sydney reached her car, she spotted one other vehicle parked on the far side of the lot near the water. A lone figure stood by its open hood. The man wore white shorts and a white T-shirt that glowed in the inky light. A strange outfit even for this warm night in May.

"Hey!" the stranger called. "You wouldn't have any jumper cables, would you?"

Sydney let her car idle for a minute, debating. Of course she had jumper cables—her mother had drummed it into her head that you should always be prepared for a dead battery—but she'd heard enough stories about women getting kidnapped in parking lots to be suspicious.

It would be indecent not to help the guy out, though. It was probably safe to drive over there if she kept her car doors locked and her cell phone in hand. She could pop the trunk and hood from the inside of her car, then give the guy the cables and a jump without having to get out.

"Sure," Sydney answered.

It wasn't until she pulled up next to the other car that she recognized Marco. He must have been playing soccer after work, judging from his shorts and cleats. His T-shirt had the Puerto Rican flag emblazoned across the front. "Sydney!" Marco's narrow face broke into a grin, startling white against his coppery skin.

"Hey," she said. "How can you drive around without jumper cables? That's idiotic."

"I know, right? Not that I'd even know what to do with them. I was about to call Triple A when you showed up. But they always take a year to come."

"Because they have so many people like you who can't jump their own cars." Sydney felt suddenly shy; she hadn't spoken to Marco since Carrie's party. Seeing his muscular brown thighs and the way his shoulders and chest strained the T-shirt brought back the delicious feeling of his hands on her waist and hips as they danced. She felt an unwelcome flush of warmth. Thank God it was dark.

"You sure the battery's dead?" she asked, popping her trunk.

"The car won't start."

"What happens when you crank the ignition?"

He looked puzzled. "Like I said. The car won't start."

Sydney went over to his car, a modest Toyota sedan—a surprise, since she'd always imagined him driving something fast and slick—and turned the key in the ignition. Nothing happened beyond a faint clicking sound. "Okay, that's good."

"What is?"

"No sound, and the lights won't turn on. If we'd heard the engine trying to turn over, it could have been something else."

She explained what she was doing as she attached the positive red cable clamp to the dead battery on Marco's car first, then the other red clamp to the terminal of her own car battery. "After that, you do the black clamps in reverse order. First to the good battery, then to the other car. But never on the battery terminal, unless you want to see sparks fly. You can put the cable on any unpainted metal surface of the other car, but I usually just clamp it to the engine block. There. Now we start my car and let it run for a few minutes. Then we'll start your car and pray."

Sydney started her engine and then got back out to stand beside him. "You're bleeding," she noticed suddenly.

Marco rubbed his temple, smearing the blood. "Yeah. Took a cleat to the forehead when this guy tried to kick past me. Worth it, though. He didn't make the goal." That grin again.

Sydney went back to her car and came back with a tissue, a water bottle, and a box of Band-Aids. "Here. At least let me clean it and see how deep it is."

"Wow. Such a Girl Scout. Got any cookies in there, too?"

She made a face. "I'm no Girl Scout. Just a sensible person with a first aid kit in the car. As you should be." She dampened the tissue and gave it to him to wipe his forehead. "That's kind of deep," she said, frowning at the jagged cut. "Do you feel dizzy at all?"

"Only when I look at you."

Sydney rolled her eyes. "Save the pickup lines for your postgame pub crawls. I'm immune." She put the Band-Aid across the cut, gently pressing it into place, and stepped back again. "There. You'll live. Now start your engine."

He did. The Toyota roared to life, making them both laugh. "Now what?" Marco said.

"Give it a few minutes to let your battery charge. How far do you have to drive?"

"Ipswich."

Another surprise. "I grew up there," Sydney said. "Well, partly, anyway. Where do you live?"

"Out on Great Neck."

"Nice. I lived with my grandparents in Ipswich center when I was in high school."

"Where do you live now?"

"In Newbury, on the Parker River." Sydney felt a familiar twinge of regret at the thought of the For Sale sign on her lawn. "For now, anyway. I'll be moving into Gary's house once we're married." They were both leaning against Marco's car now, facing the river. It was too dark to see it, but the river smell engulfed them, the brackish water slightly sweet but sulfurous, too, because of the marshes.

"Where does Gary live?"

"On Federal Street in Newburyport."

"Easy commute, anyway," he said. "But I bet you'll miss being on the water."

This was true, but she didn't want to admit it.

"Hey, I never saw you today in the office to ask what's happening with Gary's son," Marco said. "Did he come back?"

"No, but we found him. He's at my mom's in the Berkshires for now."

"A happy ending."

"Mostly. Though we still don't know why he took off."

"Is he seeing a therapist?"

"No. Dylan was in therapy for a year after his mom died, but he's not seeing anyone now." Sydney bit her lip, studying the hazy moon winking in and out of the clouds. "I'm not sure we could get him to go back into therapy, either. Dylan's balking at anything we suggest. I have no idea how this will all play out."

"Join the club. Sometimes we can't control our children no matter how good our intentions. Too bad nobody ever warns you about how helpless you feel when your kids are born."

For the first time, it dawned on Sydney that Marco must have children. He was clearly speaking from experience. "How old are yours?"

The fog had thickened around them, as if the rest of the world were slowly disappearing. Marco turned to face her, leaning his hip against the car, the planes of his cheekbones sharp. "Nineteen and seventeen. One's in college and the other's a senior in high school. They live in Puerto Rico. My ex-wife grew up there."

"How long have you been divorced?"

"Since the kids were in preschool. My wife left me when I was still in grad school because she hated Boston and got tired of us not having any money. Plus, she didn't want to raise the kids so far from her parents. I think it all boiled down to being homesick. She came to Boston for college but never intended to live in the U.S."

"You didn't want to go back to Puerto Rico?"

He shook his head. "No. I love the island, but I'm a Nuyorican, as they say. Grew up in the Bronx. My mom's still in New York. She brought my little sisters and me to New York when I was five and they were toddlers. I put my sisters through school; they're both nurses now."

"That must have been hard, having your wife take your kids far away."

"It was. But there wasn't any way for me to fight it. She's a good mom, and back then, judges almost always granted custody to the mother. It worked out okay. My ex met someone else, a nice guy. She's happy. And at least my kids are surrounded by aunts and uncles." He reached up to rub his forehead.

Sydney grabbed his wrist to stop him from touching the Band-Aid, then dropped her hand immediately when he grinned. "God, don't you ever stop flirting?" she said irritably.

"Not when a beautiful woman is trying to hold my hand." His eyes danced.

"I wasn't! I was just trying to stop you from bleeding all over your white shirt!"

He gave her a sweet smile and shifted his weight. "I know, I know. *Cálmate, mujer.*"

"So how often do you see your kids?" Parenthood was safe ground, at least.

"I used to fly to San Juan every weekend when they were little. Then, as they got older, they started coming here to visit me. We get together every couple of months now."

That explained the modest car: Marco was not only helping out his mother and sisters, but also supporting his children through college. On top of that, he was buying plane tickets on a regular basis. No wonder he was happy being a bachelor with a different playmate each month. Why would he want to shoulder more responsibilities?

"You're cold," Marco said as she shivered in the breeze. "We should sit in the car."

It was tempting to stay here, to continue talking with Marco in this quiet, dark place where the fog hid them from the world, but Sydney shook her head. Gary would be back from the hospital by now.

"I can't. I need to get home. Your car should be fine now." She showed him how to take the cables off in reverse order. His car continued to run without a hitch.

"Thanks for sparing me the Triple A wait, and especially the embarrassment," Marco said as he reached up to lower the hood. "Imagine what a tow truck driver would say if he saw some macho Hispanic guy stranded out here."

"*Macho?* Ha! You didn't even know how to jump a car." Sydney handed him the cables. "Here. Keep these in your trunk. I have a spare pair in the garage."

Marco's expression softened for an instant before he quickly arranged his features into their usual quick grin. "*Gracias, mi amiga.* I owe you," he said.

"Send me a new client." Sydney turned to get into her car. Before she could open the door, though, she felt Marco's light touch on her shoulder and turned around.

"Sure you can't stay?" he said. "We don't have to sit here. We could get a drink or something."

She felt her face go hot. Of course Marco, being who he was, would naturally resort to his standard MO and ask her out, even knowing she was engaged, she thought irritably. "No, I've really got to get back," she said, adding pointedly, "Gary's expecting me."

"Sure, of course. I'm sorry," he said. "That was inconsiderate. I hope you don't think I was hitting on you or anything. It's just that I enjoyed our dance, Sydney. And I hope you know how much I value you as a colleague and love talking to you."

"Dancing was fun," Sydney said, her face on fire now. "I've been thinking about hiring the same band for my wedding."

"Good idea. Save me a dance on your special day," he said.

The look on Marco's face caused Sydney to drop her gaze and climb into the driver's seat so hurriedly that she slammed the hem of her tunic top in the door. She didn't bother opening the door again to release it. Better to drive away now, before she could give in to her own desire to touch him.

To be touched by him.

The window was still open. "I'm sorry," she heard Marco call again as she left him, his words carrying clearly on the scent of sweet, pungent river air.

Hannah was up before dawn. She'd had trouble sleeping after Dylan's footsteps in the hall woke her around three a.m. He was trying to be quiet, nearly shuffling, but she heard him regardless. She'd always been a light sleeper. What was he doing up so late?

She thought she knew the answer. Hannah confirmed her suspicions when she gave up on sleep and went downstairs at five o'clock. Yes,

Dylan had logged on to her computer again without her permission despite her clearly delivered ground rules.

You'd think a kid that smart would know enough to erase his digital footprint. But Dylan must think she was too prehistoric to check his history. Everywhere he'd been was plain to see, a map of manic social media: Twitter, Facebook, YouTube, Skype.

In the kitchen, Hannah made a pot of coffee and mixed up a sour cream coffee cake. As she worked, she thought about how she'd threatened to expel Dylan from Haven Lake if he broke her rules governing computer use, yet he'd done it anyway.

She'd always been a big believer in rules being made to be broken, but this felt different somehow. Not because Dylan was taking advantage of her—though he was—but because some instinct told her that whatever Dylan was doing on the computer was causing him distress.

Now what? Should she confront him and follow through on the consequences by sending him home? At least that way he'd be his father's headache. And Sydney's. No, she didn't want to do that to the poor kid.

Maybe she could pretend she didn't know, and see if he confessed? She dismissed that idea instantly as well. It seemed underhanded.

Wait, a sly voice added. *There's a third choice, too. You could tell him you know and give him a second chance. That's what you really want to do, isn't it?*

No. That wasn't an option. According to Gary, he'd been ladling out second chances like canned soup for years. Maybe it really was time, as Gary had pointed out so adamantly, for Dylan to own up to his mistakes and suffer the consequences.

God, how she hated this bullshit. Hannah shoved the cake in the oven and was glad when her cell phone buzzed on the kitchen counter and Liz's number flashed on the screen.

Hannah remembered that Liz had offered to help her transport the young rams to a broker in Burlington. The broker would auction the spring lambs to area butchers. Maybe Liz was calling to arrange a date to do that.

When Hannah answered, however, Liz was clearly in a knot about something else. "I need you to talk me off the ledge," Liz said at once. "I'm freaking out big-time."

"Why? What's happened?"

"I had a date last night."

"What! You're kidding. Why didn't you tell me?" Hannah dropped onto one of the kitchen chairs. Oscar came out from under the stove and begged to be picked up. As she scooped the woodchuck up in her arms and stroked his back, she was aware of a fleeting and unwelcome sense of betrayal as she listened to her friend talk.

Like her, Liz hadn't gone out with anyone in years. She and Hannah had declared themselves done with relationships. For different reasons, though: Hannah had found marriage to be soul-consuming, exhausting, and ultimately destructive. She'd dated casually after Allen's death, but then she'd gone out with Les—the memory of which she shoved away every time it approached as if it were physically burning her skin—and "withdrawn from the field," as Liz put it, without knowing the real reason.

Liz, on the other hand, had been loved deeply and unconditionally by Susan, and she had loved Susan with equal ardor and devotion. Some rough patches, yes, but Liz and Susan had quickly become committed to each other after meeting in college.

"My soul mate from the start," was how Liz described her former partner, mourning only that they'd never had the chance to marry because legalization of gay marriage had come too late in Massachusetts. Susan was gone by then.

Now Liz was babbling happily about another woman, someone she'd met through the classifieds in one of the alternative Northampton newspapers. A baker from Greenfield. They'd gone to dinner last night, taken a walk, sat by the river. Held hands. Her name was Cate.

"She's happy and blond and has a sweet round face," Liz said. "But, my God, she's so serene and domestic, Hannah. It would be like dating June Cleaver!"

"Pearls, too?"

Liz laughed. "No, but she does make her own beaded necklaces! She gave me the one she was wearing last night when I admired it. I'll show it to you. Gorgeous!" Her voice suddenly turned glum. "It was one of those nights you hope never ends, because you know it can't happen again. Happiness never lasts."

"What are you talking about?" Hannah asked. "You, of all people! You were happy for decades with Susan. You're wonderful, and Cate sounds terrific. You're a great judge of people. If you had a good time, Cate must have enjoyed herself, too, right?"

The woodchuck was nibbling the hem of Hannah's shirt; she put him down despite his squeaks of protest. Billy nosed through the kitchen door as if on cue and came over to lay his wet muzzle on her knee, right where Oscar had been sitting. The dog reeked of some dead animal he'd rolled in.

Delightful. Susan had Cate, and what did Hannah have? An illegal pet woodchuck and a hyper dog that smelled like death.

"I know I sound like some tortured teenager," Liz said, "but I'm so rusty when it comes to romance that I know I'm going to botch it. If Cate comes over, she'll realize that I smell like a barn and have to scrape cow patties off my boots every night. Also, I love meat, and Cate's a gluten-free vegetarian. What would she do if she knew I was helping you truck cute little lambkins off to a butcher this week?"

Hannah laughed. "Just tell her you had to help a desperate friend in need. A friend who can make you smell like roses by comparison. Right now, I reek of woodchuck musk and corpse cologne." She sighed. "I was actually having my own second thoughts about taking the lambs this week. I'm afraid Dylan will be upset."

"Why?"

"One of the rams, the smallest white one, follows Dylan around like a puppy. I think Dylan's gotten pretty attached to him."

"Well, no point in glossing over the truth. You're the one who's always reminding people that sheep are livestock, not pets, right? You'd go under financially if you tried to keep every lamb born at Haven Lake."

"I might go under anyway," Hannah said.

"Not when every woman in a book club is reading yarns about knitting."

"Oh, ha-ha. How long have you been waiting to spring that little pun?" Hannah said, but she was laughing. "Look, come over in an hour. I promise to be honest about your stink. We'll talk about Cate and when to take the lambs. Then we can run over to the co-op together."

By the time Hannah had hung up and was making her way down to the barn, the cake had only another twenty minutes. Rays of bright yellow sunlight were fingering their way over the hills and diamonds of dew sparked on the grass. She let the hens out of their house and scattered grain for them in the yard so she could collect eggs while they were happily pecking.

Afterward, Hannah set down the egg basket and went through the ritual of checking water buckets before letting the sheep into the pasture. The llama led the way out of the barn, giving her his usual bucktoothed grin and baleful look, as if to say, "Guess I'm on duty again."

The ewes followed the llama in a tidy line, surprising her, as always, with their delicate dancelike movements despite their heft. The lambs gamboled around them. She laughed at their antics even knowing Liz was right: this was livestock, not her family.

Still, despite her own pragmatic outlook, Hannah got attached to every sheep born on Haven Lake. How could she not? She'd assisted in delivering many of them, watching their heads and knees emerge from mucus sacs once she'd put her hand in to help guide them free of their mothers. Then there were the navels to clip and dip, the vitamin shots. Bottle-feeding when some mothers wouldn't take on their young.

Right now, she noticed that Brownie, her biggest tan ewe, needed attention for fly-strike. There were the telltale green and black fleece stains on her left haunch, a sure sign that the ewe had a festering wound filled with maggots. It was early for a blowfly infestation, but the weather was warming up quickly and they'd had a lot of rain. Flies loved damp.

Hannah made a mental note to ask Dylan to help her separate

Brownie from the flock later today. She'd have to shear the spot and treat it as soon as possible. Then she'd put the ewe on antibiotics. They'd have to examine the other sheep, too. Always a time-consuming job.

She already felt tired and her day had yet to really begin. Hannah began walking slowly back toward the house, keeping to the fence line and watching for thistles to pull. Hand spinners loved her fleeces because they were free of debris; she was always careful to check the pastures for weeds that might compromise the wool's quality.

Halfway along the path between the barn and the end of the first fence line, she spotted something odd: a row of three heart-shaped stones. The stones were palm-sized and nothing native to this area. More like the granite you'd find in a quarry. Even weirder, these were polished stones, their black specks gleaming against a white background, their surfaces as smooth as eggshells.

She picked one up. She had found a few heart-shaped stones around the farm before, but these rocks weren't just randomly lying on the ground; they had been set in a line and buried partway. She had to use her nails to pry the rock free. It was already warm from the sun and heavy in her hand.

She set it down again quickly, feeling jumpy now, and picked up another one to examine it. Someone had deliberately gathered these particular stones and brought them here to set in a row the way you might line up flagstones for a garden path. What's more, they'd placed the stones where she was sure to see them. Who would do such a thing?

Her first thought was so unpleasant that bile rose in her throat: Les. It had been so awful running into him at the co-op the other day. Now she remembered his threat to pay her a visit on the farm. Had Les put these stones here to play with her head?

She dismissed the idea as ridiculous. Les wasn't that clever. He was the sort of man who might resort to underhanded tactics, like spiking a woman's drink to get what he wanted, but he wouldn't have the patience to do something like this.

So who'd left this romantic trio of rocks?

Dylan. He must have carried these rocks in his backpack, maybe intending to give them to that girl. They looked like they could be native to the Massachusetts North Shore; she remembered seeing similar stones in Rockport. Or maybe someone else, a former resident of Haven Lake, had brought them here, and Dylan had found them while nosing through the cabins and tent platforms. Dylan could have laid the stones down as an homage to his lost love.

That had to be it. Hannah took a deep breath and replaced the middle heart-shaped rock in the dirt, tapping it firmly in place with her foot before returning to the house.

CHAPTER TEN

Catching Casper was easy, but carrying him took more muscle than Dylan had expected. The lamb was a lot heavier than he looked.

Casper had followed him around the pasture, butting his head against Dylan's thighs because he knew Dylan often carried corn in his pockets. It was a simple matter to lure the lamb away from the grazing herd and pick him up. Dylan knew he had to move fast after that, before Casper started bleating and alerted the llama or brought his mother, an ornery black-and-white ewe named Oreo, trotting over to investigate.

He grabbed the lamb around the middle and sprinted for the gate. Casper panicked and started kicking, drumming sharp little devil hooves into Dylan's thighs. Dylan ignored the pain while he unlatched the gate, darted through it, and latched it behind him again. Then he glanced up at the house to make sure Hannah hadn't returned from wherever she'd gone with Liz.

He hated the idea of sneaking away like this, when Hannah had been so cool about everything, but no way could he let Casper go under the knife. And now he had another reason to go home: Kelly had finally texted him, saying she'd made a mistake. *Must see you,* she'd texted. *Come by the house tonight. Alone.*

He couldn't believe she'd actually contacted him. Maybe Kelly had finally realized Tyler was subhuman. At least she was willing to talk. Someday, he and Kelly could be friends, and after a while they could be more. But only if he went back now, before Tyler got to her and she changed her mind.

Now Dylan tried running up the hill to the driveway with Casper clutched to his chest, keeping the lamb's skinny legs bunched together, but the animal thrashed and bleated like Dylan was the one slaughtering him. The ewes were freaking out and racing in circles around the pasture. Larry the Llama had raised his head and was watching Dylan with a "Don't mess with me, fucker" look.

"Screw you, Larry!" Dylan yelled. "I'm just trying to save a life here!"

He shifted Casper into a fireman's carry, the way you'd hoist a victim's body around your neck and shoulders. With the lamb's front legs dangling on one side of his neck and its back legs dangling on the other, the weight was distributed better. Other than trickling a little pee down Dylan's back, Casper also seemed calmer in this position. Or else maybe he was paralyzed with fear. Whatever. Dylan was able to run the rest of the way up the hill with the animal hanging around his neck like a bulky scarf, though the effort made him pant so hard he nearly passed the hell out.

When he reached the driveway, he stooped down, keeping his back straight so the lamb wouldn't flip over his head and onto the ground, and grabbed his backpack from under the bush where he'd stashed it after overhearing Hannah and Liz in the kitchen that morning talking about butchering the lambs.

Hannah wasn't any different from his dad: she wanted to teach Dylan how the real world worked. But why would he want to learn those lame lessons? He already knew the world sucked.

He couldn't save every lamb here, but he and Casper could start a new life out west, where sheep roamed free in the Rockies. He'd start his own computer company there instead of Seattle. Way less competition and it would be cheaper to live there, too, than on the West Coast.

Dylan smiled a little as he carried the lamb and his backpack down the driveway toward Hannah's truck, imagining how he'd cross the Colorado border with Casper and find a sheep ranch where he could work. At night he'd brush up on his programming skills and invent cool new apps for mobile phones. He might take up running and lift weights, too. Weights were a cheap investment. Maybe he could train Casper to run with him the way some people ran with their dogs. He'd stay thin and strong.

Thin, strong, and safe.

Hitchhiking would be impossible with a lamb. That's why he had to steal Hannah's truck. He hadn't expected it to be so easy, since Hannah almost never left the farm. But Hannah had said she and Liz were going to the co-op for supplies before the two of them transported the rams to another farm in Vermont. She didn't say why they were moving the rams, and Dylan didn't ask because he already knew why from listening in on their conversation.

Hannah and Liz had invited Dylan along, of course, but he offered to do chores around the farm instead, saying he'd already seen the co-op. "It'll be more efficient if I get things done here," he said. "Besides, I just got up and I haven't eaten anything yet."

He knew Hannah would be pleased by the idea that he was planning to eat. She didn't hound him about food like Sydney did, but Dylan could feel her eyes on him, counting every calorie he chose to stuff into his piehole. She was a mother, after all. A weird mother, but still. All mothers worried about what all kids ate. Saying he needed to eat gave him the perfect excuse to stay home alone.

Not that he'd actually eaten after they left, of course. He needed to stay light on his feet. He'd managed to ignore the coffee cake on the counter by slipping out the back door and saying he'd do the chores first, then come in and shower and eat. He had gotten the hell out of there and waited until Liz and Hannah drove off. When they took Liz's truck instead of Hannah's, he knew it was destiny: time to execute his plan.

Now, Dylan quickly debated whether to put Casper in the back of the battered pickup or in the cab with him. The front would be safer, he decided. He didn't trust the crazy little dude not to jump out of the truck bed and try to run back to its mother. To certain death.

Jesus. The very thought of somebody *eating* Casper made Dylan want to puke. "Come on, little man," he said gently. "In you go."

He hoped Casper would understand by his tone of voice that there was nothing scary about riding in trucks, but the lamb wasn't buying it. As soon as Dylan set him down on the seat, Casper head-butted him and tried to leap out the door.

Dylan caught him just in time, flinging his body over the lamb's to pin him onto the seat. He managed to push Casper to the passenger side, swing his backpack onto the seat between them, and slam the truck door closed within seconds.

There. He was sweating like a pig, but he'd done it: he was behind the wheel of Hannah's truck, the lamb on the seat beside him, trembling but alive.

"You're not going to be anybody's lamb chops," Dylan promised Casper. Then he plucked the truck key off the visor, where he'd seen Hannah store it when they drove to the co-op.

Briefly, he rested his head on the steering wheel before starting the engine, overwhelmed by guilt. He pressed his forehead hard enough against the rigid plastic that he imagined a dent in his skin when he lifted it.

Guilt, guilt, guilt: he felt shitty for stealing Hannah's truck. It was a piece-of-crap truck, but it was still hers. He'd have to find a way to get it back to her. Dad was going to be pissed about the stealing, too, but since his main thing was wanting Dylan to go back to school, maybe that would make up for it. The lamb could either live in the backyard—he could make a stall in the garage—or they'd find a home for it.

Whatever. He would work that out later. Right now, he had to man up with Kelly and win her heart.

Hannah would understand. That's what Haven Lake was all about: people following their hearts, living with passion, shrugging off stale traditions, saying no to war and yes to living off the land. Dylan wanted to do all of that activism stuff, too. But first he had to prove himself to Kelly. She wanted to see him tonight!

He sat up and felt around with his foot for the brake. Three pedals! What a dumb ass! The truck was a manual transmission! He hadn't anticipated that. He'd begged Dad to teach him how to drive a stick, but no, Dad was always too busy, even on weekends. Now what?

Dylan took a deep breath to steady himself and tried to ignore the pitifully desperate baaing from the lamb on the seat beside him that sounded just like the noises he was making in his own head. Why the hell hadn't he noticed this was a manual transmission?

He pondered his options. Carrying the lamb back to the pasture and pretending this had never happened was the easiest course of action. But he couldn't let Casper go to the butcher. And he couldn't chance Kelly thinking he was staying away because he was too chickenshit to take on Tyler.

That left only two possibilities: try hitching with a lamb under one arm, or learn to drive a stick right now. As in, this minute.

He couldn't quit. Not now, when he had the perfect plan and a golden opportunity to act on it. *Come on,* he urged his pathetic self. *How hard can it be to drive a standard? You know lots of morons who drive sticks.*

Dylan studied the pedals and the gearshift, then put the car in neutral. At least the driveway sloped downhill. He pressed the clutch pedal a few times, feeling how far down he had to depress it to shift, then released the emergency brake and started the engine with the car in neutral and the clutch engaged. The car started rolling forward slowly.

After a few stutters and one stall, he managed to ease the truck out of the driveway and down the road toward Northampton. He could pick up Route 9 east there and take that to Boston, then head north on Route 95. He couldn't chance taking the Mass Pike because of the cameras; in fact, he should probably stay off toll roads altogether. Especially if Hannah decided to report her truck as stolen.

No. She wouldn't do that, would she? Not Hannah. Once she saw

Casper was missing, she'd figure out why he'd had to run away and save the lamb. Maybe she'd even feel a little bit proud of him.

Once he got the truck into fourth gear, it felt like driving a regular car. Just higher and bouncier. The motion seemed to calm Casper down, too, thankfully. Now the lamb was curled on the seat like a dog and peacefully nibbling a strap on Dylan's backpack. Soon Dylan was confident enough to take his hand off the lamb—he'd been holding him in place—and turn on the radio.

The radio was tuned to a station that played folk music. *Figures that's what Hannah would listen to,* he thought with another little guilt spasm. Dylan jabbed at the radio buttons. Finally he found a rock station and left it there. You sure as hell wouldn't find any EDM out here in the Happy Valley. No dubstep for hippies.

He set his phone GPS for Northampton. The lamb's eyes were closed now, its little head nodding like one of those creepy bobblehead animals people put in the rear windows of their cars. Casper's eyelashes were long and pale. Dylan smiled. If nothing else, he'd done something good in the world by saving this one special lamb.

An hour later, Dylan was on Route 9 somewhere in the Brookfields, sandwiched between a semitruck and a slow Volvo, when he realized his head was nodding like the lamb's. He was zoning out because the adrenaline rush he'd felt while escaping the farm was over. He also had to pee.

Now what? Dylan didn't trust himself to pull over and get out of the truck without the lamb making a dash for it. He'd have to grab Casper before he opened the door, then hold the lamb while he took a piss and hope nobody driving by would think he was up to some kinky fun with a sheep in his arms.

The lamb probably had to piss, too. Why hadn't he thought to bring a dog leash? Billy's leash had been hanging right by the kitchen door.

Dylan narrowed his eyes against the glint of the silver Volvo. Was that stupid car going even slower than before? Should he pass it?

Suddenly, the Volvo's brake lights lit up. "Shit!" Dylan yelled, and slammed his own brake, forgetting all about the clutch. The pickup shuddered to a halt.

There was a sudden blare of a horn—the truck behind him—then a terrifying smash and jolt. Dylan felt the seat belt nearly cut him in half as he was thrown forward when the truck behind him barreled into the back of Hannah's pickup, propelling him into the Volvo's rear bumper.

Dylan shielded his face with both arms as the lamb's body was flung against his, Casper bellowing in his ear, a hoof slashing his neck. Then everything went black.

Somehow, thirty-seven felt a lot older than thirty-six, Sydney reflected as she parked in front of the restaurant. No more being thirty-something and happily professional and single, on the move. At thirty-seven, you were marching steadily toward forty. Her skin seemed drier overnight and she'd had to throw out one of her bras this morning because the hooks were digging into her fleshy back. One of her knees was aching, too.

"I'm a middle-aged woman," Sydney said aloud as she grabbed her purse and locked her car. She hated that idea. To be fair, she was tired tonight. You always felt older when you were underslept.

Plus, her life felt so much more complicated than it had a year ago. Twice during the drive south to Boston tonight, she'd nearly phoned her friends to cancel this birthday dinner. She had a raft of excuses on hand, all of them true: she'd been having a tough time with the whole Dylan thing and was wrung out from worry; she'd had to testify in court this morning for one of her clients, and the lawyer had played hardball; Gary was in Europe for a conference and all she wanted to do was go home to her *own* little house, which wouldn't be hers much longer, since the Realtor had three showings already lined up for the weekend. She wanted to soak in her tub with a glass of wine.

On the other hand, she, Gwendolyn, and Fern hadn't missed celebrating their birthdays together since meeting in grad school a decade ago. No matter what was going on in their lives, they maintained this precious touchstone, the three of them meeting at the same restaurant in

Somerville—a Spanish tapas place—to reconnect and discuss how their lives were progressing. She didn't want to be the first to break their tradition.

Besides, she'd probably just mope if she was alone all night. She'd been concerned enough about Dylan to finally call Hannah this morning, since Dylan wasn't answering her texts.

"He's fine, Sydney," her mother said. "I haven't seen him use his phone since he's been here. Maybe it isn't charged. Anyway, I'd let you know if something was wrong. Give me that much credit, can't you?"

"Of course, Mom. Sorry to have bothered you," Sydney said stiffly. "Go back to your life," she added before hanging up, then felt horrible for acting like a snotty teenager when her mother was actually doing them a huge favor by providing Dylan with a sanctuary.

Why had she gotten irritable so fast? Because her mother hadn't remembered her birthday, and because, no matter how many years passed, Sydney still felt abandoned. "And happy birthday to me," Sydney said aloud, feeling that same ridiculous sense of childish hurt she always did where her mother was concerned.

When had her mother *stopped* remembering her birthday? At Haven Lake, her parents and Uncle Rory had made a fuss over it. There were newspaper party hats, cookies decorated to look like zoo animals, a hand-carved wooden flute Rory made for Sydney and then played while she and her mother danced.

Her favorite birthday gift—she still had it, somewhere, one of the few childhood keepsakes she'd taken when she left the farm—was a mermaid costume her mother made Sydney when she turned nine. Hannah made a green tail for Sydney and a blue one for Valerie. The tails were made out of glittering cloth; Hannah had cleverly sewn flippers into the tails so Sydney and Valerie could swim like the mermaids they still half believed were real.

Today the only person who'd remembered her birthday, other than Gwendolyn and Fern, was Gary. He'd given her a beautiful gold watch at breakfast—much too expensive for her to feel comfortable wearing it—and scribbled a heartfelt message in a card:

I only want to live in a world with you in it. You're the reason I do everything.

He'd even asked if she wanted him to postpone the trip. "I hate leaving on your special day."

"It's fine. We'll celebrate next weekend when you get back." Sydney had wrapped her arms around his neck, standing on her toes to press the full length of her freshly showered, bathrobed self against Gary's blue pin-striped suit and starched white shirt. "Besides, you can't stay home. You're giving a paper that will make you the most famous surgeon in the U.S."

He laughed. "You don't even remember what it's about, do you?"

She kissed him. "No. But if you wrote it, I'm sure it's amazing."

"Repeat after me: supraglottic laryngectomy."

When she did, Gary laughed again and lifted her up onto the counter, opening her thighs and giving her the rest of her birthday present before he left, a spontaneous session of lovemaking that left her skin humming.

The restaurant was noisy and crowded, and she immediately felt better just by being there. It was set up to look like an authentic Spanish *mesón*; there were hams and necklaces of dried chorizo sausages hanging above the bar, and the tables were topped with brightly colored tiles.

"Beautiful birthday girl!" Gwendolyn called from where she and Fern had managed to snag a table. They both stood up to hug and kiss Sydney, and poured her a glass of sangria when she sat down. The sangria was ruby red with fruit segments floating in it; Sydney took a long sip and felt better still.

Her friends had already ordered the first round of tapas. Within minutes the small plates began arriving: figs and sausage, Tortilla Española, bread with a hot goat cheese and spicy tomato dip.

Soon Sydney was feeling practically gleeful as she and the others ate and swapped stories. They had been right to create this ritual for themselves back in grad school, before all three of them had such busy lives. Fern, especially, was entertaining: she was a slender blonde with a spray tan who loved dating professional athletes, but was always disappointed when they didn't measure up conversationally—something Gwendolyn and Sydney teased her about mercilessly.

"If they'd only keep their mouths shut, I could be happy just looking at them," Fern had said more than once.

Tonight she launched into a tale involving her latest conquest, a pro golfer she'd met at a friend's country club. Hearing Fern talk was like listening to country-western songs, those twangy ballads filled with lust and betrayals and broken hearts.

Gwendolyn was more serious, even, than Sydney, a brunette who was plain to look at until you noticed her brilliant blue eyes. She'd been married only four years, but already had two small children. Her husband had gotten a promotion and was traveling more for his sales job.

"That sounds hard, being alone with the kids at night," Sydney said sympathetically.

"Oh, no, it's great," Gwendolyn said. "I love Karl to death, you know I do. But a girl likes to curl up by herself with a good glass of wine and a reality show now and then."

They ordered the next round of tapas and another pitcher of sangria. Then it was Sydney's turn to be quizzed. She started by holding up her new gold watch and talking about the frustration of trying to shop for a wedding dress, prompting both women to complain that they hadn't been invited along.

"We're the bridesmaids, after all," Fern said, pretending to pout, which caused the Spanish waiter to come rushing over in his ruffled pink shirt and tight black trousers. "What can I do for you, señorita?" he asked.

"Oh, honey, let me think about that," Fern said, batting her lashes at him and making the others—especially the waiter—laugh.

Finally it was time for cake and the one ritual Sydney hated more than any other, but couldn't imagine doing without: the waiters trooped over to the table with a lit candle in a tall brass candlestick shaped like a frog, singing and clapping and causing the other diners to join in. She blushed furiously and blew the candle out in a hurry.

It wasn't until Sydney was back in her car after dinner that she checked her phone and saw that she'd missed several calls, all from Hannah. Had she remembered her birthday after all?

Well, that ship had sailed. Her mother's birthday wishes could wait.

Sydney started the car and began weaving her way through the congested streets of Somerville. Suddenly, though, she had a panicked thought: Hannah had said she'd call if Dylan was in trouble.

Sydney hurriedly pulled over and hit the button for messages. Several were hang-ups, but two were from Hannah, sounding breathless, her voice shaking.

"Sydney? God, Sydney, pick up," she said in the last message. "I'm calling because Dylan took my truck and the police just called. There's been an accident. He's okay, but he's at UMass Medical Center in Worcester. Can you call me when you get this, please? I'm going to the hospital now, but I don't have any of his insurance or medical information. Please! Call as soon as you can."

Sydney stared at the phone as if it were a foreign object, then pulled back onto the street, dialing her mother's number as she pulled a U-turn at the next light.

Hannah hated hospitals. She'd spent too many hours in them as a child watching her mother dying of pancreatic cancer, senseless with morphine, to ever want to set foot in one again.

This afternoon she'd had to go to the ER first, where Dylan was brought by the ambulance, and where she'd felt helpless and frustrated as the staff asked questions she couldn't answer: Did Dylan have a history of seizures? Did he take any medications regularly? Was he allergic to anything?

By the time Sydney finally called back, Dylan had been moved out of the ER and into a patient room on the surgical floor. They were keeping him overnight for observation due to his concussion and neck injury.

She sat beside Dylan's bed while a young black nurse with strong arms and hair wound in a complicated braid bustled around, checking the machines that kept track of whatever was being pumped into Dylan's veins. "Will he wake up soon?" Hannah asked.

"Probably not," the nurse said. "He's not in a coma and the CT scan didn't show any sort of trauma to the brain. But we're giving him something for the pain, so it might be a while." Her accented, lilting English sounded like water trickling from tree branches after a rain. "Want to go home? We'll call you when he's awake."

"No, that's fine. I'll stay here," Hannah said. "I don't want him to be alone."

"I understand." The nurse left, then returned shortly with a cup of coffee and a pat on the shoulder for Hannah, her touch as gentle as her voice, nearly reducing Hannah to tears.

Once she was alone again, she was flooded with unpleasant memories. Allen had been hospitalized several times during their marriage, always for injuries he'd inflicted on himself, though they'd managed to keep that from the doctors. Once, she'd actually talked him into admitting himself to the VA hospital for a psychiatric examination, but that place was the worst of all: a maze of incompetence and grim desperation.

Hannah pulled the sweater she'd been working on out of her bag and began to knit, the needles moving furiously in and out of the yarn. A doctor had told her Dylan would recover fully from the accident, but lying there under the white hospital blanket, with his swollen, bruised face, sunken chest, and skinny limbs, he looked frail enough to be a victim of chronic illness or abuse. His bony arms were skeletal and nearly as white as the sheets, and his narrow torso was diminished by the thick brace around his neck.

When the police had called after finding the registration in the truck's glove compartment, they'd asked if Hannah wanted to press charges. "The truck's totaled," the officer said.

"That's all right," she'd said. "It's not worth much. Who was driving?"

Like she didn't know. When the officer told her it was Dylan, and that Dylan had only a permit, no license, she'd winced but gamely said, "That's my grandson. No, he didn't have my permission to drive the truck on the road, just on the farm fields, but I don't want to charge him with anything. I'm sure he only meant to borrow the truck, not steal it."

"That's fine, but we'll still have to charge him with operating a vehicle without a license," the cop said, not unkindly.

Hannah had called Sydney instead of Gary, because Sydney's cell phone number was all she had in her phone, and she knew they didn't have a landline. Liz had given her Susan's silver Acura to drive to Worcester. "The car's just been sitting in the driveway," she said. "I haven't had the heart to take it off the road. You can keep it."

"I can't accept a car from you! But I'll borrow it," Hannah said.

"Don't worry about a thing. Stay as long as you need. I'll do the animals, even psycho Billy," Liz had promised.

"Why aren't you a man?" Hannah said. "I'd be so happy with you."

"Why aren't you gay?" Liz answered.

"You've got June Cleaver now," Hannah reminded her. "Maybe she even vacuums."

Sydney arrived in Dylan's hospital room just before eleven o'clock. Understandably, she looked frantic, her mascara in raccoonish rings around her eyes.

It was her daughter's birthday, Hannah remembered suddenly. That thought was a fist to her throat. She tried every year to ignore this date. Otherwise it was too painful to remember how Sydney wanted nothing to do with her.

Even now, her daughter ignored her and went straight to Dylan's bedside. As Sydney stroked the boy's forehead, Hannah looked away, remembering the pain and chaos of Sydney's birth in the farmhouse at

Haven Lake, the midwife coaching her, Allen laying Sydney on Hannah's bare belly after it was over. Sydney had cried immediately. Then, when Hannah murmured, "It's all right, baby, everything's fine, I'm right here," she'd stopped and opened her eyes to stare into Hannah's face.

They'd named her for the city they loved most while backpacking around the world. Allen had hovered over them, arms dangling at his sides, radiating pure joy. He and Hannah were both overcome by the fact that they'd made a little person who could benefit from their own life lessons. Sydney could revel in the peaceful childhood they'd give her at Haven Lake.

"Epic fail" was what Dylan would call that delusion of theirs.

Hannah continued knitting until her daughter turned around. Then she tucked the yarn and needles back into the bag. Sydney's mouth was puckered like an old woman's, her gold hair scraped away from her face, her cheeks and eyes hollow with fatigue.

Sydney stood in front of her, hands balled at her sides. "What the hell, Mom? Why did you let Dylan drive your truck?"

"I didn't *let* him!" Hannah said. Her back and thighs were damp from sitting and worrying for hours in this slick plastic chair the color of flesh, and this was the thanks she got? "For your information, your kid took the truck without my permission, so you can cut the accusatory crap out right now. Dylan stole one of my sheep, too, by the way."

"What? Oh my God." Sydney sank into the chair opposite Hannah's. *"Why?"*

Hannah felt sorry for her daughter, seeing the bewilderment in Sydney's bloodshot eyes and the stain of something red—was that *ketchup*?—on her voluminous beige top. Sydney was coming undone, caught up in an emotional tornado beyond her control, touching down where she least expected it. Hannah knew all too well what that felt like.

"He was trying to save it, I think," she answered. "It was one of the lambs I was planning to butcher. I think he must have overheard me talking to someone about transporting the lambs today."

Sydney wrinkled her nose. "Ew, Mom. I can't believe you kill the poor things."

Hannah pointed to the red stain. "Did you eat that ketchup on vegetables?"

Sydney's face colored. "Where's the poor lamb now? Did it survive the crash?"

At last, something to smile about. "Yes. Apparently it broke a leg, but the cops felt sorry for it. They took up a donation and brought it to a vet. I have to pick him up tomorrow."

"And then what?" Sydney looked worried. "I'm afraid if you kill it, Dylan will take it really hard."

Hannah sighed. "I know. I guess I'll have to take it home for now. Then we'll see." She glanced at her watch. "Where's Gary?" She had assumed he was filling out papers, but now it occurred to her that Sydney might have driven to Worcester alone. "Was it too inconvenient for him to come?"

"Don't be sarcastic, Mom. You know Gary's not like that."

"I'm sorry. It's just that I don't think this should be your problem to shoulder alone. Dylan isn't even your child."

Of course this was the wrong thing to say. Sydney frowned and fixed the pins in her hair, her mouth clamped in a straight line. She looked professional but untouchable, and much older than thirty-seven. Her poor daughter, thinking pins and flat shoes and briefcases could keep her emotions in check.

"In case you've forgotten, Gary and I are getting married this fall," Sydney said. "We practically live together already. I love him. And I love Dylan. Gary's not here because he's at a conference in Europe. He has to give an important talk tomorrow afternoon. Then he'll take the first available flight back to Boston. He asked me to bring Dylan back with me when he's released tomorrow and Gary will meet us at home."

"Oh. Well, that's good." Hannah stood up, peeling her jeans off the backs of her thighs.

"Wait. Where are you going?"

Hannah stopped in surprise. "Back to Haven Lake. You and Dylan don't need me here. You've just said you're taking Dylan home. That's probably the right thing to do."

To her shock, Sydney's green eyes filled with tears. "Please don't leave, Mom. Not yet." She tried to brush the tears away with the back of one hand, but they were coming too fast, the mascara flowing in little rivers so that her face was a spiderweb of black lines.

"Oh, honey, oh no. Don't cry. Of course I won't leave. I just thought you'd want me to!" Hannah reached for the tissues on the table beside Dylan's bed.

She'd meant to hand Sydney only one, but in her haste she tugged an entire fistful out of the box. White tissues lofted free and fell like snow onto Sydney's head and lap, making it possible for Hannah to touch, just briefly, her daughter's hair as she helped her pick them up. "Some birthday, huh?"

Sydney's head was bowed, but Hannah heard her sharp intake of breath and saw the shudder across her daughter's shoulders. "You remembered."

Hannah felt her chest constrict, as if someone had wound a rope around her rib cage. "Of course I did. I remember every one of your birthdays. You were crying that very first birthday, too, greeting the world with a hell of a yell, all six pounds of you. But then I talked to you and you stopped crying. Just like that!"

"I knew your voice?"

"You did, and why not? I'd been talking to you ever since I knew you were there. You were everything to me, baby girl. You still are," Hannah said, and then she was crying, too. Not delicate spiderwebs of black like Sydney's tears, but great, gulping, noisy sobs that caused her whole body to shudder until her knees threatened to give out. She sat down again in the chair and buried her face in her hands.

After a moment, she felt a tentative hand on her arm, and Sydney said, "Have a tissue. I think I have a few to spare."

Hannah grabbed it and blew her nose. Then the two of them started laughing.

CHAPTER ELEVEN

The cop who took his statement at the station the day after the accident was cool. "The truck driver was clearly at fault," the officer explained, since that guy had rear-ended him. However, Dylan got his permit taken away and had to pay a fine.

The police had removed his gear from the truck before Hannah's pickup was towed away. Now they turned his backpack over to him at the station with little yellow evidence tags on it. Like he was being sprung from prison.

At least they were letting him say good-bye to Casper. After he and Sydney were finished at the police station, they went to meet Hannah at a veterinarian's office. The cops had brought Casper there after the crash, and seeing Casper in a leg splint made Dylan's eyes blur. He'd wanted to save the lamb, not maim him.

Despite his injuries, Casper looked alert and energetic. If the cops hadn't intervened, the vet would have probably put him down. Now what would happen? Dylan was afraid to ask. Probably Hannah would still cart him away to the butcher. What did it matter if you ate an animal's broken leg? It would still be leg of lamb.

Again, Dylan's eyes swam with tears. *Loser. Dribbler.* He'd texted Kelly a dozen times today to apologize for not showing up, to say he'd been in an accident, but she still hadn't texted him back. Case closed. She'd have nothing to do with him now, probably. He'd screwed everything up.

Still groggy from pain meds and awkward in his neck brace, Dylan felt dizzy when he bent down to cup the lamb's face between his hands and stare into Casper's liquid brown eyes, clutching the soft wool between his fingers. "Sorry, little dude."

The vet had put some kind of harness and leash on Casper. Hannah had brought a crate, and now she led Casper over to it and urged him inside with a handful of corn. Then she lifted the crate into the back of the car she was driving and came back over to Dylan. To his shock, she hugged him.

"I know you were trying to do what you thought was right," she said, so softly that probably even Sydney couldn't catch the words in the windy parking lot. "You just went about it the wrong way. That's the thing about risks. You never know if they're going to pan out. But it's still better to try and fail than to stand by and do nothing, wishing you'd acted. I'll keep Casper so you can visit him."

"Thanks," he mumbled. "Sorry, Hannah. I didn't mean to hurt your truck." And then he couldn't help it—he was so grateful that he started crying for real. Dribbling in public all over again, but Hannah didn't seem to mind. She pulled him close with her strong arms and he rested his head on her shoulder, breathing in flannel, hay, and sheep.

In the car, Sydney asked how he felt and whether he wanted a pillow—fine, he answered, and no—then didn't speak as she navigated through Worcester. She was probably pissed off at him. Sometimes you couldn't tell what Sydney was thinking because her face was a mask. Her eyebrows and mouth looked frozen, like that sphinx guarding the pyramid he'd seen with his parents on a trip to Egypt when he was ten. He'd been afraid of the sphinx. Dylan rested his head on the window, wishing he'd asked for the pillow after all. The vibration of the car was like a spike through his skull.

Suddenly, Sydney asked, "Do you wish you were going back to Haven Lake?"

Dylan thought of Kelly, of how maybe he could convince her to see him, still, even after he stood her up last night. "No. I need to go home. Anyway, I know I screwed up. I can't ever go back."

"Not true. Mom won't hold this against you. But I'm glad you're coming home."

Dylan glanced at her. Sydney looked different today. It took him a minute to work out why: her clothes. She was wearing work jeans, the kind with big pockets and a loop for a hammer, and a T-shirt with a flannel shirt over it, just like Hannah. Maybe those *were* Hannah's clothes. Sydney's long hair was down, too, instead of up the way she usually wore it. She had Disney princess hair, gold curls streaked with blond and whipping around her face because the window was open. She looked younger. Better.

She turned and raised one eyebrow. "You okay over there?"

He nodded. "I was just thinking that you probably hate it that I'm coming back."

"I do not! I *want* you to come home. I hope you know how much I care about you."

"Oh, right. Because I make your life so easy."

"You don't make my life hard. Your own, maybe, but not mine."

She shut up after that. At first Dylan thought Sydney was silent because she was shifting lanes and the afternoon traffic merging onto the highway was syrupy slow. But her mouth was tense, the lines around it deep enough that Dylan realized she'd made herself stop talking.

That sucked. When Sydney was back in Newburyport, she'd probably plaster her hair tight to her head again and turn back into a mom wannabe: *How was school? Did you do your homework/take out the trash/make your bed? What have you had to eat today? How are you feeling?* Talking to adults made Dylan feel like he was standing under a blow-dryer with people using megaphones to shout in his ears.

He didn't want to go back to that crap with Sydney. He liked how she was right now, like one of his younger, hip teachers at school. Like his Spanish teacher, Miss Moira, who'd lived in Guatemala and wore shirts that looked like rainbows. Miss Moira always looked like she was listening not just to what you said, but to *you*.

If Sydney could be looser, like she was right now, it wouldn't be so bad at home. He had to keep her talking while he could. "Your mom seems pretty cool," he said.

Sydney's mask cracked a little as she made a face. "Now, maybe. She wasn't so cool back when I was your age."

"Why not?"

"Long story."

"It's a long, boring drive back to Newburyport," he reminded her. "At least, I hope this drive will be more boring than my last one."

Sydney's mask finally cracked wide open as she tipped her head back and laughed. "You're right. It is pretty boring." She glanced at him, gathering her hair in one hand to hold it down on her shoulder and away from her face. "Did you fall asleep at the wheel? Is that what made you crash?"

"No. I just spaced out a little. When the car in front of me slowed way down, I hit the brakes and forgot about the clutch. I'd never really driven a stick."

"Yet you thought you could do it."

"Yeah, I did. I've always been pretty good with machines. That's what I liked about being at the farm, really. All those cool machines. Did you work with them when you were a kid?"

Sydney shook her head. "My dad wanted everything done by hand."

"Like the Amish?"

"Something like that, yeah."

After being with Hannah, Dylan had started to like the idea of making everything yourself, growing everything you ate, using only tools that didn't require gas or electricity or even batteries. He could get into living like that. What did Hannah call it? "Off the grid."

"Did you like growing up on the farm?" he asked.

"Sure. I was happy at Haven Lake. It was like heaven when I was a kid."

This answer confused him. "Why didn't you keep on living there, then? I mean, I know your friend died and your dad killed himself. But why did you leave?"

There was such a long silence that Dylan thought maybe Sydney would play the adult card and say, "None of your business." But he could see by the way her green eyes went narrow behind her oversized yellow sunglasses that she was just thinking about how to answer. Or maybe remembering.

He knew what that was like: you started to remember one thing, and that memory opened a door to a new room with more things for you to see and feel. And maybe wish you could wipe off your memory's hard drive.

"I left Haven Lake because I couldn't deal with my mother," Sydney said at last. "After Dad died, she drank every day, sometimes even in the morning. She stopped taking care of the animals and planting the fields and cooking. We were running out of money. She didn't call anybody to come help us, either. I took care of the cows and the chickens and the house while she drank and cried until she passed out. I got tired of having to take care of Mom like she was two years old. I was only fifteen."

Dylan was stunned. Not by the anger in Sydney's voice—who could blame her?—but because he couldn't picture Hannah so out of control. How had she quit drinking? And would his own mother have stopped, too, eventually, if she'd lived? Was there anything he could have done to make that happen?

"Where did you go when you left?" he asked.

"To live with my dad's parents. Grammy Bishop hated my mom, but she'd always been nice to me. When she came out to the farm to get some of Dad's things, she saw how it was and told me I should come back with her to Ipswich so she could take care of me."

"But that was, like, twenty years ago. Didn't you ever want to go back? I mean, after Hannah stopped drinking?"

Sydney shook her head. "No. I was too angry." She swallowed hard. "I still don't like being on the farm. Too many memories and questions.

Not so much about Dad—he'd been depressed for years—but about why Theo died."

"I thought it was an accident."

"That's what the police said, but I always thought there was more to the story." Sydney said this so softly, it was like she was talking to herself.

"Why?" Dylan couldn't turn his neck all the way with this humongous brace on it, so he swiveled his entire body on the seat to look at her.

"Because Theo knew the pond really well, and he was on the swim team at his high school."

"So what do you think really happened?"

"I don't know." Sydney pressed her lips together.

"Have you tried to find out?"

"How would I? The case is closed."

Dylan was getting excited: this was like a cold case on TV. "Yeah, but you could talk to other people who were there that night. Like Theo's sister or your dad's brother. Maybe there's stuff they never told the cops."

"My dad's brother is dead. Valerie went back to Rhode Island with her mother and I never heard from her again. They didn't even invite us to Theo's funeral."

"What was Theo's last name?"

"Sinclair." Sydney signaled and turned into a rest area. "You hungry? I'm starving. Let's get some dinner."

Dylan was too busy thinking to bother answering. Now he had a way to repay Hannah and Sydney for helping him: he could help them find out what really happened to Theo.

Gary had called last night to let Sydney know he'd booked a Delta flight leaving Amsterdam the next morning with a layover in Paris. "Eleven hours of plane hell," he said. "See you around two o'clock, probably."

Sydney dropped into a sound sleep after two glasses of wine swallowed in a stupor during a recorded television show she forgot the minute she switched off the TV. She woke around ten o'clock feeling restored.

She had already cleared her appointments for today, knowing she'd want to stay home and keep an eye on Dylan.

The house was quiet. Dylan must still be asleep. No surprise, given the pain meds they'd put him on for a few days. Only Tylenol with codeine, but still. She was glad for the peaceful house. She could eat and catch up on work before showering and getting dressed. Plenty of time before Gary arrived. She'd make Dylan breakfast whenever he got up.

Sydney pulled on the same clothes she'd worn home from the hospital—her mother's jeans and flannel shirt—and went downstairs, where she made coffee and fixed a bagel with peanut butter and banana. She was carrying her mug and plate from the counter to the kitchen table, where her laptop sat at one end, when she noticed the notebook propped against her computer. She nearly dropped the dishes. That was Dylan's notebook, his handwriting marching in loopy blue ink letters across the page. Another good-bye note?

Don't be ridiculous, she chided herself. *The kid's on pain meds and wearing a neck brace.*

She picked up the notebook carefully, as if it might crumble between her fingers before she could read Dylan's message: *Attorney Valerie Sinclair. 85 Dorrance Street, Suite 12, Providence, RI.* Then a phone number and a Web site.

Sydney sank into the chair in front of her laptop. So Valerie was still in Providence.

Not that she was completely shocked. She'd lied to Dylan yesterday. While it was true that she and Valerie had never spoken again after Theo drowned, once online searches were possible, Sydney had stalked her in secret. She knew, for instance, that Valerie had attended Brown University and then Tulane Law School before clerking for a judge in Florida.

She understood why Dylan was trying to help her; he must have questions, after spending time with Hannah. Even her own curiosity was stirred up by seeing Haven Lake again. But what good would it do to pick at old scabs? She'd moved on. She was content with her life.

No, you're not, a small but powerful voice hissed in her ear, making Sydney shiver and pull her mother's flannel shirt closed over the faded camisole she wore to bed whenever Gary was out of town. She stared at the laptop for another minute, heart hammering. Then she typed in the Web address.

Valerie's business site popped right up. Well designed, green-and-white background. Valerie Sinclair was a partner in a law practice that specialized in criminal law. Not what Sydney would have expected, given Valerie's timid nature as a child.

She sat for so long staring at Valerie's name on the screen that the letters seemed to liquefy. When she pulled herself back to the present, the vast Victorian kitchen felt cavernous and cold.

She should eat, but she'd lost her appetite. She should shower and dress, too, before Gary came home. But here was Valerie's Web site on her computer, her phone number in bold green letters.

Sydney picked up her cell phone and dialed the number even while telling herself that Valerie wouldn't answer. She was probably in court. With a client. On vacation.

Or, even if she was there, Valerie wouldn't want to talk to her.

She gave her name to the receptionist and was put on hold for a few minutes of piano music moving across the upper octaves like ants crawling across a picnic blanket. This image made Sydney picture the tea parties she and Valerie used to have on her mother's old Indian print bedspread beneath the chestnut tree on the farm. Ants everywhere, but they didn't care. They loved using the cracked china teacups and bowls Hannah had found in the free box at Goodwill. She and Valerie drank with pinkie fingers raised and spoke in accents, adjusting tattered scarves they wrapped around their bodies like capes and gowns.

Valerie's voice suddenly came on the line, deep and slightly husky. Not shy or timid anymore, yet the same breathless Valerie, as if she were standing right here in Gary's kitchen, swaying her blue-jeaned hips in front of Sydney like she'd done that last summer, moving her new woman's body like a stranger's.

"Sydney Bishop! Is that really you? I can't believe it," Valerie said. "I'm not dreaming?"

"Yes," Sydney said. "I mean no. You're not dreaming." She pressed her cell phone against her cheek, rendered nearly mute by the voice of this woman who had once helped her build fairy houses in the woods. A woman who'd shared sleeping bags and mattresses with her, everything always damp and slightly moldy with the scent of pines and pond water, sometimes sleeping with their sticky limbs entwined. She didn't know what to say.

"I don't know what to say," Valerie said.

Sydney smiled. Valerie had always known how to divine the words on Sydney's tongue, as if they'd kissed and tasted each other, transferring their words that way. Something else they'd practiced as girls: kissing.

"Me, either," Sydney managed. "I didn't think you'd be there, or that you'd take my call if you were." She wished she'd eaten the bagel. Her stomach burned from coffee and nerves.

"Well, now that I've taken your call, what do you want to say?"

"Um, how are you?"

"Very original. I'm fine, Sydney Bishop. Thank you for asking. Um, how are *you*?" Valerie parroted back.

Fuck you, Sydney thought. She wanted her friend Valerie—the shy, sweet one—back again. Not this snarky voice. This *lawyer.* "Actually, Valerie, I'm calling because I've been thinking about the farm. Some things happening in my life recently have led me back there, and seeing Haven Lake made me wonder how you're doing," she said, desperate for Valerie to again divine the words she couldn't find, the questions she couldn't ask.

"You went back to the farm? Huh. Well, like I said: I'm fine. Couldn't be better."

Sydney dug the nails of her free hand into her palm, but couldn't stop herself from blurting, "Why are you being such a total bitch?"

A brief silence, then Valerie said, "As if you don't know."

"I don't!" Sydney felt desperation rise, a sour taste at the back of her throat. "I don't know anything about what happened to you. Theo died, my dad killed himself, and then you and your mom went away. I don't know anything about your life after that."

"For the record, we left before your dad killed himself, actually," Valerie said.

This stopped Sydney. That couldn't be true. Surely she remembered Valerie comforting her after her father shot himself? Or had she only imagined Valerie's presence, their arms around each other as they sat on the dock and rocked each other, watching the mist rise on the pond, both of them grieving? As a teenager, that sorrow was so acute and foreign that it felt like a physical sensation, as if someone had surgically shaved off her top layer of skin, leaving her nerve endings raw.

Was Valerie there or not? In some ways it didn't matter. Memories, once retrieved, were altered. The more you examined a memory (as Sydney knew from her psychology studies), the more your mind changed it in subtle ways. What mattered was the essential truth that emerged from that stew made of complicated, often conflicting emotions and facts.

"Whatever," Sydney said. "I don't understand why you sound so pissed off at me."

Valerie sighed. "I'm not, really. Just too busy to have this conversation. I'm at work, Sydney. Obviously you know that, since you called me at the office. This isn't the time or place for me to get into anything."

"What would you get into if it were the right time and place?"

"Look, I'm not doing this over the phone. But you can come to Providence if you really want to get into it."

Get into what? "I could do that," Sydney said. "When?"

"Do you work?"

"I'm a psychologist," Sydney said. "I'm in a group practice, though, and I make my own hours. What's your schedule? Just tell me what's good for you and I can probably make it happen."

"My schedule is nonstop. I work too many hours and don't make any of them myself. How about Friday night for a drink? We could meet in Boston. Halfway for both of us."

"Fine," Sydney said, and they set a time and place.

It wasn't until after they'd hung up that Sydney realized Valerie must have searched for her at some point, too. Otherwise, how could Valerie have known that Boston was halfway between them?

Shaken by the conversation, Sydney forced herself to choke the bagel down cold. The best way to distract herself from worrying about meeting Valerie on Friday would be to dig into work. She opened a report on her laptop. Reading it over slowly drew her back into the case. Soon she was absorbed in editing what she'd written previously.

She was still seated at the table, working on her second report and deep in thought, when a car pulled into the driveway. Startled, she glanced at her computer clock. Only one thirty. Could Gary be here already? Damn it! She hadn't even showered! She stood up and went to the kitchen window.

It was Gary, looking tired but clean-shaven, his gray suit still holding its sharp creases despite him spending the night on the plane.

Sydney opened the kitchen door and felt a little jolt of joy as he came toward her, smiling. Gary was going to be her husband. Whatever happened with Dylan, with Valerie, with everything else in their lives, they could handle it together.

"You're up!" Gary set down his suitcase and briefcase inside the kitchen door and kissed her. "I was expecting you to be sleeping in, after everything you went through yesterday. I'm sorry I wasn't here to help you deal with Dylan. I feel terrible that you had to go through that alone."

"Don't. It all went fine. And you're here now. That's what matters."

"So how is he?" Gary asked as they moved into the kitchen, where she sat down again and he leaned against the counter, arms crossed.

"Bruised and sore, but he only has to wear the cervical collar for a few more days. He'll be totally fine. Insurance will cover the damage to the truck, since the driver behind Dylan was considered at fault for rear-ending him. I told Mom we'd have Dylan pay her five-hundred-dollar deductible. Otherwise, the only penalty is that Dylan lost his permit.

He'll probably be fined—we're still waiting to see how much—and he might not be able to get his license for a year now."

Gary shook his head, wincing. "What a mess. Well, he was lucky." He took a glass from the cupboard, filled it with water at the sink, and gulped it down, then said, "We were all lucky. Dylan could have killed himself. Or somebody else. Maybe the accident will wise him up a little."

"I know. I tell parents that every teenager should have a minor car accident. We can warn them until we're blue in the face, but that's the only way they stop feeling immortal."

"You're right. God knows nothing I've said has gotten through to that kid." Gary set the glass down on the counter.

"I don't think that's true. Teenagers are always listening, even if their actions are impulsive sometimes. That's why we have to keep talking to them."

"If you say so, Doc."

Sydney smiled, noticing that his name tag from the conference was still pinned to his suit. "I can't believe you got a flight back so quickly."

"You can always find something if you're willing to pay top dollar. But what else could I do? Dylan's my son, Sydney." Gary's voice dropped to a rough whisper. "How could I have such a screwed-up kid?"

"Stop it! You didn't do anything wrong, honey. All teenagers act out." She went to him and put her arms around his waist. "You've supported him in every way since Amanda died. You're a great dad." Marco's words came back to her: *Sometimes we can't control our children no matter how good our intentions.* "We forget that our kids are living their own lives," she said. "By adolescence, their journeys have to be separate from ours and we've got to let them learn from their mistakes."

"I know you're right." Gary stepped away from her and shrugged out of his jacket. "Even if you do sound like a crystal-fondling hippie. I can tell you've been with your mother."

Sydney winced. That stung. "Ouch! Take it easy on the help."

"Sorry! I was teasing. Forgive me. I'm so tired, it feels like I'm walking through soup." Gary reached out to stroke her hair.

"I'm sure." She rested her head on his shoulder. "How did the presentation go?"

"People seemed to like it. One of the editors from *The New England Journal of Medicine* was there and asked if I want to write up my work as a paper and submit it to them."

"That's fantastic!" Sydney tipped her head up, admiring the sharp contours of Gary's face. "Want some food? I could make you a cheese omelet. We might even have a few mushrooms."

"No, thanks. I'm too beat to think about eating." Gary edged away from her, an odd jerky motion, filled his glass with water again, and took a small vial out of his pants pocket. He popped two capsules out of the vial and into his mouth, swallowing them with the water. "Is Dylan up? I should have a word with him."

"I haven't heard him yet." Sydney grimaced. "It was scary, seeing him attached to those machines at the hospital, with his face all swollen and bruised. He has a terrible cut on one arm, too. And I don't even know if the blood will ever come out of his clothes. He's on painkillers for a few days, so he might not be up for a while. They make him sleepy, he said."

"What's he taking?" Gary looked alarmed. "Those can be pretty addictive."

"Relax. Just Tylenol with codeine. The doctor said he should be fine to go back to school by tomorrow, so he'll be able to make up his work and take his finals the following week. I've already called the school and talked to the guidance counselor about it."

"You're a marvel," Gary said.

Sydney smiled, pleased. She hadn't done too badly after all, looking after Dylan. All parents went through crises with their kids. Maybe she was getting the hang of parenting after all. "You should go lie down while the house is quiet."

Gary shook his head. "I couldn't sleep now. I just took something to help me stay awake. I'll have jet lag if I don't stay up and go to bed at a normal time."

"Really? You couldn't let yourself nap for a little while? Just close your eyes and rest? You must be exhausted."

"I'm fine!" he barked. "Jesus! Let up, will you? I'm a doctor, Sydney. I know what my body needs. And I definitely know what my son needs: he has to see that I'm on his case the minute he's awake. Dylan has to hear it from me that he can't pull any more of these stunts. That's exactly how his mother died, doing something stupid behind the wheel."

"His mother was an alcoholic," Sydney said. "Dylan isn't Amanda, honey."

"I *know* that." Gary began pacing the kitchen, a muscle in his eye twitching. "At least he's not Amanda *yet*. The question is, how do I keep him from turning out like his useless mother?"

Sydney was shocked enough to sit down at the table and stare at him. "You can't keep saying things like that, Gary, or Dylan will start believing he's useless."

"Please don't give me that crap." Gary stopped his pacing to glare down at her.

She flinched a little but held her ground. "It's not crap. I've seen it happen over and over in my practice: when parents believe kids can't do any better, can't *be* any better than who they are already, those kids give up on themselves."

He waved a hand. "Yes, yes. I know: the old self-fulfilling prophecy theory of parenting comes back to bite me on the ass. Well, I don't buy it. Kids are lost without rules. You may have grown up without boundaries, but I didn't, and neither will my son."

"I know you love him and want to teach him right from wrong," Sydney said, deliberately gentling her voice. "I'm just trying to remind you that Dylan loves you. He wants to please you. I see it in his eyes every time he looks at you. Don't you think he's already afraid of letting you down? Of turning out like Amanda? At the same time, Dylan loved his mom, so when he thinks something like that, he probably believes he's betraying her."

To her shock, Gary sank into the kitchen chair next to hers and buried his face in his hands. His voice was muffled. "Stop it, Sydney, just stop talking about Amanda," he said, his voice hoarse with strain. "Jesus, why did I ever marry that woman?"

"Why did you? You've never told me. I don't even know how you first met."

"College." Gary lifted his head and gave her a pained expression. "Amanda went back to college after her modeling career didn't pan out. She was a few years older than I was, but she was in my freshman psychology class. I was afraid to talk to her until she asked me to help her study for a test. Finally I got the nerve up to ask her out at a party. It was like being hit by a meteor, being with Amanda. She was so beautiful," he said. "So happy, too. Everywhere she walked, it was like she was dancing. She actually walked on her toes. I'd never met anyone like her." He laughed, a sharp bark. "How would I? Me, Gary Katz of Queens, the beloved only child of Myra and Ben, a Jewish butcher and the son of a butcher? How would I meet the daughter of a guy who grew up with the Kennedys on the Cape? A girl whose allowance was bigger than my dad's salary?" He blinked back tears and laughed. "Did I ever tell you how my mother said she'd be sitting shiva if I married Amanda?"

"No," Sydney said, hurting for him, but feeling petty, too, because, in this vulnerable moment where Gary was so open to her, his openness was like a knife dipping in and out of her soft flesh. Had he ever felt about her the way he did about Amanda? As if he'd been hit by a meteor and would let his own mother pronounce him dead if he defied her and married Sydney?

No.

Not that this would be an issue now, since Gary's mother was addled by Alzheimer's and his father had ceased to care about much beyond his daily game of chess with his friend Mort and watching the Mets. But still. Gary, she was certain, had chosen her not because she inspired the same intensity of passion he'd felt for Amanda, but because of the very opposite: Sydney made him feel safe. He'd said that to her once and it had made her supremely happy. She wanted, always, to be the place Gary called home. Because that's what she wanted from him.

Or thought she did. Now, watching Gary's shoulders shudder as he buried his face again and wept, saying, "If I hadn't defied my mother and broken her heart, none of this would have happened," she wondered: Had she ever felt about him, about anyone, the way he had once felt about Amanda?

Definitely not.

Sydney stood up, as much to collect herself as to give Gary space with his grief. She cleared the dishes from the table, rinsed them, and put them in the dishwasher. Then she wiped the counter, which was already sparkling—the maids must have been here while she was in the Berkshires, she realized, and felt both guilty and relieved about this. She had never imagined herself as the sort of woman who would have maids. But she hated cleaning.

Gary wiped his face on a napkin and gave her a sheepish smile. "Boy, I really lost it. Sorry."

"You don't need to apologize. I understand. You miss her. You're still grieving for Amanda, Gary. Grief is a process that can take a long time. We all do it in our own ways. You're moving through the stages."

She was parroting the words and he knew it. Gary's face clouded. "Don't psychoanalyze me, Sydney. I'm not one of the children you see. I don't need you to take care of me."

That was the biggest lie either of them had told this morning, but Sydney nodded. "I know."

Gary swallowed hard, then narrowed his eyes. "What are you wearing? I've never seen that outfit."

Sydney looked down, confused. Her mother had brought an overnight bag to the hospital for herself and Dylan. This surprised Sydney; she'd never thought of Hannah as being especially organized. In the bag were two changes of clothing; her mother said she'd brought them because she didn't know how much time she'd have to spend at the hospital. She had given Sydney this blue flannel shirt and jeans, which were probably loose on Hannah but snug on Sydney.

Still, Sydney was grateful to have clean clothes after sleeping in that hospital recliner while her mother stretched out on the room's other bed, miraculously empty. She bristled a little at the expression on Gary's face. He wasn't quite wrinkling his nose, but almost. "These are Mom's clothes," she said. "I drove straight to the hospital from my birthday dinner in Boston. I didn't have time to come home and pack an overnight bag."

"So you'll be returning them to your mother after they're washed, I assume." The corner of Gary's mouth turned up in a half smile. "That's good. You look like you should be wielding a pitchfork. Especially with your hair down and all crazy like that."

Sydney ran a hand through her curls, self-conscious but also feeling annoyed with him now. "Some people like my hair down."

"Yes, but I love you more than they do, and I don't."

"I'm going up for a shower," Sydney said, wanting suddenly to be away from him. "Then I'm going over to visit Grammy Bishop, since I canceled my appointments for today and I never made it to see her for her birthday last weekend."

"I'm sure she'll be happy to see you." Gary was distracted, already multitasking, flipping intently through the stack of mail on the table. "I'm going to wait here and speak with Dylan when he gets up. Then I've got some things to catch up on in the office."

"You're going to the hospital?" Sydney was shocked; she had imagined them sitting down with Dylan this afternoon and talking through the events of the past few days. "Why? You weren't due back from your trip until Friday. You can't have any appointments scheduled."

"That's why I want to go in. The one upside of this whole thing is that now I have a little time to think about how to write up that paper and submit it."

"How long will you be there?"

"Just a few hours. What would you say to steaks for dinner? I can stop at Tendercrop and pick up a couple of rib eyes on my way home."

When Gary looked up at her, his face was bathed in the sunlight streaming in from the kitchen window. With every crease and wrinkle highlighted, the whites of his eyes shot through with red lines, and his face so thin that his cheekbones looked sharp, Sydney could easily imagine the outline of his skull beneath that thin layer of flesh. When she'd seen him for the first time, Sydney had thought Gary's face looked elegantly sculpted. Today he just looked old. Or was that only a reflection of the way she felt about him right now? She hoped so.

"Sounds great," she said. "I'll throw some baked potatoes in the oven."

"Don't bother with one for me," he said absently, patting his trim waist. "I had enough carbs in Amsterdam to last me a week."

On her way upstairs, Sydney thought about the time she'd flung herself into Gary's arms from the middle step and wrapped her arms and legs around him, nearly knocking him off-balance. He had come home early that day to surprise her with tickets to a show and an armful of flowers. Only a year ago. Seemed like forever.

She hated feeling so separate from him. This should be a joyful time in their lives, these last months leading up to the wedding. Well, never mind, she told herself. Gary couldn't help being testy and distracted. He had so much on his mind.

And so do you, she reminded herself, remembering Valerie and their meeting on Friday.

CHAPTER TWELVE

"A meatless meal to pay penance for our bloody crime," Liz said, making Hannah laugh, though she still felt wobbly after giving each lamb one last good-bye pat on the head.

It was two days after Dylan's accident, and Liz had taken the day off from school to help Hannah truck the rams—all except Casper, left behind to peacefully munch hay in a stall next to the llama's because of his splinted leg—to the broker in Vermont. The broker's farm was on the outskirts of Burlington, Vermont, where surprisingly robust communities of Africans and Eastern Europeans created a brisk demand for lamb meat.

They left right after morning barn chores and made the trip in less than three hours. Both of them were starving by the time they dropped off the lambs, so they drove straight to their favorite vegetarian restaurant in Burlington and ordered grilled cheese and tomato sandwiches on thick homemade wheat bread.

Hannah might as well have been eating sawdust. She was still feeling bad about dropping the lambs off to be butchered—she went through this every year, but it didn't get any easier—and she was worried about Dylan. No word from Sydney, but that was no surprise. Sydney seldom called and she had a lot on her plate right now. Hannah had tried calling

Dylan's cell number twice—she discovered it still on her own phone from the night Dylan had called to have her pick him up when he was hitchhiking—but he wasn't answering. Maybe Gary had carried through on his threat to ban all of Dylan's electronic devices and now the poor kid was cut off from his friends.

Not that he seemed to have many.

Hannah took another bite of sandwich and chewed too fast, biting the inside of her cheek in her hurry to banish this surprising surge of mother worry, something she'd never expected to experience again after Sydney reached adulthood. But motherhood was a chronic illness, like arthritis or Lyme disease: it could flare up and debilitate you when you least expected.

For instance, one look at Sydney curled up in that hospital chair, her ropes of blond hair in a tangled mess around her shoulders like some crazy sea creature, had brought such a gut punch of emotion that Hannah had to turn away. Now she was fretting over Dylan.

So pointless! Dylan wasn't even her own blood. Who knew if Sydney would even stay with Gary? Dylan might vanish from Sydney's life and from Hannah's, too. That's how it was with relationships these days.

The weather had turned warm enough that she and Liz wrapped their sweatshirts around their waists after lunch as they hiked down to Lake Champlain's shoreline. Burlington, home of the University of Vermont, was buzzing with angsty teenagers and twentysomethings zipping around on skateboards and bikes, passing joints in the park, tossing Frisbees, or bouncing Hacky Sacks on their knees. Sunbathers were stretched out on towels anywhere there was grass and sometimes even in places where it was just cement.

Hannah could remember doing the same her freshman year of college. Her dorm room at UMass had a window that opened onto a flat roof; the dorm residents had cut through her room to climb out the window and sunbathe. She'd felt like she was melting into the tar beneath her, but she didn't care.

Dope, sex, music blasting from windows and cars and boom boxes:

that was the early seventies. That small window of time when sex wouldn't kill you and most of her friends happily hallucinated on mushrooms, sped around on cocaine, or tripped on acid without worrying about dying. Nixon had been booted from office the August before she started college, and soon after that, President Ford announced clemency for draft dodgers in exchange for two years of community service. The world seemed like it might finally be righting itself on its axis. College students felt powerful because they'd forced the government to respond to protests about civil rights and Vietnam, even coed bathrooms in the dorms.

Then Allen came home from war and it was as if he'd brought the blackness and terror of it back with him.

Looking at the youth spread around her in Burlington made Hannah mourn that lost time, her perky braless boobs and music with a message, not all this electronic crap with the ominous thudding bass lines. More than that, she missed the hope and power she'd felt as a young woman.

Now, at fifty-nine, she felt old. Sometimes she felt hopeful about the future, but more often than not, she suspected things would just keep getting harder: the climate, the economy, the terrorizing of women around the world, more wars ahead. Harder not just for herself, but for everyone.

She and Liz passed a lanky boy in blue jeans and a black T-shirt strumming a banjo; his long hair was gathered with a strip of rawhide and hung over one shoulder, reminding her of Rory. Of the three of them—Allen, herself, and Rory—Rory was always the optimist, the one with the biggest heart. She thought again of his last note to her, gathering dust in his guitar for so many years. What did he mean, keep her safe from the truth? What truth? How could he possibly think her life would be better if he wasn't in it?

There was nothing in that note to indicate where he had gone, or if he had ended his life. She shuddered, imagining again that deliberate leap into San Francisco's unforgiving bay, because Rory never would have fallen.

"Why do you stay here?" she'd asked Rory during one particularly bad night on the farm, a night when Rory had to run after Allen and bodily tackle him to the ground, because Allen had seen the red sun hovering over the low-lying hills and been convinced they were the mountains dividing Vietnam from Laos.

Allen had started babbling, something about his bloodied flak jacket and a guy named Steve. Then he began running toward the cornfield, shouting, "Check the tree line for kills and weapons! Come on!"

Rory had been sitting on the back porch playing his guitar when he saw Hannah chasing Allen, trying to stop him from hurting himself or someone else. Rory outran her and brought Allen down with a thump and a curse. By the time she reached them, Allen was lying on the ground, sobbing quietly, and Rory was sitting several yards away from him, his lip split and bleeding.

"How could I leave?" Rory had asked in response.

"What do you mean?" Hannah sat down on the cooling, fragrant dirt beside him. "You get to leave any time. I married him. I chose this life. You're free to go."

She'd been angry, saying that. That night was the start of her realization that she was truly pissed off at everyone: at Allen, at herself, at everyone on the farm who made her life difficult. Especially the people who came and went, treating the farm like a summer camp: Lucy, Josh, Donna, Keith, Noah, Sandra, Adair. The list was endless. An infinite line of people with their hands out and their mouths open. Sometimes Hannah pictured the transients of Haven Lake as baby birds, stretching their necks, mouths opened wide, peeping in desperation: *Feed my need.*

"He's my brother," Rory had said simply.

Allen was still sitting where Rory had left him, arms wrapped around his knees, rocking a little. Humming. He did that sometimes to comfort himself. Hannah never did figure out the tune, but it was always the same.

"Lots of people have brothers," Hannah said. "That doesn't mean they have to live with them. Really, Rory. I want to know why you're still here."

What had she wanted Rory to say? That he was staying for her? He couldn't—wouldn't—do that. Rory was too good. Too ethical. Despite the frequent couple swapping at Haven Lake, Rory rarely even touched her. Not that she would have let him anyway. They both knew that would destroy Allen.

Rory had cocked his head so that his long brown hair, shot through with copper highlights, spilled around one shoulder. "Allen never told you, did he?"

"Told me what?"

And that was the night she'd found out: attorney Ron Bishop, father of Rory and Allen, husband to Georgia Bishop of the garden club, longtime resident and selectman of Ipswich, was a bastard. The kind of bastard who beat his boys in the basement with a belt or a two-by-four while his wife cleaned the kitchen upstairs, pretending to be oblivious to their screams.

"Dad always said he did it to make men out of us," Rory said.

"Oh, God, Rory," Hannah had said, tears streaming down her face, flinging a terrified glance at Allen, afraid he'd overhear them whispering. No. He was quiet now, staring up at the stars in his usual postrage trance. "But I still don't understand why that would make you stay here now."

Rory sighed and stretched his long body out on the dirt beside her, crossing his arms behind his head and relaxing after he, too, had done an automatic check of Allen's position and mood. "Allen was there for me as a kid. Always. I was younger and smaller than he was, so he would step between Dad and me and say *he* was the one who'd done whatever Dad was beating me for. Then Dad would start wailing away at Allen and forget all about me. The weird thing was that it made Dad love him so much more, because Allen 'took it like a man.' And you know what's really fucked up? Even though I was glad Dad left me alone, I was jealous, too, because Dad clearly loved Allen more than me."

"But that's sick, Rory. Why didn't your mom do anything?"

"She pretended not to know. She made it her business to never go down those basement stairs when Dad was 'disciplining' us."

Rory fell silent. His shoulders were so broad and his arms were so muscled in his faded green T-shirt that Hannah couldn't help herself: she lay down beside him the way she used to when they were teenagers counting stars while everyone around them was getting high and making out, and rested her head on his shoulder. Just for a few minutes, she pressed her body against his to comfort him. To be comforted.

She'd completely forgotten about Liz walking beside her, until Liz suddenly stopped abruptly and said, "God. Look at those girls over there. Did you ever wear a bikini like that?" She pointed to a trio on the grass, their breasts and buttocks plump and glistening golden brown, like fresh dinner rolls just buttered.

"Every chance I got," Hannah said. "My favorite was a white halter top. I wore that suit everywhere, even pumping gas at my dad's station."

"Me, too, even though I never had the body for it," Liz said. "It's hardly seventy degrees. You'd think those girls would be cold, but I guess they have to bare their flesh while they can. It's been a brutal winter and they know summer lasts about ten seconds in Vermont."

Hannah was scarcely listening. She'd spotted a boat on the lake and was thinking about that white bikini and how she'd worn it canoeing on the Ipswich River with Rory and Allen the last time the three of them were together in 1972, the summer Allen went to Vietnam after high school graduation.

"Can't wait to catch me a monkey. It's gonna be all jungle, all the time, boys and girls," Allen said, leaning back in the canoe while Hannah paddled and Rory played his guitar. "Just me huntin' down the Commies like squirrels and keeping you safe."

Rory had laughed. "Come on, Al. You don't seriously believe the North Vietnamese are going to attack the U.S. That's such bullshit."

"Don't laugh," Allen had said, pointing at Hannah.

"I'm not." She pressed her lips together to keep from giggling. Like Rory, she thought the idea of the North Vietnamese somehow toppling their neighboring countries and making it as far as the U.S. was absurd. She was facing Allen, who was rowing, aware of his eyes on her breasts in the bikini top, of the heat beneath the small triangle of fabric between her legs.

"You know the Soviets are equipping them, man," Allen said. "I'm fighting for you, Hannah. And for you, too, dickhead, so the Commies won't rule the world."

"The domino theory?" Rory challenged. "Really, that old song? Again, the shit of the bull."

Allen chugged the rest of his beer and tossed the can onto the riverbank, where it rolled into the brackish water. "The Commies take Southeast Asia, they'll be swimming up the Ipswich River soon enough. Anyway, don't believe me. I don't care. You'll get to see how it all goes down for yourself, little brother. The army's got your number. What'cha gonna do if they come for you?"

In answer, Rory broke out Phil Ochs's "Draft Dodger Rag" on his guitar, then moved right into "I Ain't Marching Anymore" even when Allen threatened to throw him and the guitar into the river.

Rory's number hadn't come up, though. He'd gotten lucky in the lottery.

She and Liz reached the lake and sat cross-legged on the grass. There was a frothy white chop on the water created by the breeze. Sailboats flitted back and forth like butterflies on the vast blue expanse of Lake Champlain. It wasn't the ocean, they agreed, but it was something.

"So listen, Cate wants to meet you," Liz said, nudging Hannah's shoulder.

"Uh-oh. Things are getting serious, huh?"

Liz didn't answer. Her gray hair had grown out enough for it to ruffle in the breeze, and her tattoos stood out against the sleeves of her bright purple T-shirt. She wore overalls and her usual bright sneakers. This pair was red.

Hannah studied her fondly, imagining Liz as a child wearing a similar getup, and said, "You've got it bad, darlin'."

Liz covered her face with her hands and said in a muffled voice, "Jesus Christ. I'm too old for this."

Hannah laughed and put an arm around Liz's waist, pulled her close. "Too old for what? For falling in love? Even people in nursing homes fall in love. That's what humans do. Nobody's immune."

"You seem to be." Liz dropped her hands. "So will you come to dinner and meet Cate?"

"I'd be honored," Hannah said.

"There's one more thing."

"Anything. You trucked my lambs to slaughter and gave me a car. Whatever you want, it's yours."

Liz smirked, her brown eyes bright in her elfin face. "Cate has a brother."

Hannah pulled away. "Shit, no. Not that."

"Come on. All you have to do is be civil to the guy. We're not expecting you to fall in love. We know that's unlikely. Though, as you point out, nobody's immune to the possibility of love, right?" Liz's voice was hopeful.

"If anybody is, it's me," Hannah said glumly.

Now it was Liz's turn to study her. "Why?"

Hannah shrugged. "Been there. Done that."

"Yes, but it's more than that, isn't it? I mean, you were dating for a while."

"When I was drinking," Hannah said. "Dating and drinking just seem to go together. Kind of like matches and kerosene."

Liz didn't laugh. "What happened?"

Hannah studied the water. One of the sailboats was heeling low, dangerously close to the water. The lone sailor in the boat leaned to the opposite side, his entire body nearly out of the boat as he struggled to counteract the wind. That's how she felt right now: in danger of losing all control. Then she thought of Dylan, of whatever was coiled up inside his body, of how hard Dylan was fighting to contain his memories and emotions. Like Allen, in a way. Sydney, too. She didn't want that for herself.

"It wasn't anything, really," she began, then realized, no, that was a lie: it was something. Something awful. She started again. "Something horrible happened a couple of years back. I'm over it now."

"No, you're not," Liz said at once, turning to face Hannah, her arms crossed like a playground bully's. "If you were, you would have told me about it."

"I'm telling you now," Hannah said. "Ergo, I must be over it."

"Ergo?" Liz snorted. She pulled the truck keys out of her jeans pocket. "Ergo, I go, so you might as well tell me right now, ergo you can hitch home."

Hannah sighed and glanced around. There was no one close enough to hear them. "There was this guy I saw a couple of times, Les Phillips."

Liz frowned. "I don't remember him."

"No, you wouldn't. I met him in a coffee shop in Amherst. We started talking, and I went out to dinner with him. He seemed like a real sad sack. I wasn't going to see him again, but he kept calling me." Hannah had to stop here to close her eyes and take a deep breath.

She opened her eyes again immediately, not wanting to picture Les's face as it had looked when he was fucking her, or how smug he'd been when he saw her at the co-op.

"So you saw him again?"

Liz's voice was gentle, but Hannah could hear the dread in it. Hannah tracked the sailboat she'd been watching and was relieved to see that it was under control, no more at an angle than any of the others, the sailor safely back in his boat. She could do this.

"I did," she said. "I went to his house, fool that I am. I wanted to be friends, just that, and I thought the conversation might go better in person. We had drinks first, a lot of drinks, and then, well. I got drunk. I think he might have spiked my drink, but the bottom line is that I went to his house, got drunk, and got stupid."

"He raped you, didn't he?"

Again, Liz's voice was soft, but laced with an icy undertone. She was seeing it all unfold, had perhaps been in the same circumstances. A date rape, an assault in an alley, a boss, an uncle, a professor: every woman had stories.

Hannah's story was this: she'd gone to Les's house because he'd wanted to cook for her. It was an undistinguished red ranch in a university neighborhood of houses just like it. She had protested when Les took her hand to lead her to the bedroom, but it didn't matter. He half carried, half dragged her into one of the back bedrooms, a paneled room with an orange-and-brown quilt that would have spruced up a roadside motel, maybe, but looked absurd in a real house. Les had turned angry and mean.

"You can quit protesting," he'd hissed in her ear. "I know why you came here. Women don't like to admit it when they're horny, but I could tell it from the moment I laid eyes on you that you just need a man to tell you what to do in bed." Then he'd forced her facedown onto that ugly quilt.

Hannah had tried bucking him off, but Les was too heavy and her limbs were weak from the alcohol and fright and who knows what drug. The room was spinning like a carnival ride and she was afraid she might puke. That would fix him, she thought.

She thought about screaming, but who would hear? And who would believe her story anyway? She'd come here willingly in her own car. He'd made her dinner. They were both adult and single, and she was definitely old enough to know better. Besides, Hannah knew there were still people around who remembered the community at Haven Lake as a bunch of blissed-out hippies into free love. Who would believe her word against his?

And so she'd given up. She must have blacked out, because at some point she woke up with her face pressed against the awful quilt, the fibers in it sharp as fingernails against her cheek, and she was naked. Les was gone.

"He did," Hannah said, and held up her hand as Liz started sputtering in outrage. "Before you ask why I didn't report it—"

"I wasn't! I was going to call him names and tell you I want to string him up by his filthy balls! But, okay. Why didn't you report it? Or at least tell me about it? I could have set his house on fire."

Hannah laughed despite the hollow pit in her stomach. "Because I felt like such an idiot," she said. "You would have believed me, but I certainly didn't want you to get involved. And who else would have taken me seriously? Me, the hippie shepherdess whose husband went nuts and killed himself?"

"Hannah, that was twenty years ago!" Liz protested.

"People have long memories, especially in the Berkshires," Hannah said. "Anyway, now you know."

"You could still file a report with the police. Maybe protect some other poor woman."

"It was a long time ago, and there never would have been enough evidence to convict him even then. The one good thing it did was make me stop drinking and hooking up."

Liz put her arms around Hannah and pulled her close. "That is good," she agreed. "Though I bet some of that was fun."

Hannah smiled. "A lot of it was fun."

"Good. Then you'll come to dinner and meet Cate's brother," Liz said.

"I'll come to dinner and meet Cate," Hannah said, "and I'll be my most charming self with anyone else who happens to be at the table. Even her brother."

For her belated birthday lunch, Grammy picked the Clam Shack, a white cube of a restaurant on Route 1A in Essex just south of Ipswich, where Grammy lived alone now in the big house. Sydney had asked why she didn't move to something smaller after Grandpa Bishop died, but Grammy shrugged and said, "Allen and Rory are still here." She'd preserved their rooms just as they were in high school.

On summer weekends, the line out the door could be fifty people deep at the Clam Shack despite the picnic tables accommodating overflow diners on a deck above the river, where if the greenheads didn't eat you alive, the marsh mosquitoes would carry you away. Grammy never sat outside; she'd rather eat in the car if it came to that. She wasn't about to battle insects. At eighty-four, she still dyed her hair blond and was proud of her well-guarded, powdery complexion.

Sydney guided her grandmother carefully through the nearly empty restaurant to the prime half-dozen tables by the windows overlooking the Essex River. The tide was out; the riverbank mud was a rich chocolate and thatched with bright green grass. A great blue heron stood in one of the inlets slicing through the marsh, feathers glinting bright and metallic in the sun, as if the bird wore a suit of armor.

Grammy had had a stroke soon after Grandpa Bishop died and still suffered weakness on her left side that caused her to rely on a cane. Sydney walked behind her, alarmed by the older woman's shaky progress and keeping both hands ready in case Grammy fell. It hurt to see this; her grandmother had always been athletic, playing competitive tennis well into her late seventies.

When their number was called, Sydney went to the counter for their food, loading up the tray with salt, lemons, and tartar sauce. Her grandmother had ordered her usual fried clams and French fries; Sydney chose scallops with onion rings.

"You missed my birthday," Grammy announced once they were eating. "I suppose you were busy as usual."

That was the thing about her grandmother that Sydney found both irritating and endearing: she never minced words when you displeased her. "Yes, I know. I'm so sorry," Sydney said. "I had to drive out to the Berkshires that day."

At this, Grammy glanced up, her pale blue eyes sharp. "To see your mother?"

Sydney nodded, watching Grammy dunk a French fry into her miniature fluted paper cup of ketchup before putting it between her trembling lips. She wondered how much to say about what was going on. She didn't want to worry her about Dylan.

Oh, who was she kidding? Sydney ate another scallop. She was more afraid of having Grammy turn against Dylan than worry about him. Grammy was a black-and-white sort of woman. You were either right, meaning you agreed with her, or wrong. So far Gary had ranked high on Grammy's approval rating because he was a doctor, wore suits to work, and had given her an expensive bracelet for Christmas.

Gary was "a catch," Grammy said, and his son was "polite and civilized." This last was based on the fact that Dylan knew enough to put a napkin on his lap during dinner and seldom spoke.

"It's been a good long while since you've been out to the farm," Grammy was saying, smoothing out the paper napkin she'd tucked into her shirtfront. "Twenty years, is it?"

"Yes." Sydney was sure her grandmother knew exactly how long it had been, probably to the minute. Surely she hadn't forgotten the day she arrived at Haven Lake to find Hannah passed out on the sofa at three o'clock in the afternoon, and Sydney trying to put a brave face on things by making lunch and boxing up her father's few belongings and her uncle's, too, for Grammy to bring back to Ipswich.

"How time flies," Grammy said. "What was the occasion for your visit?"

Sydney squeezed more lemon onto her scallops, wondering about how much to tell her. "Dylan was staying with Mom for a few days. We went out there to see him."

"Whatever for?" Her grandmother looked up again, plastic fork poised to spear another clam.

"A project for school." She was surprised by how the lie rolled off her tongue, but she felt fiercely protective of Dylan. "He's back home now."

"Oh, honestly. What could Gary's son possibly learn on that filthy farm? Your mother could only be a bad influence. Well. I don't have to tell you that, do I?"

"Mom's better now. She's sober and working hard. And Dylan's sixteen. Old enough not to be so impressionable."

"Oh, you'd be surprised. My Allen was about Dylan's age when he met your mother. She made a big impression on him, all right." Grammy's face darkened. "Her in those tight blue jeans and no bra. And that god-awful Greek hair! I don't think she ever brushed it. Hannah was no lady. I'd wager she's not much different now. And there's nothing worse than an old flower child. Thank God I could intervene with you. You'd be on welfare otherwise."

Sydney might have reacted badly to this, except she'd heard this kind of rant from her grandmother many times. When she was younger, she had been grateful to have a clean bed and an orderly house; she'd loved attending a real high school and having structure to her days, nice clothes, and a car of her own. Her grandparents took her to the country club and taught her to play tennis. They doted on her, really; having never had a daughter of their own, they spoiled her with trips to the mall and manicures.

She had missed her father, but not his rages; she missed her mother, too, but was grateful not to have to cope with her weepy breakdowns and boozy breath, and told herself she was better off in Ipswich until she was old enough to live on her own.

Her mother had only attempted to bring her back to Haven Lake once. She came to Ipswich straight from some rehab clinic to pick her up, but Sydney refused to even come downstairs. Then there was a standoff between her grandparents and her mother that lasted until the police showed up and threatened to handcuff her mother if she didn't leave the property.

Sydney had hidden her head under a pillow as her mother drove away with a spray of gravel she could hear beneath her bedroom window, the blue lights of the police car flashing in the driveway. She sat up when she heard the low voice of the police chief, a friend of her grandfather's, advising the Bishops about what to do if Hannah came back. "I'd suggest a restraining order," the chief said. "And you have good grounds to go after custody if she's that unstable."

"And what about assault and battery with a dangerous weapon?" Grammy had demanded. "That crazy woman slapped my husband. You see that mark there? That's from her car keys! She slapped my husband with keys in her *hand*! That woman should be locked up!"

As the months and years went by, Sydney began to see the chinks in her grandparents' relationship—the way they seldom spoke even at breakfast, when it was only the three of them, and how her grandmother went to bed at seven o'clock while her grandfather played cards with a group of men down the street or tinkered in the basement. But for her, the fact that their routines never varied was a blessing. She no longer had to worry about taking care of herself because these quiet adults were in charge.

Her mother, meanwhile, had abandoned her. They never spoke, except for the occasional Christmas or Easter, where Hannah would go to Grandpa Leo's, and Sydney would join them for dessert after first eating with the Bishops. Then the conversation was formal and perfunctory: How were her classes? Had she finished her college applications?

Once she was in college in a different state, there was no reason for her to see Hannah at all, and it would have been difficult anyway without a car. Meanwhile, Sydney tried to imagine her own future as a happy one. Married with children, certainly. Not on a farm, with drifters and would-be farmers, and not in a buttoned-up New England house with two elderly people who seldom spoke to each other, but in a small house with a garden and a dog. Her own vision of this home was embarrassingly like the idealistic crayoned pictures her young clients did in her office, all of them with picket fences and a single apple tree, smiling suns blazing yellow in one corner of the page.

"Did you always hate my mother so much?" she asked her grandmother now. "Or did she do something wrong that made you feel that way about her?"

"Hannah was just a child, so it's probably unfair to say I hated her. But I knew the minute I laid eyes on her that she wasn't our kind of people. Greek, as you know. They do things differently." Grammy waved a gnarled hand, dismissing the entire culture. "Your grandfather Leo was a decent sort of man, not educated, but very helpful at the garage. Though he never should have let his daughter pump gas. What was he thinking? Especially when she wore next to nothing all summer! 'Dressed in grease and not much else,' your grandpa Bishop used to say about your mother. Not that he minded getting an eyeful himself. Men can't help themselves when it's on offer like that. We warned the boys off your mother, of course, after that first time Rory brought Hannah home, but boys can't help themselves once they sniff out an easy girl."

"Careful, Grammy," Sydney reminded her, appalled by the sudden vitriol in her grandmother's voice. "This is my mom you're talking about."

"I'm sorry if you find that offensive, but I'm not telling you anything new, am I? Boys lose their minds and just follow their noses when they're on the trail. Speaking of smell, does your mother still have all those stinky goats?"

"Sheep. Mom raises Icelandic sheep now."

"At least she finally got rid of all those stinky people."

Sydney couldn't help it; she laughed. "You're right. There *were* a lot of stinky people on the farm," she said, then waited, curious to see what her grandmother might say next. Usually she pretended the past never existed.

Her husband, for instance: Grammy spoke of Grandpa Bishop infrequently, but always in glowing terms. His fine cars. His table manners. His waltzing. His family money, which had originated with textile mills and been gradually woven into politics, banking, and real estate across Massachusetts.

Grammy Bishop was eating another clam, dipping it into her little plastic tub of tartar sauce before conveying it to her mouth. The old woman chewed with such obvious delight that Sydney had to turn her head away. Too intimate, all of that sucking and dripping. Like watching someone else have sex.

After she'd swallowed, Grammy geared herself up to speak again, straightening her skinny shoulders in their layers of scarf, blue sweater, and white polo shirt worn against the chill of any weather under eighty-five degrees. "It wouldn't have been so bad, you know, if your mother had married Rory. Rory was a dreamer. Hopeless from the start. You couldn't tell that boy anything." She said this fondly, dabbing tartar sauce off her chin with a napkin. "Your grandfather and I both agreed that if things went on between him and your mother, we wouldn't bother putting a stop to it. Rory wasn't going to amount to much anyway."

Hearing her grandmother say this about Rory was an unpleasant echo of Sydney's earlier argument with Gary about Dylan. What caused parents to give up on their children?

Her grandmother was still talking. "I know I sometimes sound harsh when it comes to your mother, Sydney, but you should know that I, for one, never believed for one second that Hannah was trying to trap Allen into marriage," she said. "Hannah was never a schemer like some girls. She just didn't understand how easy it was for men to lose their heads over her."

Sydney tried to recall what her mother had told her about her wedding day. She'd been under the impression that Grammy Bishop had thrown a fit.

"Your grandfather, though, was convinced Hannah was after the family money," Grammy said. "Oh, that man was beside himself at the wedding! He didn't want Allen signing up for the army, either, but Ron thought that would make a better man of Allen, said the army turns boys into men faster than anything else. I didn't want Allen to go, of course, but we were both sure he would finish college when he came home from Vietnam and take over the law practice, make something of himself. Then Hannah came along."

"Come on. You can't blame everything on Mom."

"Oh, but I do." Grammy Bishop shook her head so hard that the white curls unwound. "Hannah was the ruin of our family. It was one thing for Allen to agree to travel with her—I'm sure he was doing the gentlemanly thing, knowing she'd be safer in male company—but he never should have agreed to marry her and stick around once she was pregnant. We would have been happy to help with her support. Those two absolutely weren't ready for children. They were just children themselves, and him so soon back from the war. That was the beginning of the end for Allen: your mother talking him into traveling to those godforsaken parts of the world instead of staying in school."

"Mom always told me it was Dad's idea to drop out of school and travel."

"Lord, no. That was just Hannah's way of isolating Allen from us." Grammy Bishop leaned forward to add, "It was spousal abuse, is what it was."

"But Dad only hit her when he was hallucinating or freaking out. He was suffering from post-traumatic stress disorder. I know that now. He should have had therapy. Medication, too, probably."

"Your generation puts too much stock in pills." Grammy raised her penciled eyebrows, thin brown seams arching over her eyeglasses. "I don't know anything about your father hitting anybody. That doesn't sound like Allen. No, I mean it was the other way around, dear. Hannah isolated Allen deliberately out there in the mountains after the war. We hardly saw our own sons once she convinced Allen to buy that farm."

"Who? Mom?" Sydney was thoroughly confused now. Her father always talked about how he'd been the one to stumble on Haven Lake during a solo hike through the Berkshires.

"Yes! Your mother wanted that farm in the worst way. Allen bought it with his trust fund just to keep her happy. He would have done anything for her. If your father did hit her, she must have given him a reason."

Sydney felt the color drain from her face. "That's a horrible thing to say!"

"I'm sorry if that's hard for you to hear, but it's the truth." Grammy Bishop laid her soft knotted fingers over Sydney's wrist. "You were too young to understand that relationship. If your mother had been different, maybe acted more like a real wife and kept a normal house, your father would probably still be alive today. She was always provoking him into a foul temper. I saw it happen once when they visited. Poor boy felt like he couldn't do anything to make her happy. That's why he shot himself. If it weren't for your mother, my Allen could be celebrating my birthday with us right now. Enjoying these delicious clams." Tears ran down the crevices of her papery cheeks and she patted them dry with a napkin.

There were a million reasons to argue with her grandmother. But, when faced with an old woman who was hunched and weeping—Grammy, who had given her sanctuary when she needed it most—Sydney couldn't bring herself to do it. Fortunately, her grandmother recovered after a few minutes and went on to talk about her bridge club, describing the clever ploys she used to handle her partner's failing memory during tournaments. They finished eating and Sydney drove her home, taking her time on 1A because she knew Grammy liked seeing the marshes, the houses, and the gardens now that she could no longer drive herself and had to rely on a woman who came to the house to run her on errands and to doctors' appointments.

In the driveway of her grandmother's stately Colonial, Sydney parked the car and helped Grammy Bishop lever herself off the passenger seat. She handed her the cane and trailed her closely up the brick walkway so she could catch her grandmother if she fell. They made slow and steady progress, Grammy pointing out the new flowers coming up in her garden and lamenting her neighbor's habit of composting leaves and brush along the fence separating their yards.

"You know, compost piles can spontaneously combust," Grammy complained. "You can't ever be too careful about fire. Well, I don't have to tell you about fires, after that farm of yours nearly burned to the ground. It must have been terrifying to lose everything like that."

Startled, Sydney hastened her stride to get to the front steps before her grandmother, where she opened the screen door and held it wide while Grammy fished in her suitcase of a beige handbag for the house key. "What do you mean? The only fire we ever had was in that little barn. There was nothing much in there."

Grammy leaned on her cane as she stepped up over the threshold. "Surely you remember, child? It wasn't just the barn that burned. It was everything in it. All of my son's possessions! Allen's tools and papers were in that barn, your mother said. Even his high school trophies. Everything but his clothes. All gone now." She sighed and began her slow progress through the front door, clasping the threshold with one hand and her cane in the other.

Sydney had no idea if that was even true. Had her mother purposefully piled her father's belongings in that barn and then set fire to the whole lot? The thing was, she could imagine Hannah doing this, as a sort of last good-bye ritual, a private memorial between herself, her husband, and the sky. She shuddered, remembering her father's brown eyes gleaming with intelligence, as unmistakable as a ray of light shining beneath a door.

"Thank you for making time to have lunch with me," she managed, her throat tight with loss, new questions thick as bread in her mouth.

"Oh, no. I should thank you," Grammy said. She swiveled on her cane to kiss Sydney's cheek. "Whatever else I may have lost, I'm grateful for you, my girl," she said, and gently closed the door behind her, leaving a whiff of lemon.

On the way back to Gary's, Sydney turned off 1A down the road to her house in Newbury, rationalizing that it was on the way and still early. Inside the cottage, she stripped off her clothes, which reeked of fish, and showered the grease off her skin. She washed her hair twice but still imagined she could smell fish, so she washed it again and applied a rosemary mint conditioner. That did the trick.

She towel-dried her hair and sat at the kitchen table in her robe, sipping a glass of iced tea while listening to her messages. It was a relief to have a few blissful minutes to herself.

Not that the messages were restful. Three clients had called, desperate for appointments because the school year was drawing to a close. But it was the final voice mail that made Sydney's pulse rate jump.

"Dr. Bishop, this is Barbara Shield from Eastern Shores, your listing agent." Her Realtor's voice sounded crisp, smugly pleased. "I'm calling because we've had a solid offer on your home. Please get back to me at your earliest convenience so we can go over the terms."

Sydney deleted the message and looked around at her kitchen wallpaper with its colorful birds. She didn't want to give up her cottage. She wasn't ready to live with Gary full-time. Hell, maybe she wasn't even ready to marry him.

There. She'd let herself think those awful, disloyal thoughts. She was experiencing prewedding jitters. That was normal, right?

Now she'd better go to Gary's and let him know about the offer. He'd be thrilled; Gary had been pushing her to move in with him before the wedding.

But not just yet. First she had to smell the sea. Sydney slipped on a pair of ragged sweatpants and a T-shirt. She left the house in bare feet despite the late afternoon chill.

She walked down the grassy path behind her property to the edge of the marsh, breathing in the tingling salt air. In the glistening pools among the whispering marsh grasses stood white egrets, arrow-sharp against the blue sky. There was a rookery just to the left of her backyard and egrets were starting to gather in the trees. The first time she'd seen them there, she'd thought they were plastic bags blown into the branches by the wind.

Redwing blackbirds buzzed from their waving cattail perches. Sydney closed her eyes, feeling her limbs and neck relax. It was all she could do to hold her head up straight; she could almost fall asleep standing here, locking her legs in place like a horse.

She wondered if Hannah felt this same sense of peace at Haven Lake. She must, as she stood out on the hill behind the house. Hannah would watch the bobolinks and hear their irrepressibly gleeful songs. She'd listen to the wind in the pines sigh across the valley and feel, as Sydney did right now, like she was one with the land.

Sydney curled her toes into the cool mud and lifted her damp hair off her neck to let the breeze dry her skin beneath it. She thought about the night she and Theo and Valerie had sneaked down to the pond and found a party in progress. She and Theo were thirteen, so Valerie must have been fourteen. They'd hidden behind the pines to watch the adults tripping on acid, gathered around the water for some pagan ritual led by one of the newest women to arrive that summer, a ritual that involved sound healing with Tibetan bowls and a baptism in the pond.

The people of Haven Lake had gathered with guitars and drums and wooden flutes. They were dancing naked around a bonfire, having shed their clothes to go "acid dipping," as they called it when they swam while tripping. Some were in the water already, floating on their backs. The women's pale breasts reflected the moonlight, flat and shining like giant coins as the women lay faceup in the black water beneath the plum-colored sky. The men standing on the beach were reduced to children again, their penises small knots of harmless dangling flesh as they gathered around the Tibetan bowls, alternating between "om" and giggling or weeping, depending on how the acid hit.

Sydney had watched with Valerie and Theo from the edge of the woods, entranced. She could easily imagine how her own body might dissolve into the black water studded with its starry reflections, like sinking into a jeweled blanket.

And then her mother saw them standing at the edge of the pond. She came out of the lake, slashing at the water as if her arms were knives, and pulled a long shapeless dress on over her head as she hurried to the edge of the woods, waving her arms at Sydney and Valerie and Theo as if she could scatter them like pigeons, shouting, "You kids get back to the house and go to bed!"

The other adults tried to call Hannah back into the water. Several followed her, emerging from the pond with sinewy bodies dripping with weeds. "Let the children be true night creatures," one man suggested. "I got a few tabs left."

"Yeah, man, the kids need an acid dip, too," another suggested from somewhere near the dock, a woman's voice, disembodied and slow. "The water's like molasses. So sweet and slow. Let them feel the sugar."

"They're teenagers, man," Josh called out, his voice blurry. "Time for them to get down with us big kids and feel the magic."

Sydney had crept forward, hearing this, with Theo and Valerie beside her. Sydney pulled off her rainbow tam, releasing her snarled yellow hair. Then she started tugging off her top, pleased to be included. It was no big deal. She'd been skinny-dipping in Haven Lake all her life, with anyone and everyone. But this time Hannah rushed at her like a linebacker, scolding and shaming, telling her to keep her clothes on and go to bed.

There was a shocked silence around the pond. Shaming was against the rules at Haven Lake. It said so right in their community manifesto, posted in the kitchen in purple ink:

Be Here, Be You, Right Now
Peace, Harmony, and Understanding for All Kinds
Live the Life You Always Imagined
No Guilt Trips
Question Authority
Question Yourself Most of All
Live with Love, Not Shame

Hannah didn't seem to care. She took Sydney by one arm and started to grab Theo and Valerie, too. But Lucy intervened, emerging from the purple dark near the dock as if she were a shadow creature come to life, like the wayang puppets Millie had brought from Bali.

"Theo and Val, come to Mama, my precious babies," Lucy had purred, beckoning them into the water, her slick, pale body no bigger than theirs. "Josh is right. It's time for you to feel the magic."

Hannah had let the other children go, but marched Sydney up to the house, her black hair ropey and her cheeks ablaze with color, her profile as fierce as a hawk's. Sydney had been frightened but furious at her mother for days. Now, though, she was shocked to remember this incident and see it in a different way.

Her mother had been trying to protect her that night: from drugs, from having sex too young, perhaps even from seeing her father with other women. It must have taken courage for Hannah to ignore the others and take her daughter up to the house, where she pretended Sydney wasn't having a stomping tantrum and made her a cup of hot chocolate laced with mint. Afterward Hannah lay down with her until Sydney, bewildered by her mother's sudden intense attention, had no choice but to fall asleep.

What else would she remember differently, if she let herself? Sydney wondered, as she hurried back to the cottage, pinned her hair up in its usual twist, dressed in slacks and a blouse, and filled her bag with clean clothes. Then she drove to Gary's house to see how he was managing with Dylan.

Gary wasn't there. He'd left a note saying he was at the hospital. Sydney went upstairs to see if Dylan was awake. She found him lying in bed but dressed in jeans and a *Star Wars* T-shirt, stretched out on top of the blanket. His hands were folded over his concave chest as if he were lying in a coffin.

"Hey. Did you see your dad?" she asked.

"Yeah. We talked. That's what you want to know, right?"

"That, yes, but I also wanted to ask how you're feeling."

"Okay."

She doubted that. Dylan's expression was bleak and his blue eyes were dark hollows in his pale face, which bloomed like a wilted yellow rose over the startling white cervical collar he still wore around his neck. Sydney decided not to push him to talk. They would have a family dinner and she could engage him in conversation then.

She went back downstairs, filled a glass of milk and arranged gingersnaps on a plate with a few slices of apple, and carried the food up to his room. "Eat a little," she said. "Remember the doctor said those painkillers can be hard on your stomach."

"I'm not taking them. They make me feel like somebody hit me in the head with a hammer."

She sympathized with this; Sydney didn't like taking anything, either, even cold medicine. "Still, you should eat. You need your strength."

"Yeah, like it takes a lot of strength to lie here."

She was taken aback by Dylan's harsh tone, but decided to treat it as a joke. She rolled her eyes and smiled at him. "See you at dinner," she said.

In the kitchen, she put potatoes in the oven and went to her laptop. She was absorbed in work when Gary came back from the hospital, a grocery bag slung over one arm, pumped up over the writing he'd gotten done at the office on his journal article. "Amazing what you can accomplish without distractions, isn't it?" he said.

He nearly danced in front of the grill as he seasoned the steaks and waited for the coals, sharing the specifics of his research, but using surgical terms too technical for her to follow. Gary's energy made her nervous and she was irritated with him besides, wondering why he hadn't spent his precious time off with his son, who was so clearly in a bad way. Nonetheless, she sat out on the deck with a glass of wine and kept him company.

She went in to make the salad while Gary grilled the steaks, then called Dylan to join them. He protested, but eventually thumped downstairs and slouched into one of the kitchen chairs.

Sydney filled her wineglass again—a surprisingly decent Cabernet given the price—and offered a glass to Gary, but he shook his head. "Early surgery tomorrow," he said. "Better not." His eyes flicked over to Dylan, who sat with his hands folded over his waist, nearly prone in the chair. It was an eerily similar position to the coffinlike pose he'd maintained in his bedroom.

"Please sit up, son," he said. "We're at the dinner table."

"I can't. My neck hurts."

Dylan's expression was sullen. Sydney's heart went out to him; he probably *was* in pain if he'd stopped the pills. His narrow face was a riot of colors, the bruises as spectacular as spring pansies, gloriously purple and yellow and green. "At least you'll be able to take that brace off tomorrow," she said.

"Won't matter. I'll still feel like shit."

"Don't swear at the table," Gary said, chewing his steak vigorously.

"I call it like I see it."

"Not while I'm around, you don't. It's time you learned that the rules of this household aren't meant to be broken. This isn't Haven Lake."

Sydney realized she was watching this tense interaction with her wineglass clutched in one hand; she deliberately set it down. "Let's just try to have a nice dinner," she said.

"I'm not hungry," Dylan said. "Those pain pills made me sick to my stomach."

"Wait. You said you stopped taking them," Sydney said.

"That's why I quit taking them, because I felt sick. But it hasn't been that long. I need time for the pills to leave my system. Right, Dad?" Dylan slouched lower in his chair, his blue eyes hooded as he looked at his father.

Dylan was provoking Gary deliberately, Sydney realized. She picked up her wineglass again and drained it.

Sure enough, Gary suddenly launched himself out of the chair and came around to Dylan's side of the table. "I said. Sit! Up!" He grabbed Dylan's shoulders with both hands on either side of the brace and hauled him to a sitting position.

"Ow! Dad, stop!" Dylan said, as his father nearly lifted him right out of the chair.

"Gary, don't," Sydney pleaded, but she was paralyzed, her mind working overtime. Something was off-kilter. Gary was wild-eyed and furious. Not himself. "I thought we were just going to have a nice dinner. As a family."

"How could we do that? We're not a family," Dylan said.

Gary cuffed him on the back of the head, not gently. "Don't you dare say that. Sydney has done more for you than you deserve. You apologize."

Dylan looked at Sydney, his mouth set in a thin line. "Sorry," he mumbled.

"Like you mean it!" Gary ordered, still standing over him.

"Gary, really, it's all right," Sydney said. What the hell was going on here? She'd never seen Gary this agitated and belligerent. Was it just Dylan's defiance, getting to him? That, combined with the jet lag? He should have had a nap instead of going to the office and getting himself all worked up about that paper.

"I'm sorry, Sydney," Dylan said.

To Sydney's surprise, Dylan sounded like he meant it this time. Her shoulders relaxed a little and she nodded at him. "Thank you," she said. "But I don't blame you for saying that. You're right. We're not a family yet. We're more like friends. It'll be a long time before we really know each other."

Gary, appeased, came back around to his place at the table and began compulsively carving his steak into small strips, then cubes, all the same size, while Dylan and Sydney, who had also lost her appetite, sat in silence and watched.

Eventually Gary realized they were staring at him and looked up. He smiled, but it was more like a grimace. "So, back to school tomorrow," he said.

"Yeah. Can't wait," Dylan said.

"It'll be good to see your friends, anyway, I bet," Sydney said, then felt stupid. It was clear Dylan had few friends, if any, who were more than 2-D apparitions on his computer.

"Have you caught up on your assignments?" Gary asked.

"Dad. I've been on pain meds," Dylan said. "I can hardly keep my eyes open. Besides, I haven't had a chance to talk to my teachers."

"You should have found a way," Gary said. "You can e-mail them tonight, can't you? And your assignments are probably on the portal. It's junior year, son. Think you'll get into college if you let your grades slip?"

Dylan was watching his father with an expression Sydney couldn't decode. "Yeah? Is that what you're worried about, me not getting into college? Come on, Dad. There's always ZooMass."

"The University of Massachusetts is a damn good school," Gary countered. "And, with tuition the way it is, a lot of smart kids choose state schools now. There won't be many places for slackers even at UMass, mark my words. You could be out of luck."

"I can always raise sheep," Dylan said.

He was needling Gary again. Sydney eyed Dylan's plate. He hadn't touched his food. She wondered when he'd last eaten. Yesterday, at the rest stop on the way back from Worcester? No wonder he felt sick.

"I expect you to do more with your life than animal husbandry," Gary said. "It's time you started thinking seriously about your future."

"Gary, maybe we should talk about something else. Everybody's tired and it's getting late." Sydney stood up and cleared her plate from the table. "Finished, honey?" She gestured toward Dylan's plate.

"Yeah, I am, thanks. Sorry I couldn't eat."

She took their plates but left Gary's; he was eating his broccoli now, severing the heads and popping them into his mouth one at a time. Sydney went to the sink and rinsed the plates, then put them in the dishwasher. The problem with this kitchen, she thought, was that it was too efficient: cleanup hardly took any time at all, especially when Gary grilled the meat.

"I'm just trying to get you to see that your future's going to be here before you know it, son," Gary said.

He pushed his plate away and Sydney took that, too, and deposited it in the dishwasher directly. There was nothing to rinse off; he had nearly licked the plate clean. Maybe he had skipped his fiber bar, she thought, then immediately chastised herself for being mean and petty. *She* was the one who should eat fiber bars for lunch. Not fried scallops. God.

"The future is now, Dad," Dylan said. "Today is the first day of the rest of my life, right?"

"Do not mock me," Gary said, wagging a finger. "I have given you everything. I deserve some respect around here. And I will not sit idly by and watch you throw your life away."

Oh, God, Sydney thought, seeing Dylan roll his eyes.

Gary shot out of his chair again and pushed his face close to his son's. "You think this is funny? Do you?"

"No," Dylan said.

"Good. Because this is no joke. This really is the first day of your life, Dylan. Now you're going to go upstairs and hit the books. I expect you to be prepared for school tomorrow. Tomorrow, and every day, buddy."

"Dad, I told you. I can't study. I can't even keep my eyes open."

"Too bad. Find a way to make yourself stay awake."

Slowly, Dylan edged out of his chair, carrying his glass to the sink, walking stiffly, as if balancing a plate on his head. He deposited the glass on the counter and said, "You mean like you do, Dad? With pills?"

"What?" Gary said.

To Sydney's surprise, though, Gary sounded enraged, but he didn't move. If anything, he looked panicked. Cornered. His eyes pinged between Dylan and Sydney as he stood frozen to the spot beside Dylan's chair.

"What are you talking about, Dylan?" Sydney said, keeping her eyes on Gary. "What pills?"

And then the pieces fell into place: Gary's jerky movements, his bloodshot eyes, his irritability, his aggressive behavior. Her mind raced. He'd been acting this way for weeks. Those capsules he'd taken after flying back from Amsterdam to "stay awake" had been clear, with little orange beads inside them.

Dexedrine? Had to be. She saw kids who took that for ADHD. A lot of them, the older teens especially, sold the pills to classmates who wanted to stay up all night and study for tests.

Sydney felt Dylan and Gary watching her and looked up. Dylan's expression was apologetic. She nodded at him once, to show she understood: Dylan had staged this scene deliberately, so she'd find out about Gary's drug abuse. But why? Was he helping Gary? Or hoping Sydney would leave him?

It killed her that she didn't know the answer to that.

Gary still hadn't moved. He strained in her direction like he was waiting for someone to unhook him from an invisible leash. "Tell me," she said.

"It's nothing," Gary said. "Dylan's overreacting, as usual. I take a prescription medication to help me stay alert for surgeries, that's all."

"What is it? Dexedrine?"

She could see by his expression that she was right. "How much are you taking?"

"Just what I need. That's all. I swear." Gary was nervous, half-grinning. Or was that the drugs, too?

"You aren't yourself," she said. "You haven't been for a while. You must be taking too much of it."

"You have no idea what I need!" Gary roared, and turned to Dylan. "You, either, you little shit!"

Dylan stared at his father for a minute, then ripped off the cervical collar and tossed it at Gary's feet before running out the door. Sydney stared at the foam doughnut where it rolled between them, tempted to laugh, but afraid of what might happen next if she did.

CHAPTER THIRTEEN

He'd gotten his cell phone out of his father's desk by using a paper clip to pick the lock of the center drawer. Piece of cake. Dylan had charged it overnight by plugging it in behind his bed so Sydney and his dad wouldn't see it; on Friday morning before classes, he texted Mark to say he was coming to Mark's track meet after school.

Y? Mark texted back.

B/C

OK

Dylan breathed a sigh of relief. He was still feeling down about Kelly, even worse now that she'd stopped tweeting about him, which was weird. He wanted to talk to somebody about her and Mark always had his back.

He knew Kelly was done with him, but he texted her anyway. Just once more, he promised himself: Hey, out of the hospital and home now. Want to talk?

To his shock, she texted back immediately. Sure, when?

Dylan frowned. He didn't want to make Kelly think he was stalking her, even though he totally was. So he texted her about Mark's track meet and suggested meeting him there.

Again, her reply was instant. OK.

Going back to his own school today didn't totally suck, especially knowing he'd be seeing Kelly later—a fact that made him want to whoop in the hall. Whatever happened, this sick nightmare was over. Kelly might not want to hang out with him—he was pretty sure she wouldn't, actually—but at least they could talk about what happened and be friends or whatever.

Nobody at his school seemed to care, or even notice, that he'd been gone for a week. That's how invisible he was and he intended to keep it that way. He hadn't eaten anything in eighteen hours, so his khakis—his school uniform, khakis and a polo shirt, which he couldn't believe kids hadn't mutinied against—were belted on the last hole around his waist and ballooned around his legs like a friggin' skirt. But he felt lightheaded, close to happy.

Taking that stupid collar off his neck was a major bonus. Though he would have liked it if that brace was metal or something. The foam hardly made a sound when it hit the floor last night. No drama. So typical of him: a major statement turned squishy. Why didn't he turn over a chair or pound his fist on something? Loser.

He felt bad about upsetting Sydney. He really did. But it was better if she knew Dad's all-day glow wasn't love—it was an amphetasheen.

Dylan made it through his classes without having to fake it too badly. The guidance counselor called him into her office after lunch to make sure he'd signed up for the June SATs, since he'd missed the May test date. The counselor was a lumpy woman in a too-tight jacket with orange hairs on it that made Dylan picture her sleeping with cats. He felt sorry for her and cooperated.

At lunch, a lot of kids who never bothered talking to him started asking about the bruises on his face. Dylan had wondered if he should make up something cool, a fight or whatever, but he wasn't quick enough. Didn't matter. The car accident freaked a lot of people out. A lot of juniors didn't even have their permits yet, claiming to be too stressed over SATs and final exams to bother learning to drive until summer.

"I'm, like, ready to die," one girl said. "I took that SAT prep course and did worse on the SATs than on the pretest! How is that even possible?"

"Yeah, me, too. Kill me now," another agreed. "And now they expect us to do finals?"

Tiffany, the skinny dancer chick from English who'd tried to help him purge a few months ago, went all gooey-eyed when Dylan said he almost died trying to save a lamb, so Dylan tested the story out on some other girls.

Suddenly some senior girl who was pretty hot sat down next to him and called all her friends over to hear about Casper. Dylan didn't know what to do, surrounded by so much hair and girl chatter. It was like suddenly finding a secret door into the monkey cage at the zoo. Fun, maybe, but you couldn't turn your back. You never knew when a monkey might throw its shit at you.

It had started raining by the time Dylan made it to Mark's high school. He was always amazed when he stepped onto the grounds of any public high school that it was just like one big Disney musical. The jocks clustered together in one corner, alpha males slapping backs and butts; the fat goth girls giggled in the shade of the creepy pine trees; the hot chicks flipped their hair and floated like Victoria's Secret angels; and the geeks had their noses in phones or books or computers. Really, they should just start singing. Nobody would be surprised.

He made his way down the path between the pine trees that led to the track behind the school, ignoring the goth girls as they offered him weed. He still couldn't believe that Mark, of all people, was doing a sport, but even Mark seemed to be buying into the whole college thing now, determined to pump up his applications even if it meant huffing around a track in a lame superhero's outfit.

Dylan hung over the chain-link fence and tried not to break his neck looking everywhere for Kelly. He had to play it cool. She might bail, just to get him back for standing her up the other night.

He watched Mark do the long jump, three times of running and flinging himself in the air and landing in the sand. Mark had already done the 400m and wasn't on again until the 800m; he came over and they walked to the snack shack, where Mark bought a water. Then they went and sat under the bleachers to keep out of the rain.

"Shit, how far was that last jump?" Dylan asked. It was an effort not to check his phone or look over his shoulder for Kelly, even though by now he was pretty sure she wouldn't show.

"Seventeen feet and some change."

"You're a fucking kangaroo."

"Turns the girls on. What can I say?" Mark drained the water bottle, then gave Dylan a sideways glance. "You look like you've been finger-painting. Like, all over your face."

"Turns the girls on. What can I say?"

They high-fived, then Mark said, "Seriously, dude. What happened to you?"

Dylan told him everything, starting with Kelly and Tyler and going to Haven Lake, and finishing with Kelly texting to say she wanted to see him, which was why he'd stolen the truck and tried to bring Casper with him.

Afterward, Mark said, "So I'm guessing you didn't come here just to watch me jump or run in circles."

"I didn't want to say, but yeah."

Dylan was grateful that Mark looked sympathetic, not pissed. "She's probably playing you. You know that, man, right?" Mark said.

"Yeah." It was raining harder; even under the bleachers, Dylan was getting soaked. "I really want to talk to her about some stuff, though. Do you even know who she is?"

"Of course, dude. Once you told me she worked at the drugstore, I did some checking on your behalf." Mark was peeling the label off the water bottle, making the plastic crackle in his hands. "You do realize that girl's a bad idea in every possible way, right? Some guys say she even slept with a teacher last year. He got fired. Kelly's hot, but more like a hot mess."

The sound of the rain drumming on the bleachers filled Dylan's brain like a train roaring through his mind. "She wouldn't sleep with a teacher," Dylan said, but he knew it could be true.

Mark shrugged. "Whatever, man. That's the buzz, all I'm saying. And now there's Tyler, King of the Assholes. He already punched the lights out of two kids who said they went to Kelly's house and smoked with her. You'd think he'd get expelled, but you know how it is."

"Yeah. MVP lacrosse. Plus he probably beat them up someplace else, not school."

"Right." Mark gave Dylan a worried look. "Don't mess with him, man. He's trained to kill. The guy's a major badass, and who are you? Mr. Lamb Savior."

Dylan stared at him, pissed off for a second. Then Mark made that dork face that always got him laughing, and they were still laughing when one of Mark's teammates, a freshman even skinnier than Mark, came trotting over to say it was time to get his ass back on the field.

He didn't have anywhere he needed to be—Sydney and Dad thought he was in SAT prep class—and he'd pretty much given up on Kelly, but Dylan decided to hang around just in case hell froze over and Kelly showed up. He watched the relay race and the 1600m, loving how everybody cheered the guys who sprinted past their rivals like horses on a racetrack, heads thrust forward and chests puffed, arms pumping.

Maybe he should have done track this year. By next year he'd be too old to start. He should have done a lot of things. His dad was probably right that he'd screwed up, wasted a shitload of time on the computer.

That was the thing: once time went by, it couldn't ever be yours again. This minute, right now, when he was waving good-bye to Mark? That was gone now. That part of his life was over.

Dylan wandered back to the front of the school along the same narrow dirt trail between a stand of pine trees, head down and thinking about biology. Just before he went to Haven Lake, his class had talked about Charles Darwin, who went around the world on the HMS *Beagle*, sending home species of plants and animals from parts of the world nobody in England had ever seen before. Dylan liked the idea of being the first to do something, or of at least being in a place so far away that nobody knew where he was.

At Haven Lake, he'd felt a little like Darwin: happy to discover a small pocket of the world where there was still beauty and meaning. Maybe Hannah had the right idea. He should go back to Haven Lake and throw himself on her mercy, promise to work his ass off for free. There was nothing for him here. He'd be fine without Kelly.

No sooner had he thought her name than Kelly appeared like a mirage at the end of the path. Her blond hair was soaked to a dark silk curtain. She wore a short black skirt and her yellow top glowed like somebody was shining a spotlight on her.

She was here! She had kept her promise to meet him! What did that mean? What could he possibly say to make Kelly see that he was worthy?

Dylan felt panicked, not knowing how to approach her. Or if he should. What if she wasn't really here to meet him, but just happened to be walking in the same place?

No. That was stupid. Kelly was walking toward him, not turning around. She had definitely come to find him. Him, Dylan.

He felt the corners of his mouth turn up even though his breath was coming in short, nervous pants. Kelly must have been standing in the shelter of the trees on the parking lot side. That's why he hadn't seen her before.

"Hey," Dylan called out as they approached each other, wondering why she hadn't said anything yet. Maybe she was nervous about seeing him, too. That thought made him feel better. He quickened his step.

Quit being a pussy drama queen, he thought. He was just going to talk to Kelly. She was only a girl. This was the start of his new life. What a mistake he'd made before, thinking he'd have to start life over in Seattle. This was where he was meant to be!

"Hi," Kelly said at last.

She'd stopped walking and was looking around, fiddling with her hair. Why? Was she afraid she looked bad? That girl could never look bad. Not to him. He would tell her that, after they were talking for a while, when things were okay.

He stopped maybe a foot away, reminding himself not to spook her. This was sort of like approaching a ewe, he supposed. You didn't want to get in that zone where she thought you were a predator. "I was afraid you might not come," he said. "I'm glad you're here."

Dylan was proud of himself for sounding so normal. But Kelly crossed her arms under her breasts—did girls do this on purpose, holding their boobs up like melons on a platter just to torture guys?—and didn't say anything, just narrowed her eyes. "I came for a reason," she said. "I need you to get the message."

Was it his imagination, or was Kelly looking as jumpy as he felt? She kept glancing over his shoulder, giving him the creeps. "Okay," he said slowly. "What message?"

"This one," she said.

Dylan focused on her pink mouth gaping suddenly open, and then heard feet pounding toward them and Tyler shouting, "Hey, you little fuck! Get away from her!"

He dove through the trees, but not fast enough. Tyler was on him, punches landing like bricks on his head, slow motion at first, while Kelly stood over them with her phone. There was a roaring like the ocean until his nose was on fire and his vision went. At last a bright light started shining in his eyes and the pain stopped, so that he thought maybe he'd died at last.

Then the world went away.

Hannah couldn't wait to get outdoors lately. The house was a living, breathing creature to her, with its moans and creaking floors, its chips and cracks, the lives of its previous inhabitants still embedded in its walls. Oddly, she had been only vaguely aware of this until Dylan came to live with her. While he was in the house, the ghosts had been banished by new life taking root.

But now he was gone and her presence was no longer enough to fill the empty rooms. Hannah didn't like this change. She supposed she just had to get used to being alone again. In the meantime, she rushed out of the house every morning after breakfast, eager to pull on her boots and tend to the sheep and garden and endless litany of chores.

Today, after she finished in the barn, she was going to start preparing the house trim to be painted. That meant chipping off the peeling paint and sanding the window frames and doors. She didn't much like getting on the ladder to do the second floor, but she'd gotten estimates from painters and liked those even less. She'd do it herself.

In the barn, she was about to let the sheep out to pasture when she noticed that Queenie, one of her most productive ewes, was limping badly. She was usually skittish, but today Queenie hung around by the gate, her placid face aimed in Hannah's direction. This was also unusual. Hannah edged over to her and saw the problem right away: a cracked hoof.

She let the sheep into the pasture and then went for her hoof trimmers and a bucket of corn. She always built a small temporary pen out of hog panels in one corner of whatever pasture her sheep were grazing. She used the boot-top rule for deciding where they were grazing, letting sheep into a pasture when the grass was as high as the top of her rubber boots and moving them when they'd grazed the grass down to just over her toes.

"Come on, Billy," she yelled. The dog darted out of the shadows and heeled. "Stay now," she commanded, walking ahead of him and opening the gate of the small pen, where she kept a low trough. She poured the corn into the trough.

"Okay now!" she yelled, and Billy shot forward toward the sheep, herding them forward. Queenie, as always, led the herd. Hannah managed to drop the gate behind Queenie before the others made it into the pen. "Sit!" she yelled at Billy, and he did, quivering in the grass, alert and waiting for his next command.

She haltered Queenie as the ewe went for the corn and tied her to the fence so she could clip off the cracked nail with her hoof trimmers, feeling exhilarated, as always, by her small success. Nothing kept you in the moment like having to capture an animal and tend to it.

By the time she started scraping the house, it was hot enough for Hannah to wear a T-shirt and shorts. She'd forgotten sunscreen; by afternoon she was parched and her skin had reddened. She went inside and drank several glasses of water, then put on sunscreen and went back out for another two hours. By then her arm was lame from scraping clapboards and it was time for afternoon chores. She'd also promised to bake a lemon poppy seed cake for Liz's dinner party on Saturday night. Tomorrow. Well, she could do that in the morning.

She walked down to the pasture, Billy at her heels, and looked longingly at the pond. When Dylan had asked if she swam there, she'd told him no. That was the truth. She hadn't been in that water since Theo died and couldn't stand the thought of it now. Yet she could admire the water from this distance, the large, heart-shaped body of water with its island in the center, the mountains rising in the distance behind it, the tall pines in the woods to one side. Paradise. Nobody would ever expect, looking at that scene, that Haven Lake had been the site of a tragedy.

She turned away from the pond and watched the sheep for a few minutes. The ewes were peacefully chewing their cuds and the lambs had fallen asleep in a pile, exhausted from their own antics in the pasture. Looking at her contented flock made Hannah breathe more easily, as if the world had righted itself again. The sheep were at peace. She had done her job.

She and Billy moved the sheep into the barn, where she checked their water and gave them a little hay to keep them happy. Then she slid the barn doors closed and walked up to the house.

Her toe caught on something as she was going up the hill by the wisteria that grew on the trellis over the bench Allen had built—one of his first projects when they bought the farm, even before they'd patched the roof of the old brick house. They used to sit there at sunset, just the two of them, before everyone else came. Allen was tender with her then, communicative. They talked about the books they were reading, their own developing spirituality, farming. Parenthood. God, they were young. Allen could be so gentle with her, cupping her face as if she were a flower he'd never seen before.

Later, as the wisteria grew to become vines as thick as her arms, he trained the plant to grow around the sturdy trellis so that, in early summer, the blossoms hung like a lavender waterfall, creating a dappled purple room below. Hannah sat less often with Allen beneath the trellis as more people came to Haven Lake, because the two of them had so little time alone together. But she still used the bench for lessons whenever children stayed on the farm.

Now she bent down and picked up the rock she'd stumbled on. It was as big as her hand and flat, a black heart-shaped stone that seemed to pulse with heat. She dropped it as if the rock had burned her fingers. The grass was still green beneath the stone, so it couldn't have been lying here long. A day, maybe.

Hannah heard her own heartbeat thudding in her ears. Who the hell was leaving these rocks for her to find, and why?

Sydney stayed late at the office on Friday. Valerie had postponed meeting her until Monday because she had to be in court. Her voice in the message sounded brusque, professional, but Sydney decided not to read anything into that, especially because Valerie had added that she could drive to Boston for lunch. That would be easier than Sydney having to drive to Rhode Island after work anyway.

She had been to Brianna Carlson's middle school earlier in the week, per Mr. Carlson's adamant request, to observe Brianna in her seventh-grade classroom and talk with her teachers and guidance counselor.

Brianna's teachers had issued glowing reports. As her father had pointed out, Brianna wasn't an A student, but she did reasonably well in her classes. More important, she got along well with others and seemed gifted in music. Her teachers seemed to care about Brianna's progress in a way that made Sydney wish more middle schools were like this one.

The only person to voice a negative view was the guidance counselor, a baby-faced guy with pictures of his little baby-faced clone children on his desk. He had nothing negative to say about Brianna, only about her parents. "Some damn thing's going on in that house," he said. "Brianna came to us as a happy sixth grader. Chatty and all that. Now she's quiet, almost guarded. Plus she's packed on the pounds. I don't think it's normal middle school pudge, either. A couple of the teachers have reported finding food hidden in her desk during clean-out days and seeing her binge at the corner store after school, buying like six candy bars. Maybe you can find out what's going on. If nothing else, I'd like to have the parents take her to a nutritionist."

Mrs. Carlson had never called Sydney for a follow-up appointment. Sydney only had Jack Carlson's office number; she Googled the residence and found the home phone, making sure to call early enough in the afternoon to catch Mrs. Carlson alone. She was in luck. Mrs. Carlson answered and was shocked enough by Sydney's request for an appointment that she made a date.

Sydney had half expected the woman not to show. But she did, at eleven o'clock this morning, quivering like a bird in a net and keeping her eyes on her shoes. As they talked, Sydney assured Mrs. Carlson first of how well liked Brianna was at school. Then she told her that the probability of being able to convince a judge to pay for private placement was slim, given Brianna's good grades and her teachers' glowing reports. Mrs. Carlson seemed to relax as they talked. She even smiled a little when Sydney said how impressed she'd been, hearing Brianna play the flute in music class.

"Your daughter's a very talented musician," Sydney said.

Mrs. Carlson's hazel eyes were bright with pride. "She can try out for the North Shore youth orchestra, her teacher says."

"That's great," Sydney said. "And the high school where she'll be in just another year has a great music program, from what everyone tells me. Their jazz band won some state contests last year."

"So you don't think we should change schools?"

By the strain in the other woman's voice, Sydney knew that Mrs.

Carlson was probably thinking about how displeased her husband would be by this report. "No, I don't. Of course, you always have the option of having Brianna apply to a private school, but you won't qualify for funding, since Brianna isn't experiencing any significant learning issues where she is now. Also, you should think carefully about moving her. Girls can have a tough time adjusting to a new school. At least you know she's happy and well liked where she is now."

"Mr. Carlson won't be pleased."

"If it'll help, I'll speak to him for you and explain everything," Sydney offered. "There is one other thing, though."

"What's that?"

"Is anything going on at home that might be upsetting Brianna? Fighting, money problems, an illness in the family?"

"No. Nothing. We don't fight, Mr. Carlson and me." The woman said this flatly, the light going out of her eyes.

"What about your husband and Brianna? How do they get along?"

"He loves her." Mrs. Carlson fingered the silver cross she wore on a chain around her neck. "She's Daddy's girl. Mr. Carlson spends a lot of time with Brianna. Especially when I'm away at my sister's. She's sick, you know, the cancer has come back. Jack is like Brianna's best friend. They even have slumber parties in the basement."

Sydney felt like she'd swallowed a handful of stones. Sexual abuse? That could explain Brianna bingeing on junk food and not wanting to talk to any of her teachers. Who knew how far things had gone? Mrs. Carlson, like so many timid wives, might not want to acknowledge that she knew, even to herself. Because then what?

"All right," Sydney said, forcing a smile and thinking fast. "That's all good information. But, look, there is one more person Brianna should see right here in my office. A psychologist."

Mrs. Carlson looked alarmed. "Why? You're a psychologist. You already did all the tests."

"Yes, but I'm an educational psychologist. My colleague is a clinical psychologist who talks to kids about things that might be upsetting them. Brianna might not be having difficulties with her schoolwork, but there could be other things bothering her. Girls go through a lot of transitions at puberty that aren't just physical, and things can get tough with the social pressures."

"You mean somebody might be pressuring her to do drugs or have sex?" Mrs. Carlson nearly yanked the cross off its chain in distress.

"Well, I don't know about that. I'm just saying your instincts are good, Mrs. Carlson. You and your husband brought her to me partly because Brianna doesn't seem happy, right?"

"I guess so."

"So she might be experiencing another difficulty at school. Maybe bullying," Sydney suggested, feeling terrible about lying, but still, she had to get Mrs. Carlson to agree to therapy for Brianna.

Thankfully, this seemed to work. The color had returned to normal in Mrs. Carlson's face. "All right. If you think that's best."

"I do," Sydney said firmly. "I'll have the therapist give you a call. His name is Dr. Baez." She handed Mrs. Carlson one of Marco's cards. "I know Brianna will benefit from working with him. And I'm sure it would be covered by insurance," she added to dispel the lingering doubt on the other woman's face. "We want to make sure Brianna is happy, don't we?"

"Yes, we do," Mrs. Carlson said, her voice small, and tucked Marco's card into her purse.

Afterward Sydney wrote up her report on Brianna and e-mailed a copy to Marco. Even as she was writing, she was conscious of feeling lonely at the office; Ella had disappeared for a long weekend without saying why, so she hadn't had a chance to tell her about Gary and the ugly scene at dinner the night before.

When the report was done, she stared at her cell phone. It was six o'clock and there were two missed calls from Gary and another from the Realtor. She still hadn't called back to hear about the offer on her house. Now she sighed and dialed the Realtor's number.

They talked for only a few minutes. The offer was solid, as Barbara had promised in her messages. Just five thousand below the asking price. "You could hold out for full price, but I wouldn't advise it," Barbara said. "These people are first-time home buyers and they've already been cleared by the bank. Shall I fax the offer to you, or would you rather come into my office to sign it?"

"I need another day to think about it," Sydney said.

"All right, but remember, you've only got another twenty-four hours."

They hung up. As Sydney started to tuck the phone back into her handbag, she noticed another missed call from Gary. He must have called while she was talking to Barbara.

She dialed his cell, even though she was still undecided about what to say to him. Last night they'd talked for a while, but Sydney had been too upset to spend the night and had gone home over Gary's protests. She went up to say good night to Dylan before leaving, but he had pretended to be asleep. She knew he wasn't; she'd seen the glow of his cell phone beneath the bed. He must have somehow managed to get it back from Gary. She suspected Gary didn't know about this, but she didn't have the stamina to deal with another confrontation. She decided not to say anything. Maybe Dylan had someone to call. A friend. She hoped so.

Now they got right into it. Gary must have been in the car, maybe on his way home from the hospital; she could hear the whoosh of traffic or wind as he told her again that she was overreacting about his drug use.

"Every surgeon I know needs a pick-me-up now and then," he said. "You know the hours we keep and the stress we're under. It's perfectly safe, what I'm doing. You must have tons of kids on Adderall, right? That's basically Dexedrine. Plenty of college kids take it, too, when they want to focus on exams. I wish I'd had it in medical school."

"Doctors don't prescribe stimulants just to help kids study," Sydney argued. "There has to be a constellation of factors before that happens. Older kids might be buying stimulants like Ritalin, but they're doing it illegally. So are you."

"I have a prescription! Diane Shoreman wrote one for me when I said I was having trouble focusing."

"Oh, come on!" she said. "You know damn well that you have no medical condition that warrants that prescription, other than wanting to be the smartest guy in the room and as skinny as a twenty-year-old."

A brief, tense silence followed. Finally Gary said, "Look, Sydney. I am a doctor. A very well-qualified doctor. I don't abuse drugs. But if this really bothers you, we'll talk it through some more. I'm on my way home now. Let's have dinner early, just the two of us. Dylan has SAT prep class after school, so he'll be late. Please, Sydney. I need you to understand where I'm coming from."

Sydney was quiet for a few minutes, but she still couldn't formulate an answer. She didn't know how she felt, other than wanting the old Gary back. And their old life, both of them working hard during the week but looking forward to leisurely hikes or biking on weekends, Dylan supposedly happy and doing his schoolwork, everything running smoothly. She'd felt fulfilled, almost like a wife and mother, when things were going well between them.

What if Gary was telling the truth? What if it wasn't really the drugs making him twitchy? What if he, too, was stressing out over Dylan and their wedding, which had seemed absurdly far away when they set it for October, but now felt alarmingly close?

In any case, Sydney needed some time to think about things. "I'm sorry. There's a lot going on. I need to sleep in my own bed, Gary. Alone."

"Come on. Don't do this." There was a note of panic in Gary's voice. "I love you, and I know you love me."

"Of course I love you," she said. Saying the words aloud should have felt like a declaration. Instead, they were as cold in her mouth as ice chips rattling between her teeth. She wanted to spit them out or swallow them.

What if she didn't really love him the way he'd described loving Amanda? That description still haunted her. Maybe the drugs were Gary's way of coping not just with work and Dylan, but with her, with the reality that he felt less for her than he had for his wife.

"If you loved me, you'd come be with me tonight," Gary said. "You wouldn't be avoiding me."

"I'm not! I just need a break," she said, the phone pressed close to her cheek. "You and I both need to think about things."

"What things?"

"Everything! About Dylan. About us," she added.

"So that's what this is really about? Not the drugs, but how you feel about me?" His voice had risen in pitch. "If that's it, I don't see how us being apart will solve anything."

"It might not," Sydney agreed. "But I need time to think."

To her shock, Gary started yelling. "Really? You want to think about things? All right. I will, too. See you Monday. Have a good weekend," he said, and hung up.

Stunned, Sydney sat there for a few minutes, trying to breathe. What had just happened? How had they reached this precipitous place in their relationship? Was this just typical wedding jitters, or the sign of something irreparably wrong in their relationship?

No, she couldn't jump to that conclusion. Gary was a good man. A kind, loving, thoughtful, intelligent person. Yes, he'd used a physician's loophole to help himself along with pharmaceuticals when he needed to perform stressful surgeries. But maybe that wasn't so different from, say, her drinking wine to relax at night or coffee to wake up in the morning.

She considered calling him back, but didn't. They both needed a little time apart to think about what really mattered in their relationship.

What to do with herself, though, to stop fretting? She picked up her phone and started to search for Fern's number, then put the phone down again. She didn't feel like driving into Boston. Besides, her friends would quiz her relentlessly about Gary.

Maybe she should just go straight home and have a soak in the tub. She could finally have a bubble bath and read, a glass of wine at her elbow. Normally this idea would have thrilled her. But she felt panicked, too energetic to sit.

"Jesus, leave yourself alone," she muttered, just as a knock on her office door startled her.

It was Marco. He poked his head in when she called hello and raised an eyebrow. "What are you doing here so late? I hope you're not still working." He was dressed casually, but that was no clue to Marco's activities, since he typically wore black jeans and T-shirts to the office, with an occasional sweater as a nod to school administrators if they went to a team meeting.

"I could say the same to you." Sydney smiled. "Actually, I was just packing up to leave. Did you get my e-mail?"

"About that seventh grader, Brianna?" Marco nodded. "I called her mother and set something up for next week. What's the deal, do you think?"

"I don't really know anything other than what the guidance counselor told me, but I do think the girl's in distress for some reason."

"I'd say trust your gut. If you think something's up, it probably is, Sydney."

Marco rested his lean frame against the doorway, arms crossed, and chatted with her about a couple of other clients they had in common. As always, she was impressed and surprised by his insights into the families. Yet she felt uncomfortable doing something as ordinary as packing her Tupperware containers into her bag in front of him. Marco always made her feel that way, she realized: fluttery as a teenager. She was as bad as the other women in the office around him. How stupid.

She was finished in here. She switched off her laptop and tucked it into her briefcase, then stood up and gathered purse, briefcase, and sweater before switching off her desk lamp. She hadn't remembered that the overhead light was off. Sydney hated buzzing fluorescent lighting and hardly ever turned on her ceiling lights; now it was dark outside, nearly eight o'clock, and that meant it was unusually dark in the office. She felt her way around the desk toward Marco and the light in the main reception area.

"So where are you off to now? Home?" he asked, moving with her across the waiting room.

"I guess. How's your car running these days?"

"So far, so good." He reached the elevator before she did and pressed the button. "Why? Need a ride?"

She shook her head. "I have my car."

Marco must have heard something in her voice. "What's wrong? You can tell me, you know. We're friends. Or at least I hope we are."

"We are." Sydney suddenly wanted more than anything else to lean her head on his shoulder. It was the warmth in his voice. No wonder the kids all trusted him. "It's nothing big. Everything's fine, really. Just, you know." She felt the words stick in her throat, nearly choking her, but she managed to spit them out. "Gary and I are taking a break this weekend. We've been through a lot with Dylan. As you know. And he's very stressed at work."

"And you? Are you stressed over Dylan and work?"

"Dylan, yes. Work is actually winding down a little, now that the school year's almost over."

"And what's going on with Dylan?" he asked as the elevator doors slid noiselessly open. He put his hand on the small of her back to guide her inside.

It was a light touch, but Marco's fingers burned through her blouse. Sydney stepped quickly into the elevator in front of him and took her time turning around so she could mask her expression of shock at the physical sensation he'd provoked.

"I don't really know," she said as the elevator lurched downward, leaving her stomach on the floor above. "Dylan's face is still banged up, but he was able to take the brace off and go back to school today. Hopefully he'll be able to catch up on schoolwork over the weekend. Finals are next week."

Marco made a vague humming sound.

"What?"

"It's just that I'm not sure Dylan will be as determined to catch up on schoolwork as you are to have him do that."

"I didn't say I was keen on it."

"No?"

Sydney sighed. "No, I'm not. I want him to pass, of course. But Dylan has other things he has to sort through before he can think about college. It's just that Gary is very focused on Dylan's grades and college applications. He really wants Dylan to do well in life."

"Understandably. I'm sure you do, too." They had reached the lobby; again, Marco held his hand as if to guide Sydney through the doors, but this time she was too quick for him to actually touch her. "College isn't for everyone," Marco said. "Maybe there's something else that interests him. Or maybe he'll take a gap year and be more focused on college later. It's a mistake, I think, to equate college with success for every child."

"I know. But I don't think Gary believes that."

"So you've been fighting?"

Sydney gave him a look that made Marco put up both hands and smile. "Sorry," he said. "None of my business."

"That's right," she said curtly. "See you Monday. Have a great weekend."

"You, too, Sydney."

She started striding across the parking lot to her car. This brisk, urgent movement away from Marco was less effective as a good-bye gesture than it could have been, because she somehow managed to drop her oversized shoulder bag as she was fumbling for her car keys. There was an explosion as her bag hit the ground and everything from file folders to her lipstick went flying.

"Goddamn it," Sydney said.

And there he was again, Dr. Caretaker, on his knees and helping her gather her things, tidily stacking the file folders and even finding the cap to her lip balm before handing it to her. "One of those days, huh?" he said.

That was all it took, that one last expression of sympathy, for Sydney to unravel. She had been on her knees, too, never mind her nice black linen slacks and white blouse, but now she sat down on the ground and buried her face in her hands, weeping, her shoulders shuddering so hard that her teeth chattered and she bit her tongue, which made her cry harder.

Marco didn't say a thing. He just sat down in the parking lot and put an arm around her shoulders, pulling her close. She resisted at first, then gave up and let him hold her until she'd finished crying. Then he handed her a handful of Kleenexes he'd extracted from one of her bags and waited patiently for her to dry her face and blow her nose before saying, "Now tell me what's going on."

So she did, all of it: her visit to Haven Lake, her uneven relationship with Hannah, Dylan's accident and homecoming, and yes, God help her, about discovering Gary's drug use, too.

Afterward, she laughed shakily and said, "I think that's it. I imagine my session's up by now anyway, right?" She started to stand, but he pulled her down beside him again and pulled the pins out of her hair.

"What are you doing?" she said, but didn't try to stop him.

"Your head will hurt less if you let your hair down. My sisters always say so."

She let him massage her head. Then he ran his fingers through her hair, combing it down around her shoulders. "You're right," she said. "That is better."

"Kind of like loosening a vise around your forehead, I imagine," he said.

"So what do you think?" she asked.

"About which part? It's a lot to process."

"I don't know."

"Well, which thing seems most urgent? Gary?"

"Or Dylan."

Marco thought for a minute, then said, "Well, about Dylan I can't really offer an opinion. Something definitely went down that made him run away. You already know that. Will you ever find out what it was?" He shrugged. "Maybe not. Sometimes we never know what's going on in a teenager's world. All you can do is keep a close eye on him."

"And Gary?"

Marco sighed. "Look, I hate to tell you this, but I've known a lot of doctors who've gotten into trouble with meds. I also know a lot of them who manage it pretty well, taking what they need when they need it. You're going to have to watch him closely, too, to find out which camp he's in."

"That's the thing," Sydney said, standing up abruptly and brushing off her pants. She picked up her bag and looped it over one shoulder. "I don't *want* to babysit Gary. I don't mind watching out for Dylan. Dylan's a child. But I don't want to be with a man I can't trust."

Marco stood up, too, his expression, usually so devilish, surprisingly solemn and sweet. "Good. I'm glad you realize that you deserve more."

Sydney turned away, glad her hair was down to hide her ravaged makeup. "I grew up with a father who raged at me, at my mother, at everything. It was no fun. And in the end he killed himself. I don't think Gary's depressed enough to do that, but I don't want to live with him if he's under the influence of drugs that make him unpredictable."

Marco nodded. "You need to trust your own instincts."

"Jesus, don't shrink me, okay? I hope you and I don't talk in those clichés when we're with clients."

He laughed, his old mischievous expression back. "All right, then. How about if we just go out tonight? Let's go dancing. There. Does that sound less like a shrink?"

"Dancing? Are you insane?" Sydney tried to glare at him, but couldn't because he was grinning. Just standing there and grinning, waiting for her to change her mind. Knowing he'd win.

That pissed her off. She pissed herself off, too. She was a terrible person, confiding her fears about Gary to this man she was obviously attracted to, despite her best intentions. But who did Marco think she was? Did he honestly believe she'd spill her guts, then turn around and go dancing with him?

"I'm not at all crazy," he was assuring her. "It's just that I happened to be heading over to one of my favorite salsa clubs tonight in Lowell with my cousin, and I know you like to dance."

"Your *cousin*?" She was too surprised to stay offended at him for hitting on her. "That's the best you could dig up on a Friday night?"

"What's wrong with that? Juan and I both like to salsa. There aren't a lot of women who know how. We go to the club together and it's easy to find dance partners there."

"Why don't you take Carrie?"

"Carrie and I are just friends. And she doesn't really dance."

"And you can't meet other women who want to go out with you? Women who like to dance?"

Marco raised his dark eyebrows and folded his arms. "You know, you've said a bunch of things to me lately that make me think you believe I'm a player."

She snorted. "Marco, everybody in the office *knows* you're a player."

"Thanks a lot." He was honestly angry now. "Anyway, sorry I asked you to dance, if it offends you. Hope you sort things out with Gary. Have a great weekend." He stalked across the parking lot to his car.

Sydney watched him go with a confusing soup of emotions: remorse that she'd upset him, confusion that her image of him kept changing, and—most alarming—a sudden desire to go dancing. A night of harmless flirtation and fun with Marco would take her mind off Gary and Dylan just for a little while. What could be the harm?

"Wait!" Sydney said. "What do women wear at a salsa club?"

Marco turned around. To her relief, he was smiling. "You'll be fine the way you are."

That was almost true. The women, it turned out, were casually dressed at the club, but they wore as little as possible, mostly skimpy skirts and camisoles and tall shoes. Sydney had never felt so elephantine, plodding around in her flats and wide trousers. But Juan and Marco didn't seem to care, and both were brilliant partners, moving her around the floor until her back was damp with sweat and her hair fell in ringlets around her shoulders.

Juan was shorter than Marco, stockily built, with a scar down one cheek that she was afraid to ask about; he was jolly, though, with a belly laugh that jiggled his tight white T-shirt, and he wore an array of gold chains. He seemed to be far better known at the club than Marco. Everywhere they went, Sydney heard, *"Oye, Juan, qué dices?"* or something similar, followed by quick raining phrases in Spanish that she couldn't follow.

The club was housed upstairs in one of Lowell's old textile mills. The massive industrial pipes along the ceiling were strung with brightly colored lights, and by eleven o'clock the place was packed and everyone was dancing full throttle. Sydney finally took off her tunic and danced in her camisole, a move that made Marco's eyes go straight to her breasts. Sydney didn't care. Most of the women wore less than she did and it was a lot cooler this way.

Then the music slowed and both Juan and Marco were circling, as well as another man she'd danced with twice, all three of them begging her in Spanish to dance with them, making comically exaggerated faces. Juan even fell to one knee, his hands clasped in prayer, making her tip her head back and laugh. Marco edged the other men aside and took Sydney in his arms, pulling her close.

He moved her expertly around the floor until Sydney felt slightly dizzy; she closed her eyes to follow him better and then it was like floating, the music all around them, as if the music were embedded in the colored lights and in the bodies of the people pressing against them, as if they were one being, and suddenly she felt as she had riding horses with Theo, at one with another being, sensual and filled with joy, her body surrounded by music, every nerve ending on fire.

When Marco kissed her, she didn't resist. She let him trace her lips gently with his tongue, then slide his mouth down her neck, pressing himself harder against her now, until Sydney thought her knees wouldn't hold her through the waves of her desire.

She pulled away then, stricken. "No," she said.

Marco, for once, wasn't teasing or grinning. He had been serious about kissing her, and now he was tender as he let her pull away. "Sorry. I was taken over by the moment," he said. "By you, *mi querida*."

"I need to go home," Sydney said, overwhelmed by sensations she couldn't remember experiencing since she was a teenager and with Theo in the cornfield, in the barn, in her room, and suddenly remembering Gary as if she'd just awakened from a dream and realized this moment wasn't her real life. Her messy, chaotic, dissatisfying life.

Juan, whom they'd picked up in Haverhill, said he'd find another ride home, so Marco drove Sydney back to her car. He rested his arm across the back of the seat but didn't touch her again. They talked haphazardly about Juan, the club, Lowell, the music, dancing—anything but each other and what they were doing, or had done, together. At last they arrived and Marco waited until she'd opened her car door and started the engine before waving and driving off.

Sydney sat in the car for a minute with the engine idling and put her head on the steering wheel. What the hell had she just done?

CHAPTER FOURTEEN

Where was he? What the hell was that bright light?

Didn't people say you saw a bright light when you died? Was he dead?

"I think he's awake!" someone's voice said. Mark's?

Dylan tried to answer, but his lips and tongue felt like they'd been stung by bees, swollen and burning. He couldn't breathe through his nose. That was a problem when his tongue felt like a sneaker in his mouth. The room was spinning. He tried to sit up and vomited into a silver pan thrust at him.

"Take it easy, son. Here, let me get you some water."

His father's voice. Hearing that made Dylan want to die again. This couldn't be heaven if his father and Mark were here.

He must be in the hospital. Shit. Death would have been so much easier.

"Son? Here, drink this. Please. Sit up. Just a little."

Dylan took a few sips of lukewarm water and threw up again. His head whirled and ropes were tugging at his arms. His dad and somebody else, a woman, started shouting as he dropped his head flat and everything went dark.

The next time he woke, the spinning had slowed in his brain. He could see a little better, too. A relief not to be blind, but why was everything so blurry and small? Was there a bandage or something around his head? Or were his eyes swollen? He could only see through little slits and his nose was in the way.

Dylan finally remembered: Tyler. A look in his eyes like a rabid dog's. Tyler must have broken his nose. Dylan ran his tongue over his teeth to see if they were all there. They were. That was something. His retainer had probably held them in place.

He made a noise, just clearing his throat really. Instantly his father was next to the bed, his face close to Dylan's but fuzzed out. "How are you feeling?"

Dylan tried to form a word that came out sounding like "thisttsrd." As soon as he made the sound, he couldn't remember what word he was trying to say. He threw up again, heaving a few teaspoons of liquid into the silver dish.

"That's all right," Dad said. "You'll be better in the morning. We'll talk then. Go back to sleep."

Dylan couldn't have stayed awake anyway. It was like somebody was hammering nails into his forehead.

The next time he opened his eyes, the room was brighter. He could open one eye all the way now. Enough to see Dad wasn't with him. He was able to sit up when a nurse came in and offered to unhook his arm from some tubes.

With her help, Dylan stood up and hobbled across the room to the bathroom, embarrassed by the hospital gown flapping open over his bare ass. He had vertigo and wanted to vomit, but nothing would come. Just dry heaves. Pissing hurt, but not as much as his face. The nurse was old, at least, so it was less strange having her help him than if she'd been young and pretty like Kelly.

Kelly. Her name came roaring back like a hurricane in his head. Did Kelly see Tyler pound him? She must have. Dylan struggled to remember. They were talking on the path and Kelly looked scared. She had her phone out. Filming? Now it occurred to him that maybe she wasn't just scared about what Tyler would do to him, but to her, too.

The police came to his room a little later and wanted a statement.

"I didn't see the guy," Dylan said. "He came at me from behind."

They didn't believe him. He didn't get why they wouldn't leave him alone. Wouldn't their jobs be easier if they didn't investigate?

Dad kept pushing Dylan for a name, too, but Dylan wouldn't budge. If he ratted out Tyler, he knew it would be Revenge City. Tyler might find a way to get back at him even in the hospital. Nobody policed visiting hours.

Plus, if the cops talked to Tyler and Kelly, Kelly could spin it so Dylan would be the one in trouble. For all he knew, Kelly had filed some kind of sexual harassment report on him already. She could say Tyler hit him because he was defending her.

His memory was coming back in disorganized, crazy bits, like colored chips in a kaleidoscope. Kelly screaming. Tyler spitting on him after he'd pummeled Dylan into the dirt. Staying conscious long enough to watch a robin hop around his head.

Mark found him. Dylan's eyes had opened for a minute when they were loading him into the ambulance because they jostled him onto the stretcher and it felt like he was being tossed into a fire pit. So much hellish noise from the siren, red and blue lights everywhere, and Mark's face, bug-eyed with fear.

Finally Sydney came to his hospital room. She looked like crap. Not bruised on the outside like him, but banged up on the inside. He could tell she felt his pain by the way her green eyes wavered between light and dark. Her eyes were like windows with a crowd of people trying to shout at him through the glass. What would she really say to him, if he could hear her muffled voice? Her hair was down, a river of yellow and gold spilling around her shoulders.

"I'm sorry," he said, managing words better now, as long as he didn't try to string together more than two at a time. He wanted to tell her why: for being stupid enough to run away. For crashing Hannah's truck. For throwing his dad under the bus. For not being nicer to her. But he was still too tired and sore to talk.

Sydney seemed to understand anyway. "It's all right," she said, putting a hand over his. "Don't try to talk right now. Later, though, it would be good if you did. Just to me if you want." Her hand was small and warm on his own bony cold one.

Dylan turned his hand over and held on to Sydney's.

Again, she understood. Sydney gripped his hand like she was pulling him out of a soupy fog. He started to cry, remembering this one last thing about his mother, about how he used to be so afraid of the dark as a kid that she always read him a story and then stretched out in the bed beside him, holding his hand while he fell asleep.

"We're going to walk into Dreamland now," Mom would say. "We'll go together. Close your eyes. You see the clouds, all blue and pink and pretty? Can you see them, honey? You can walk on those clouds when you're asleep. There's nothing to worry about, because you can never fall down. Step on the clouds. I'll be right beside you, holding your hand."

No two ways about it, Liz's girlfriend, Cate, looked like an angel and so did her twin brother, Clark: sweet round faces, straight corn silk hair, doll-like features, round blue eyes. Cherubic as overgrown children. It was easy to imagine them naked and spitting water in a fountain.

Cate and Clark were only about an inch taller than Hannah's five foot eight, but they had surprisingly thick, powerful bodies, with broad backs and muscular forearms. They owned a bakery together; probably kneading all that dough was better than any free weights in the gym.

"Where did you say you found Cate?" Hannah hissed at Liz once she'd cornered her alone in the kitchen, ostensibly to ask for help serving her lemon poppy seed cake while Clark and Cate went outside to admire Liz's garden. "And why did you ask me to bake the dessert, when your guests won the Berkshires' Best award for their bakery?"

She'd learned that little tidbit over Liz's dinner of linguine with broccoli and oil served with caprese salad. Cate and Clark had brought the wine and, of course, the bread: rosemary dinner rolls that were soft as clouds on the inside and crusty on the outside, nearly bringing Hannah to her knees.

"Your cakes rock," Liz said. "And Cate found me, actually. Through an ad. She wouldn't let go once she had me, even though I'm too old for her and too ill-tempered for relationships." She sighed happily.

Hannah burst out laughing. "You're in deep."

"I'm in where I want to be and the water's fine. Let me drown."

"Listen, speaking of love, have you been leaving heart-shaped rocks around my place? I know that sounds strange," Hannah added quickly, catching Liz's startled look.

"No. I've done a lot of bizarre things in my day, but not that. Where are you finding them?"

"All over. I found the first couple of stones about six months ago, one near the sheep barn and the other where the small barn used to be. Then, when Dylan was here, I found three heart-shaped rocks in a row. Yesterday I found another big one by the trellis. They're beautiful, actually."

"Maybe they're just natural stones that happen to be heart-shaped."

"No. These rocks didn't come from around here. They look like they came from quarries. A couple of them look like Vermont marble."

"Could they have been dropped around the farm by one of your WWOOFers back in the day? By some crazy European backpacker with a heart-on for the world?"

"Ha-ha. No, I don't think so. I would have found them before now. If nothing else, I would have hit them with the mower. Especially the last one. It's bigger than my hand."

"Gifts from heaven, then," Liz said. "Or a secret admirer?" She gave Hannah a wicked grin.

"God, I hope not." Hannah nervously scrubbed at her face with both hands.

Liz put down the plates she was carrying and stared at her. "What is it? You don't really think you have a stalker, do you? That awful guy you told me about?"

"No."

"Then what?"

Hannah sighed and looked at her. "I forgot to tell you something. Dylan found a note from Rory to me."

"*What?* Where?"

"Inside his guitar. He obviously wrote it just before leaving." Hannah's throat tightened at the thought of the poor Martin, dusty and forgotten under Rory's bed. She wished now that she'd insisted on Dylan taking it with him. "The note said he was disappearing to protect me in some way."

"From what?"

"I have no idea."

Liz picked up the plates and came over to give her an awkward one-armed hug. "I still say he was cowardly to run off and leave you to deal with Allen's death, the farm, Sydney. Everything! That man, at the very least, should have been your friend."

"He was," Hannah said. "Rory was my best friend. If he left, it was because he had no other choice."

Liz gave her a sympathetic look while at the same time prodding her with an elbow. "Come on. Put on your happy face and let's eat cake."

The cake was a hit. Liz served grappa and coffee with it on her back porch, where she and Cate sat together on the swing. Hannah perched on the steps with Clark, balancing her plate on her knees and trying not to notice when Liz and Cate fell silent and kissed during a break in the conversation.

Hannah was pleased to see Liz so happy, but it was still difficult when it was Cate who lingered with Liz on the porch, not her, as Hannah walked home that night. In the past, Liz might have asked Hannah to stay and watch a movie; there were many nights when Hannah had dropped off to sleep on the sofa or in the guest room. As Liz waved good-bye, one arm slung around Cate's shoulders, Hannah felt lonely and oddly bereft. Rejected.

Don't be an ass, she scolded herself sternly. Liz was right. They both needed to move on, not hang on to the past.

Clark insisted on walking her home. Hannah didn't protest, knowing he was probably as desperate as she was to escape the lovefest on the porch. He was good company, but she wasn't the least bit attracted to him. She felt sorry for him, actually; it might be even worse to see your twin in love than it was to see your best friend so preoccupied.

Along the way, Clark talked about how he and Cate had traveled to France for a study-abroad program and fell in love with Parisian bakeries.

"That was our downfall," he said. "Cate and I both had our hearts set on learning how to make the perfect croissants and French bread. We wanted to train in Paris. You can imagine our father's reaction: four hundred grand spent on college educations for his kids, and all we wanted to do was put on aprons and stand in front of a hot oven all day."

Hannah laughed. "Good for you. And you've made a success of it."

"Well, if you call being successful driving an aging Honda and owing a mortgage on both a house and a shop, then, yes, I'm absolutely at the top of my game."

She told him about the sheep as they reached her property and were hit full force by the fragrant lilacs along the stone wall. As they turned down the driveway, a barred owl hooted in the rustling trees and Hannah thought, as she often did, how easy it was to imagine the trees having faces in the bark, as if at any moment they could grab at her with their limbs like long, wrinkled arms.

On the porch, there was no awkward moment when neither of them knew what to do. They both seemed to understand there was no chemistry between them. After saying good-bye, Hannah quickly pulled out her key and stepped through the screen door. Clark waved and went on his way.

Hannah peeled off her clothes upstairs. At least she'd managed to forget all about Dylan and Sydney during dinner. Now she wondered what they were doing with their Saturday night. Maybe she'd give Sydney a call in the morning. Families called each other on Sundays, didn't they?

A tradition, she thought groggily, preparing for bed, suddenly feeling drowsy and full. She could start a new family tradition.

The dog woke her from a deep sleep. Billy was barking his fool head off, hysterical about something. Coyotes, maybe. Hannah was just about to shush him—Billy was downstairs in the hall by the front door; she could hear his nails scrabbling about on the wood floor—but then she heard footsteps on the porch and someone knocked on her door. Maybe Clark was back.

"Hang on," she yelled, as much to calm Billy as anything. The dog whined but quieted. She pulled on jeans and a sweatshirt.

Downstairs, she snapped the porch light on and was about to open the door when a strange shiver ran up her spine.

She went into the living room and peered out through the window onto the porch. To her horror, Les Phillips was standing there, in a baseball cap and flannel shirt tucked into his jeans, swaying a little as he knocked on the door again.

Hannah came back out to the hall to check the door, terrified. Had she remembered to throw the dead bolt?

She had. Her heart was pounding so hard, she could feel it in her throat. She went back into the living room, opened the window a crack, and yelled, "What the hell are you doing here, Les?"

Les jumped at the sound of her voice, then grinned and came over to the window. He bent close enough that she took a step backward, even though she knew he probably couldn't see her, because she was in a darkened room and he was standing under the porch light.

His voice was amiable. "Just thought I'd stop by and pay you a friendly little visit, like I promised. Maybe have a nightcap."

"Get the hell off my porch or I'll call the cops." Hannah's heart clawed at her chest. The dog, hearing the fear in her voice, started a low growl next to her.

"Call the cops for what?" Les widened his eyes in false astonishment. "To tell 'em a friend stopped by to visit? It's not a break-in." He knocked on the window frame, making her jump. "Not yet."

"It's the middle of the goddamn night and you're not welcome here, you bastard."

Les clucked his tongue. "The mouth on you, darlin'. You need a spanking. Come on, now. Ten o'clock on a Saturday night is hardly uncivilized for two consenting adults who want to have a little fun."

"I've seen your kind of fun. No, thank you. Get out of here, Les. I'm serious. I'm picking up the phone right now." Hannah hated the quaver in her voice.

She also hated the fact that she'd left her cell phone upstairs, along with the unloaded shotgun under her bed. Now she wished she'd brought both down with her. Even more, she wished she'd loaded the gun.

"No, you're not," he wheedled, swaying again as he bent forward and rested both big hands on his knees. "You're not going to call anybody, because then you'd have the cops out here, and who knows what they'd find in your house. Let me in and we'll catch up. It's been too long. You were so sweet, comforting me after my divorce. I don't know how I would have gotten through that bitch leaving me without you. She took my son, Hannah." His voice broke.

"You raped me!"

"Come on, now! You know you came to my house for a little hanky-panky. You have a rep around town. I can see why, too, all the people you have coming and going from this place. I was just passing by tonight, like I do sometimes, minding my own business. And what do I see? Your gentleman caller skipping up the driveway. No bigger than a minute, but he got what he came for. Now it's my turn." He rattled the window frame. "You know these screens can't keep me out. Open the door."

Now Hannah frantically wished she'd let Clark stay. "I will report you for breaking and entering, and for assault." She was shaking so hard she had to wrap her arms around her body. Would Les really break in? Could he, if the doors were locked?

Probably. It was an old house. The bulkhead doors didn't even have a lock on them. She'd never worried much about burglaries. What did he mean about the cops finding something in the house?

Pot. Les must think she had drugs in here.

He was still talking. "You report me. Go ahead. I'll tell my good friend, the chief of police, that it's not easy for a woman to make a living these days. Sometimes a girl's gotta do what a girl's gotta do to get by. Like I said, everybody in this town knows all about you and Haven Lake, Hannah." He gave the screen a good tug and the frame bent outward.

Hannah ran up the stairs so fast it felt like she might pass out from lack of oxygen. She grabbed her phone off the table and slid the shotgun out from under the bed, then pounded back down the stairs, where Les was trying to wedge his fat fingers between the screen and the window to pull it out of its frame.

She unbolted the door. Billy was barking again now that she was running around. She opened the front door, put the shotgun to her shoulder, and emerged, shouting, "Go on, Billy! Get him!"

Billy hurled himself onto the porch and leaped up at Les, grabbing on to the man's thick forearm and drawing blood. Les managed to pry the dog's jaws open and shake him off, then aimed his boot at Billy's side, but the dog was too quick for him. Billy snarled and went after Les's leg, but Hannah called him off. She didn't want Les to be unable to escape.

"Enough, Billy! Come. Good dog."

Billy gave her an incredulous look, but whirled back around to sit beside her, growling at Les.

He backed away with his hands raised, eyes on her gun, blood oozing out of his arm. "Jesus, all right, already. I can take a hint. I'm going," Les said, then turned and ran for his truck.

He roared out of the driveway. Hannah sank onto the porch steps, the gun across her knees. Billy edged over to press himself against her. She looped an arm around the dog and said, "We did all right, Bill. He'll think twice before he comes after me again, won't he?"

The moon came out from behind a cloud then, illuminating the trees standing guard, withered faces winking as they shook their branches overhead.

. . .

Dylan would be in the hospital until Tuesday afternoon. Given the circumstances, the school had offered him extensions on all of his finals and papers.

Sydney stopped by the hospital on Monday morning with his books and assignments. Dylan was still groggy, but his face was less swollen. He gave her a reassuring smile when she said she'd be back after lunch. Something had shifted between them. She didn't know how or why, but Sydney knew he trusted her now. She was determined not to let him down.

With Gary, things were awkward but civil. He had called Sydney as soon as he heard from the police. Apparently Dylan's friend, Mark—a boy Sydney didn't even know existed until now—had been the one who found Dylan unconscious at the school and called 911.

Sydney was back at her cottage by the time Gary called to report all of this, after she'd gone dancing in Lowell with Marco. She rushed over to the hospital, where she met Mark, a short, skinny boy with thick eyelashes and a mop of black hair who looked like an orphan in a Dickens novel. She could tell by the way Mark wouldn't meet her eyes that the boy knew more about the incident than he was saying, but she didn't want to push him while Gary was badgering the poor kid for information.

Gary wanted to punish whoever had done this to his son. Sydney didn't blame him. Privately, though, she thought they were more likely to get answers from Mark and Dylan if they talked calmly with the boys alone, and didn't involve the police until they knew more.

She and Gary had spent the weekend running between his house and the hospital, being polite but having conversations with little content. Gary was agitated and tense, talking about how frightened he'd been seeing Dylan in the hospital. Sydney sympathized. She'd had the same experience in Worcester. However, she was also feeling guilty about Marco and wary, wondering if Gary's anxiety was due to pills, Dylan, or him sensing she'd been with another man. She didn't want to distress him more by asking about the drugs, but found herself watching him closely, especially when he was drumming his fingers on the kitchen table or his knee was bouncing. Had he always been this hyper?

Sydney didn't want to acknowledge it, even to herself, but it was the truth: she loved Dylan and was concerned about him, but her feelings for Gary had changed. She didn't trust him, and she was more unsure than ever about marrying him.

She pushed these thoughts aside while she was at work. Then she kept her lunch date with Valerie. She'd cleared out the afternoon to make room for it, and with Dylan still in the hospital, there was no reason not to keep it.

At Valerie's suggestion, they were meeting at the Procrastinator's Café in Boston. The café had floor-to-ceiling windows that opened onto the street and was staffed by skinny, tattooed lesbians dressed mostly in attitude accessorized with piercings. The music was deafening.

She'd thought that, even after twenty years, she would know Valerie's walk or her heart-shaped face and brown eyes, but she didn't. It was Valerie who walked up to her, finally, when Sydney had been waiting by the counter for ten minutes.

"Hey, Sydney," Valerie said. "How weird is this?" She shook Sydney's hand.

Valerie had a cyclist's calves and wore a tailored, no-nonsense gray suit with close-toed black heels. Sydney felt underdressed in her black pants and beige blouse. At least her hair had stayed up this morning.

Valerie's smooth bob was highlighted with copper streaks and she wore the makeup of a woman who'd spent years perfecting the art: green and beige eye shadow in careful arcs, a brown-toned lipstick. Everything about Valerie seemed sharp, from the cut of her skirt to the pointy toes of her shoes and the razored edges of her chin-length hair.

The only off note was her eyeliner, which had been used under one eye but forgotten under the other, giving Valerie's face an asymmetrical look. Maybe she'd been nervous this morning, too.

"You look almost the same," Valerie said, giving Sydney the once-over from her hair to her flat shoes. When Sydney didn't answer immediately, Valerie snorted and added, "Yeah, I know. I look like I've got a stick up my ass. Goes with the briefcase."

Sydney laughed and some of the tension in her shoulders fell away. They both ordered salads at the counter and then found a seat near the windows, where the music was quieter.

"Thank you for meeting me," Sydney said.

"No prob. I would have called you eventually."

"Liar." Sydney studied her friend's shifting brown eyes. "You already knew how to find me, didn't you?"

"Yes. I've always known." Valerie's mouth tightened at the corners.

Sydney forged ahead anyway. "I mostly knew where you were, too. Like I said, I called you now because I finally went back to Haven Lake."

"This wasn't the first time, was it?" Valerie sounded suspicious.

"Yes. I was living with my grandparents after Dad died, and after a while, it seemed easier not to go back at all."

"I understand. I've certainly not had any desire to see the farm again."

Their number was called. They went to the counter to retrieve their food and find silverware and napkins, salt and pepper. Sydney's fork slipped out of her hand, damp and slippery with nerves, and clattered to the floor. She picked it up and wiped it, intending to use it anyway, then caught Valerie's look and went to get a clean one.

There was so much she wanted to ask, but where to begin? Sydney seized on a question that seemed neutral. "So where's your mom living these days?"

"L.A." Valerie waved a hand dismissively. "She moved to California after Theo died. Well, first she had to do a couple of self-healing stints at ashrams in India and Bali. You know Lucy. I stayed with Dad, then moved to California to live with her when she got settled in Los Angeles. I came back after three months because I couldn't stand her. Or L.A. All that sun and traffic. But it suits her."

"What does she do there?"

"Yoga instructor. Naturally."

Sydney wanted to laugh, but Valerie's head was bent to her salad, so she couldn't tell if the other woman was trying to be funny or simply stating facts. She decided to play it safe. "It must have been so hard for both of you after Theo drowned. For years, I've wanted to see you, to tell you how sorry I was. We weren't invited to the memorial service or I'm sure we would have come." This last sentence came out more accusatory than she'd intended.

"Yeah. Well. My mom and dad fell apart. We all did. I can't believe your mom stayed at Haven Lake, frankly. I'd have nightmares out there. What's she doing?"

"She's raising sheep now. Not much of a living, but she's always been good at living close to the bone."

"Yeah, that early seventies mind-set," Valerie agreed. "Good for her. I'd had enough of that hair shirt act by high school."

Sydney smiled. "I remember how starstruck I was when you came back to the farm that last winter. You seemed so grown-up and experienced. I was still being homeschooled and protected from the heathen influences of things like TV. I coveted your Walkman and all that music you brought. Michael Jackson, Mariah Carey! My God, Madonna! It was a revelation."

Valerie smiled for the first time. "And Duran Duran. God, I had a crush on them."

Sydney laughed. "And you'd just gotten your license. Remember how we sneaked out one night in your mom's car and went to see *Alien 3*? I still don't know how you got us into that theater. It was an R-rated movie."

"I gave the ticket seller a blunt," Valerie said. "Of course, Theo was even more freaked out by that movie than we were," Valerie said, and dropped her eyes. "He always was a wimp." Her eyes filled.

"I'm sorry. I didn't mean to upset you." Impulsively, Sydney reached across the table to touch Valerie's hand.

Valerie snatched her hand away. "You didn't. I'm sad every day, thanks to your dad."

"What do you mean?"

"That man was a raving lunatic." Valerie picked up her fork and stabbed at a cherry tomato. "Your father broke up my parents and my brother drowned himself because of it. I suppose you must miss him, but frankly, I'm glad the guy shot himself. If only he'd done it sooner, my brother might still be here."

Sydney drew in a painful, shocked breath. "That's a horrible thing to say. And completely untrue. You can't seriously believe your parents got divorced because of my *dad*? That's ridiculous! Your mom is the one who came to the farm alone every summer and screwed any guy who'd have her!"

Valerie threw down her fork with such a clatter that several of the other diners turned to stare. "Why do you think I didn't want to come back to the farm that last time?"

"Because of your stupid boyfriend! You told me you were going to *die* if you had to live without him one more day! You were finally in love and having *sex* for the first time!"

Valerie widened her brown eyes. "You believed that? Shit, Sydney. I had sex when I was thirteen with that airhead Josh! Remember that loser in his jeans skirts? I just made that stuff up about a boyfriend because I wanted Mom to take us home. Your dad was like a drug to her, and not a happy drug, either. Every time she tried to quit him, he came after her."

"That's a load of crap," Sydney said, her voice rising. "My father was never with your mom. But everybody else was. She was always dancing or playing that stupid flute, putting on her breakable act. Worked like a charm with any guy she wanted. I saw Lucy with Uncle Rory and a lot of the other men. Once, out in the cornfield, she was screwing *Josh*! So, nice job hitting on your mom's lover. My dad suffered from PTSD, but your mom was certifiable. He never would have touched her."

Valerie stood up so fast that her chair fell over with a loud bang. "My mother was a vulnerable woman struggling in an abusive marriage!" she barked. "Your father was a controlling, egotistical shit! You must have had blinders on, thinking your dad wasn't shagging her. Theo probably went out looking for your dad that night because he didn't want my mom hooking up with him again. After that, Theo was so fucked-up, he went swimming. *That's* what made him drown. Your fucking father!"

"It was Uncle Rory she was sleeping with," Sydney said, trying to hold on to her own conviction as she stared up at Valerie. With her shoulders thrown back and her square-cut hair and bangs, Valerie looked as powerful as Cleopatra. Sydney half expected snakes to appear and wind themselves around Valerie's arms.

"No, it wasn't!" Valerie said.

"I saw them together," Sydney insisted, "and I told Theo. *That's* why he went out to find her. He didn't want your mom to be with Rory."

Valerie leaned over the table, putting her face alarmingly close to Sydney's. "Theo was with *you* that night?"

"Yes." All the air seemed to have been pushed out of Sydney's lungs. Her mind was working overtime. Had her father really been sleeping with Lucy? How could her mother have let that happen?

Valerie picked up her chair and sat down on it again as Sydney told her everything: about going to bed with Theo that night, then saying the one thing that could have made Theo get up and leave her. "So you see, even if my dad and your mom were lovers, it wasn't my dad's fault your brother drowned," she finished. "It was me. I'm the reason."

Valerie was staring at her, holding her face so stiffly that for a minute Sydney imagined the skin cracking and shattering off her bones. Finally she said dully, "No. It wasn't your fault, Sydney. You loved Theo. You never would have deliberately done anything to hurt my brother."

Sydney hadn't realized that this was what she'd been waiting to hear from Valerie: forgiveness. She tasted salt and wiped her damp face on a napkin. "I did love him, Valerie. So much."

By now everyone in the café was openly staring at them. "Come on," Valerie said. "Let's get the hell out of here."

They began walking blindly in the direction of Boston Common while Valerie told Sydney her version of events from the night Theo drowned.

"I was on the porch for a while, hanging out with a couple of cute guys from Israel," Valerie said. "They'd just finished their military service and were talking about how cool it was to shoot a gun. I wanted to try it, so they told me to find a rifle and they'd teach me. I left them on the porch and went looking for Rory."

"Wait. Why Rory?" Sydney leaned closer, trying to hear every word over the rush of traffic on Boylston Street.

Valerie shrugged. "I thought if there was a gun on the farm, Rory would know where it was kept. We were just going to go out and shoot some cans, you know? Target practice. Anyway, when I found Rory at his cabin, he was bleeding, his face and arms all cut up. He said he'd gotten into a fight with my brother and wanted to know if I'd seen him anywhere. But I told him I hadn't."

"What was the fight about? Did Rory say?"

"My mom, just like you said. The weird thing is, Rory was about the only guy Mom never went to bed with, because he'd have nothing to do with her. They were just friends. Later, Mom told me Rory wouldn't sleep with her because he was in love with your mother."

"What?" Sydney was shocked, but only momentarily. She supposed she'd always known this on some level, just as she must have been subconsciously aware of her father and Lucy being together. The pieces were all falling into place now. Between gigs and farm chores, Rory always seemed to be helping her mother around the house or kitchen garden, running errands for her, or just sitting in the kitchen and playing his guitar while she baked. Sydney had always perceived their relationship as a love between friends. But, in retrospect, it was Rory who had acted like her mother's husband.

Valerie was still talking. "Yeah, Rory was crazy about Hannah. I think that's why my mom was so in love with your dad and determined to have him. Allen was charismatic and handsome and energetic. Sexy as hell. Even as a teenager, I could see that. But, more importantly, Allen was Hannah's husband, and everyone at Haven Lake was in love with her. Your mom just had this quality of knowing how to make everybody feel welcome. Hannah was the real heart of Haven Lake. Naturally Mom envied her. I think she wanted to *be* Hannah."

Sydney knew this must have been true, hearing Valerie say it like this. "I don't think Mom thought that way about herself," she said. "She told me once that she never felt like she was in control of anything at the farm except the garden and me."

Valerie nodded. "I get that. But my mom grew up as the only child of wealthy parents. She always wanted to be at the center of things. It killed her that my dad played around, that he made so much money and used it to control her. It was her own fault for wanting the money without wanting to work for it, I know. But the point is, she was never with Rory. When Theo didn't find Mom with Rory, he must have gone looking for your dad."

"Maybe he thought I'd been mistaken and seen Lucy with Dad instead of with Rory," Sydney mused, thinking this through. "They had similar builds."

"That's possible. Anyway, on my way to see Rory that night, I passed Theo running through the woods toward the lake, but I never told anyone. Not even Rory when he asked."

"Why not?"

"Because, as he was running, Theo turned his head to look at me and made a circle with his fingers." Valerie demonstrated the gesture with her fingers.

Sydney had to take two strides for every one of Valerie's. She wanted to tell her to slow down because she had a stitch in her side, but she didn't want Valerie to stop.

At the same time, she wanted Valerie to say no more, because now the two of them were reliving that night again, and it could have only one terrible ending. What was the point of going back there?

Because you both need to know the story, Sydney reminded herself, and clung to Valerie's arm as she struggled to keep up. *You may never know the one real truth, but with many truths, you'll come close.*

"What did the circle mean?" she asked.

"It meant that whatever happened at that moment couldn't be shared beyond us," Valerie said. "Theo and I had kind of a sign language as kids, because we were only a year apart and our parents, well, living with them was like living in a war zone. We were like little spies with our own world and our own language. Putting your fingers in a circle meant that we were asking the other to keep whatever was happening from the adults. Your fingers were like a fence. Or maybe a force field, a bubble to keep you safe."

Sydney nodded, picturing this: Theo with his long legs and bare feet carrying him through the forest, his eyes black as embers as he wove between the tall pines toward the lake, seeing his sister and holding up his fingers in that circle.

"So there was this crazy moment in the woods when I passed Theo running like some kind of storybook creature, half man, half deer." Valerie turned to Sydney and brushed her bangs off her forehead. "You see? It's not your fault that Theo died. It's mine. If I'd told Rory I'd seen which way Theo was running, Rory might have gone after him, and Theo wouldn't have drowned."

They walked in silence, arms still linked. Finally Sydney said, "I don't think it was your fault, either, Val. You loved your brother. You kept silent because of that love. You were loyal and good to him, always. What's really amazing to me is that none of the adults seem to really know anything about what happened that night. Why didn't anybody wonder why Theo never came back to the house and went to bed? Were the adults all high that night, just out screwing in the cornfield or playing music?"

Sydney was getting so worked up that she had to stop suddenly at a corner. She didn't move even when the light changed and pedestrians streamed around them to cross the street. There were so many unanswered questions, still. "I need to go back to Haven Lake and see my mother again. You should come with me."

"No," Valerie said. She made no move to cross the street, either, just stood next to Sydney, panting slightly in the heat.

She wasn't just hot. Valerie was afraid, Sydney realized. "Come on," Sydney said. "I'm sure Mom must know more than she's told me. Did you know she burned down the barn where my dad shot himself?" she asked abruptly. "As a lawyer, doesn't that seem like the act of a guilty person?"

"Or the act of a grieving one," Valerie said, drawing Sydney into her arms and blocking out the traffic, the people passing by, and the whole bright blue sky above them.

CHAPTER FIFTEEN

It was Monday afternoon and his hospital room was empty for once. Sydney and Dad must still be at work, and Mark had another track meet today.

The problem with being stuck in a hospital bed and held hostage by tubes feeding into your arms was there was too much time to think. Dylan imagined Mark walking up to the track from the high school gym, stepping on his own blood speckling the path under the pine trees. Pieces of himself now mixed with dirt.

Once, when Dylan was in fifth grade, he'd found a dead opossum by the side of the road. He hadn't told any of the other kids at the bus stop about it. Instead, he used to lag behind and wait until everyone was gone, then poke at the animal with a stick, fascinated by the stiff hair and pink snout, the way the tongue protruded, and the opossum's long comma of a tail.

What really got him, though, were the animal's tracks, like a child's bloody handprints showing where the animal must have dragged itself from the road to this bush to die after getting hit by a car.

Every day, he'd gone to see the opossum, ignoring the stink to watch it rot and attract flies. He'd watched the eggs puff up and the maggots emerge, white as toes, to wriggle around and feast on the opossum's rotting meat. Gradually, the animal's flesh disappeared, and as more time passed, the opossum became nothing but bones and a bag of skin made dusty by passing cars. It didn't even stink anymore.

After Tyler's beating, he'd drifted in and out of consciousness, unable to pick himself up off that dirt path, and imagined being eaten by bugs until his skin was flat and his bones were shiny. People might not see his bones and just crush them under their feet on the path. Eventually he would turn to dust like his mom, whose soul he hoped might be watching him sometimes. That idea had its appeal.

But death sucked. He could see that now.

For one thing, there was Mark. Mark had come to the hospital every day, even though Dylan knew his friend must be cringing every time that hospital smell hit him. Mark hated pain and was terrified of needles. One year in elementary school, they'd all lined up for flu shots and Mark had run away. They'd sent the security guard to catch him, but the guard had returned breathless, red-faced, and empty-handed. Mark had been that scared. Yet here he was. For Dylan. What would his death do to Mark?

Or to his dad? His father visited him every day, too, looking pinched and uncertain. He hadn't bitched Dylan out for stealing his cell phone back, even though he must have seen it charging on the hospital nightstand. Dad looked like he hadn't slept in a week, twitchy and jumping up every time the nurses came in. Of course, he knew a lot of them, so maybe he was just embarrassed about his own kid being there.

Then there was Sydney. Dylan could tell by looking at Sydney's eyes that she was pulling for him. He wondered if Sydney would break up with his dad now that she knew about him using drugs. He'd feel like crap on toast if that happened. But he still wasn't sorry he'd told her. It wouldn't be fair if he and Dad knew, but she didn't.

Anyway, the point was this: he had to keep living. This whole stupid thing with Kelly and Tyler had shown him that. Tyler was an a-hole, but Kelly was even worse: a betrayer. He'd trusted her, but she'd obviously set him up. He wasn't in love with her anymore. Now the only thing that mattered was staying away from both of them and getting his head on straight so he could stop disappointing the other people in his life. The ones who mattered.

The afternoon dragged on, the sun shifting so that the lower roof of the hospital wing glittered against the pink sky. He wondered who lay in those rooms below that sparkling roof. A hospital was a layer cake of pain and sickness. How did his dad stand working here?

Finally he was bored enough to do homework. Dylan pulled his laptop out of his school backpack, which Sydney had heaved onto the table beside the bed so he could reach it. He'd just opened the computer on his lap when somebody came into the room and moved swiftly to stand in the narrow space between his bed and the windows.

Dylan looked up and nearly had a seizure when he saw Kelly. "What are you doing here?"

"You don't sound too happy to see me." The sunlight coming in from the window behind her gave Kelly a gold halo like those paintings of the Madonna he'd seen in his art history class, but she was standing funny, stiffly, with her arms at her sides.

"I'm not," Dylan said, imagining Tyler leaping out from under his bed. He didn't really think this would happen. On the other hand, he hadn't thought Kelly would set her bonehead boyfriend on him like an attack dog. He wished, for the first time, that his dad were here. His dad would know what to do. Or Sydney.

"I came to say I'm sorry." Kelly reached over to close his laptop lid, then sat down on the bed beside him. Now he could see her face: creamy pink cheeks, black-rimmed eyes, bright red lips. "I wanted to make sure you're okay."

"Do I look okay to you?" Dylan wanted to fold his arms, but when he tried, the IV tube pulled tight, so he stopped.

She blinked hard at him. The black stuff she wore around her eyes was thick and smudged, like she'd crayoned around her eyelashes. "I *do* care. Listen, none of that was my idea. Tyler just said he wanted to see you, to tell you to quit trying to get with me in person. He made me text you."

"Yeah, well. I guess he saw me, right?" Dylan tried to smile, but he was getting nervous again. What if Tyler came flying through the hospital door? It somehow seemed worse that Kelly didn't have any control over him.

She seemed to be worrying about the same thing, because Kelly glanced over her shoulder and then twisted her hands in her lap, saying, "You can't talk to me anymore. Or text me or anything. I want you to unfollow me on Twitter, too."

On impulse, Dylan grabbed his cell phone off the table and threw it across the room. The back came off and the battery went skidding out into the hallway. "There. Happy? Consider yourself unfollowed. But you don't own Newburyport. Neither does Tyler. If I see you, I see you." Something occurred to him then. "Did you take a video of the fight and post it?"

He could tell by the way she dropped her eyes that she had. Jesus. Kelly's nails were long and blue, the same color blue as her eyelids and that Gatorade he used to drink until he found out that one serving had fourteen grams of sugar. He almost felt sorry for her. If she'd been dumb enough to post that video on Twitter, the cops might see it. They'd be looking at the closed-circuit cameras behind the school, too. The cops could recognize Tyler from the footage. How could Kelly be that stupid?

And how could he have ever thought he was in love with her? Today she looked like a stranger to him. A Disney mean girl who wasn't even that hot. Definitely not hot enough to die for.

"Okay, then," he said. "We're done here. Get off my bed. Unless you're waiting for Tyler to come find you and make another romantic action video."

To Dylan's shock, Kelly jumped off the bed like she'd been stung by a bee, springing almost straight up in the air and landing on her feet. Her blond hair was filled with static from the polyester hospital blanket; strands of it stood almost straight up. "It's not *like* that," she said. "I never meant for you to get hurt!"

"Right," he said slowly. "So, just out of curiosity, if that's true, why didn't you stop Tyler from pounding my face into the ground?"

"I tried! Didn't you hear me yelling? What was I supposed to do, huh? Jump on him?" Kelly was standing in that strange position again, rigidly straight, arms at her sides. "Then he would have gone after me, too! And I tweeted that stuff about you to keep him away from you, moron. You're not a bad kid, and I was scared shitless Tyler would come after you if you tried to see me."

"I don't get why you don't leave him. Not for me. But for you."

Tears began sliding down Kelly's face, bringing black goo from her lashes with them like sooty raindrops. "I can't. He'd kill me."

"There's got to be a way," Dylan said warily.

"There isn't. I'm fucked."

He couldn't trust Kelly, Dylan reminded himself. This could all be an act. But then he thought of Sydney, of how she was trying to stick with his dad even though she probably didn't trust him now, either. Hannah had gone out in the middle of the night to help Dylan, not just once, but twice, and she'd fed him and taught him about sheep and put up with him hacking into her computer at the farm. And his dad? His dad was still coming to the hospital every chance he could, even after all the shit Dylan had pulled. Even when somebody let you down, you should try to help that person. "Have you told anybody that you're scared Tyler might hurt you?"

Kelly smacked her own forehead with one hand. "Yeah, right. I forgot. I could go to an adult!" She gave a manic grin. "Like who? My druggie mom, who gives me pot so I won't bust her for dealing? My *guidance* counselor, Dr. Compassion, who'll just remind me that I've got six detentions already for missed homework and might not graduate?"

"Come over here," Dylan said.

"What?" She stared at him, spooked enough to claw her hands into fists.

"Come here," he said again, fishing around in his backpack. "What, are you afraid of me now that I've got tubes in my arms and I'm wearing this polka-dot nightgown that shows my bare ass when I get up to take a leak?"

Kelly giggled nervously, inching forward until she was standing next to the bed. Dylan tore a piece of paper out of his notebook and scrawled Sydney's name and number on it. He handed it to her. "Call this person," he said.

"Why?"

"Because she's my friend," Dylan said. "I think you met her at the drugstore. Her job is helping kids with problems. You can trust her. She'll help you. I promise."

"I doubt it," Kelly said, but she took the paper, folded it, and jammed it into her pocket. "Why would you want to help me, anyway?"

Dylan laid his head back against the pillows. "Because I can."

On Monday night, Hannah harvested the asparagus out of the patch behind the barn. She was carrying the stalks up to the house when she was stopped by the sight of a leggy doe. The doe saw her at the same time and picked up its head, ears twitching.

Suddenly a fawn that must have been curled in the tall grass by the doe's legs struggled upright, its white spots gleaming like daisies against its caramel coat. Hannah froze and held her breath until the doe decided it was safe to bound away, the fawn leaping after its mother, their tails waving like white flags in the purpling dusk. The deer ran into the woods next to the pond, where the animals were easily camouflaged in the dappled light and disappeared instantly. It was as if they'd never existed.

When Hannah started walking again, she realized the deer had been grazing around the foundation of the small barn. There was nothing left of it now but the pit that had once been a pigsty and the old fieldstones around the base of the building, spotted with lichen.

She had walked by this spot nearly every day in the twenty years since Allen's death. It pained her every time, like a sore tooth she sought to avoid. Usually she kept her head down to keep from seeing it.

Today, though, she stepped on a branch that cracked loudly beneath her feet, a deafening retort in the peaceful valley. The noise brought her to a sudden halt, her heart pounding as the doe's must have been, though her predator wasn't a live thing, only memory rearing its black shadow.

Hannah willed her legs to move forward, but her body remained as solidly in place as the chestnut tree now flowering behind the house, its white blossoms startling against the darkening sky as if someone had lit a thousand white candles in the branches. She had no choice but to relive the moment if she wanted to move forward. It was her mind playing tricks, she knew that, but sometimes people were as furiously primal as animals when it came to fear.

Everyone thought she was afraid of Allen, but she wasn't. Not ever. She had understood, even the few times he hit her, that it wasn't her he was after. He was not himself during those ugly moments, but some other more primitive being, one awash with fear or rage or confusion, depending on what had triggered his mood.

Most of the time she was able to talk him through it. Or, with Rory's help, they could get Allen outside. Sometimes he removed himself, too, running through the hills, an increasingly tiny figure racing across the fields and up the dirt paths carved into the acreage behind the house, beyond the pond. Allen sought open spaces and silence. She and Rory knew that, and they could usually find him.

But not that last night. They were nearly alone on the farm, other than Rory and a couple from Norway, new arrivals. The others had left Haven Lake soon after Theo drowned, convinced—possibly by the sudden and unwelcome police presence—that their Haven no longer existed.

A child's tragic death marks everyone forever, surprising you like icy spots in an otherwise warm and welcoming pond. Allen had felt the shock of Theo dying more than anyone but Lucy, probably. He was upset not only because he'd been Lucy's lover, but because Theo's death brought down the entire community he'd worked so hard to build. A single tragic death had smashed his dream of a better world as surely as a boot crushing a rose blossom.

For a few days after Theo drowned, Allen had held himself together, despite constant questioning by the cops. But at night he would crawl out of bed and stumble toward the doorway after pulling on his jeans and boots.

"Going out," he'd say. "Need some air."

If Hannah tried to follow or pleaded with him to come back to bed, Allen would snarl at her, his words guttural, sounding smashed. But Allen didn't drink. Not after the war. He'd seen what booze could do to men, starting with his father.

For days, this went on, Allen unable to sleep, Hannah waking up with him and then dropping back into bed exhausted. With their help mostly gone, she was working harder on the farm, and saw no end to the labor. They would have to advertise, she was thinking that last night. Hire people to help over the summer if nobody showed up, as they usually did, through word of mouth.

Practicalities. She was thinking practicalities. Meanwhile, her husband, six days after Theo drowned, went out of his mind with grief, disappointment, guilt, anger, or some combination. She still didn't know what had finally triggered him to end his life. She only knew that she'd been lying in bed, doing petty mental accounting when she heard the sharp report of a rifle.

He must be shooting rats. That was Hannah's rational mind coming up with an explanation for the noise shattering the peaceful night. But her body understood before her mind did that it was impossible; Allen would never hunt rats at night. He rarely fired a gun at all, too freaked out after the war. He usually left that sort of thing to Rory.

Her body somehow got itself out of bed while her mind considered other possibilities. Maybe Allen had seen a fox near the hens, or maybe that sound was actually a car backfiring on a neighboring farm. Sound traveled at night.

But the noise had come from the barns.

Hannah had dressed hurriedly, tugging a sweater on over her nightgown and yanking boots onto sockless feet before running down the dew-slick hill from the house to the small barn, to this very spot where she stood right now with her arms full of sweet green asparagus stalks, their feathery tips tickling her skin.

She'd found the doors to the small barn wide open. That set off alarm bells immediately: she knew she'd closed them that night after milking the cows, as she always did.

A second mental alarm sounded when she realized the cows weren't in the barn anymore. Someone had let them out into their pen to one side of the barn without opening the gate from the pen to the pasture. Now the poor spotted beasts were huddled outside and making a din, mooing in terror, their enormous eyes rolling white in the dim light.

Hannah darted into the barn and slid on something—blood, she realized later—catching herself with one hand on the rough barn wall inches from Allen's body. Her husband's face was nearly intact, but the back of his head was blown apart. Later, the cops would tell her that's how soldiers killed themselves: they aimed downward into their mouths, not straight back, because they knew that would be the quickest and least painful way to hit the spinal cord.

"Kind of the way you'd want to shoot a horse with a broken leg," one of the officers told her, not unkindly. "Your husband didn't suffer."

But he did suffer! Allen had been suffering for years! Hannah wanted to tell the police that, to rail against their kindness, against the practical, efficient way the cops cataloged the scene and then told the ambulance guys to take Allen's body away. She had remained silent throughout, her body numb with cold and shock despite a blanket one of them had put around her shoulders, not wanting to cooperate with the police because, even then, she was used to mistrusting their authoritarian uniforms. She knew it was too late to help Allen anyway.

Maybe it had always been too late to help him. Even when he first returned from Vietnam at twenty.

With this last thought, Hannah sighed and lifted her foot experimentally out of the grass. Yes, she could move again. One foot in front of the other. She took halting steps up the hill without looking behind her at the deep pocket of shadow that threatened to swallow her whole each and every day.

In the kitchen, she mechanically boiled water for pasta and sliced and sautéed the asparagus. She ate the pasta and asparagus tossed together with olive oil and shaved Parmesan, then did the dishes.

This effort exhausted her. She stood for a minute at the sink, staring out the window. The sheep were in for the night, but bushes humped like animals, dark and bristly beneath the full moon gleaming against the rapidly darkening horizon. Hannah couldn't relax. She wondered if she should have her bath now and be done with the day, even though it wasn't quite seven o'clock.

Just then she heard a car turn into her driveway and snapped to attention.

Billy was barking. Oscar had been sitting in the fireplace, grooming himself; now the woodchuck disappeared under the stove. The sound of a car arriving at night brought back the memory of Les showing up on her porch. Hannah's mouth went dry with fear and she wished she could hide under the stove with the woodchuck.

She grabbed the shotgun she'd started keeping in the closet by the front door. The gun was unloaded; still, holding it made her feel braver as she secured the dead bolt on the front door and hurried to the front window.

The car was an ordinary blue Honda. Not Les, then. Sydney had a car like that, but it couldn't be hers.

Yet it was. There was her daughter, stepping out of the car and looking around as if she might jump back into it and drive away if something spooked her.

Hannah realized she'd been holding her breath only when she felt suddenly light-headed. She ran to the door and threw it open. "What are you doing here?"

Sydney stared at her, wide-eyed. "What's that for? Are you trying to send me a message?"

Hannah had forgotten she was still holding the gun. She hastily ducked into the house and stowed the rifle in the front closet, then returned to the door and held it open. "No. I'm glad to see you, honey. Just surprised."

"Obviously." Sydney rubbed her arms as she walked up the porch steps. Her hair was pinned up, but tendrils had come loose and curled around her face. "What's with the gun?"

"Coyotes." Hannah didn't want to say too much or ask any questions, for fear that whatever words she spoke might chase Sydney away. Why was she here?

Something must have happened at home to cause Sydney to drive all this way. Hannah felt nearly sick with anxiety. Not once, in twenty years, had Sydney come to see her, until Dylan was here.

Dylan! Had something happened to him?

Patience, Hannah chided herself. *You'll know soon enough.*

Sydney had entered the house and was following her into the kitchen, where Hannah offered leftover pasta and tea or coffee. Sydney said no to the food but agreed to a cup of mint tea.

Hannah was relieved to have something to do, though she fumbled awkwardly, catching the spoon of dried mint leaves on the edge of the canister and scattering them across the green Formica counter. She spooned too much tea into a pot and started the electric kettle, then filled a couple of mugs with hot water to warm them, and arranged shortbread cookies on a plate.

She turned around only when she could trust her own expression to be pleasant and welcoming. Hannah was startled to see that Sydney was still standing up, staring as if she'd never seen her own mother before.

"Oh! Sit down! Please," Hannah said, her voice too loud. "We'll have tea."

The words echoed between them, as ridiculous as dialogue in a theatrical farce. Finally, though, Sydney scraped a chair away from the table and sat with her hands folded primly in front of her. Oscar, sensing treats, came waddling out from under the stove, stretching and baring his big front teeth in a yawn, then sat and cleaned himself next to Billy.

The dog lay motionless with his head between his paws, his worried eyes fixed on Hannah.

She began to smile at the dog to reassure him, but Sydney was still watching her in that detached, clinical way, so she stopped. The silence between them stretched tight, nearly unbearable as Hannah turned her back again and finished making the tea.

Once she'd poured it into cups, there was nothing else to do. She sat down at the table and Oscar immediately hurried over to beg. She scooped him into her lap, taking comfort in the warm heft of the woodchuck on her knee, and fed him a bit of cookie, ignoring the crumbs spilling into her lap.

"So," Hannah said. No point in pretending. "Why are you here? Has something else happened? I've been wondering about Dylan."

"Really? You could have called if you were concerned." Sydney sipped her tea and made a face. "Ouch. Hot."

"I did just boil the water." Hannah, immediately on the defensive, was disproportionately glad that her daughter had burned her tongue. What had she done, after all, to incur Sydney's snippy tone? "I didn't call because I know how busy you are, and how much you don't want me interfering. I tried Dylan's cell a few times, but he never picked up. I assumed Gary had confiscated it along with the computer. That seemed to be his plan."

"For a little while." Sydney blew across the top of her cup. "Dylan stole it back."

"Oh." Hannah barely stopped herself from smiling. Clever kid. "I'll try calling him again, if Gary lets him keep his phone."

Sydney nodded, set down her cup. "He will. The phone is the least of our concerns right now. Dylan was attacked. He's all right now," she added, seeing Hannah's expression. "He'll come home from the hospital tomorrow, probably."

"What do you mean, he was *attacked*? When?"

"Friday night."

"But today is *Monday*." Hannah couldn't believe she was just hearing this now. "Why didn't you tell me?"

"I'm telling you now. That's partly why I drove out here."

"But that was days ago! Didn't you think I'd want to know? Dylan must think I don't even care about him. Is that what you think, too? That I don't care?"

Sydney shrugged. "Oh, I know you *care*. I guess I just didn't think you'd care that much."

"That's unfair." Hannah's anger was a prickling sensation that started at her hairline and moved rapidly down her spine like hot fingers. "You're wrong," she said. "About as wrong as you could be."

Sydney's face paled at her tone. "Calm down, Mom. I'm sorry, okay? I didn't mean to upset you. It was an oversight! Everything happened so fast. We didn't even leave the hospital all weekend. He was drifting in and out of consciousness for the first twenty-four hours."

"Dylan was *unconscious*?" Hannah's voice was loud enough that Billy raised his head to stare at her.

"Yes."

Poor Dylan! Hannah felt sickened by a mix of sorrow, helplessness, and fury at her own stupid missteps. Why hadn't she kept trying to reach Dylan? Why had she let her own pride keep her from calling Sydney to check on him? She couldn't stand the idea of Dylan feeling so alone.

Especially because that's how she felt: all alone. Had felt, for years.

Hannah put the woodchuck down hastily and moved rapidly to the counter, carrying her cup with her and keeping her back to Sydney as she dumped the tea into the sink and rinsed out the mug.

"Is he all right now?" Hannah asked when she'd composed herself.

"Mostly. He's still banged up, but nothing's broken. They kept him in the hospital because the CT scan showed a concussion. The brain trauma was causing him to lose consciousness. And then, whenever he was awake, he kept vomiting, so they had him on an IV as well. I don't even know how much Dylan remembers about the fight. He can't, or won't, tell us who attacked him."

Hannah heard the fatigue in Sydney's voice and sat down again. "But you don't think it was random?"

"No. I absolutely don't. I think Dylan's just afraid to say who it was. He's either protecting someone or protecting himself. Maybe he's afraid his attacker will go after him again."

"Oh my God. The poor kid."

They sat in silence for a minute. Hannah noted the dark blue circles under Sydney's eyes; her daughter's hair needed washing and her blouse was twisted in a funny way around her body. Hannah regretted having lost her temper—really, what good did that ever do?—but didn't apologize.

Sydney should have called me, she thought stubbornly, picturing Dylan, bruised and bleeding. "Are the police involved?"

Sydney nodded. "They're going over surveillance videos to see if they can identify the attacker."

Hannah remembered her conversation with Dylan in Rory's cabin, how he'd confessed that he was afraid to go home because of a girl. "Did Dylan say what the fight was about? Was it somebody who knew him?"

"He hasn't said anything at all, no. Why?"

"While he was staying here, he said one reason he didn't want to go back was because he was obsessed with a girl and wasn't sure he could stay away from her. Do you think this fight could have something to do with that?"

Sydney bit her lip, looking thoughtful. "I do know who the girl is, and yes, maybe. She has another boyfriend. God. I really don't know. I'll have to ask his friend Mark."

"He has a friend? That's good."

Sydney smiled. Not much of a smile, but it was there. "Yes, he's the one who found Dylan after it was all over. Mark has been very loyal, coming to see him every day."

I would have been there every day, too, Hannah thought, but it was pointless to say it. If she did, Sydney would view her as needy, and Hannah knew from experience what Sydney thought of needy mothers. Sydney had left Haven Lake because Hannah was too needy.

And because you were a sloppy, witless, irresponsible drunk, a shrill voice blared in her head.

All true. She was an awful mother after Allen died, too intent on curling up and trying to disappear to take care of anyone. If she hadn't had a child, Hannah knew she might have disappeared just like Rory. Started a new life or thrown herself off a cliff. As it was, she did whatever it took to stay numb after the horror of finding Allen's mangled body.

She should have stopped him from leaving their bed that night. Or followed him, no matter how hard he shook her off. Allen never would have shot himself if she'd been with him.

That's what Hannah wanted to believe, anyway. But another, saner voice in her head whispered otherwise: Allen might have killed her, too, if she'd followed him to the barn. His mind had snapped.

"Have you tried talking to the girl?" Hannah asked.

Sydney's smile disappeared. "No. The police were pretty clear about not wanting us to contact anyone who was potentially involved. They want us to give them names, if Dylan says anything, but to otherwise stay out of this and let them go about their business."

"Well. Of course they'd say that," Hannah said.

"Don't, Mom."

"Don't what?"

"Don't act like you don't believe in the justice system! You're too old to rebel against authority."

"I'm not." Hannah thought about Les and his threats. "It's just that sometimes things are too complicated for the police. You might find out more on your own."

"I'm not about to play detective. I don't want to do anything to compromise the investigation." Sydney picked up a shortbread cookie and crunched on it.

Her daughter might have come here to talk about Dylan, but Hannah could tell by Sydney's rigid posture that she had another agenda as well. She was chewing that cookie as if it were made of glass, chomping straight into it and wincing with each bite.

Oscar had come over to her chair again and was pawing at her leg. Hannah bent down and picked him up, cradled his fat body against her chest.

Finally, Sydney set the half-eaten cookie down and said, "Speaking of cops, I saw Valerie for lunch today."

Hannah was confused for a minute, until she realized Sydney must be talking about Theo's sister. That was the only "Valerie" they both knew. "Oh? How is she?" Hannah swallowed and continued stroking the woodchuck; Oscar was trying to burrow into her sweater.

"Seems like her life is going well."

"Have the two of you kept in touch?"

"It was the first time I'd seen her since Theo died." Sydney stumbled, but went on. "I didn't even recognize her at first. She's a lawyer now and dresses like one. Very tough and professional looking."

Hannah couldn't imagine this; Valerie had always been such a nonentity around the farm. Well, until the last few years, when her mother started encouraging her to do drugs and "explore her sexuality." Jesus. Lucy: what a piece of work.

"Was she with her mother?" Hannah asked.

"No. Lucy's living in California now."

Doing what? Hannah wondered briefly, then realized she didn't want to know. With Lucy, the less she knew, the better. She didn't trust her emotions not to flare up where Lucy was concerned.

By now Sydney was sitting straighter in the chair, her hands folded again on the table in front of her like a school principal's. She'd had a manicure but not recently, Hannah noticed; the red polish was badly chipped. Hannah was on edge, too. She said the most neutral thing she could think of: "It must have been interesting to see Valerie after all this time."

Sydney gave her a look to let Hannah know just how stupid any neutral remark between them sounded. "I arranged to see Valerie after coming back to Haven Lake, because being here again made me realize how much I didn't know about the night Theo died."

"He went swimming and drowned. Millie found him floating out by the little island. It was an accident. He probably hit his head. You know all that. What else is there?" Hannah felt claustrophobic. The kitchen walls seemed to be closing in and she could smell the compost in its bucket under the sink. She'd forgotten to take it out; maybe she should do that now. Anything to leave this room.

"None of that makes sense, though," Sydney said. "For starters, how would Theo have hit his head? If he dove in from the dock and did hit his head, maybe on that big rock we all used to love to stand on as kids—and even that seems unlikely, because Theo damn well knew where that rock was—he would have knocked himself unconscious right away. I've read up on this, Mom. He would have sunk where he drowned. He wouldn't have floated to the island."

"I thought the same thing at the time," Hannah agreed. "But the forensic pathologist said Theo died with water in his lungs, so he definitely drowned. The pathologist actually speculated that Theo dove into the water from the island and hit his head that way."

"You mean he swam across the pond, got out of the water at the island, then dove back in and hit his head? Is that what you really think happened, Mom?" Sydney's voice was patient. Her therapist's voice, probably, the one she used to soothe anxious parents and troubled children.

It did sound far-fetched, Hannah knew. It had been a chilly, rainy May night. If Theo did swim out to the island, he never would have gotten out of the water in that cold air. He would have just swum back to the dock. "No. I never believed that, either."

"So what's your theory, then?" Sydney asked.

"I don't know." Hannah was having trouble taking a full breath. She'd never really talked things through with anyone; she had been in shock immediately after Theo's death, she supposed, and numb throughout the investigation, with cops crawling all over the farm. Then there was Allen's suicide.

The woodchuck suddenly felt as heavy as a bear against her chest. She set Oscar down on the floor despite his squeaks of protest. "I thought it was strange, too, that Theo's body could float halfway across the pond, especially that night. And I didn't think he'd get out of the water and stand on the island. It was too cold. Plus, it's so shallow around the island that he wouldn't have tried diving in. He knew better, didn't he?"

Sydney nodded. "We all did."

"The only thing that makes sense to me is that Theo must have been swimming underwater fast," Hannah continued. "He was a competitive swimmer in high school. Because it was night, maybe he plowed into a rock headfirst. Or maybe he did a racing dive off the dock and went farther than he ever did before. That might have given him enough momentum to float to the island."

"Interesting ideas," Sydney said slowly, though she obviously didn't agree with either one. "So where were you when he died?"

The question surprised Hannah. "I was up at the house, same as you. Millie's screams must have awakened us at the same time, because we saw each other in the hallway when we came out of our rooms. Remember? We both ran down to the pond at the same time."

Sydney gave an impatient shake of her head. "No, I didn't mean that. I know where you were when we found out Theo drowned. But where were you when he went swimming? Go back. You tried to get me to unlock my door earlier, remember, and I wouldn't do it."

"Why not?" Hannah had her suspicions.

Now Sydney confirmed them, saying, "Because I was in bed with Theo. We were planning to have sex. We were both virgins and we wanted to be each other's first time. But then he and I started talking, and something I said upset him, so he ran out of the house."

"You were having sex?" This thought derailed Hannah. Her daughter having sex at fifteen! Of course she'd wanted to do the same with Rory; from the early seventies, birth control pills were being handed out like candy. Girls could do whatever they liked. Why should she be shocked? But she was.

"No, Mom. I'd never had sex before then. Like I said, we wanted to be each other's firsts. That was our plan. But then Theo freaked out and ran away."

"Why? What did you say to upset him?" Hannah was picturing it all: her daughter's fair head on the pillow, her limbs entwined with Theo's own longer, darker arms and legs. If she'd been able to design her daughter's first time, that would have been it. She knew how much Sydney loved Theo.

Sydney had been folding and refolding the dish towel on the table; now she answered the question before Hannah could ask it again. "I upset Theo by telling him that his mom was sleeping with Rory. He left to stop them. He wanted his parents to stay together."

"Lucy and Rory were sleeping together?" This news came like a punch to Hannah's head, startling and painful.

"No. That's the thing." Sydney picked up another cookie and crumbled it onto the plate, the crumbs falling like sand through her fingers. "I *thought* Lucy and Rory were sleeping together, because I'd seen them together a few times at Rory's cabin in the early morning and Lucy wasn't wearing much."

"She never wore much." Hannah hated the bitterness in her own voice, and hated it even more that Sydney noticed and glanced up. "But I don't think Rory slept with her."

"You're right. He never did. Val just told me that. But when I told Theo that I thought Lucy was with Rory, he went mental. He was afraid his dad wouldn't take Lucy back if she was sleeping around, and said Lucy was crazy without his dad."

"Her husband was a bastard. Lucy should have left him years before that night." If only she had, Hannah thought sadly, things might have turned out differently.

"Anyway, Theo left my room to stop them. Apparently he and Rory fought. Valerie saw Theo running through the woods afterward—she was on her way down to Rory's cabin for a different reason—and he was covered in blood. Theo seemed to be headed for the pond. He must have been looking for Dad. I guess he realized I'd made a mistake, or maybe he thought I'd told him on purpose that it was Rory, when really it was Dad who was sleeping with Lucy, wasn't it?"

When Hannah didn't answer, Sydney took a deep, shuddering breath, as if repeating this question was as painful for her to do as it was for Hannah to hear. "Did Lucy sleep with Dad?" Sydney asked.

Hannah ran a hand across her face, wishing she could run from the room rather than confront this ugly truth one more time, especially with Sydney, whom she'd always tried to protect from this one thing about her father. "Why do you want to dig around like this? What's the point, honey? I thought the reason you stayed away from Haven Lake was to avoid having to remember all this."

"Turns out, I was wrong about that. I need to know these things, Mom."

And there it was. Hannah had been expecting Sydney to ask questions, but years ago. She had never thought it would take so long for them to have this conversation. Yet, now that they were, it seemed to have sneaked up on her and thrown a blanket over her head. An itchy, damp blanket that she wanted to tear apart with her bare hands before she suffocated.

"You're sure you want to know?" Hannah asked.

"Yes."

Hannah nodded. "Okay, then. Yes, your father slept with Lucy. Not just once, but many times."

"How could you have let that happen?" Sydney cried.

"You have to remember the context," Hannah said. "Your father created Haven Lake out of his disillusionment after the war. He believed that American society was corrupt at its core and that it was our generation's job to reconfigure the rules our parents had been following, and our grandparents before that. He was very much a child of the sixties."

"I don't get how sleeping around would fix society." Sydney sounded sullenly adolescent.

Hannah smiled. "I never did, either. But I loved your father, and to be with him meant believing in what he did. He hated the whole concept of territoriality—over land, people, resources—because he believed that sole ownership would just lead to more bloodshed on both small and grand scales. Nobody should own anything, in his view. Especially not husbands and wives. As he saw it, that was the only way to give peace a chance. He was trying to give everyone equal power."

"Jesus. I mean, I guess I sort of understood his philosophy on some level as a kid, but it all sounds so strange now. Yet you bought into that, too?"

Hannah spread her hands. "I did. So, yes. Your dad slept with Lucy and with some of the other women at Haven Lake, too."

Sydney looked like this idea made her sick to her stomach, but pressed on. "Did you screw other guys?"

By Sydney's harsh tone, Hannah knew she was aiming to wound her for some reason. She couldn't blame her. What kid wants to know the inner workings of her parents' relationship? Hannah refused to lie, though. "No," she said. "I never slept with another man while I was married to your father. But I thought about it. And I came close a couple of times."

"With Rory?"

"Yes. But I never would have done it." Hannah flinched inwardly. She and Rory had never made love, true, but there was so much more to love between a man and a woman than just sex.

"Where was Dad the night Theo drowned? Was he with Lucy? Did Theo see them together? Is that why Theo and Dad fought? Josh heard them arguing."

Hannah stood up to give her lungs more room to expand. "I don't know where your father was. I never asked him questions like that if I could help it, because often I didn't like the answers."

Sydney wound her hands together one way, then another. "But he wasn't with you?"

"Earlier that night, yes. But not later."

"So how do you know he wasn't with Lucy?"

"I've already told you. I don't." Hannah crossed her arms and kept her eyes on her daughter's face. Such a beautiful, sad, worried-looking woman, her daughter.

"Tell me what happened that night, Mom!"

"All right." Hannah wasn't sure she could take much more of this, and yet for Sydney, she had to go on. "Your dad and I were on the porch for a while with the others after dinner, but then I asked him to walk down to the pond with me because I needed to talk to him in private. It was never easy to find time alone with him, not with so many people around."

Sydney gave her a scathing look. "Yeah. Whose fault was that? I wonder."

"Don't make this any harder than it is," Hannah said sharply, and sat down again.

To her surprise, Sydney held up her hands and apologized. "Sorry. Go on, Mom. What happened at the pond?"

"He and I went to the beach and sat there for a while. We used to meditate, you know—we both learned how while we were traveling in India—but as things got busier at Haven Lake with the business, we stopped meditating. Still, it was almost as good, sitting quietly by the water. We both loved how peaceful it was on the dock." She closed her eyes for a minute, picturing it all and trying to describe it for Sydney. "Down in the valley by the pond, it could often feel like you were trapped in a bowl of stars, the way the sky was reflected in the water, as if you were in the middle of the universe instead of tethered to the earth. And I always loved the sound of the wind in those pines along the shore."

Sydney nodded. "Me, too. I always loved the pond at night. It was that kind of healing place."

"Your father named it Haven Lake for a reason, remember?" Hannah said with a smile. "Anyway, I asked your dad to go down there that night because he always seemed more restful by the water, and I needed him to really listen to what I had to say." She clasped her hands around one knee to steady herself. "That night, I told him I was going to leave him and take you with me if he didn't stop sleeping with Lucy. I made it clear that I expected him to tell her she had to find somewhere else to live."

Sydney was staring at her, green eyes wide. "So you did care about him screwing around."

"I cared when it was Lucy." Hannah's own ferocious jealousy came charging back, leaving her with trembling hands. "Your dad was shocked. I was essentially issuing an ultimatum—me or her—and I'd never before imposed any sorts of restrictions on him. Allen was smart and generous and talented in so many ways, but he could be oblivious, too. I don't think he'd ever fully realized how jealous and hurt I was when he spent time with Lucy until that night."

"He was oblivious to a lot of things," Sydney said. "Dad lived in his own world most of the time. After living with his parents, I always thought maybe he turned out like that because his parents put him on such a pedestal."

"You're probably right," Hannah said, but she was thinking of the beatings in the basement, of the ugly secrets in the Bishop household. She had put Sydney at risk, letting her live there. Yet, some part of her had always known that Sydney's grandfather would never feel threatened by her. Only by his own sons.

But Hannah didn't want to get into that, so she kept talking, hurrying her sentences so that one tumbled into another. "Your dad was furious with me that night," she said. "He couldn't believe I actually expected him to kick Lucy out. We argued for a while, and then I left, since obviously nothing I said mattered to him."

"So you went back to the house and left Dad on the beach?"

Hannah shook her head. "I didn't go back to the house right away. I couldn't. I was too upset and there were too many people around."

Sydney waited. When Hannah didn't speak again, she prompted her. "Where did you go, Mom?"

"Oh God," Hannah said, and buried her face in her hands.

She heard Sydney scrape her chair away from the table and walk to the sink, where the tap ran for a few seconds. After a moment, her daughter put a glass of water next to Hannah's elbow. "Tell me," she said gently.

Hannah dropped her hands. Her eyes were dry but stung as if she were facing a heater. Through the open window, she heard a pair of barred owls calling; when she'd first moved to Haven Lake and heard that raucous, nightmarish noise, she'd thought it was coyotes and Allen had pulled her into his arms because she was so scared.

He was so tender sometimes, stroking her hair. Comforting her. Hannah's eyes filled with tears.

"Where were you that night, Mom?" Sydney was seated in a different chair now, the one next to hers.

Hannah had never spoken of this to anyone. She cleared her throat, trying to choose her words carefully. "I left your father on the beach. I'd crossed him in some unforgivable way, and I knew he was going to be in one of his moods. I didn't want to deal with it anymore. Or him. That night, I didn't think I could ever love him again. Not if he was going to keep on with Lucy, despite knowing how much that hurt me." Even now, she remembered the bewilderment she'd felt when Allen just laughed off her demands. "So I went to the only place that felt safe."

She could see by the look on Sydney's face that her daughter understood, so she waited until Sydney said, "Rory's cabin."

"Yes. He was there, but he was in terrible shape."

"He fought with Theo, Valerie said. Theo had a knife."

"It was Rory's knife, the one he always wore on his belt," Hannah said. "Rory told me Theo managed to grab it while they were fighting. He wanted to kill Rory because he thought his mother, well. You know all that."

Sydney drank from the glass of water she'd brought to the table for Hannah, noisy gulps. "How badly was Rory injured?"

"Bad enough. I tried to get him to the hospital for stitches, but he wouldn't go. Rory didn't want to get Theo in trouble. So I helped him clean up and we tore up an old T-shirt to bandage his arms. Then, I don't know. . ."

Sydney's hair was coming loose from its pins; she must have sprayed it, because it stood out in stiff strands around her face. "You don't know what?"

"I don't know why we didn't go after Theo," Hannah said, hearing her own voice break as she said the words that had been jaggedly lodged in her throat for years. "Rory told me Theo was looking for your father and we'd better follow him. But Rory was bleeding so much that I stopped him. I was afraid for him. And Theo had that knife."

"But Theo was running through the woods when Valerie saw him. Why wasn't he hurt, too, if they'd had a physical fight?"

"Your uncle Rory was big and very strong, but he was a pacifist. He and your father couldn't have been more different in that way."

"So Rory did nothing? Just let Theo cut him up?" Sydney sounded disbelieving.

Hannah looked down at their hands on the table. Sydney's were young-looking still, smooth, the fingers long and delicate. Her own hands had ropey blue veins protruding along the backs of them. Strong, but care-worn. The hands of a woman who knew about labor and harvest, tending and letting go.

"That's exactly what Rory did," she said sadly. "Until he finally convinced Theo that he'd never been with Lucy. He didn't say anything about Allen—Rory told me that, and I believed him. But Theo figured you'd mistaken your dad for Rory and went looking for him."

"And we know Theo found Dad, because Josh heard them fighting. Was Dad still at the beach when they fought?"

"I don't know."

"How can you not know?" Sydney asked, her voice too loud for the quiet kitchen. The barred owls started calling to each other again, making both women jump.

"Because I spent the night with Rory in his cabin," Hannah said finally. "I didn't want him to get hurt, and I didn't want to face the people at the house, or your father. I figured your dad had probably gone to be with Lucy, and you were in your room with the door locked, safe, so I stayed. I didn't want to be anywhere that night but with Rory."

"All night?"

"Yes." Hannah smiled a little, thinking of Rory's flannel shirt, soft and smelling of him. He'd held her in his narrow rope bed, cradling her on his shoulder while she told him she was leaving Allen, that she couldn't stand it anymore, she had to leave the farm and Allen and the whole idea of Haven Lake. Hannah couldn't bear being Allen's wife one more day, she'd said.

They hadn't made love. She'd wanted to, but just like when they were teenagers, Rory refused. She pleaded, but he shushed her and told her they could talk in the morning if she still felt this way, that she was upset and not thinking clearly. All true, she knew, and so she'd asked if she could just sleep with him, nothing more, just feel his body against hers, his blue-jeaned legs pressed to her own bare ones, his thigh between her knees, pushing up against her hot dampness, his hand on her hips, his breath coming too fast in her ear as he held himself still, so still, and tried to pretend not to want her as desperately, as urgently as she desired him.

Somehow they'd fallen asleep on the narrow rope bed. And then had come the screams from the pond when the morning light was pale green, filtering through the trees in shredded bits of sunlight caught on the dew-heavy pines, and Hannah had cried, "Sydney!" and left him, fled from Rory in bare feet, cutting her foot on a rock along the pine-needled path but not caring, running until she had no breath left in her, until she reached the house and raced upstairs and found Sydney just emerging from her bedroom. For that moment, it was enough. She felt as though she'd been spared a terrible fate, seeing her daughter safe, sleepily stumbling out of her bedroom.

The shrieks continued, however, and Hannah and Sydney ran down the stairs together to find Millie hunched over on the beach, and the men dragging Theo's body in from the island with the rowboat. They'd tied a rope around the boy's body because it was waterlogged, too heavy and awkward to bring him into the boat, Josh had explained, but Hannah wasn't listening, not really. She was too busy searching the shoreline for Allen until she found him, as shocked-looking as the rest of them, his mouth moving but no sound coming out as he sought her out, too, and came over to fold her into his arms.

Hannah had tried not to shrink from her husband's touch. She kept her eyes on the body that turned out to be Theo's, and realized in that moment that she would never be able to leave Allen now, because he would need her even more.

The sunlight, so bright and glittering before, had paled as Lucy ran toward the pond, also from the woods, where she might or might not have been with Allen. She threw her entire body over her son's as if he were her soldier come back from war, and with that one gesture she became all of them, and they became Lucy, grieving and lost.

CHAPTER SIXTEEN

Sydney left Haven Lake that night over her mother's protests. She still couldn't imagine spending the night in that house, and their conversation had shaken her to the core. Just sitting in the kitchen, she'd been awash with memories.

When she first sat down, for instance, she'd rested her elbows on the table and conjured an image of her father sitting across from her, the way he always did in the evenings. Scraggly beard, blue work shirt, dark eyes merry as he challenged her to a game of hearts. He'd become addicted to that game in Vietnam during long hours in-country. Dad would let her win, but just barely, and the two of them would laugh so hard that Sydney would get the hiccups. God, she had loved him, loved her father's true self, capable and intelligent and earnest.

Dad never talked about the war unless she asked questions when he was in one of his bright moods. Then he told her what he loved about Vietnam: the beauty of the sunrise over emerald rice paddies, the surprising friendships formed with men he might not otherwise have ever known or trusted. His friend Hank, for instance, who had died there, a twenty-year-old pig farmer who loved bluegrass and beer.

Her father was an infantryman in a combat platoon. They were sent mostly on search-and-destroy missions. When she was a child, this had sounded glamorous to Sydney, as if her dad were James Bond, a spy she'd read about as a child in tattered paperback novels left by some of the WWOOFers stopping over at Haven Lake. But Dad assured her it was not. Once, he'd lost his temper when she made the mistake of saying she thought it was cool, what he'd done.

"Look, we were just clearing trails of mines and booby traps," he yelled, "or burning hootches and watching the gooks scatter like ants in their black pajamas. Now don't say that again."

Her dad told her about the bugs in the jungle, how there were so many you couldn't help inhaling them in big clumps, a thought that made her almost gag. Sydney loved hearing about something called "elephant grass," though, which was what hid them from the enemy, and about the "wait-a-minute" vines, plants that sounded like something out of Dr. Seuss.

"What were they, really?" she'd asked. "Why did you call them that?"

"Because those damn vines would tangle around your legs so tight you couldn't move," he said. "You'd have to say 'wait a minute!' so everybody would wait for you while you cut your way free. Kind of like your friend Valerie, always telling you to wait because she's so slow. She's kind of like a vine around your legs, isn't she, kitten?"

"Dad!" she'd scolded him.

He let her boss him around when they were alone at the kitchen table, playing cards while Mom did the dishes or hung out with Uncle Rory on the porch. This only happened off-season, when nobody else was around but their own small family; when they were too exhausted from all that farming to do more than just go to bed by sunset, bleary-eyed and sore from chores.

Sydney turned her windshield wipers on high as she drove east on Route 2 into a hard rain, continuing to mull over the bits and pieces of story she'd gathered from her mother and Valerie. Thinking about the night Theo died felt like one of those thousand-piece jigsaw puzzles Grammy Bishop loved doing, the kind where half the picture was made up of different shades of the same color, like a sky or an ocean or a field.

There was something missing, still, a jagged gap. But Sydney didn't have a clue what it was or how to find it.

The wind had picked up and the car shuddered. Maybe she should have spent the night with her mother after all. This was a terrible night to be driving out here in the Berkshires, and there had been a rare intimacy between them tonight, sitting at that table, despite her feelings of claustrophobia and tension as she stumbled through new revelations.

On the other hand, she owed it to Gary to go back. He hadn't wanted her to drive out here in the first place. "You'll just get yourself worked up over things again," he'd said when she called him after work to say she was going to Haven Lake. "What's the point of rehashing things with your mother? Leave it alone, Sydney."

She couldn't do that. Not after seeing Valerie. Plus, there had been no reason to go to Gary's house right after work. Dylan was still in the hospital and Gary was working late to catch up on patient rounds, phone calls, and his new paper.

Before hanging up, they had agreed to talk about their relationship when she returned from the Berkshires. This would be their last evening alone before picking up Dylan, and—though this was left unspoken between them—Sydney needed some kind of reassurance about Gary curbing his drug use. Gary maintained that his dependence on medication was under control. But, now that Sydney was aware of it, it seemed like everything he said or did—his increasingly zealous attention to detail when housecleaning, for instance—could be explained by him being amped up.

She didn't want to feel this suspicion. If nothing else, Sydney was determined to find out exactly what Gary was taking and why. They would discuss that tonight, she vowed.

Route 2 seemed to last forever. When she finally merged onto Route 495, that highway seemed giant by comparison, since she had three empty lanes to herself, but she still had to proceed with caution to prevent hydroplaning in the heavy rain. She turned on the radio. There was nothing on but dire weather predictions about terrible storms and flooding, thanks to Tropical Storm Annabelle forming off the coast of Cuba, the summer's first hurricane. She turned the radio off again.

By now the rain was coming down in great sheets of water blowing across the road like curtains lit occasionally by oncoming headlights. Sydney squinted through the windshield and kept both hands on the wheel as she wondered where her father was the night Theo died. Hannah truly didn't seem to know. Had Theo found him with Lucy and succeeded in attacking him?

Unlikely. Her father was quick and agile—once a soldier, always a soldier—and she didn't recall him having any injuries that night.

Theo had suffered a blow to the head, somehow, while he swam in the pond. Sydney shivered, feeling her skin crawl with damp and cold as the rain drummed on the car roof and she thought about Theo thrashing alone in the water beneath the unforgiving night sky.

Or had he fought at all? Not if he'd hit his head. In that scenario, Theo would have simply breathed in water, as they had always imagined doing as children. She and Theo and Valerie wanted to have gills so they could swim with the frogs in Haven Lake, bending their knees and jumping from stone to stone, until that last final splash into the water when they would frog-kick their way across the pond underwater.

Was that what Theo was doing? Swimming underwater, frog-kicking through the silent deep, shivering through the cold springs and relaxing in the warmer parts of the pond until he hit his head and took one last, shuddering gulp of water? Was his death like falling asleep? She hoped so. Sydney wanted to imagine Theo dying peacefully, if nothing else.

How young he'd been. Dylan's age.

How young they had all been that night. Even her parents.

Sydney felt the tears she'd been holding back all night start to fall, sliding down her cheeks. She stabbed at the radio knob with her finger to turn it on again. Anything for a distraction.

By now she was close enough to Boston to tune into her favorite NPR station. The news was still all about the weather, the reporters focused on the building hurricane and the storm lashing the East Coast. They talked about waves pounding the coastline, rivers flooding, and power outages until Sydney started to feel nervous and silenced the radio again.

Now she was worried about her cottage. Had she left the windows open?

Damn it: yes. Sydney remembered opening them on Friday night when she came home from dancing with Marco. Then things got so crazy, shuttling between the hospital and work and Gary's house, that she hadn't been back to her house to close them.

She had phoned Barbara to decline the first offer, but the Realtor had lined up two more showings this week. She had ignored Sydney's fumbling protests about maybe not wanting to sell the house after all. To be fair, Sydney herself was no longer sure what she wanted to do, but either way, she'd better go home and close the windows or there could be significant damage.

She had slowed to thirty miles per hour because of the poor visibility. At least there wasn't any traffic. Sydney kept her eyes on the road and one hand on the wheel as she fumbled in her purse for her cell phone and hit the button for Gary's number.

He answered on the second ring, sounding tense. Hopped up? She hated not being sure, and hated it even more that he'd managed to fool her for so long.

"Hey," she said, "I'm on my way back from Mom's—"

"I still can't believe you drove out there," Gary interrupted. "What the hell were you thinking? Didn't you pay attention to the weather reports? It's a tropical storm, Sydney. No joke."

It had started to rain harder, true, but otherwise there wasn't anything that unusual about the storm so far. "It seems wet but okay here," she said. "It's probably worse along the coast. I'll be fine. I'll be home soon, but first I have to stop at the cottage. I just realized I left the windows open."

"Don't you dare drive more than you have to," Gary said. "So what if the rugs get wet?"

"It's not just the rugs! It's the wood floors, the furniture, the woodwork. Everything!" Sydney said. "And I've got two more showings this week. Look, you're the one who wants me to sell and move in with you, right?"

There was a brief silence, during which Sydney was aware of the car shuddering in the wind, as if a giant hand had grabbed the roof to shake it.

"About that," Gary said finally. "Maybe this isn't the right time for us to live together."

Sydney tightened her grip on the steering wheel. "What do you mean? Why not?"

"It's just that, with everything going on with Dylan, I don't know," he said.

"You don't know what?" she pressed. "You don't know about me? About us living together? Or about the wedding?"

Sydney let several miles go by without pushing him to answer her, while the wind now seemed to howl not only outside, but inside the car, too.

"I love you," Gary said finally. "But I don't think Dylan's ready to have another mother."

"I wouldn't be replacing his mother!" Sydney said. "I'd be your wife and Dylan's friend!"

"You're good with him, of course," Gary said. "And I think Dylan loves having you around. But his behavior lately—"

Sydney cut him off. "I don't think Dylan's behavior has anything to do with me."

"How can we be so sure?" Gary sounded agonized.

Sydney didn't know the answer to that. She just was. "I think he's going through something we don't even know about," she said. "Maybe with that girl he was seeing. So does Mom."

"Oh, so the hippie shepherdess is a parenting expert now?"

"That's not what I'm saying." Sydney was having trouble hanging on to the last shreds of her patience. "The thing is, Mom really cares about Dylan, and he seems to like and respect her, too. We need to honor that relationship."

"Honor that relationship?" Gary repeated. "God. Listen to yourself! I guess you can take the girl out of the tofu-eating Berkshires, but you can't take the tofu out of the girl."

"Shut up!" Sydney shouted. "Why are you being such a jerk? You and I may have our issues to work on—"

"Like what?" he interrupted.

"Like you popping pills to get through the day, for one thing!"

This time the silence lasted long enough for Sydney to pass another exit on the highway. She was nearly to Newburyport. "Are you still there?"

"Yes," he said. "Look, I'm sorry. You're right. I went too far with that remark about your mother. I shouldn't criticize her or jump to conclusions about why Dylan ran away or got into a fight. We'll have to talk to him at some point. Maybe his doctor knows something we don't. We'll find out tomorrow. Go home and close the windows in the cottage if you think you can make it. But then stay put, all right? Don't try to drive to my house. I don't want you out on the road longer than necessary. Just be safe, and I'll meet you at the hospital tomorrow for the appointment with Dr. Wong. Then we can go to lunch and talk everything over."

She heard the stutter of panic in his voice and realized he must be thinking about Amanda's car accident. This wasn't the time to press him about anything. Tomorrow they'd both be calmer and thinking more clearly.

"All right," she said. "I'm sorry, too. I didn't mean to make you worry. I promise to be careful. I love you."

"I love you, too," he said.

By the time Sydney reached Newburyport, the wind was so powerful that she had to grip the steering wheel with both hands as she navigated onto Route 95—safer than going on Route 1 closer to the coast, she thought—and inched her way south. She took the Scotland Road exit, but skipped her usual shortcut to Newbury in favor of staying on wider roads. She didn't want to risk having a tree fall on her car. The rain had let up a little, but the trees were swaying, bent nearly double in places.

Gary was right. She should have spent the night at Haven Lake. Let the ghosts come and get her. It was stupid to be driving in this weather.

But she was almost home now, and Sydney was still glad she'd made the trip. She would have hated leaving her house unprotected, its windows open to the roaring elements.

She turned left by the veterinarian's to go to Route 1A. As she passed the elementary school, there was some flooding but nothing remarkable, just deep puddles along both sides of the road. There wasn't any other traffic, so she kept her car at the highest point along the yellow dividing line.

Her house was on a road that turned east from Route 1A. As she neared the intersection, she gasped in terror as a tree branch snapped and fell onto the back of her car with a solid thump. The branch rolled off as she kept driving.

A few minutes later, Sydney spotted a familiar dark blue Toyota pulled over with its hazard lights blinking. That looked like Marco's car. But how could it be? What would he be doing in Newbury?

Then she remembered: Marco had been in the Newburyport courthouse all afternoon, testifying on behalf of a mutual client. He was probably on his way back to Ipswich. It would make sense that he'd be on this road if he'd stayed in Newburyport to have dinner with one of the lawyers.

She eased her car into the breakdown lane ahead of his. Marco came running out of his car, his coat over his head, and climbed into her passenger seat. The wind slammed the door shut before he could pull it closed.

"Thank God you came along!" he said. "Wow! This is brutal. I thought my car was going to get picked up like one of those spinning houses in *The Wizard of Oz*."

Sydney laughed. "This is a hurricane, not a tornado," she said. "What happened? Did your car break down again?"

He nodded. "I was coming back from dinner when the lights and the dashboard panel started to dim. Then the car suddenly stopped. It was like I ran out of gas, but that can't be true. I just filled the tank."

"Your alternator's probably dead."

"And here I was all set to jump the battery with those cables you gave me."

"I doubt anybody would have come along anyway. And you won't be able to get a tow truck out until the storm dies down."

"Well, I can hardly ask you to drive me home to Great Neck in this weather. Want to drop me at the Newbury police station? I could call a cab from there."

"I don't think you'd get a taxi out now, either."

"In that case, the cops will have to drive me home. That's fine. I've always wanted to ride in a police car."

"Look, my cottage is close. You can stay at my place. I have a guest room. They're saying the weather should ease up by morning."

The minute the words were out of her mouth, Sydney regretted making the offer. Her cheeks were flaming, her body acutely conscious of Marco's strong thighs so close to her own in the car. But it was too late now.

Marco was grinning. "Thanks," he said.

As they drove slowly down Route 1A, Marco told her about the court case. He seemed perfectly relaxed, even oblivious to the storm raging outside the car, but Sydney's knuckles were white as she clutched the wheel and held the Honda steady against the buffeting winds. At last, though, they were pulling into her driveway.

The rain drenched them both as they ran for the door, where Sydney fumbled her key into the lock. Then they were inside, where—no surprise—the power was out.

"Nice place," Marco said.

"It looks better when the electricity works." Sydney slipped off her shoes in the hall while Marco did the same. The rain was clattering like hooves on the porch roof.

She moved quickly down the hallway and into the living room, where she dug around for the pair of battery-powered lanterns she stored in the closet. She set one on the side table in the living room and carried the other into the kitchen, then found two flashlights in her junk drawer and handed one to Marco.

When Marco insisted that she should shower first while he built a fire in the living room, Sydney had to laugh. "How many fires did you build in the Bronx?"

"Hey. Thank the Fresh Air Fund camp for getting poor kids like me out of the city. I can make a mean fire. I can even shoot a bow and arrow."

"Less useful," she said, but left him to it and went around the cottage closing windows before heading for the shower.

The hot water stung and then tingled against her icy skin. Sydney luxuriated in the feeling, then dried off and covered up in her most matronly blue flannel pajamas. She deliberately chose her ancient floor-length pink terry-cloth robe to wrap around her, too, determined not to send Marco the wrong signal.

She lit a few candles and tended the fire—which was well built and blazing, as promised—while Marco showered. He emerged in the dry clothes she'd given him, gray sweatpants and a navy blue ribbed sweater that was big on her but snug across his chest and shoulders. They both laughed at the sight of his feet in the only pair of oversized socks she had: black socks with pink cupcakes that Ella had forgotten to take home after spending a night at the cottage a few weeks ago.

"I knew Ella was a woman of mystery, but truthfully I never once pictured her in cupcake socks," Marco said. "She seems more like the seamed-stocking type. Who do you think she spends time with when she's not queening around the office?"

They were in the kitchen, where Sydney was arranging crackers and cheddar cheese on a plate. "Me, for one," she said. "Ella's helping me plan my wedding."

"Sure, but who else? She never talks about the guys she sees, only makes rude noises about her hot dates. Do you think she actually goes out with different guys every weekend? Or does she stay home and binge-watch recorded TV shows like the rest of us?"

"You don't do that," Sydney said. "You're out dancing."

Marco rolled his eyes. "There you go again, confusing me with some kind of playboy. You know I only go out dancing once in a while, and even then it's with my cousin. Other than being kicked around in soccer matches, I live a sedate life."

"Yeah? So did Clark Kent. But give him a phone booth, and watch out."

Marco laughed. "Seriously, though. What about Ella?"

Sydney frowned, considering. She had wondered this before, too. "I don't know. Every time I ask her personal questions, Ella gives me vague answers. And I've never met any of her dates," she admitted. "I always assumed she deliberately put a wall between her work life and home life. I suppose most of us should do the same, given that we're constantly dealing in emotional currency. I don't know about you, but I'm wrung out sometimes. So many unhappy kids and families in the world, right?" She took down a bottle of brandy and two glasses from the cupboards over the fridge.

"Sure," Marco said. "But I wouldn't say I have any strict verbal boundary between my clients and me. I know that doesn't sound very professional, but when I see kids, especially teenagers, if I think it'll help for them to hear about some of the mistakes I've made, I go ahead and share those. I think it helps kids to know that it's possible for everyone to be better than they are during their worst moments."

"That's a nice message," Sydney agreed.

Marco helped her carry the food and brandy into the living room, where Sydney spread a blanket on the floor so they could sit closer to the fire. "By the way, I saw your client," he said.

"Which one? I referred two of them to you this month." They were facing the fire with their backs against the couch, the plate of cheese and crackers on the floor between them, brandy glasses cradled in their laps.

"Brianna Carlson. The mom brought her in to see me this morning."

Sydney pictured Brianna, earnestly talking about her music, and rubbed her arms even though she wasn't cold anymore. "I know you can't share specifics, but what do you think?"

"I think you were right to send her to me. There's definitely something going on at home."

They sat in silence for a few minutes, looking at the crackling fire. Sydney wondered if Marco was thinking, as she was, about all the kids like Brianna who came and went in their lives. You could only try to find them the right support, then hope like hell that a child's resilience would win over whatever adversity, or even horrors, their own parents might inflict on them.

Marco reached out and touched her arm. "Don't think about it right now. I just wanted you to know I'm looking out for her."

"Thank you. That means a lot."

"Sure. But, Sydney, I'd advise you to have backup if you see her father again. Things might get ugly."

"All right. Thank you."

The fire popped, startling them both and making them laugh. Marco got up to poke at the flames, though they were already vigorous. Sydney had been worried about opening the flue in the storm, but the rain didn't seem to be coming down the chimney. The wind was blowing in off the marsh, hitting the house's back side and making a steady deep whistling.

She relaxed against the sofa, cupping the brandy glass between both hands. If only someone like Marco had reached out to help her father, things might have turned out so differently. She felt her eyes well up and took another sip of brandy, swirling it in her mouth and enjoying the burn as she swallowed.

Marco sat down beside her again, his eyes on her face. "What are you thinking?"

Sydney smiled. She wasn't used to a man asking her that question. Usually she was the one knocking on whatever door Gary had tried to close. "Oh, just about all of the people in the world who should get help, but don't find it in time."

"A cheerful thought."

"I know. Sorry." She shifted her weight to look at him. The flickering firelight accentuated the sharp contours of Marco's face, his elegant nose, his sensual mouth. Sydney was painfully aware of wanting to lean forward, of her desire to press her lips to his, to drink in his warmth.

Every woman's dumb fireside romantic fantasy, she scolded herself, and forced herself to sit up straighter. "What about you? What are you thinking?"

"That you're beautiful," he said.

Sydney laughed dismissively. Marco was a player, despite whatever he said to the contrary. Yet she felt the brandy glass tremble in her hand. She twisted around to set the glass down on the end table next to the couch. "That's right. Nothing's sexier than terry cloth."

"Nothing's as sexy as terry cloth if you're the one wearing it," Marco said, and reached for her.

Not for her body—she could have, and would have, resisted that—but for her face. His long fingers slowly traced her brow, her cheekbones, her chin, ending on her lips before he dropped his hand to his lap. "You look like a mermaid, with all of those yellow curls and your green eyes."

"Don't say stupid things to me. You know I don't like it." Sydney pulled the robe closer and stared at the fire to avoid looking at him. "I'm getting married in a few months, remember?"

"You're not married yet."

Her eyes filled with tears. "But I will be."

"*Oye, chica*, don't cry. I didn't mean to upset you. I was just teasing. What's wrong?"

"Nothing." A sudden gust of wind rattled the windowpanes, making her jump. "Gary and I just have some things to work out."

"Every couple has things to work out. That's part of the challenge of being a couple, right? Hey, how's Dylan doing? Ella told me he was in a fight of some kind, bad enough to land him in the hospital. Is he okay?"

"He will be. He's coming home tomorrow." Sydney thought of Dylan there now, with only nurses for company, and felt even worse.

She had called Dylan before leaving for Haven Lake tonight, to ask if he wanted her to stop by. "No, I'm just going to watch a movie with this other kid they put in my room," he'd said. "You should just go home after work. I heard the weather's going to suck."

Marco had asked her a question; she asked him to repeat it. "I was wondering what went down during the fight between Dylan and that other kid," he said.

"I'm still not sure."

"Have you talked to the girl? Does she know anything?"

"I gave the police her name and they were going to interview her."

"She might open up more to you."

"That's what my mother thinks, too. Maybe I'll try to track her down tomorrow."

"Good. Let me know if I can help. I could always stop by the hospital and visit Dylan or something if you want." Marco turned to set his brandy glass on the other table. As he swiveled his body away from her, the sweater rode up above his narrow hip bone and revealed a long scar, pale against his coffee-colored skin.

"What happened there?" Sydney reached out to touch it, but quickly drew her hand back.

"Where?"

"That scar on your side."

"Oh. That." Marco shrugged, his eyes hooded. "It's from a knife fight."

"*What?* How old were you?"

"Fifteen. I have others, too. Want to see my medals of honor?"

When she nodded, Marco raised both sleeves of his sweater to reveal a series of jagged scars, then lifted the hem to show her a crosshatch pattern of scars on his chest and stomach. Sydney stared at him in horror. "My God. Did somebody attack you?"

"More than one somebody. And more than once. I did my share of the attacking, too, though. I wasn't always the victim. I was in a gang for a while when I was a kid. That's what you do, when you need a posse to survive on the streets."

"I guess I'm going to have to revise my opinion of you yet again."

"What do you mean?"

She told him, then, about how her perceptions of him kept shifting. For instance, how he seemed like the sort of man who would drive a new sports car, but instead had a sensible, if unreliable, used Toyota. "You look like the kind of guy who'd buy yourself toys, maybe flat-screen TVs or fancy sound systems," she added, "but instead you take care of your mother and put your sisters through college. I thought you were probably some kind of soccer prodigy as a teenager, but now you're telling me you were in a gang. I don't know what to think. I've been wrong every time about you."

"Is that good or bad?"

"I'm not sure. You keep me guessing."

"Better than boring you."

"You could never bore me," Sydney said, and then she was the one to reach for him, tracing her fingers slowly down Marco's face and neck, then pausing to dip her fingers in the hollow of his collarbones, feeling his heat through the cotton sweater before moving her fingers beneath the soft knit to stroke the scars on his side and chest. Marco sat very still, scarcely breathing, until finally she could stand it no longer and leaned forward to kiss him, tasting brandy and heat.

Then she was on his lap, moving to straddle him at the same time that Marco reached to lift her onto him. She kept her mouth on his, feeling his hands move through her precautions of flannel and terry cloth to her bare skin, sliding up to caress her breasts, making her inhale sharply with pleasure. She leaned into his palms and continued to kiss him, tasting those lips that she had wanted to feel on hers for so long, without even knowing how much she'd wanted them. Wanted him.

Her hair spilled around Marco's face and her robe slid down her shoulders as he untied the belt and tugged at the fabric, eventually freeing her of the robe and of her pajama shirt, too. She was moving more urgently now, pressing against him, too much time going by until he rolled her off him and tugged off the pajama bottoms as she pulled his sweatpants down. Soon they were both naked and lying on the floor on top of the blanket, his hand between her legs, her desire making her tip her head back and say his name in a whisper that felt like a shout.

And then, suddenly, Marco pulled away. He put both hands on her shoulders, his face so close that their foreheads touched. "You don't want to do this," he said, his voice hoarse.

"What do you mean?" Her own voice cracked. "How can you say that? I want you more than I've ever wanted anything. Or anybody."

"You don't want to do this," he repeated woodenly, dragging the words out of his mouth in a way that she could see caused him physical effort. "You're going to marry Gary. You will regret this if we keep going, Sydney. I know you."

And that was it. Sydney wept a little as she tugged her pajamas back on, ashamed, contrite, but most of all frustrated, because she had known, and still knew, that her body longed for Marco's, and that some part of her would never be satisfied until she knew how it felt to make love with him.

But he was right. That wouldn't be fair to Gary. To Dylan. Or to herself, most of all, because if she made love with Marco, she would have to tell Gary or live with that secret for the rest of her life, and she couldn't imagine how she could do either of those things.

"I'm so sorry," Marco said, running his hands through her hair.

She shook her head, blind with tears, pushing her face against his shoulder. "No. I'm the one who should apologize."

"You did nothing wrong. I wanted you. I want you, still," Marco said. "But the problem is that I want all of you, not just a part of you for only one moment, one night. I'm sorry."

"Stop apologizing!" Sydney shouted, suddenly feeling deranged with humiliation and frustration. She whacked Marco hard enough on the shoulder to make him gasp and grab her wrist. Then she broke down completely, weeping so hard her teeth chattered.

It was all too much. Everything was wrong.

She was wrong, most of all.

. . .

It had become clear, after Dylan left, just how much easier it was around Haven Lake with another pair of hands, so Hannah hired Sloan, the girl from the farm down the road, to come by for a few hours on weekends and after school. Once school got out in another week or so, Sloan promised to work more hours.

"What about your dad? Doesn't he need you?" Hannah asked.

Sloan shrugged her narrow shoulders beneath her two thick plaits of dark hair. "I do my chores at home, too. But he knows I need money for college."

The girl arrived each day on a small but noisy motorcycle, startling the sheep with its buzz at first, but by the third day the ewes mostly ignored the noise. The lambs, always curious to investigate something new, would trot toward the sound and then, delighted by their own audacity, would spring away from the gate as if the bike might chase them, making Sloan and Hannah laugh.

At first she'd asked Sloan to help with fencing and clearing the pasture of poisonous plants, pleased that Sloan could easily identify most common culprits, like milkweed, pigweed, goldenrod, lupine, and roses. The girl was also strong enough to heave hay bales around, despite her slight build, and Sloan found so many things funny that her piercing laugh became a welcome new soundtrack on the farm.

The day after Sydney made her surprise visit, Hannah had Sloan help her deworm the sheep and trim their hooves, thinking the intense work involved in those tasks would keep her from dwelling on last night's conversation. She'd been up half the night wondering whether she'd told Sydney too much, especially about Allen and Lucy. She was still worrying about Dylan, too, who had yet to answer her calls. Maybe she should just drive out there and, if Sydney protested, remind her that she was the one who'd started this new trend of ambush visits.

Sloan helped herd the sheep into the confinement pen, where Hannah showed the girl how to catch the ewes one at a time and immobilize them. This required approaching them cagily from one side, lifting their heads up, and easing them onto their rumps by pressing down on their hindquarters, tipping the sheep backward against her legs.

Sloan laughed at the absurd sight of the first ewe sitting down, her legs looking spindly and useless against her bulky, woolly body. "Why isn't she struggling?" she asked, as she held the animal upright so Hannah could get to the hooves.

"Sheep are prey animals. Their only defense is to run. She knows she can't run in this position, so she's just going to stay limp and hope we think she's dead and boring," Hannah explained as she scraped the muck off the hooves and then trimmed them with her shears.

"How do you know when to trim the hooves?"

"If the outside nails have started curling under the toe, they're too long. Or when they're cracked and the sheep is limping. Trimming the hooves keeps poop from getting caked inside there. What's really interesting is that there's a tiny scent gland located at the front of the hoof, right where a sheep's toes come together. See this? That part can get inflamed if it's not clear."

"Cool. Did you ever think about becoming a vet?"

Hannah shook her head and reached for the dewormer. "No." She lifted the ewe's head, inserted the tip of the drenching syringe into the animal's mouth, and emptied it slowly enough for the animal to swallow without choking. "Okay, you can let her go. Why do you ask? Are you thinking of becoming a vet?"

"Yeah, a large-animal vet."

"It's a lot of years of school," Hannah said. "I admire you. I never even finished college."

"Why not?"

"A man."

Sloan burst out laughing. "You're the last person I'd expect to say that."

Hannah straightened her back and smiled. "Why's that?"

"You just seem so, I don't know. Like you don't need anybody."

"Well, right now I need you to help me catch that ewe over there,"

Hannah said easily, thinking that, even a month ago, she would have agreed with Sloan. Now, though, Hannah was newly conscious of her empty, echoing house and the vastness of the woods and fields around her. She longed for company.

"Listen," she said as she knocked the next ewe on its rump, "I might have to go away tomorrow. Would it be possible for you to come by and bring the sheep in for me?"

"Sure," Sloan said. "I'd like that."

Hannah left at dawn the next morning after turning the sheep out in the pasture, bright green and sparkling with dew, and calling Liz to see if she was free to look in on Sloan and the sheep that afternoon. "You're sure you don't mind?"

"Are you kidding me?" Liz had said. "You should have gone out to see Sydney long before this. And Dylan needs to know you're thinking about him."

"I've been leaving him messages."

"Yeah, well. Kids aren't great about checking voice mail, IMHO."

"What the hell does 'IMHO' mean?"

"'In my humble opinion.' Come on, Sheepgal. Get with the program."

"I'm too old," Hannah complained.

"No. Just too stubborn," Liz said with a chortle, and hung up.

She *was* stubborn. Hannah knew that. She'd always been headstrong; when her father had pleaded with her to stay in college, after working so hard to earn scholarships, she hadn't listened, had she? No, she'd dropped out to travel with Allen. Maybe that's why she felt a certain connection to Dylan and his restless nature.

She hadn't been to Newburyport more than a handful of times, but Gary's house was easy to find. She'd hoped to arrive before Sydney left for work, but neither car was in the driveway and nobody answered the door when she rang the bell.

Maybe they were at Sydney's. Hannah backed out of the driveway and took the only way she remembered, heading south along Route 1A past enormous, stern-looking Federal houses, elegant Victorians, and prim Colonials that set her teeth on edge because they reminded her of the Bishops and all they had done to harm Allen and Rory. Their mother may not have been the one disciplining them in the basement, but she'd pretended not to know, and she had wielded a different but equally powerful stick with her constant disapproval of them.

And of Hannah. But Hannah pushed that thought away—a stupid woman, why dwell on her?—and continued driving until she reached the lower common in Newbury, the one with the little old schoolhouse, where she knew to turn left toward the water. Sydney's neighborhood was made up of modest Capes and cottages, and even a trailer, painted bright Bermuda blue. Everyone had a garden and dogs wandered the road like they owned it, which they probably did.

Hannah was disappointed to find Sydney's driveway empty. Damn it. She'd have to call Sydney instead of taking her by surprise. Calling was a risk: it would make it easier for Sydney to say she was too busy, or Gary was too tired, or Dylan was, well, whatever Dylan was. Hannah just hoped he was all right. She was determined to see him for a few minutes, at least, after having come all this way.

First, though, she needed to pee. That was a lot of coffee and a long drive. Hannah got out of the car—she was still driving Susan's old car, thanks to Liz—and went to the front door. Did Sydney bother locking her door in this quiet neighborhood?

She did. Hannah rattled the knob in frustration, then noticed the pot of geraniums at her feet. She bent down and slipped her hand beneath it, searching for a key.

Nothing. But maybe there was a back door. If not, she'd just have to pee in the yard. She hadn't seen any gas stations or restaurants between Newburyport and Newbury along Route 1A, and she was that desperate.

Hannah made her way around the side of the house. She had been here only twice before. She'd forgotten how magnificent the view was. A shame Sydney had to sell it. She'd been so excited when she bought the cottage that she'd even invited Hannah to a housewarming party. A disaster of a night: Hannah hadn't known anyone and Sydney hadn't seemed to want to introduce her.

But her daughter seemed more approachable now. More forgiving.

Hannah walked across the little brick patio behind the house, nicely set up with a pair of teal Adirondack chairs and more containers of flowers, and went up to the sliding door. Eureka! Unlocked!

Inside, Hannah removed her shoes and glanced around. She'd never seen such a clean house, other than Gary's; where were the magazines on the tables? Then she remembered the Realtor's For Sale sign and blanched. How horrible, to have strangers traipsing in and out of your home at odd times, judging your furniture, your rugs, your roof. Another reason not to sell Haven Lake. They'd have to carry her out feet-first.

She found the bathroom, peed with a sigh of relief, washed her hands, and returned to the kitchen. She was standing at the kitchen window, admiring the view and drinking a glass of water, when someone knocked on the front door. Oh, dear God. The Realtor?

Maybe it was just a UPS guy or something. In any case, she wasn't going to answer the door. Hannah rinsed out the glass and hurried out the back door without bothering to put on her shoes first, sliding it shut as soundlessly as possible. She was hovering there, her shoes in one hand, waiting to hear the sound of a car pull out, when a man came around the corner.

He stopped at the sight of her, looking as alarmed as Hannah felt. He was a striking man, with sharp features and a tangle of dark hair, dressed in black jeans and a blue T-shirt. He was handsome in the fierce way of a musician or a cowboy, all angles and long legs, bronze skin, a sharp chin with a shadow of beard. His eyes were very dark beneath the thick black brows. He didn't look like a house burglar, certainly, but the guy wasn't carrying tools, either. Was he one of those insurance adjusters? A meter reader?

"Can I help you?" Hannah asked, trying to sound breezy.

"I'm looking for Sydney."

"You must know she's not home. I heard you knocking."

"You were in the house?" He looked understandably confused, probably wondering why the hell she hadn't answered the door.

"I was just leaving." Hannah put on her shoes as proof. "Would you like me to give her a message?"

The man was staring at her, his eyes narrowed. "You're Sydney's mother," he said abruptly. "What are you doing sneaking around her house?"

"I wasn't sneaking," Hannah said testily, wondering how this man knew who she was. "I stopped by to see if Sydney's here, since she wasn't at her boyfriend's." She emphasized the last word.

"But you were in her house."

"So? I'm her mother."

"I've heard a lot about you." The man crossed his arms.

"Have you? And who are you?" Hannah demanded, hating the heat flaming in her cheeks. What had Sydney told this guy about her? Nothing good, surely.

"Marco Baez."

Hannah quickly tried to recall anything Sydney had told her about this man and failed. "Well, she may have told you about me, but I haven't heard one thing about you."

She was shocked to see the downcast expression on the guy's face. He must be sweet on Sydney! She felt the corners of her mouth twitch at this idea. Sydney's love life must be more complicated than she let on. Good for her.

Marco quickly recovered, though, and said, "I don't imagine you would. We just work together."

Hannah eyed him from head to foot. "You do more than that, I'm guessing."

It had been a guess. But she wasn't surprised when Marco blushed and turned away. "Yeah, well. Please don't tell Sydney I was here. I should just go."

"Wait!" Hannah hurried to catch up with him. "I'm sorry I upset you. Whatever is between you and my daughter is none of my business. I'm looking for her, too. Do you have any idea where she is?"

He looked at her, dark eyes assessing. "No."

"What about Dylan? Is he all right? That's really why I came. Dylan was staying with me for a while."

"I know. You were good to take him in when you did." Marco's voice had softened. "You know he was attacked and has been in the hospital?"

"Yes. That's why I drove out here to see him. I called the hospital and they told me Dylan had been discharged, so I went to Gary's house first. Then I came here."

"Gary's taking Dylan to an eating disorders clinic today. A day clinic down in Beverly."

This didn't exactly come as a shock, but still it hurt to take in this news. She should have known. But Dylan had eaten at her house. Had eaten a lot, in fact. What did that mean, that he ate at her house, but not here?

Nothing. Nothing she could understand, anyway. She'd never known anything about teenagers. Not even about her own. Obviously. "I'm sorry," she said.

"Don't be. It's the right course of action. He'll be in a day program for a few weeks. Then they'll determine what kind of support he needs. It's a good thing overall."

Hannah felt comforted, as much by Marco's kind, no-nonsense delivery as by his words. "Did Sydney go with them?"

"No. I thought she might be here, since she wasn't in the office yet."

Hannah nodded. She wasn't about to press him about why he was looking for Sydney. She liked this man. She felt Marco's compassion, warmth, intelligence, and the depth of his feelings for Sydney. "Look, I know this is none of my business, but you should tell Sydney how you feel about her."

Marco looked startled, but smiled and brought an envelope out of his pocket. "I already have. And I was planning to tell her again. I wanted to leave this note for her if she wasn't home."

"The back door's unlocked."

They looked at each other for a minute; then Hannah nodded. "I'll leave and let you get on with it."

CHAPTER SEVENTEEN

His dad picked him up at the hospital to drive him to Beverly. Dylan didn't want to go. He even thought about running away again as he waited for his dad to sign the papers to release him from the hospital. But he was too sore. Plus, Dr. Wong said she'd send him to the clinic by ambulance if he didn't go voluntarily.

"This is an intervention," she'd said earlier that day when he and Dad and Sydney met with her. Dr. Wong wore her badass grim reaper face. "Dylan, you are severely underweight and anemic. Your blood pressure is too low. Tests have also shown a reduction in bone density. You have an eating disorder called anorexia. Perhaps you have heard of it?"

"We learned about it in sixth grade," he'd mumbled.

"We must all work together to get this under control, Dylan, or there will be serious health consequences."

No lie, he was pissed when Dr. Wong said those tubes up his arm had been pumping calories into his body as well as antibiotics. No wonder his jeans fit funny. The nurses wouldn't bring him a scale, but he could tell by looking in the mirror that his face was fat and white, like those weird white pumpkins with warts and green streaks his mom used to bring home at Halloween because she felt sorry for them. The nurses probably felt sorry for him, too.

Still, the truth? Dr. Wong had scared the crap out of him.

"Okay. I'll go," he said.

For the first time, he saw Dr. Wong smile in a way that didn't look like something she practiced in the mirror to avoid scaring patients. "Very good," she said. "A positive step on the road to your recovery."

Dad steered the car with both hands on the wheel in that "nine and three" safety pose they taught in driver's ed. Watching him, it was hard to believe Dad ever used to race his Mustang against his brother's Camaro. Even before Mom died, Dad had been the poster child for auto safety. Except for his special cocktail of pills. Was he still taking those? Wouldn't taking speed impair your driving? Make you drive faster, ha-ha?

You couldn't tell if a person was on drugs just by looking, not unless he did something. You couldn't tell if a person was insane like Tyler, either, or fucked-up like Kelly, as long as the person was holding things together.

Human bodies were like those shells with hermit crabs in them. When he was little, he used to go to a beach in Gloucester with Mom to find hermit crabs. They'd fill buckets with them, then line up the crabs on the beach like race cars and bet on which one would make it to the water first. It wasn't always the crab with the smallest shell. Also, once the hermit crabs were mixed in with the other shells, you couldn't tell which shells had animals inside and which ones were empty until they started moving. Just like people: you couldn't predict what was inside their shells just by looking.

Dad cleared his throat like he wanted to say something. Dylan noticed new creases around his eyes. He'd never thought of his father as old, but today he looked it. "Sorry about everything, Dad."

His father kept his eyes pinned to the road, as if the highway might start swinging like a jump rope in front of him. "It's fine, son. Getting you the right help is more important than work. Sydney had concerns about your weight a long time ago. I should have listened. We'll get this all straightened out. Don't you worry."

Okay, that was his old dad talking: the Guy Who Gets 'Er Done. Why hadn't he listened to Sydney? Dylan wondered. Was it because she didn't have enough letters after her name, like stiff Dr. Wong, who moved like a puppet on strings in her red high heels?

Or maybe Dad just didn't want to think there was a problem so big, he couldn't solve it himself. Whether he was hiking a mountain and the weather turned bad, or trying to fix a broken body on a dirt floor in Haiti, Dad always believed he could make things better. When he was little, Dylan had believed that about his dad, too.

But sometimes you couldn't control what happened. Not if you had other people in your life. People you cared about. People didn't always say and do the right things. Everybody had to live their own lives. His dad, Hannah, Sydney, him, Kelly, Mark, even butthead Tyler: every person was on a different path, feeling the way forward one toe at a time. If you were lucky, your path would cross the paths of other people who cared about you and you'd catch each other if you fell. If you weren't, people might trip you up.

But you didn't have any control over that, either.

"I'm not saying I'm sorry about your having to take me to the clinic, Dad. I was just trying to say I'm sorry you're unhappy."

"You think I'm unhappy?" Now his father did look at him, a quick sideways jerk of his head.

"Aren't you?" Dylan said.

"Of course not." His father's voice was fake-cheerful. "What gave you that idea? I'm not unhappy. I'm never unhappy!"

"Yes, you are, Dad. Otherwise you wouldn't be taking those pills."

Dad swiveled his head to look at him again, too fast this time, causing the car to swerve. The driver in the SUV beside them honked and sped up, giving them the finger.

Dad didn't seem to notice. "I'm not taking antidepressants," he was saying. "I've explained this to you. I work long days and take medication to help me stay alert. You know the hours I work. I have a prescription. You had no cause to worry Sydney about that."

"We're not talking about Sydney. *I'm* worried about you."

There was a long silence where his father said nothing and Dylan imagined various scenarios: his father lashing out to strike him, causing them to crash into another car, or shouting him down for mouthing off. The only scenario he didn't imagine was what happened next.

His father shuddered and kept his eyes on the road, saying, "I never should have put those things of your mother's in storage."

"What are you talking about? What things?"

"Everything." His father's hands twisted the wheel erratically, causing the car to shimmy between lanes. "I kept it all." Another car honked behind them.

"Dad. Dad!" Dylan glanced between his father and the road, wondering if he should grab the wheel. "Pull over, okay? Listen, let's get a snack. I'm hungry." It was the only thing he could think to say that might work.

It did. His father signaled and shot off the next exit ramp. They drove a short way down the road and found a Dunkin' Donuts.

Inside, his father went to the bathroom and came back with his face still dripping with water. He ordered a black coffee and Dylan, after deliberating, asked for a yogurt smoothie. He looked around while they waited, at the pink and orange decor here, in Newburyport, everywhere. Ten thousand of these pink and orange restaurants around the world. Over thirty countries. All so people could eat fat and sugar and make their hearts go bump in the night.

He'd asked for the smoothie instead of water not just to make his father feel like he was trying to get better, but because he knew it wouldn't take much to push his weight into a zone doctors would call "normal." He'd eaten a gallon of ice cream just before Sydney took him to the pediatrician last year, and drunk a quart of milk. That had added two pounds instantly and the doctor hadn't said anything about him being underweight. If he drank this smoothie, there was a chance they'd shake their heads at the clinic and send him home again.

A fat chance. Or would it be a slim chance? Dylan nearly laughed, that uncontrollable kind of laugh you get when you're freaked. His freak-out wasn't about the clinic, though. It was about his dad, who, always solid, seemed to be crumbling in front of him. In public! The guy's hands were shaking so bad that he could hardly grab his wallet out of his back pocket. What had he meant about keeping Mom's things in storage?

They carried the drinks outside, where his father stood blinking in the bright sunshine next to the driver's side. Then, just as Dylan was about to get into the car, his dad's head disappeared below the roof of the Lexus. Whoosh! One minute there, the next, gone.

"Dad! Dad!" Dylan ran around the car. His father hadn't fallen, but he was stooped over and muttering like a homeless person, tipping the coffee in one hand so it dripped brown tears onto the pavement.

Dylan took the cup out of his father's hand and set it down on the pavement. "What's wrong? Talk to me! Jesus, are you okay?" He wished Sydney were here, but Dad hadn't let her come. He'd heard them arguing in the hospital hallway after the first appointment with Dr. Wong. Dad had told Sydney he needed "quality time with my son," like he and Dylan were going on a fishing trip.

Now his father couldn't seem to put words together. Was it the pills? Was he having a stroke? Dylan glanced around the parking lot to reassure himself that other people were around. Should he call somebody?

Dylan pulled his cell phone out of his pocket. He'd put it back together after Kelly left; now he scrolled through his contacts, keeping one eye on his father while he searched for Sydney's number. There!

He was about to press it when his father suddenly looked up at him, his eyes lasering into Dylan's, blue on blue. "I don't want you to be sick," Dad said. "It's my fault you have an eating disorder. I never should have kept your mom's things from you."

Dylan turned the phone off again but kept it in one hand. "What are you talking about? What things?"

"Her clothes. Jewelry. Photographs. Her favorite rocking chair." His father spidered his fingers through the air as if he were a magician who could conjure these objects in the parking lot. "She loved to sing to you in that chair."

"You have her *stuff*?" Dylan felt dizzy in the sun and thought he might be sick. "I thought you threw it away. Or gave it to Goodwill or whatever."

"No. I wanted to, but I couldn't."

"Jesus, Dad," Dylan said, loudly enough that a family of two normal-looking parents and two kids, a family that probably went to fucking church every fucking Sunday, stared at him as they walked across the parking lot. "You mean you've been *hiding* Mom's stuff from me?"

"Not from you." His father sank to the curb beside the car, never mind his new khakis with the creased fronts and his clean dress shirt. "I was hiding it from *me*."

Dylan felt rage building as he stood over him. He wanted to strike his father, or at least kick over his coffee. Two things stopped him: a bald spot the size of a quarter on the crown of his father's head, where the skin was sunburned a bright tender pink, and the fact that his father's shoulders were as rigid as if someone had stuck a broom pole inside his shirt and that broom was the last thing holding him upright.

Was his father trying not to *cry*? Here in a fast-food parking lot? When he hadn't even cried at Mom's *funeral*?

Dylan's anger ebbed away. He suddenly felt like he could collapse here, too. He sat down on the curb next to his father, wincing at the rough feel of it biting through his board shorts. "So where is everything?"

His father looked over at Dylan, his eyes red-rimmed and bleary. "In a storage unit in Rowley."

Rowley. Close enough to Newburyport that he could have ridden his bike there if he'd known. Dylan pictured himself hammering on steel doors, picking a lock, torching a hole in the roof and dropping down among his mother's boxes. "Why didn't you tell me you still had Mom's stuff?"

"I was afraid you might want to see it."

"So?" Dylan was furious; he had to bite the inside of his cheek to act calm. "What would be wrong with that?"

"Because then I'd have to see it, too." His father looked down at his clean brown doctor's shoes with the thick rubber treads and shook his head. "I didn't think I could survive having to see her things. I kept meaning to tell you. But time went by and after a while it seemed easier for both of us to leave it there. I was still angry. So angry! I couldn't believe Amanda would do a thing like that to us!"

"She didn't do it *to* us, Dad," Dylan said. "She just did it. She was having a good time."

"That was the problem! She was always having a good time!" his father shouted, red-faced now. "Your mother couldn't ever take life seriously! Even after you were born! All she wanted to do was play, play, play!"

Dylan thought of his mother's laugh, of her shining hair the color of chocolate. Of how she'd run through sprinklers with him, even in her clothes, or pretend she was a horse and let him climb on her shoulders so they could canter around the yard. He felt her watching him, still. Every day. He hoped he always would.

"But that's why we loved her, Dad. Isn't it?"

"I know." His father's voice sounded scratched and broken.

Maybe he was broken, like Dylan had been. Because his father turned to him then and put his arms around Dylan, and it was something Dylan had never experienced before: his father leaning on him, needing to be close, asking to be forgiven, to be loved, to be heard.

Sydney was in a good mood as she drove back to Newburyport from her last school visit of the year. This one was to Quinn's school in Topsfield, where the team meeting couldn't have gone better. The teachers and guidance counselor were on board with her plan for learning strategies and behavioral interventions. She felt optimistic that Quinn would thrive in school next year.

Everything had gone so well, in fact, that her irritation at Gary for insisting on taking Dylan alone to the clinic today had waned. Maybe it had been best for all of them. She'd already taken a lot of time off work because of Dylan, and wasn't she the one who'd been urging Gary to spend more time with him?

Back in the office, she wrote the report for Quinn's parents. Ella had left for another long lunch—"Don't be such a Nosey Parker," she'd sniffed when Sydney teased her about having so many steamy dates—and everyone else was gone as well. Sydney couldn't go home because the Realtor was planning to show her house sometime between one and two o'clock, so that left her alone to forage in the office fridge for lunch.

She found a limp salad in a plastic container with a Post-it note reading "Eat me"—Carrie's, probably, since Carrie's idea of a fatty lunch was an extra crouton—and a can of Coke. She ate the salad standing up, staring out the window at a sleek white boat motoring along the Merrimack River and wishing she were on it, then dug around in Ella's candy jar for the few caramels still mixed in with the hard candies. She washed these down with the Coke.

Afterward, Sydney checked Ella's book to see if Marco had scheduled an afternoon appointment and was disappointed to find nothing marked. They hadn't spoken since the night of the storm. On the off chance he was working in his office, she walked down the hall, her heart hammering in her throat, but the door was locked and nobody answered when she knocked.

Better that way. She'd acted like such an idiot. And a hormonal idiot at that. As humiliating as that night was, Marco had done the right thing by reining her in. What was wrong with her? She was never impulsive, and she certainly wasn't the sort of woman who'd ever cheated on a boyfriend.

No, being with Marco was a mistake. She had to figure things out with Gary, not abandon herself to a few hotheaded moments of passion with a colleague at the potential cost of shattering a steady, loving relationship she'd been nurturing for two years. She was getting married, for God's sake. There would always be temptations.

But oh, those moments of passion! Sydney had relived the night she spent with Marco—the two of them finally falling asleep curled on the blanket in front of the fireplace—more often than she'd ever admit to anyone. He had left her house by the time she woke; he must have called a friend or a cab to pick him up. She didn't try to follow, too mortified both by her behavior and by the ongoing buzz of her own desire. Even now, the memory of Marco's hands on her breasts and hips made her feel feverish.

What. An. Idiot.

She slouched back to her desk. Only one more report to write, and then she'd be free for the afternoon. *Focus, Sydney.*

She'd just opened the new file on her computer when she heard the outer door to the reception area. Heavy footsteps thudded into the waiting room, then hesitated. She held her breath. A client? Marco? No, that didn't sound like Marco. He was light on his feet.

The footsteps advanced down the hall. She didn't have anything else scheduled today, but it might be a parent arriving early for a postlunch appointment with one of the other psychologists. She should probably go out and greet whoever it was, since Ella wouldn't be back for a while.

Just as Sydney started to get up from her desk, her own office door slammed open against the wall with a bang. Jack Carlson lurched through the doorway, red-faced and sweating, reeking of beer, his necktie half-undone and his suit jacket twisted. "You had no right! No *fucking* right!" he shouted. "Do you realize what you've done, you little bitch? You've ruined my life!"

Sydney's first impulse was to dive under the desk—what if he had a gun? In her job, she always had to consider that possibility. But she held her ground. He could shoot her just as easily under the desk, and maybe she could talk him down.

She frantically tried to remember the cognitive behavior training she'd learned long ago from a laid-back professor with a goatee and a hypnotist's voice. He had lectured Sydney and other therapists-in-training on strategies for dealing with angry patients. *Talk them down. Be calm. Elicit their thoughts and reinforce them positively.*

She forced a smile and gestured to the chair in front of her desk. "Hello, Mr. Carlson. Please sit down. You seem very upset."

"You bet your fucking *ass* I'm upset!" he bellowed, but, momentarily sidetracked by her welcome, he sank into the chair.

Sydney let herself take a deep breath to keep her voice from wavering. "I'm so sorry to hear that. Would you like to tell me why?"

Mr. Carlson pursed his lips, mimicking her for a moment: *"Would I like to tell you why?"* Then he dropped his voice again and leaned forward. "Okay, sweetheart. How's this for starters? My wife kicked me out of my own fucking house and now they're saying I can't see my little girl. *That's* fucking *why*!"

Sydney's mind raced. Something must have provoked timid Mrs. Carlson to stand up against her husband, but what? "That sounds very difficult. I'm sorry to hear that."

"You're *sorry*? Fucking right, you'll be sorry!" he shouted, but thankfully he remained rooted in the chair, his bulk pressed against the arms of it. "Sorry you were ever born!"

Her professor's voice droned on in her head like a static-riddled radio program. *Remain pleasant and engaged. Express empathy. Help your client problem solve. This can be a teachable moment for both of you.* "Mr. Carlson, I'm sure you could use some support at a time like this. Would you like me to call someone for you? A friend, maybe?"

"I don't have any fucking friends! Now they all think I'm a pervert! What's *wrong* with you, huh? I came to you in good faith to help my kid in school, and what do you do? You break every confidentiality rule in the book, seeing my kid behind my back! I ought to have your license revoked for fraud!"

Sydney nodded. "Making an official complaint is always an option, certainly. You could even report me to the police if you like. In fact, why don't we call them right now?" She reached into her handbag for her phone.

But Mr. Carlson was too quick for her, lurching forward over the desk to slap the phone out of her hand. "Oh, no, you don't! No goddamn cops! I've seen enough cops today! You think that was pleasant, huh? Having those bozos march into my office and serve me with papers while everybody watched, even my boss?" The big man's eyes filled with tears as he loomed over the desk across from her.

Now everything made sense. Marco had tried to warn her. After Brianna's mother had taken her to see him, Brianna must have told Marco something that required him to call the Department of Children and Families. Psychologists, like teachers and health professionals, were considered mandatory reporters by the state.

Good for Marco. Brianna would be safe now.

No sooner did Sydney think this, however, than Jack Carlson started pounding his fist repeatedly on her desk, yelling, "You cost me my family, bitch! I don't care about my wife. She's a useless sack of shit. She can do what she wants to me. She can take everything I have. But she can't take Brianna! I love my little girl! She's *everything* to me! You fucking reported me. Said I was a child molester, huh? Well, you can't get away with lying like that about people. Not in my book!" He was still on his feet, chest heaving.

"Mr. Carlson, it sounds like you really do love your daughter." Sydney deliberately kept her voice low and spoke slowly, almost humming the words. "I'm sure things will work out as they should. If there's an investigation and you've done nothing wrong, the report will clear you of wrongdoing. But I'm afraid you're mistaken about me being the one to file any kind of report." She took deliberate, shallow breaths to funnel enough oxygen into her body to keep herself from panicking and passing out. "I did no such thing. My role has only been to assess Brianna's academic progress, as you requested."

"If you didn't do it, who did?"

Her head was starting to pound. "I have no idea."

"Liar!" he yelled.

So much for cognitive behavior role modeling, was Sydney's next, fleeting thought, as Jack Carlson came around the desk at a speed she wouldn't have thought possible for such a big man. He grabbed her around the throat with both hands and began choking her, nearly lifting her off her feet.

With her senses on high alert, she was keenly aware of every detail, as if things were happening in slow motion: the droplets of water gathering on Jack Carlson's reddened forehead, the sound of her computer humming as it backed up her work, her own heartbeat cantering like a miniature horse. Later, she would wonder if the adrenaline of that moment had opened a door in her mind she'd previously been unaware of, but in any case, as Mr. Carlson tried to strangle her, she remembered coming into the kitchen and finding her father with his hands around her mother's neck, shaking her like a rag doll while Hannah made sounds like she was gargling water. Her mother's feet were nearly off the ground; she looked like a ballerina *en pointe* in jeans.

Sydney remembered what happened next, too, and in that instant mirrored her mother's actions: she brought the heel of her hand up as hard as she could under Jack Carlson's nose, smashing his nose into his face and causing him to release her and stagger backward, blood gushing from his nose.

"You filthy little cunt!" he howled, and then he was falling. This, too, seemed to happen in slow motion, until he hit his head on the corner of the desk. Blood gushed from his scalp and nose as Mr. Carlson lay whimpering at her feet, legs curled to his stomach.

That's how Marco found them, Carlson on the floor as Sydney dialed 911 and told Jack Carlson everything would be just fine, even though she knew that probably nothing would ever be all right for this man again.

After the police took a statement and left, leading Jack Carlson away in handcuffs, Marco suggested a drink. Sydney had been to the ladies' room twice, but still felt soaked in Carlson's blood and sweat. She shuddered. "I need a two-hour shower," she said. "I just want to go home."

"I'll drive you."

She remembered, then. "I can't go there. The Realtor's showing my house."

"What about Gary's?"

Sydney thought of the empty Victorian with its high ceilings and skating rinks of gleaming counters in the kitchen, the neat rows of magazines on the coffee table in the living room, the sofa pillows just so. She couldn't imagine sitting in that house by herself.

Before she could speak, Marco nodded. "All right. Not Gary's. My place, then. Is that okay with you?"

She nodded mutely, her mind too numb to consider alternatives, and let Marco guide her downstairs with a protective arm around her shoulders. Outside, the sun was too bright and the day looked almost cartoonishly cheerful with its metallic blue sky, the seagulls wheeling overhead, and the office garden with its absurdly orange poppies and purple irises. It was as if she had stepped into that moment when the *Wizard of Oz* movie goes from black-and-white to color.

In the car, she took a shaky breath and said, "I can't believe that man came at me like that. I felt so sorry for him."

Marco's expression was grim. "Don't. That guy deserves whatever he gets, and then some, for what he's done."

She covered her face with her hands, then smelled Carlson on her own skin and immediately dropped them back into her lap. "So it was you who reported him."

"Yes. And I had reason to, Sydney. That man belongs behind bars. I'm sorry you had to get mixed up in this, but maybe everything will come out sooner now, and he won't have access to Brianna again."

Sydney felt chilled and wrapped her arms around her shoulders. "I didn't mean to hurt him. I was afraid I'd killed him, the way he was lying there in all that blood."

"Scalp and facial wounds always bleed like crazy." Marco glanced at her, smiling a little. "I can't believe you took that guy down, Sydney. He probably weighs twice what you do! How did you do it?"

Sydney studied her hands, wincing at the sight of blood crusted under one nail. "I don't know. It was really weird. It's like I was channeling my mother or something. I just shoved him in the nose the way I saw her do to my father once."

At hearing the absurdity of her own words, Sydney started laughing. The laughter quickly became hysterical and turned to tears. Marco handed her a Kleenex out of the glove compartment and continued driving south on 1A. They passed the road to Sydney's cottage and then went over the bridge, the Parker River glittering blue beneath them, a lone red kayak paddling upriver like a child's toy in a creek. Great white egrets stood in the marshes.

Rowley's town common was green and inviting, the bandstand surrounded by roses. Then they were in Ipswich, passing her grandmother's Colonial in the congested center of town. The old Ford that belonged to Grammy Bishop's caregiver was parked behind her grandparents' silver Buick. Minutes later, they were wending their way along Jeffrey's Neck Road, past the yellow seventeenth-century Paine House on its marshy estate and Strawberry Hill.

The pressure on Sydney's chest finally eased enough for her to breathe normally. This lasted long enough for her to absorb the fact that, once again, she was alone with Marco. They would have to talk about the other night and clear the air.

A shower first, though. And a drink. God, yes. A drink.

Sydney leaned her head back against the seat, vaguely wondering what time it was. The sun was still fairly high, so it couldn't be more than three o'clock. Gary wouldn't be picking Dylan up at the clinic in Beverly until seven o'clock. The clinic operated almost like a camp. Clients ate all three meals under supervision and spent the rest of the time doing schoolwork, nutrition counseling, therapy, and recreational activities. She hoped the program would take; at least Dylan seemed to go willingly. That was half the battle.

She unrolled her window and let the tangy sea air fill the car. She was dimly aware of Marco looking at her now and then, but she tried not to care. She'd left her computer and cell phone in the office in her hurry to leave. Nobody knew where she was. Good.

More than anything, Sydney wanted to savor this moment, to stare at the ocean and be lulled by the shushing sounds of the waves against the rocky shore below, the sound like that of a beast drawing in breaths and blowing them out again; by the hum of car tires on the road; and, most of all, by the fact that right now she felt far away from everything, here with Marco on this peninsula jutting into Plum Island Sound. It was such a clear day that she could see Mount Agamenticus in Maine.

Marco seemed to sense her mood and didn't try to make conversation. Once they were on Great Neck, he turned down a road toward the Ipswich Bay Yacht Club.

"Do you have a boat? Is that why you live out here?" she asked.

"No. I did for a while. But owning a boat is like having a job."

"Oh, come on."

"No, really! It takes hours and hours every week to keep your boat shipshape, so to speak," Marco said. "Only your income is reversed: money goes from you to the boat, never the other way around. That boat nearly sank me in more ways than one. I finally sold it. Now I have friends with boats. Much better."

"How did you end up living on Great Neck?"

"A friend of mine from grad school, his parents had a summer place on Little Neck and I always loved it out this way." He turned the car left, navigating a road so narrow that two cars would never be able to pass. "How about you? Why are you here instead of out in the Berkshires? You grew up there, right? Ella told me."

"Yes. Long story. But basically I came to live with my grandparents in high school and never left. This part of the state has always appealed to me more."

She'd never been able to describe it to anyone, really, that feeling of heaviness, of near claustrophobia, she'd felt in the mountains that she hadn't even known she felt until seeing the ocean for the first time.

Now, Sydney took in a sharp breath at the view: sparkling Plum Island Sound and, beyond that, Sandy Point Reservation, a long finger of sand and undulating dunes thatched in green. "Wow," she said as they pulled into the driveway of a house that could have been the big brother of her own: the same classic style of shingled cottage with a screened porch in front. The porch ceiling was painted light blue and pots of scarlet geraniums stood on either side of the stone steps. "Gorgeous place," she said.

"I knew you'd like it, since it's so similar to your house." Marco turned off the ignition. "I still can't believe this is me, a Puerto Rican kid from the Bronx, living here."

She laughed and got out of the car. "You done good."

The downstairs rooms were small, but with such generous windows that they seemed larger. A window seat overlooked the ocean in the living room, where hardwood floors gleamed beneath bright scatter rugs. The furniture was mostly Mission-style with leather cushions and bright patterned pillows. The kitchen, separated from the living room by a copper-topped counter, had white cupboards with blue sea glass knobs.

"Marco, I can't believe this. It looks like something out of a magazine."

He waved a hand, looking sheepish. "That's because it *is* out of a magazine. When my sisters heard I was house-hunting, they kept sending me pictures they'd cut out from different decorating magazines. The house was a wreck when I bought it, which was why I could afford to live out here at all, but I had fun doing it over."

"Did you do the actual work?" Sydney asked, feeling more astonished by the minute.

"I know, right? I can't even jump my own car, yet somebody lets me rent a power sander. Amazing." Marco flashed a grin.

The only bathroom was upstairs. It was small, too, but neatly done in white subway tiles with blue and green iridescent accent tiles. Marco showed her the cupboard with the towels, gave her a clean pair of sweatpants and a T-shirt, and said, "Take your time in the shower. The hot water won't give out, I promise."

Under the shower, Sydney felt the remaining tension drain from her neck and shoulders. She washed her hair and scrubbed her entire body twice, then used the unscented lotion she found in one of the drawers, wishing she had makeup or at least her comb. She ran her fingers through the snarls as well as she could. The bathroom was so steamy that she had to keep swabbing at the fog on the mirror with a corner of the towel; finally she opened the narrow window. Here, too, was a view of the ocean, the waves cresting white on a sandbar.

She couldn't stand to put on any of her own clothing, not even her bra and panties, so she wrapped them along with her pants and bloodstained blouse and stuffed everything into the plastic bag Marco had given her. Then she slipped into his soft black T-shirt and gray sweatpants, rolling up the pant legs to make them fit, and went downstairs in bare feet.

She felt more like herself again. But she also felt jittery with nerves. What could she possibly say to Marco about the other night that would allow them to stay friends? For she wanted that.

No, you want more, a stubborn little voice said in her head. *And this is your chance.*

She scowled at her reflection in the hall mirror at the base of the staircase. "Forget it," she said aloud.

One drink. Then she'd ask him to take her home, back to Gary's where she belonged. She was going to marry a good man, the kind she'd always dreamed of marrying: reliable, smart, compassionate. Yes, they were going through a rough time, but didn't every couple? It was always easier to be lovers than to stay in love.

Marco was out on the brick patio overlooking the ocean. Sydney stopped for a minute to take in the view, watching the sea foam up on a sandbar and thinking that nothing much about this view would have changed between now and when the first settlers landed here in the seventeenth century.

A row of yellow tree peonies bloomed like hundreds of miniature suns at the edge of the patio and a pair of green metal camp chairs was angled there to face the water, a small white table between them. Marco had mixed a pitcher of gin and tonics. Now he handed her one and touched his glass to hers with a smile. "Feeling better?"

"Much. I feel like I'm at a resort," Sydney said. "I bet you have a tough time getting rid of women after you bring them here."

"No, I don't."

"No?" She was taken aback by his tone, suddenly serious. "Why not?"

"Because I don't bring women here. You're the first woman I've invited home in two years, Sydney."

She didn't know whether to be flattered or alarmed. Neither, she decided, taking a long gulp of the icy drink and turning away from him, pretending to admire the view. This didn't count as a date: she was engaged and he was a friend helping her after a crisis. "We should talk about the other night."

"No need. I know the score." He, too, was looking at the water, his jaw set.

"I just wanted to apologize—"

"Stop," he said, cutting her off with a sharp sideways motion of his hand. "You have nothing to be sorry about. I was in the moment and so were you. These things happen between friends. I respect you too much to make more of it than it was, all right?"

"All right." Feeling the gin in her knees and the sun on her face was making her sleepy and meek. Sydney slid into one of the chairs and said, "Tell me something that will make me forget how embarrassed I am right now."

He laughed and sat down in the other chair, setting his glass on the table. "Nobody needs to be embarrassed, okay? We both did what we did because it felt right at the time. But, sure. How about this: Did you know there were once giant piles of clamshells here on Great Neck from the Agawam Indians? And that the stubborn Pilgrims wouldn't eat clams no matter how hungry they were?"

"That is stubborn," she said.

"Like someone else I know."

Sydney watched him tip his head back and finish his drink, admiring his sharp features and his strong hands on the glass. Everything about Marco was wiry and quick and compact and strong. It was easy to imagine him on a soccer field. His black hair gleamed in the sunlight and she longed to feel its silkiness between her fingers. She closed her eyes to force herself to stop looking at him. "I assume you mean I'm stubborn. Why do you say that?"

"Well, look at you. Your whole life is about taking a stand. You keep dogging away at those schools until they give your clients what they need. You convince parents to advocate for their kids. And you take on a male attacker twice your size and deck him." Marco rattled the ice in his glass, then added, "Oh, and you're stubborn enough to refuse to see what's right in front of you, because you're determined to follow reason instead of passion."

Infuriated, she stood up. "What do you mean by that?"

"You know what I mean." He crunched an ice cube, noisily.

"I'm not being stubborn about us. How can you say that? I acknowledge what I feel for you: lust. Heat. Desire. We want to fuck like dogs. Like goddamn *teenagers*. Is that what you want me to say? Because, oh yes, I'll say that and more." She stood in front of him now, hands on her hips. "I want you, Marco. You know I do." Her face and neck were prickling with heat. She dug her nails into her palms. "But you're all wrong for me."

"Why? Because I'm not a surgeon with a big house? Because I don't present papers at international conferences and go on mission trips around the world? What does Gary have that I don't, besides a six-figure salary? If you really loved him, Sydney, if you really were committed to Gary, you wouldn't have let me bring you here today. You would have called him."

She was astounded. "I couldn't, okay? Gary's in surgery!"

"You didn't even *call* him, Sydney! I was with you every minute this afternoon, and unless you called Gary from the shower, I know you haven't even told him what happened to you today!" Marco said. "If you were my girlfriend, do you think I wouldn't want to know when you were in trouble?"

"I couldn't call him," Sydney repeated. "How can I expect Gary to take care of me, when he's trying to take care of his son, who, as you know, is hurting right now, huh?" She set her glass down on the table hard enough that the table, made uneven by the grass, wobbled and fell over. "You're my friend, Marco. That's why I let you bring me here. I like you and I trust you. And, yes, part of me wants very much to sleep with you. I admit that. But Gary is the man I'm going to marry."

Marco righted the table and picked up her glass. "All right. You've made your point. It is what it is, right? Come on. I'm sorry I upset you. That wasn't the idea. Let me take you home. I shouldn't have said what I did."

"No, but you did!" Sydney wanted to kiss him. She wanted to slap him. She was paralyzed.

"It's all right," Marco said, backing slowly away from her. "Really. Things will be fine. We've established that we're colleagues who want to get it on, like who knows how many other coworkers, right? Good for us. We're healthy, lusty humans. Nothing wrong with that. Now let's go. I'm sure you need to be home for dinner."

For all the right reasons, and all the wrong ones, too, Sydney didn't want him to walk away. "We need to keep talking, Marco."

Marco's dark eyes were nearly black. "Why?" he said softly. "What's left for us to say? I want you, Sydney. You want me. Whether we talk about it or not won't change that. We'll just have to live with that attraction and hope it dies a natural death. You're getting married and you can't see the truth."

"What truth?"

"That you don't love Gary. If you did, this wouldn't be happening."

"But I do love Gary! We're getting married!"

He crossed his arms. "You keep saying that, but those are two different things."

"For some people, maybe, but not for me. I wouldn't marry a man I didn't love!"

Marco sighed. He looked suddenly exhausted, his shoulders slumped. "All right. Fine. Have it your way. You're in love with Gary and you're going to marry him. There's nothing else to discuss." He turned and started walking away from her again, faster this time.

For a moment, Sydney watched his determined athletic stride and imagined herself running after him, begging him to listen. But what would be the point? He was right. She was going to marry Gary. There was some part of her that didn't trust Marco because—and she knew this sounded irrational—he made her feel too much pleasure. Passion and fun were temporary states.

She and Marco would continue working together. They would be polite, friendly. He would find someone else.

That thought made her feel sick.

She followed behind him, the grass cool beneath her feet, and picked up her bag of clothes and purse.

As they pulled out of the driveway, Marco acted as if nothing had gone on between them. He turned on the radio and mentioned something about a soccer practice that night, a championship game that weekend. He was living like a college kid, she wanted to tease, but her heart wasn't in it: she knew him better than that, now.

Sydney glanced at the clock on the dashboard and saw it was just after five.

She wondered how the showing had gone at her cottage. Better if it sold sooner rather than later. She was in limbo, that was her problem. Gary had hinted at putting off the wedding. She had no wedding date, no dress. Everything she owned, except for a few articles of clothing and her sewing machine, was still in her own little house, as if the cottage were a safety net. It was time to walk the tightrope without a net. Was that the metaphor she was looking for?

She hoped not. It sounded terrifying.

Hannah hadn't planned to show up unannounced at her mother-in-law's house. But there was nowhere else to go while she waited for Sydney to appear, or to at least return her phone call. She'd been to Gary's house and Sydney's office again this afternoon. Finally she'd left a message for her daughter, saying she was determined to see Dylan before driving back to Amherst. She wanted to make sure Dylan was all right, and to let him know her offer for coming out to live on the farm was always open, Gary be damned.

She'd spent a couple of hours in Newburyport, a relentlessly cheery town of brick and window boxes overflowing with bright annuals. She hadn't really spent much time in this tiny North Shore city despite growing up in Ipswich, just a dozen miles south. Her own parents never went out—her father was always at the garage—and she worked after school and spent summers pumping gas or at the beach. Besides, back in the seventies, Newburyport had been grim and down-at-the-heels, a place artists favored for the cheap rents. Now you'd have to be a millionaire to afford one of those big houses in town.

She bought a sandwich and ate it on one of the benches along the boardwalk, marveling at the size of a yacht tied there and at the tourists descending from a whale-watching ship, filming everything, even the trash can overflowing with orange paper cups from the frozen yogurt place. Finally, she'd grown bored and decided to drive to Ipswich. Dad would like it if she saw the old house and called to tell him what the new people had done with it. On the way, Hannah phoned Liz to ask if she minded doing the evening chores with Sloan.

"Everything's fine here," Liz said. "Take a day off, for God's sake. The world won't end if you do. Stay overnight if you want. I'll help Sloan out in the morning. No worries. It'll be payback time next week, when I tap you to help me bring my calves to auction."

Hannah thanked her and hung up. She thought about her father as she traveled south to Ipswich. He wanted her to meet his new girlfriend, Celia, who did nothing but giggle any time Leo put her on the phone or made her step into the camera's path when they were Skyping. Celia was silver-haired, short, round, peppy, and a die-hard fan of pastel sweaters. So different from Hannah's own dark, quiet, bookish mother. She was glad her father had found a companion, but felt lonely and bereft as she drove past their old house, a tiny Cape with a postage-stamp yard. The new owners had taken down the ancient rose trellis, which probably needed doing, but they'd replaced everything with vinyl. That would kill Dad. Maybe she wouldn't tell him.

Of course, being in Ipswich and feeling so melancholy made her think about Rory and Allen, and those memories led her to the Bishops' door. Hannah parked her car in the driveway and saw that the silver Buick Mr. Bishop had cared for like a prize pig, washing and polishing it, feeding it special fluids, still sat in the garage. Behind it was an older Ford sedan she'd never seen before. The lawn was a tidy green square around the house. There was an ancient perennial bed, and stately rosebushes around the porch. Yet it felt like something essential was missing from this house: a heartbeat, maybe. Everything was too stark and neat to feel lived in by humans.

She hadn't seen Georgia Bishop for years, not since Sydney left for college and Hannah could finally stop negotiating with that woman for permission—permission!—to visit her own daughter. The only other contact they'd had was through the letters she continued to mail to Rory, all of which Georgia Bishop had returned with "address unknown" stamped across their faces. Hannah sometimes wondered if she had bought that stamp precisely for those letters, and imagined the woman's laugh as she pounded that sucker onto the envelopes, red ink staining her fingers like blood. Eventually Hannah stopped sending them.

Now, as she sat in front of the house with the engine idling, a squat, sturdy-looking woman exited the kitchen door carrying two netted bags stuffed with laundry. Hannah backed her car out of the driveway, then pulled it in to one side so she wouldn't be blocking the other vehicles. She got out of her car. "Need help? Those look heavy."

"No, no. I'm fine. Getting my workout, that's all." The woman's face was flushed but cheerful, her lank brown hair lifting from her head in the breeze. "Can I help you?"

The woman looked familiar, but Hannah couldn't quite place her. "I'm Hannah Bishop," she said. "I just stopped by to see my mother-in-law."

The woman's face cleared. "Oh! Hannah! Of course! Do you remember me, dear?"

Hannah squinted for a minute, puzzling out the woman's features. Finally she had it: the school nurse from the high school. She must be working privately now. Sydney had said something not long ago about Georgia Bishop living at home after her husband died and relying on caregivers after a stroke. "Mrs. Falconi! I'm so sorry. I didn't recognize you."

"I don't blame you. Look at me! It's after midnight in my life and I've turned into a pumpkin." Mrs. Falconi patted her distended belly and her face dimpled into a smile. "Not you, though. You haven't changed a bit. You always were a lovely girl."

Hannah burst out laughing. "Keep fibbing like that and your nose will grow, too."

Mrs. Falconi laughed, too. "Go ahead into the kitchen. The missus is sitting in there with a cup of tea. You've come at a good time. I was just going to run these sheets and towels over to the Laundromat. So much easier than doing them at home because you can stuff everything in at once—don't you think? I'll be stopping at the market while the things are in the wash, but I'll be back in two ticks. It'll be good for her to have someone new to talk to."

Hannah doubted whether Georgia Bishop would agree. In fact, she was almost certain Mrs. Bishop would want to toss her out of the house. But she smiled and waved, waiting for Mrs. Falconi to back out of the driveway before she went inside, so she wouldn't hear her employer's reaction to this unscheduled visit.

Mrs. Bishop—who had always insisted that Hannah call her by that name, even after she married Allen—was doing a crossword puzzle in the newspaper. Her head was down and there was a cup of milky tea at her elbow. She must have lost some of her hearing, for she didn't look up when Hannah entered the room, only filled in a few more squares with her yellow pencil. A noisy square silver clock ticked above the stove; that clock had hung there for as long as Hannah could remember.

Other than the older woman's hair, now snow-white, Hannah might have been transported back in time. Whenever she came home with the boys after school, their mother had been in this very pose, sitting at the table with the paper while dinner simmered on the stove or roasted in the oven. Rory and Allen used to joke about their mother's cooking, saying she cooked meat until it dissolved into paste. Hannah wouldn't know. Mrs. Bishop had never once invited Hannah to stay, even though she had to know Hannah was motherless, with a father who kept the town garage open until eight o'clock.

She'd never been allowed in the living room, either. Georgia Bishop always claimed this was because of the white rug. But Hannah knew it was because Mrs. Bishop wanted to keep Hannah in her place as the progeny of the town mechanic and a Greek woman whose own family had disowned her because she hadn't consented to an arranged marriage with a second cousin.

"So you're a mixed breed," attorney Bishop had said once, clapping his hand firmly across Hannah's bottom when she was all of sixteen. "I can see why my boys like you even if their mother doesn't. I bet you're a fun little filly."

She would have hit him, but she didn't have to: Mrs. Bishop had come sailing into the room from somewhere offstage—she always seemed to be listening from a dark corner—saying, "Pet, I'm sure Hannah has better things to do than flirt with you," in a cool voice, flicking her fingers in Hannah's direction as if Hannah were an insect she couldn't be bothered to slap dead.

The pencil moved across the newspaper again, erasing this time. Mrs. Bishop looked up, frowning, and saw Hannah standing there.

"Sorry," Hannah said, as the other woman gasped and clutched her heart. "Mrs. Falconi let me in. I didn't mean to startle you."

"Well, you certainly did. A person could die of a heart attack this way." Mrs. Bishop picked up the cup, taking a deliberate sip of tea.

Hannah stood there until it became apparent that the older woman wasn't about to invite her to sit down. She sat down anyway. "Having trouble?" she suggested. "Maybe I could help." She gestured at the crossword.

Mrs. Bishop kept her pale blue eyes fixed on Hannah's face as she set the cup down on top of the puzzle, obscuring it. "I don't need help. I do a crossword a day. I never quit until I finish. Although there are no words to express what I'm feeling right now, seeing you barge into my house."

"You could start with, 'Hello, Hannah. How are you?' "

"No, I can't. Because that would indicate the desire for a conversation, and you and I have said everything that needs to be said. Why are you even here?"

"In this house?"

"No. On the North Shore. I hear from your daughter that you're still living on that godforsaken farm, raising cows."

"Sheep," Hannah corrected. "And I'm here to see Sydney."

"Well, obviously you've come to the wrong house. I assume you know she's engaged to that lovely doctor. They're practically living together."

Lovely? Hannah wondered how much the other woman knew about Gary and Dylan and what had been happening in that family. Probably nothing. If she were Sydney, she wouldn't have told her, either. "She's not there," Hannah said. "She's not at her house, either. I'm assuming she's out doing a school visit. I'm waiting until she comes back."

"They're going to be very happy," Mrs. Bishop said dreamily, as if Hannah hadn't spoken. "Sydney will be a beautiful bride. She'll have the wedding of her dreams; I'll make sure of that. It's the right sort of match for her. A professional. A surgeon! You should be thrilled. Any mother would be."

Any *normal* mother, she meant. "I'll be thrilled if Sydney's happy," Hannah said.

Mrs. Bishop's mouth tightened at the corners. "Will you? Why? You've never seemed to care about that precious little girl's happiness. Well, no thanks to you, Sydney's going to be just fine. A wife and mother soon enough. She doesn't need you."

Hannah felt a pain beneath her breastbone as if she'd swallowed something sharp and it was lodged there. She hated Allen's mother for finding her weak spot so soon. The hate felt like gritty dust in her mouth and throat; she wanted to spit it out, but couldn't because the pressure in her chest was already suffocating her.

"You still haven't said what you're doing here," Mrs. Bishop said, finally putting down the pencil. "If there's something you want, please say it and go. I like to take a rest in the afternoons. My girl will be back soon to get me settled."

Hannah hadn't known before arriving what had prompted her visit. Now, though, as she heard Mrs. Falconi's car pull into the driveway, she did. "I want to know why you sent back Rory's letters."

"Because I knew there was no point in having them here."

"Why not? He might have come home and read them. You could have kept them here for me," Hannah said fiercely, willing herself not to tear up in front of this old bat. "Didn't you hope he'd come home?"

"Of course not," Mrs. Bishop said, something like glee glinting behind the steel frames of her glasses. "How could I hold out any hope, when I knew Rory was dead?"

There was a crash behind them. Hannah whirled around to see Mrs. Falconi standing there, a bag of groceries scattered at her feet, mostly tins of tuna and soup. The small woman had paled and was staring over Hannah's head at Mrs. Bishop, her mouth open.

"Mrs. Falconi, are you all right?" Hannah got up and went to her, gently touching her shoulder.

The shorter woman put both reddened hands to her face. "Dead? Our Rory's *dead*?"

Was she having a stroke? Did she have early dementia? "Probably, yes," Hannah said gently. She stooped to gather the groceries. As she stacked the cans on the table, she added, "Remember? The police found his car in San Francisco."

"Oh, no, no, no, not Rory, too," Mrs. Falconi moaned.

Tears were streaming down the nurse's face. Hannah picked up the last of the cans and stood to guide her to the rocking chair in the corner of the room. "Sit down, Mrs. Falconi. It's all right. It happened a long time ago."

"When?" Mrs. Falconi whispered, staring at her employer. "Mrs. Bishop? Are you all right?"

Mrs. Bishop had turned to stone. She sat with her hands folded so tightly on the table that the arthritic knuckles gleamed like white marbles.

"Haven't you told her about Rory?" Hannah asked Mrs. Bishop, mystified.

Mrs. Bishop shook her head. Mrs. Falconi was still weeping softly. She yanked a tissue out of the box on the table to wipe her streaming eyes, muttering, "No, no, not Rory!"

"Why didn't you tell her?" Hannah went to the stove, where she felt the kettle for water—still half-full—and lit the burner beneath it, feeling torn between empathy for Mrs. Falconi and irritability at her mother-in-law. What a mess. "Listen, we're all going to have tea, Mrs. Falconi, and then Mrs. Bishop will explain what happened to Rory."

"When did it happen?" Mrs. Falconi said, sounding impatient now despite her tears. "How?"

"Twenty years ago," Hannah said gently. "The police don't really know how. They assume he either jumped off the cliffs in San Francisco where they found his car, or it was an accidental drowning."

"Twenty years ago?" Mrs. Falconi's head snapped up. "Did you say *twenty*?"

"Get out of my house, Hannah," Mrs. Bishop said. "You've done enough damage."

"But, missus, what's the girl talking about?" Mrs. Falconi pleaded. "Our Rory dead twenty years? What's she saying that for? Is the poor girl not right in the head?"

"Hannah doesn't know what she's saying," Mrs. Bishop replied. "That's why she needs to leave my house before I call the police and ask them to arrest this woman for harassment."

"Oh, come, now," Mrs. Falconi said, clutching her tissues. "Surely you can't mean that! The poor girl's confused, and no wonder, all she's been through."

"Confused about what?" The water behind her rattled in the kettle, about to boil. Hannah ignored it and came around to stand between them at the table. "If you mean I'm confused about Rory's death, you're right. I don't believe he committed suicide. If anything, he drowned accidentally. I think the police were mistaken."

"Well, of course they were, dear," Mrs. Falconi said, reaching one soft, plump hand over to cover Hannah's thin, callused one. "We know that. I'm glad you do, too."

Hannah's mind scrambled in all directions, forming questions, dismissing them, suddenly fearful. The kettle shrieked on the stove, startling her into saying, "Oh!" She went to the stove and took it off the burner.

"Get out, get out, get out!" Now the shrieking was coming from Mrs. Bishop, who was struggling to stand. "You've done enough, I told you!"

"Why? What have I done?" For the first time, Hannah realized the other woman relied on a cane to get around; she hadn't seen it hanging from the back of her chair.

Now Mrs. Bishop was leaning on the chair and waving the cane in the air. "Leave my house this instant! Isn't it enough that you stole Allen from us? That you ruined him? He dropped out of college because of you! You never deserved him, or Rory either."

Hannah folded her arms, trying not to appear as shaken as she felt. Standing before this enraged mother was like balancing on top of a moving train headed into a tunnel. "Allen dropped out because he was having difficulty concentrating on school after the war," she said. "I tried to get him to finish his degree, but he said he had to get out of a country where nobody understood why he was fighting in Vietnam. Least of all him."

"He was a patriot! That's why he fought!" Mrs. Bishop shook a finger at Hannah. "Allen could have made something of himself. Instead you made him buy that godforsaken farm with his grandfather's money, and you ruined him."

"The war ruined Allen, not me," Hannah said. "Did you know he got hit by sniper fire? And that a snare trap once shot a wooden spike through his right leg? Did you know he had nightmares, night after night, until we were out on the farm, and even then they came? He lashed out at me, at Sydney. At everyone! Allen never escaped the war, even out in the mountains. We did yoga, we meditated, we farmed in peace. But the act of killing damaged Allen forever. You have no idea what he went through."

"You drove my son to his grave! You're trying to kill me, too, but I won't let you." Mrs. Bishop was advancing on Hannah now, inching across the kitchen, using the cane to prod Hannah backward until she stumbled out the door and onto the steps. Mrs. Bishop's creased face was bright pink beneath her halo of white hair.

"You mustn't let the missus get all worked up, or she'll have another stroke," Mrs. Falconi said in alarm. She got out of her chair, too, rocking herself forward onto her feet, and tried to pull Mrs. Bishop by the arm back into the kitchen. "Come inside and sit down, missus, before you hurt yourself."

All three women were standing outside on the brick steps now. Mrs. Bishop whacked Mrs. Falconi on the hip with her cane, a surprisingly soft sound, like hitting a sofa cushion. "Move! Get out of my way!" she wheezed, then lifted the cane to point at Hannah again. "Out, out, out!"

Hannah lifted both hands. "All right, all right. Please, go back inside and sit down. Mrs. Falconi's right. You're going to hurt yourself if you keep this up." She edged down a couple of steps toward the yard, keeping a wary eye on Mrs. Bishop.

"That's right, dear. Listen to your daughter," Mrs. Falconi said, rubbing her hip where the cane had connected.

"She's not my daughter!" Mrs. Bishop said, clinging to the doorframe. She towered above both of them, now that Mrs. Falconi had also moved down a stair. "She killed my son!"

"You're never going to forgive me, are you?" Hannah said bitterly. She turned and took the last step onto the sidewalk.

"Now, now," she heard Mrs. Falconi saying to Mrs. Bishop behind her as she started for her car. "Hannah didn't kill anyone. It was very unfortunate, what happened with Allen, but that's what war does to some men. You mustn't blame her. Or yourself. Goodness. And you still have Rory. Rory's all grown up and doing fine. Don't you remember? You saw him last week for your birthday! You remember, don't you? We went to that lovely place on the water. We all had lobster. He helped you crack the claws, did our Rory. We all had the most wonderful time. Don't you worry about him."

Hannah turned back in shock. She stared up at Mrs. Bishop, who still stood at the top of the small staircase, her body filling the doorway. "What are you talking about? How could you have had dinner with Rory?"

"Why, he came to us, didn't he?" Mrs. Falconi said, blinking in surprise as Mrs. Bishop started shrieking again on the step above her. "Just last week, we saw him. Came all the way from Vermont for his mother's birthday."

CHAPTER EIGHTEEN

In the ten minutes it took to drive from Great Neck to the center of Ipswich, during which Marco continued to do most of the talking and kept both hands on the wheel, Sydney came to a decision. Gary was right: they should postpone the wedding. Clearly, she was having unresolved feelings about the marriage.

Just thinking this phrase—*unresolved feelings*—made her feel better, because (1) it meant her current emotional state wasn't permanent, but could be resolved with further exploration, and (2) she had applied her therapist's perspective to her roiling emotions, and was being objective rather than impulsive or theatrical. Always a good thing.

The genesis of her complicated feelings, whatever they were—and here she could list various factors, including her return to Haven Lake, Gary's drug use, Dylan's situation, and Marco—didn't, in some ways, matter. As she often told her clients, what mattered was that the feelings existed. Acknowledging them was the first step toward hurdling over whatever stumbling blocks stood between her and Gary getting married.

Or *not* getting married.

There! She'd let herself whisper that possibility, if only in her own mind: *not* getting married.

"Hey, isn't that your mom standing in front of that house?" Marco asked suddenly.

Sydney laughed. "How do you even know what my mom looks like? Anyway, Ipswich is about the absolute last place she'd ever . . . ," she began, but stopped, because Marco was right: that was definitely her mother standing on the front steps of Grammy Bishop's house.

More alarming, that was her mother banging on the door with her fist. She looked like a small child having a tantrum, with her black-and-silver hair loose and wild around her shoulders, and her narrow body tucked into blue jeans and a white T-shirt.

"Pull over!" Sydney said, though Marco was already doing that. She jumped out of the car before he'd even shut off the ignition. "Mom? What are you *doing* here?"

Hannah ignored her and kept pounding on the door. "You can't do this to me!" she was yelling. "Open this door and talk to me! There has to be some explanation. Mrs. Falconi, please! Open the door and tell me the *truth*! Somebody, please, just *tell me*!"

Sydney reached her as Hannah collapsed on the top step, sitting with her head pressed to her blue-jeaned knees, weeping. "Mom? What the hell's going on? Why are you yelling at poor Grammy?"

"Ask her," Hannah said dully.

Sydney stepped around her mother and tried the door, but the screen door was locked and the inner door was shut. Through the window in the door, she saw her grandmother standing in the middle of the kitchen, her shoulders stiff, her face enraged. Her caregiver, Mrs. Falconi, stood beside her, an arm around her grandmother's shoulders.

"Grammy?" Sydney leaned over to call through the open kitchen window. "Are you okay? What's the matter? What are you doing in there with the door locked? Why are you and Mom fighting?"

Mrs. Falconi said something to Grammy that Sydney couldn't hear. At last her grandmother sat down on one of the kitchen chairs, her posture as stiff as if she were perched on a church pew. Finally Mrs. Falconi came to the inner door and opened it, though she left the screen door locked. "I'm sorry about the fuss, Sydney, but there seems to have been a misunderstanding. Your grandmother doesn't want your mother here."

At this, Hannah shot up from the step behind Sydney and came to stand beside her. "Mrs. Falconi, this was no misunderstanding," she said, her voice thick with emotion. "That woman lied to me. You know that. You heard her yourself!"

Sydney had never imagined it would be possible to see rage the way they drew it in cartoons, like lines emanating from a person's body, but there it was around her mother: clearly visible lines of red-hot energy. "Mom, maybe if you lower your voice, Grammy won't feel so threatened."

"But I *want* to threaten her!" Hannah shouted, pressing her face against the screen door hard enough that it dented inward, making Mrs. Falconi step backward.

Sydney sighed. "Could somebody please just tell me what's going on?"

Hannah jabbed a finger at the screen door. "Ask your grandmother."

"I'm not talking to anybody," Grammy Bishop declared. "And if you don't leave, I'm calling the police."

It was an empty threat, Sydney knew: there was no weight behind the words and no phone within reach. "Grammy, come on," she said. "Don't be like this. I can see you're upset, and I'm sure you have a good reason. Open the door and we'll talk about it."

"Of course you'd be on her side," Hannah muttered beside her.

"Jesus, Mom, I'm not on anybody's side!" Sydney said. "I just want to know what's going on. What are you doing here, anyway?"

"That's what I kept asking her!" Grammy Bishop said. "But she had to keep poking her nose in our family when she wasn't wanted."

"You don't know I wasn't wanted!" Hannah shouted, punching at the screen hard enough to tear it. "You never let me see my daughter, and you just sent the letters back!"

"What letters, Mom?" Sydney said. "Did you write to Grammy Bishop?"

"No! Not to her. To Rory! I wrote to Rory, but she never gave him the letters. She sent them all back. She made me believe he was dead. But he's alive! She's been lying to me all along!"

Sydney felt faint, suddenly, a roaring in her ears. The tiny squares of the screen door felt like they were pressing against her eyes, a painful metal grid smashed onto her forehead. Then she remembered Marco and turned around. "You should go," she said. "This could take a while."

Hannah glanced over her shoulder and her eyes widened. "Oh! You found her!" she said. "Good."

Sydney looked from Hannah to Marco in shock. "Have you two met?"

Marco shook his head once at her mother, sharply, but Hannah either didn't get his signal or chose to ignore it. "Yes. We met at your house, Sydney," she said. "He went inside to leave you a note. And I definitely think he should leave it there and not go back and get it."

For a minute, Sydney stared at her mother, wondering if she'd really lost her mind. Then she looked at Marco and saw from his expression that he knew exactly what her mother was talking about: a mixture of dismay and embarrassment caused him to draw his dark brows into a frown. Then he smiled. "Damn it," he said. "All right, Sydney. I guess it doesn't matter now if you read the letter or not. You say you've made up your mind, but I want you to know how I feel about you. Call me if you end up needing a ride."

With that, he was gone, striding back to his car with both hands jammed into the front pockets of his jeans.

"I'm not even going to ask," Sydney said to her mother.

"That's good, because I'm not saying anything," Hannah said, and turned back to the door. "Mrs. Falconi? Please? I promise I'm done shouting." She took a ragged breath. "Unlock the door. I'll behave."

Mrs. Falconi unlocked the door even as Grammy Bishop said, "You're not welcome here, either of you!" from her seat at the kitchen table. "This is my rest time, you know."

"I know, Grammy," Sydney said soothingly. "We'll only stay a few minutes." She and Hannah sat down.

Mrs. Falconi did, too, pink-cheeked with distress. "I think you'd better explain to Sydney what's going on, missus," she said.

"Grammy? It's all right. Whatever it is, it'll be all right, I promise," Sydney said softly, touching the old woman's bony fingers, the skin as cool and silky as milk.

She'd expected tears and shouts, but if anything, Grammy looked impatient, her mouth set in a thin line, her movements jerky. "The long and short of it is that your mother believed Rory was dead and I let her," she said.

Sydney heard her mother gasp but didn't look at her. "What do you mean? Isn't Uncle Rory dead?" Maybe her grandmother was suffering from some kind of stroke-induced psychosis, she thought, her mind racing through a catalog of mental health symptoms. Delusional disorder? Dementia?

But Grammy Bishop's voice was firm. "He is not," she said. "We all *believed* he'd died because he parked that damn car of his on the cliffs. That's what he wanted us to think! That's why he left his wallet in the glove compartment. But Uncle Rory hitched a ride to Vancouver and lived there for a while, doing God knows what to get by. You didn't need a passport in those days to cross the border, so nobody knew. He contacted us after a few months, but told us not to tell anyone he was alive."

"I still don't believe you," Hannah said dully, immobile in her chair beside Sydney. "Rory wouldn't have done that to us. He can't be alive."

Grammy Bishop shrugged. "Believe what you want. It's the truth."

"It is," Mrs. Falconi said. "Rory has been here a few times. I've seen him myself. Mrs. Bishop said we weren't to tell anybody in town when Rory came to visit. Only I didn't know she meant you, too." She turned to her employer, scolding her with a raised finger. "That hardly seems fair on the girls, missus, keeping that kind of secret."

"I know, but it's what my son wanted," Grammy Bishop said. "'Better for everybody if I'm dead,' he said, and I couldn't convince him otherwise." She turned to Sydney and her eyes softened. "I'm sorry, honey. I know you were fond of your uncle."

Sydney pressed a hand to her forehead, as if the pressure could alleviate some of the noise in her brain. "I can't believe this," she said.

"See what I mean?" Hannah said. "Your grandmother's the worst kind of liar." She laughed, but it was a mirthless bark. "Or maybe the best kind. I certainly never suspected."

"So when did you actually see him again, Grammy?" Sydney asked.

"Not until about five years ago, after your granddad died. Those two never got on." Grammy Bishop reached out for the pencil on the table next to her crossword puzzle and adjusted it, lining it up with the edge of the paper.

"He hated his father," Hannah said. "Because he beat them both, Rory and Allen. But you probably knew that, didn't you? While you were upstairs here, cleaning your perfectly clean kitchen, your husband *beat your children* in the basement."

"Mom!" Sydney said, putting a hand on Hannah's shoulder. "Stop," she begged, because even if it was true, what was the point of saying all that now? Her poor grandmother already looked done in, pale and trembling across the table.

But Grammy Bishop lifted her chin and said, "My husband was a good father. He knew how to set limits with children and make them obey. We didn't raise our children to be weak or run wild. But you bewitched them with sex, Hannah. We didn't recognize our boys after you got your whoring hands on them. But it didn't matter in the end, did it? Rory is my boy. He came back to *me*, not to you!"

Sydney felt her stomach lurch as Hannah buried her face in her hands beside her. "Grammy, that's enough," she said sharply. "It was never a contest between my mother and you."

Grammy Bishop snorted. "It's always a contest between mothers of sons and the women in their lives."

Sydney stood up and touched her mother's shoulder. "Come on, Mom. Let's go. Don't listen to her."

"Why shouldn't she listen?" Grammy Bishop stood up, too, levering herself out of the chair with visible effort. "She came here wanting to know the truth. Now she does. Good. I'm sick of protecting her." She leaned heavily on her cane, though her voice still had some strength in it.

"Listen to me, Hannah. Rory didn't want anything more to do with you. He made that clear enough. That's why I sent your letters back. Now, if you'll excuse me, I really must lie down." She began teetering across the kitchen toward the living room, breathing heavily.

Sydney was afraid Hannah might try to stop her, was prepared to intervene if she did. But her mother sat there watching the old woman walk away, Mrs. Falconi at her side now, murmuring something they couldn't hear.

And then they were alone in the kitchen. When Hannah still didn't get up, Sydney put an arm around her shoulders. "Mom? Are you okay?"

No answer. She could see by Hannah's ashen, ruined face that her mother was in shock. "Come on," Sydney said softly. "Give me your keys, Mom. I'll take you back to Gary's house. You need to lie down."

Her mother leaned heavily on Sydney as they walked slowly to Hannah's car. She guided her mother into the passenger seat, helping her buckle the seat belt when she fumbled with it and then closing the door gently before coming around to the wheel.

As she started the ignition and backed out of the driveway, Sydney glanced at her mother. "I'm so sorry, Mom," she said. "Grammy never should have said those awful things. But I'm glad Rory's alive. Aren't you?"

When she finally spoke, her mother's voice was slightly hoarse. "How could he be alive, but not tell me?" she asked, then pressed her fingers to her eyes and wailed like a lost child.

He had to pick up his last paycheck. It hardly seemed worth it, such a pitiful amount, but his dad insisted, just as he'd insisted on Dylan giving the grocery store official notice and an apology letter when he quit, even though he hadn't worked in weeks. "Never burn your bridges," he said.

Dylan rode his bike to the grocery store early Friday evening—his clinic in Beverly ended early on Friday afternoons—and locked it to the bike rack out front. Inside the store, he shivered in the icy air and went to the customer service window to collect his check. The woman at the desk had hair the color of a raspberry slush and the air around her smelled like popcorn.

"Hello, dear," she said. "All done with school now?"

He nodded. "We finished a couple of weeks ago." He thought about adding, "And then I dove straight into therapy instead of the pool," but caught himself. That was the kind of joke kids made around the clinic. No need to freak her out. "I just came by to pick up my last check and hand in my resignation." Dylan gave her his name and the envelope with the letter in it, feeling like a fugitive, standing there while the store buzzed with shoppers and the baggers lined up at the counters behind him joked with the cashiers.

"Oh, I'm sorry to hear you'll be leaving us! Any special plans for the summer?" the woman asked, thumbing through a box of pay envelopes.

"I'm working weekends on a sheep farm in the Berkshires."

She gave him a quizzical look as she handed him the check. "How unusual."

"Yeah, well. I'm an unusual guy."

This made her laugh and wish him luck.

Outside, Dylan stood in the humid air and let his skin temperature rise to normal, keeping a wary eye on the drugstore. He wanted to go in there and ask for Kelly, see if she was okay, but he was afraid. What if she somehow blamed him for what had happened to Tyler, who was charged with assault and battery with a dangerous weapon after the cops saw the school surveillance video? Apparently Tyler had used his lacrosse stick to bash him in the head. When Dylan asked what would happen now, his dad said a lot would depend on whether Tyler was over eighteen. Dylan didn't know the answer to that. Oddly, he hadn't thought much about Tyler and Kelly in the past two weeks, since he'd been in therapy with kids a lot worse off than he was.

Like Tiffany, that girl from his English class. She had joined the program last week, her bones sharper than ever beneath her skin, her hair falling out in clumps. Dylan knew this because he'd been watching her tug hunks of it off her head during their breaks at the clinic. He'd sat on the bench next to her one day, hoping to distract her enough that she'd stop. She did. Now they spent a lot of breaks together.

In group therapy over the past week, he'd discovered that Tiffany's dad died from a brain tumor after seven years. Dylan didn't know if that would be better or worse than losing somebody as fast as he'd lost his mom. One minute there, then poof! Gone. At least he hadn't had to go through dreading his mother's death or having to act all noble. Nobody expected you to be brave when your mom or dad died in an accident. You could just rage and fucking cry your eyes out.

Or stop eating. By now, Dylan understood that he'd started to make himself disappear when she died. Eating was the one thing he could control, his therapist suggested.

He liked Cary, already a clinical psychologist but still in his twenties, with a sleeve tattoo and signed music posters from concerts he'd been to all over his office. Cary wasn't all about what Sydney called "mirroring," that kind of shit therapy Dylan had after Mom died, where the therapist just waited like a puddle to absorb whatever emotions you wanted to fling into it without ever throwing anything back at you. No, Cary always had something to say. They talked about all kinds of things: sheep and organic farming, music and math, and what it meant to do good in the world versus just existing.

It wasn't so bad, being at the clinic. Two more weeks of all-day sessions and then they'd see what came next, his dad said. In the meantime, Dylan had gained five pounds, and Cary had talked with his dad about letting Dylan work on Hannah's farm every weekend instead of staying at the grocery store. Hannah had suggested it, actually, that night she came to stay with them.

It had been less weird than he'd thought having Hannah at his dad's house; she'd mostly just sat in the living room and started knitting with yarn Sydney must have had for about a hundred years. She'd brought Dylan's yarn, too, so he'd sat with her, the two of them talking about Casper and Liz and how Sloan had started working at the farm. He'd been jealous until Hannah told him it wasn't the same, having Sloan, as it had been with him there.

"The sheep really took to you," she said.

Cary had also encouraged Dylan to make a deal with his dad: to support each other as they both "got healthy." For his dad, that meant quitting the pills. So far it seemed like he'd kept his word. Dad was acting a lot calmer and didn't look so wasted.

Last week, his dad had taken Dylan to the storage unit where Mom's stuff was. Together they'd loaded a bunch of boxes into the car and brought them home to go through in the kitchen. They'd cried, so that kind of sucked, but now he had three entire photo albums of Mom and him, plus a watercolor she'd done in college. It was sort of a lame painting, really, a sailboat crudely drawn and too flat-looking against the water, but the colors in the painting made Dylan remember going to the beach with Mom, watching her jump waves next to him, her hair slick and wet, laughing in that big way she had with her head tossed back.

Things were almost normal at home. Dad had even started leaving work early enough so they could take bike rides together after dinner, sometimes with Sydney, but more often without. He didn't know what was happening there, Dad said, "but things might not work out. Everything's still up in the air. Not your fault, son," he'd added quickly. "It's all me. I just might not be ready to get married again, you know?"

"I like her, Dad," Dylan had said. "It's okay with me if you marry Sydney. More than okay. Really."

"I know," his father said sadly. "That's not it at all. It's me."

Dylan believed him. He was sorry about Sydney, but as Cary kept reminding him, "You can't fight anybody's battles but your own."

He bent down to twirl the combination on his bike lock. He wound the chain around the handlebars and backed the bike out of the rack, glancing up just as Kelly came out of the drugstore.

"Oh," she said, and put a hand to her mouth.

"Yeah," he said. "It's me. Sorry."

She shook her head and started to duck back inside the store.

"Kelly," he called out. "What happened? I heard the police came after Tyler. I'm sorry."

"Shit," he heard her say, and then she was walking fast toward him, her eyes unnaturally bright, crayon blue against her artificial tan.

Was she going to attack him? He thought this was a possibility. Before he could get on his bike and escape, though, she'd flung her arms around his neck despite the bike between them. She smelled of cherries and coconut. "Don't be sorry," she said, her voice muffled against his neck. "Tyler's a motherfucker. I'm wicked glad the cops got him. I'm safe now." She kissed him, but missed his mouth because he jerked his head away in alarm.

"Don't," he said, and then he did back up, making sure to hold the bike in front of him like a two-wheeled shield.

"It's all right! Tyler's locked up!" she cried, putting a hand between her breasts and pressing the blouse close to her skin, against the lacy contours of her bra. "You and I can be together now!"

There was a strange humming in Dylan's ears, muffling outside sounds. It was as if he were being forced to hear his own brain whirring. His thoughts had never been clearer. "I don't want us to be together," he said. "Look, good for you, getting away from Tyler. But I'm definitely done with this. With *you*," he added for emphasis, and jumped on his bike.

He pedaled away without looking back, stopping only when he reached the street to put on the helmet clanking from the handlebars, his heart pounding as if he'd just finished one of his dad's century rides.

Hannah had been working hard all morning, starting with the usual chores related to getting the sheep out and the barn cleaned up. Now she was using the small tractor to turn the pile of manure behind the barn over to let it aerate. By fall she'd be able to use the manure as compost.

Dylan, whose father had agreed to have him spend weekends here at the farm, would normally have been helping her in the barn, but Sloan's brother had come out to cut the hay this week. A little earlier than usual, but that's when the weather felt like cooperating. Now they had to bale it and get it inside, since they were predicting thunderstorms for Monday.

After her brother did the mowing, Sloan—who proved to be as capable at operating machinery as she was at everything else, despite being barely sixteen—had returned with a hay rake attached to the tractor a couple of times during the week to fluff it up and let it dry into windrows. Today she'd come back with the baler, which essentially scooped up the hay and launched it into the big wagon being pulled behind it; Dylan was out in the field helping her on the wagon. Damn if the boy didn't look right at home standing there on the rocking wagon out in the field, like a sailor on the deck of his ship. It made Hannah so happy to see him grinning and shouting over the tractor noise at Sloan, and getting stronger and browner by the minute. This was only Dylan's third summer weekend on the farm, but what a change from when she'd first met him.

Hannah finished in the barn and then went up to see what she could do about weeding her vegetable garden. Unfortunately, the right combination of June heat and rain, so good for hay and vegetables, had also brought out the mosquitoes; as Hannah weeded and slapped at them, wishing she'd thought to put on bug spray, she thought about Allen and how much he'd hated any sort of insects.

"They're eating me alive, get them off me!" he'd shouted one night, his eyes nearly rolling back in his head with fear because the insects meant Vietnam all over again. He'd imagined maggots in the shaving cut on his cheek one night, too, and told her how some of the soldiers had deliberately rubbed jelly into their wounds to attract the fly larvae, hoping to become infected and sent home.

Allen. Hannah shook her head, closing her eyes, remembering the venom in his mother's voice: *You ruined him.* No matter what, she'd never regret having that time with Allen. Their early months together—the thrill of riding camels and wearing mirrored jackets in India, the excitement of boarding a train to whatever European city called to them next, the hope they'd felt in buying this farm and growing organic crops while building a peaceful community—she would have missed all that if she hadn't married Allen. And Sydney, too: she would never have had Sydney.

Everything with Allen was as electric and vivid as the colors of the seventies, psychedelic promises in an embittered land. There would be equal rights for all, no matter what color or sex you were. There would be no more war. There would be love and freedom and music and people power. That's what they had believed. Allen had been so strong, so committed to his vision of the future, that she had been drawn in his wake, head back, hair streaming, laughing as he taught her to be fearless when it came to standing up to authority and protesting whatever wasn't right with the world. She used to feel sorry for people who didn't know what this felt like, this forceful positive energy and unity of vision.

But she'd lost him to the war as surely as if he'd died in Vietnam. "What were we fighting for, in the end?" Allen had asked once. "A delusion, that's all. And not even our own delusion at that."

Sometimes she tried to see what he described, looking out at the Berkshires: instead of the lush rolling hills that turned green in summer and every bright color of red and orange and yellow in the fall, she imagined land chewed up by fighting and pagoda walls chipped by gunfire. Allen had survived one particular battle by hiding under dead soldiers, and had been rescued by helicopter, which she imagined hovering above the ground with the rotor whipping dirt around him like angry bees.

She had held on to the farm because it was a way of holding on to the best of Allen. It was a way of making sure that his dreams of a better world came true. Had they?

Watching Dylan shouting at Sloan from the hay wagon, watching how tall he stood as the wagon circled the field, she thought that maybe they had, if only in a different way.

Except for one thing: Rory. Rory had chosen to absent himself from their lives. She had felt such a powerful mix of disappointment and fury and hope three weeks ago, when his mother had finally confessed that Rory was alive. As stunned as Hannah had been by the news, she had gradually accepted it as the truth. She had already known it, on some level, because the world was still spinning on its axis, and she and he—Hannah'n'Rory, Rory'n'Hannah—had been inseparable for so long, she felt certain she would know if he was gone from this earth. She would have to know.

So that left just two questions: Why did Rory disappear? And did she really want to know the reason?

It had been threatening rain all day Friday, but when the weather remained muggy beneath an ironclad sky, Ella suggested frozen yogurt after work.

The Newburyport shop was throbbing with small children and teenagers. Sydney didn't usually frequent the ice-cream shops in town, for fear of running into a family she'd worked with in her office. Luckily, she didn't recognize any of the kids milling around the spigots and spiraling more and more frozen yogurt into their containers while their parents made halfhearted admonishments from the sidelines.

She and Ella joined the fray, loading their own bright orange paper cups with different flavors and toppings, giggling at the absurdity of spooning Swedish Fish and Oreo bits and caramel sauce on top of yogurt. They carried the cups down to the benches along the river. The harbor was crowded, as it always was on summer Fridays, with pleasure boats tied along the boardwalk.

"Better than the zoo," Ella remarked, eyeing an older couple in striped sailor shirts sipping tall pink drinks on a yacht bigger than Sydney's cottage. Ella plunked down on the bench in front of them. "So how's every little thing in your life?" she asked, dipping her spoon into her dish and coming up with a bite of an astonishing variety of colors and textures.

Sydney did the same with her spoon. "I don't know where to start. And by that, I mean in my life or in my yogurt."

"Surprise me. It's been a while since we had time for a real chin-wag, and I always like a little taste of everything."

Sydney had already told Ella about Jack Carlson's attack, of course, and about Marco taking her home, quickly adding, "Nothing happened. Well, almost nothing," which had made Ella beg for details Sydney refused to give her. But she hadn't yet shared the story of seeing her mother in Ipswich and discovering that Uncle Rory was still alive, or about the note Marco had left her that Sydney now carried in her wallet. She began by describing the scene at her grandmother's house.

"Mom was absolutely shattered," Sydney finished. "Not so much by my grandmother keeping this secret from her all these years, I think, as by Rory's deception." She dipped her spoon into a pool of hot fudge.

"That's unforgivable," Ella pronounced.

Sydney sighed. "It's pretty bad," she agreed. "Grammy says she was honoring her son's wishes to keep his survival a secret, but it was hurtful. I can't imagine why Uncle Rory would desert my mom and me, or the farm, even, when we all needed him."

"What was he like?"

Sydney thought for a minute. "Thoughtful. Kind. Musical. A lot more stable than my dad. That's why this is so hard to accept. In a weird way, I could believe my dad would do something like this, but not Rory."

Ella had finished her yogurt; she tossed the cup into the trash barrel beside the bench, causing a flurry among the sparrows chirping in the bush behind them. "Could Rory have been in hiding, maybe?"

"From what?" Sydney asked, startled.

"I don't know. Did he secretly grow weed? Did he have a criminal record? I would imagine Haven Lake was a Utopia for guys like that, especially since he had your dad running things and Rory could just stay in the background."

"I don't know." Sydney had never considered this possibility. "We did have draft dodgers working on the farm because they needed a place to stay, and a few ex-cons. I'm sure it's possible that some were wanted by the police. But Rory lived with us for ten years. Seems like a long time to stay in one spot if you've got something to hide."

"What about that boy who drowned? Could Rory have been mixed up in that?"

Sydney stared at her in shock. "No! Absolutely no way."

"I didn't mean anything personal," Ella said. "It's just that I know you've always wondered what really happened that night." She shifted her weight on the bench so that her black-and-white wrap dress rode up her knees, causing a man passing by to pause and stare until his wife tugged him forward.

"Not like that! I never once thought Theo was *murdered*, if that's what you mean," Sydney said. "I just wondered why he went swimming alone that night, when we all knew better, and how he could have hit his head and drowned. We knew every rock and stick in that pond—it's not that big a body of water, and there's an island in the middle—plus, Theo was a competitive swimmer in high school. The pond wasn't even over your head in most places."

"Right, you've told me all that," Ella said. "But what if your uncle saw the accident, but didn't do anything to save the boy? Or saw somebody else do something to Theo? It could be that Rory took off to avoid talking to the police. Maybe his mother's covering for him."

"I don't think that's it. Rory *did* talk to the police. A lot. Everybody did. The cops were determined to drive us out of town. Which I guess in a way they did," Sydney added bitterly. Her head was starting to ache, having these possibilities tossed her way.

"Okay." Ella held up her hands again. "You got me."

"I'm sorry. I don't mean to sound defensive. It's just that I loved Theo so much back then, and it kills me not to know what really happened to him."

"Maybe it's for the best. We can't unknow what we know, right?" Ella reached out and patted Sydney's knee. "Now what's all this about Marco leaving you a little love note?"

Sydney's cheeks burned. "God. Now I'm embarrassed I told you."

"Since when do you have to be shy with me, girl?" Ella demanded. "Don't I have your back, every second of every day?" She corrected herself hastily, adding, "Except when that foul man came after you. Lord in heaven, I cannot believe I was out of the office. Mr. Jack Carlson never would have gone after you on my watch, no sir. I would have stopped him in his ugly-ass tracks."

Sydney smiled. "I know."

"Still. I'm going to tell you this right now: I'll be running that man over with my car if he dares come knocking on your door again." Ella's handsome face was glowing with indignation.

"I believe you. Where were you that day, anyway? You never did tell me. Must have been a special date for you to take a three-hour lunch."

Ella looked away and sniffed. "Now *that* ain't none o' your business."

"What? Oh, come on!" Sydney said. "How can you say that? You've seen me literally fall flat on my face and make a fool of myself at parties. Haven't I even let you inside my *closet*, for God's sake? Haven't you pawed through my pathetic excuse of a wardrobe? And aren't you now about to read an inappropriate personal note that I should never share with *anyone*?"

"Yes, ma'am." Ella was smiling a little.

"So?" Sydney demanded. "Are we friends or not? Don't you trust me enough to share even a little bit of your life?"

Ella swiveled her head around to look Sydney in the eye. "Like I said before, once you know something, you can't ever unknow it."

"But I want to know you! You're my best friend. My other mom."

At this, Ella's face relaxed a little. "I'm honored to hear that, because I know how much you respect and love your mother."

"I do?" Sydney asked in surprise, then realized Ella was right: something had shifted in the past few weeks. She didn't know exactly when. But ever since the day Jack Carlson had stormed into her office, she'd been aware that she felt differently about her mother.

Hannah was the one who saved her that day. She had been teaching Sydney survival skills all her life: everything from how to change a tire to how to mend a shirt, from how to bake bread to how to defend herself. No mother could have taught her more. Sydney was grateful for that. And now that she'd seen her mother crumble in front of Grammy Bishop's house, had watched every wall come tumbling down in the face of Rory's betrayal and her grandmother's cruelty, Hannah seemed very, very human: vulnerable and strong.

"I *do* love and respect her," Sydney agreed, wishing that her mother could be here right now to hear this. But she was with Ella, who deserved her full attention, so she pressed on and said, "I hope you know that anything you tell me would be kept in confidence, and I would never judge you for it."

Ella nodded, making her earrings catch the evening light and sparkle against her brown skin. "I know. So here it is: I have a son doing time for breaking and entering. How do you like that? My only boy, age twenty-six, drove a getaway car when he and some of his dumb-ass friends decided to rob a convenience store. And when I go on long lunches, or have those Friday night hot dates, it's to see him in Concord prison."

Of the hundred things Sydney had guessed Ella might tell her, this wasn't even on the list. But she was determined not to let her shock show. "Well, lucky for your boy, he has a great mom who supports him. You should see him as much as you can. I'd ask for a four-day workweek if I were you."

"Thanks, baby." Ella snapped her fingers and held out her hand. "Now give me that letter. I can't spend one more second sitting here and feeling sorry for myself."

"Okay. But you can't share this with anybody else," Sydney warned, pulling Marco's note out of her bag.

"You know you didn't need to say that." Ella took the letter and unfolded it.

While she read it, Sydney focused on a cormorant standing on one of the buoys in the water, its wings outstretched to dry, a black prehistoric profile against the blue sky, and recited Marco's words to herself by heart:

Dear Sydney,

It wasn't easy to leave you sleeping in front of the fireplace after our night together, but I thought it was better. I called a cab so you wouldn't have to wake and find me in your house, or have Gary find me there if he happened to come by and check on you. Please don't torture yourself about last night. Guilt is a useless emotion, unless you accept guilt for what it really is: a catalyst for change.

We had a moment of weakness. I will behave from now on, and so will you. Just know that I want to be with you, always. Come away with me. You might be sorry if you do. But you'll definitely have more fun than you're having now.

With love,

Marco

Sydney glanced at Ella as she folded up the note, and was surprised to see her wiping her eyes. "What's wrong? I thought the letter would make you feel better!"

"It did." Ella rooted around in her handbag, a gold satchel big enough to carry a Pekingese. Finally she came up with a wad of lipstick-stained tissue and pressed it to her streaming eyes.

"Then why are you crying?"

"Because I know you too well."

"What's that supposed to mean?" Sydney asked.

"That I know you've already made up your mind Marco isn't the one for you, because he makes you feel too good."

"That's crazy talk!"

"No. Listen up: after you read this letter, I'm betting you told yourself to work harder on things with Gary, right?" Ella's tone was stern. "You thought, 'Gary is a good man, a man in pain who needs me.' Am I wrong? Stop me if I say something foolish." Ella cut her eyes at Sydney.

Sydney bit her bottom lip, thinking maybe Ella *did* know her too well.

"All right," Ella went on. "So you're going to stay the course and marry Gary, thinking that's the sure thing. You're buying the loaf of white bread instead of the wine and cheese, because you think life should be about workaday sandwiches, not romance."

"Because romance doesn't last," Sydney interrupted. "Neither does passion."

Ella folded her arms. "Maybe the fires burn down a little. But, honey, you better start with a red-hot blaze if you're going to have any hope of rekindling the flames later, know what I'm saying? You love Gary. I know that! He probably loves you, too. You want to take care of each other, and of Dylan, so you're both settling for resigned contentment instead of busting-out joy."

"That's completely unfair!" Sydney cried. "Gary and I love and respect each other. We've been together too long for me to just throw it away. Gary has never betrayed me or lied to me, except for this one thing about the pills, and he's off those. I owe it to him to work things out, one way or another."

Ella's mouth twitched. "Wait. Did I just hear you say 'one way or another'?"

Sydney nodded, somehow feeling tricked.

"Music to my ears, honey girl," Ella said.

An hour later, Sydney pulled into the clinic parking lot to pick up Dylan. During the past two weeks, she'd been the one to drive Dylan to Beverly most mornings, and Gary typically picked him up after dinner. On Friday nights, Dylan came home from the clinic early enough for dinner, but tonight Gary had wanted to take a bike ride before dark with one of the other surgeons, so Sydney had agreed to swap with him.

At the thought of Gary whizzing around on his bike, Sydney felt immediately conscious of her stomach, imagining it full of the candy she'd scooped onto her frozen yogurt. Guilt, guilt, guilt. Then she remembered Marco's note. He was right: guilt wasn't going to get her anywhere. She had enjoyed that candy. Maybe she'd take a walk tonight, work some of it off. Or maybe not.

She e-mailed a couple of her clients from her phone. When she looked up again, she saw a man standing in the shade beneath the awning; it took her a minute to recognize him as Dylan. He'd gained weight and his arms were tanned from working on the farm. Seeing him looking so healthy, and leaning like a cowboy with one foot propped against the wall behind him, arms crossed over his chest, made her smile.

Dylan looked surprised, too, as Sydney pulled her car over to the door. "Sorry, were you waiting long? I didn't see your car. I was expecting Dad."

"He's out riding his bike with Dr. Miller. He'll be home for dinner. How was your day?"

"Okay, I guess." Dylan buckled his seat belt and for a minute she thought that was all he would say. Dylan didn't typically talk much about his therapy, and she supposed that was normal. It must be exhausting to be in an intensive program like this one. But then he surprised her by adding, "I think I might be helping this girl from my school."

Sydney pulled out of the parking lot, trying not to let her curiosity show too much—the worst thing you could do with teens was hammer them with questions. Better to let them share information at their own pace. "Oh yeah?" she said. "That must make you feel good."

"Kind of, I guess. This girl's pretty nice—she was in a couple of my classes at school last year—but she told me she thinks she's fat even though she's so skinny her neck looks like a chicken's." Dylan put a finger to his mouth, started to chew the nail, but quickly brought it down to his lap again. "She pulls out her hair, too, when she's nervous. But lately I've been sitting and talking with her during our breaks, just about what video games I play or her drawings or whatever, and she leaves her hair alone. I said I thought her drawings were cool—she always carries a sketch pad around with her—and I could tell she liked me saying that. We might be friends. I don't know." He pressed his head back against the seat rest. "Is it like that when you work with kids? Do they relax and tell you stuff, and that's what helps them get better?"

"That's a big part of what I do, yes."

"I bet you're good at it," Dylan said.

She glanced at him, surprised. "Thank you. You'd be a good psychologist, too."

"I would?"

Sydney nodded. "You have a lot of insights about people, and you're very accepting."

He grunted. "Except when it comes to that jerk-off Tyler."

"Well, I wanted to run him over with my car," Sydney said.

Dylan laughed, and after a minute she was laughing with him.

As they neared Newburyport, Dylan said he was planning to see a movie that night with Mark. He'd spend the night at Mark's and then leave on the earliest possible bus to Haven Lake.

Sydney wanted to ask how her mother was doing, but she didn't like to put Dylan in the middle. She'd been mulling over that awful scene at her grandmother's; she still couldn't believe Grammy Bishop had done something like that to Hannah deliberately, but she had. And no matter how many times Sydney tried to remind herself that Grammy Bishop had always been good to her, and was perhaps deranged enough by grief after losing Allen to blame Hannah for her son's death and want to exact revenge in some way, she couldn't muster the empathy or energy to forgive the old woman. Her sympathies lay squarely with her own mother, a fact that surprised Sydney. Yet she didn't know how to express any of this, and so she hadn't even called Hannah. That, too, was unforgivable, especially after Hannah had bent over backward to reach out to Dylan.

Now Dylan was telling her of his own accord that Hannah seemed fine, if tired. "She's always working, but other than that, things are okay at Haven Lake," he said. After a brief hesitation, he added, "I think you guys should look for Rory. I could help you find him."

Sydney pulled into the driveway and shut off the car. How did Dylan know about Rory?

Stupid question. Teenagers knew everything. They were the ones born with eyes in the backs of their heads, not parents or teachers.

"How would you even do that?" she asked as Dylan grabbed his backpack from the backseat and she picked up her briefcase. "I tried asking Grammy Bishop, but she won't tell us where he is."

"Hello? Google?"

"I don't know if it's a good idea," Sydney said. "There might be a reason he took off."

"Well, duh," Dylan said, then caught himself. "Sorry."

In the kitchen, Gary, still in his bike shorts and bright yellow spandex top, was steaming asparagus and flash-frying tuna steaks. "Thanks for picking up the boy," he said, and kissed Sydney.

"No problem. Good ride?"

"Oh yeah, we were hauling. I'm beat. Chardonnay's in the fridge. Dinner in ten."

At the table, the three of them talked about Gary's upcoming bike race and the boats Sydney had seen along the waterfront. Sydney relaxed, marveling at how far they'd come as a family in a few short weeks, after what had felt like a complete breakdown. She wished Ella were here to see that *this* was what she craved most: a family that served as a sanctuary from the madness in the world.

She and Dylan did the dishes while Gary went to his office to catch up on paperwork. Then Dylan went upstairs to get ready for the movie. He clomped down again as she and Gary had just poured themselves second glasses of wine and were sitting on the couch in front of one of Gary's recorded BBC shows.

"Okay, I'm out of here," Dylan said. "Mark and I are going to a nine o'clock show at the mall. I'm sleeping over and he's driving me to the bus station in the morning. I'll text you which bus I'm taking back on Sunday night. Here." He thrust a sheet of notebook paper into Sydney's hand. "Your uncle's living in Vermont."

Her breath caught as she studied Rory's name and address. "Ever thought of being a detective? My God. How did you find this so fast?"

Dylan grinned. "Easy. I knew he was a musician, so I looked for him on Facebook. His band has a fan page. They're called 'the Copperheads' and they play at a bar in Brattleboro."

Then he was out the door, letting it slam shut behind him a split second before Gary yelled at him not to. Sydney folded the paper into quarters and tucked it into her pants pocket. "I don't know what to do with this information," she said, taking a gulp of wine.

"Burn it," Gary suggested.

Sydney hit pause on the remote and turned on the couch to look at him. "That's a weird thing to say."

He rubbed his eyes. "Sorry. Didn't mean to be flippant. Fatigue's setting in after that bike ride. But, really, why do you have to do anything? You already know the guy's alive. So does your mom. You also know Rory doesn't want anything to do with you."

"We don't actually know that."

"Oh, come on, Syd! Why delude yourself?"

Gary set his wineglass down on the coffee table and slid closer to her on the couch, slinging an arm around her shoulders. He smelled of suntan lotion and fish. She tried not to wrinkle her nose. "I'm not!"

"Yes, you are," Gary said patiently. "Think about it. Obviously your mom wouldn't be hard for Rory to find, since she never left Haven Lake. If he'd wanted to see her, Rory wouldn't have taken off and then made it look like he freakin' *died*. What kind of guy *does* that to people?"

Sydney felt a chill despite the warm evening and Gary's body pressed close to hers. Gary was right. She leaned her head back against his arm. "I know. I was sad when they told us he was dead, but somehow this is just as painful. I can't even imagine how terrible Mom must feel about it all. Rory was always so good to us. I used to wish he was my real dad, you know? My own father was so unpredictable. Even scary sometimes. But Rory was always *Rory*. Sweet and good, the kind of guy with a guitar in one hand and a book in the other. I can't believe he did this. Or that Grammy Bishop kept up this charade of grief in order to get back at my mother for her own perverse reasons. My God. How dysfunctional is that?"

"I know. I'm sorry, honey. Thank God you're more evolved than anyone else in your family."

Sydney stared at the television, the action frozen. She was more bothered by Gary's remark than she wanted to let on, so she returned to the subject of her grandmother. "I wonder if Grammy Bishop orchestrated the whole death scenario and kept Rory away from Hannah just to be rid of my mother."

"Nobody's that Machiavellian."

"You don't know my grandmother."

"True," Gary said. "But my money's on Rory just wanting to bail and asking his mother to keep his secret. He was that kind of guy, like you said. A musician and dreamer. A draft dodger."

"He never actually dodged the draft," Sydney said, feeling immediately, inexplicably defensive. "His number never came up."

"You know what I mean. From everything you've told me, your uncle Rory strikes me as another groovy longhair who grew up in the seventies and never wanted to face reality, so he kept escaping it."

"Reality being?"

Gary picked up the remote to play his show again. "Having to work hard like the rest of us. You know. Living a normal life."

Sydney felt her neck prickle with irritation. That was always the assumption by anyone with a so-called "normal" job and family life—even her own, sometimes, admittedly—that people who chose alternative lifestyles or devoted themselves to art and music didn't work hard. Yet the truth was that nobody worked harder than Rory and her parents, trying to keep Haven Lake afloat. That was still true of her mother today.

She leaned forward and picked up the remote, muting the show again despite Gary's annoyed glance. "I still think I should go see him."

"Why? For God's sake, Sydney. Haven't we had enough emotional upheavals lately, between Dylan and your mom and that whole Jack Carlson thing? What can you possibly accomplish, other than reassuring yourself that Rory is a deadbeat?"

"We don't *know* he's a deadbeat!"

Gary snorted. "He's playing music in a bar in Brattleboro, druggie capital of the druggiest state in the country. Well, maybe after Colorado. What else do you need to know?"

"I want to know why he stayed away. Was it grief? Was he angry about how everything went down? Did he see or hear something about Theo drowning that he didn't want to share with the cops?"

"Shhh. Don't get yourself all worked up, Syd." Gary reached over to put a hand on her hair, stroking it rhythmically, the way he might soothe an anxious golden retriever. "Just sleep on it. That's all I ask. We can talk about it again tomorrow."

For a moment, the only sound in the room was the steady dripping of the kitchen faucet. Sydney had meant to fix that, but kept forgetting. Now the sound was like a clock ticking inside her skull.

Her senses seemed to be on high alert. She was aware of the dryer humming upstairs and felt a breeze from the front windows lift the hairs on her arms. The moon gleamed like a white circle in the upper left pane of one of the front windows, like a button in the sky you could push to make something happen. Outside, a cat howled.

In her heightened emotional state, Sydney watched Gary watching her, and suddenly she knew: Gary didn't love her.

He might have, at one time, but he didn't now. Not anymore. Whatever they had was gone. Or, if not gone, altered forever by the events of the past few weeks, transformed into an emotion so pale and unrecognizable, there wasn't even a name for it. They had been together. Now they were not.

Don't say it, she thought, but said it anyway. "You don't love me anymore."

"What?" Gary had reached for the remote again. Now he froze with it in his hand, pointed like a conductor's baton at the TV, and gave her a wild-eyed look. That look might have communicated that he thought she was talking gibberish, if there hadn't also been a dawning realization in those blue eyes, a potent mix of betrayal, anger, hurt, and, yes, relief. Enormous relief.

"You don't love me anymore," she repeated softly.

Gary put down the remote. His face was so altered by grief that he didn't even look like himself, but like the photographs of his father, long dead, stored in a leather album in the living room closet, a hunched-over wizened man with bony knees and eyes like blue marbles.

"I tried to love you," he said, his voice as low as Sydney's. "I really tried, honey."

She felt a sharp pain in her chest, but ignored it. She could deal with the hurt later. Right now she had to keep tearing away the layers of pretense between them to get to the truth. "When did you know it was over between us?"

"When I first took Dylan to the clinic," he said, dropping his face into his hands.

Gary's beautiful surgeon's hands, the fingers long and tapered, looked old as well. He massaged his temples and ran his palms up and down his face, as if he might peel back his skin and expose another face beneath it. She'd seen a horrible movie once where that happened.

She shuddered and looked away. "Why?" she asked.

"I don't know. I think maybe what I felt when I met you was relief, more than love. I felt relieved that I could feel anything at all after Amanda. But I don't feel the same way about you that I felt for her, and that's not fair to you."

"Or to you, either." Sydney thought about this. "I wouldn't expect you to feel the same, exactly," she said eventually, "but I would want your feelings for me to be as intense. Does that make sense?"

He nodded. "I'm sorry. But I don't think that's possible. I think maybe I wasn't ready for all this." He made a gesture that encompassed them, the television, the wineglasses, and the upstairs where their bed waited, still unmade from this morning because they'd both rushed out the door to do what couples with families did every day of their lives: take out the trash, take care of a child, get themselves to work on time, make dinner, then collapse on the couch.

She had loved most of it. She had loved Gary. She was as sure of that as she was of this other fact: she didn't love him enough to marry him.

She slipped the ring off her finger and set it down gently on the table between their wineglasses.

CHAPTER NINETEEN

Bobolinks. That's what those birds were called. Sydney had bought him a birding app; now Dylan pocketed his phone, satisfied, and set off for the hill. So far he'd identified fifteen species of birds with this thing.

Hannah had asked him to check the fence in the upper pasture; she'd moved the sheep there this morning. Now she and Sydney were driving to Vermont to find Uncle Rory, after Sydney showed up without warning last night while he and Hannah were already showered and wearing pj's, knitting while the radio played that show Hannah liked, what was it called? Some insect name.

The Moth. That was it. The stories were always strange, but a lot of them were funny and he was getting used to the radio, to just listening without having earbuds dangling from his head or watching something on a screen. Weird, but cool, because he could knit when his hands and mind roamed free. His scarf was halfway done; he'd decided to give it to his father, since his birthday was in November. Dad might not wear it, but he would definitely like the idea of Dylan making him something. After this, Hannah said she'd teach him how to make a hat. He could use a striped skater hat.

Dylan had been embarrassed to have Sydney catch him knitting at the dining room table, but she seemed upset and barely noticed. Her eyes were red and puffy; she must have been crying. But, when Hannah asked why she was there, Sydney only said things were fine, but she thought it was time to go see Rory.

"I was hoping to spend the night here, and then you and I can drive to Brattleboro in the morning," Sydney said.

"No," Hannah had said at once. "Rory doesn't want to see me."

"You don't know that, Mom."

They'd argued, and somehow—miraculously, in Dylan's view, given how stubborn Hannah could be—Sydney had persuaded her mother to change her mind. She basically did that therapist voodoo thing, asking Hannah what she was afraid of, and what she thought might happen if they found Rory.

Meanwhile, Dylan kept knitting, amazed by how much two women could look and act alike but not even know it. Despite her height and thinner legs, Hannah stood just like Sydney, with her knees bowed a little and her shoulders thrown back. It was like you could run either woman over with a truck and she'd pop back up again, like that inflatable clown his mother had bought him one year. He'd loved knocking that thing over with his bicycle, back when he still had training wheels and wasn't afraid of anything.

So today Hannah and Sydney were driving to Vermont with the address he'd given them. Dylan didn't know whether to hope they found Rory or not. He couldn't stand the idea of them getting hurt. He hated it that he even cared, but there it was: his heart, all banged up but still beating away in his chest.

"Hey! What are you doing up there?" Sloan yelled from the barn below.

She must have arrived on her motorcycle; Dylan hadn't even heard the bike—he'd been thinking so hard. Sloan had given him a few rides on her motorcycle. She'd laughed when he held on to her waist, but then she'd leaned against him and Dylan had felt something stirring in him.

Yeah, the obvious physical reaction, that was part of it: Sloan was cute, even if she dressed and acted like a guy most of the time. But he felt something else, too, a response that was more about admiring her. Sloan was the coolest girl he knew. Maybe after the summer, he'd be able to drive a motorcycle or tractor the way she did.

"I'm checking the upper pasture," he called back. "Hannah was worried there might be something wrong with the current."

"Don't electrocute yourself up there," she said. "I heard it's supposed to rain."

"Ha-ha," he yelled back, but glanced at the sky and saw Sloan was right: the sky over the tallest hills to the west was turning gunmetal gray, as if a bucket of paint had been poured over the Berkshires and was slowly spreading.

Dylan used a voltmeter to test the fence when he got to the top of the hill. The current seemed fine; he checked in a couple of places to make sure, then stood there a little longer, admiring the sheep. The rams were gone except for Casper. He was still in the pen down near the barn, but his splint was off and he was getting around just fine. Hannah said she'd found a farm that could keep him as a pet, a friend of hers with a girl who didn't want anything ordinary like a dog. The girl was getting Casper as a birthday present. Dylan would be sad to see the lamb leave, but he liked the idea of some kid making a fuss over him, and no way could he bring him to Newburyport.

The sheep were getting woollier, puffing up by the day, and the lambs were big enough now that it was harder to tell them apart from their mothers. Dylan hoped he could be here for the next shearing. He thought about what Hannah had told him about wool fibers being able to bend back on themselves over twenty thousand times without breaking. Cotton broke after thirty-two hundred bends or something like that, silk after eighteen hundred. Now he couldn't help but feel proud that he was taking part in growing wool instead of, say, farming dumb silkworms.

The breeze was fluttering the leaves in the fruit trees above him. Rain was definitely coming. Millions of tiny atoms must be vibrating in the leaves, just as atoms were vibrating in his own body. In biology, he'd learned there were a hundred trillion atoms in a human cell. Weirdly, there were the same number of cells in the human body as there were atoms in each cell. That was science for you: beautiful patterns everywhere.

Those sheep, these trees? They were all made up of atoms, too. Learning this in class was different from how he felt it in his bones here, standing under the trees and waiting for rain to fall and turn the grass greener for the sheep, so the animals could eat and then breed and provide wool and compost and meat for humans.

In life, everything was connected. You were never really alone.

"Hey! You done yet or what?" Sloan was walking up the hill toward him, her dark ponytail bouncing behind her.

"Yeah, I'm done. Why?"

"I want to go swimming! Aren't you boiling hot? Let's go jump in the pond."

"Isn't it going to rain?"

She laughed. "So? Come on. I'll race you."

Wait, wait! Dylan wanted to call, watching the girl's long legs carry her in leaps down the hill, as if she were a lamb, too. What if there was thunder and lightning? Also, hadn't Hannah said nobody had been swimming in that pond in twenty years?

Dylan looked up at the bruised sky and then at the pond below, an opaque silver coin now instead of its usual glittery blue. Sloan was halfway there. She would go swimming with or without him. That's who she was.

And who was he?

Never mind that. Who did he *want* to be? The sort of kid who stood around worrying, or that guy who took risks, who rode a motorcycle and went swimming in the rain?

He took a deep breath and looked at the sheep. The sheep seemed not at all worried about the weather; they happily buried their faces in the tall grass.

Dylan took a deep breath and raced down the hill after Sloan. He made it to the beach as she was pulling off her shoes on the dock. He hesitated when she stripped off her jeans, revealing slim, muscled legs and a surprisingly round ass in black bikini pants. She looked at him and laughed, then tugged off her shirt. Beneath it she wore a blue cotton bra; her breasts were as round and perfectly shaped as her butt.

"You're not going to swim in clothes, are you?" she demanded. "You'll sink like a rock if those jeans get wet, and I am so not pulling you out." She dove into the water then, a sleek white arrow shot off the dock with surprising speed.

Dylan stepped onto the dock and stripped down to his boxers. The dock was blistered and hot and rough against his bare feet. He waited until he saw Sloan's head surface, black as an otter's, and then did a cannonball almost on top of her, laughing as he felt the icy water spray around him.

Sloan dunked him as he came up for air, then swam away toward the island in the middle of the pond. Dylan felt the weeds tugging at his legs like fingers, but raced after her, his heart pumping hard as his arms and legs pistoned through the water. Sloan was a good swimmer, but he was bigger and, to his surprise, stronger.

He caught up and, at the last minute, dove beneath the water's surface and opened his eyes, seeing her pale limbs flashing through the hazy green water ahead of him. Finally he caught her, his arms around her waist.

They bobbed to the surface, shaking the water out of their eyes, laughing hard as the rain began, the droplets sparking on the water's surface around them, endless patterns expanding around the circles of their bodies as the two of them drew close together, treading water skin to skin as the rain beat against their heads and faces, falling in sheets now across the fields and woods and pond. They were in a tunnel of gray, the rain beating a rhythm on their scalps and making Dylan whoop with laughter because there was nothing else, not anything beyond this girl, this pond, this rain, this moment, and him, yet they were part of everything in the world.

. . .

Brattleboro, Vermont, hadn't changed much since the last time Hannah was here for one of Rory's concerts back in the nineties. It still felt like a college town without a college, with its brick buildings and riverfront shops.

It was a tense ride with Sydney at the wheel and Hannah wanting to ask her to stop and let her out every mile that brought them closer. So stupid. Closer to what? They had Googled Rory's home address but found nothing, not even his name. Sydney had tried calling Mrs. Bishop again. To no avail, of course: Hannah had been vindicated, if annoyed, to hear Sydney argue with her mother-in-law and then stab the phone off with multiple jabs of her finger when no information was forthcoming.

Now they pulled up to a parking meter near the Red Barrel, the bar where Dylan said the Copperheads performed every week. And, sure enough, there was the band's name listed on the calendar of events. The two of them sat staring at the poster, equally stunned to see that it was real, Hannah suspected. She pulled her braid over her shoulder and tightened the elastic.

"Now what? They're hardly going to be playing during the day," she said. "It was stupid to come so early."

"Maybe it was stupid to come at all," Sydney said.

Her daughter sounded so defeated that Hannah immediately felt remorseful. "I'm not complaining," she said. "I appreciate you coming all the way out to Haven Lake to drive me here. I think you're probably right. We need to see Rory, if only to find out why he won't see us. It's just that I'm scared."

"I know."

Sydney's hands remained on the wheel of the parked car. She was leaning forward as if the car were still in motion, and in heavy traffic at that. Her hair, instead of being pinned in its usual knot, tumbled down her back in gold curls. Hannah had to fold her hands in her lap to resist touching it, because seeing Sydney's hair like that made her remember the feel of those thick, springy curls between her own fingers, whenever Sydney let her brush it as a child.

"Why are you doing this, really?" Hannah said. "I'm surprised you even remember Rory that well."

Sydney didn't change position. "Of course I remember him. I loved Uncle Rory." Her voice caught. "I don't get why he did any of this."

"Me, either." Hannah shook her head. "But it wasn't just wanting to find Rory that made you leave home in the middle of the night and drive to Haven Lake, was it?"

Sydney smiled a little. "Maybe you're the one who should have been the therapist."

"Look at me, Sydney. Please."

Slowly, Sydney turned her head, her green eyes flecked with gold and beautiful, but pained. "Gary and I broke up Friday night."

"Oh, honey. I'm so sorry," Hannah said, though she wasn't really: Gary wasn't the one for her daughter. Sydney deserved someone more open, to make sure she'd stay that way, too.

Sydney seemed to read her thoughts. "You're not the least bit sorry. You didn't like Gary. You did a good job of trying to hide it, but I could tell."

"See? You're the one who should be a therapist," Hannah said, keeping her voice light. "All right, it's true: I thought you could do better. But I didn't want to say anything. Obviously, I don't know what goes into making a marriage work."

"You tried, Mom," Sydney said softly. "I know that now."

Hannah's emotions threatened to spill over right here in this overheating car: gratitude, sorrow, love. She looked out the window at the stream of people on the sidewalk in Brattleboro. They looked like they could have walked here from Amherst: women with long graying hair and blue jeans or loose cotton dresses and skirts; men with ponytails and sandals. Her kind, Hannah thought with a grimace: liberals self-righteously striving to do good in the world, but hardly a blip in history when it came right down to it.

"Did you break up because of Marco?" she asked.

Sydney's face reddened. "Not exactly."

"There wouldn't be anything wrong if it was," Hannah said, wishing there were some way she could pour all of her life lessons into a glass and make her daughter drink them down, one long gulp of wisdom. "Just because you desire Marco and have fun with him doesn't make wanting to be with him the wrong thing. Does that make sense? Don't ever let need be the only reason you stay with someone."

To her relief, Sydney simply nodded. "Thanks, Mom."

"Have you told Dylan?" Hannah's heart ached for the boy, going through yet another loss, and for herself, too, because she'd been looking forward to being his grandmother. But their friendship had already begun. She would just make sure it continued to grow.

Sydney shook her head. "I didn't want to talk to him about it when I was so upset. Besides, maybe Gary should be the one."

"You have your own relationship with him, and it's a good one," Hannah said. "Maybe all Dylan really needs to know is that you and I will still be there for him. We can be his family even if you don't marry Gary."

To her surprise, Sydney leaned over to rest her head on Hannah's shoulder over the awkward span between the seats. "You're a good person, Mom. I'm glad Dylan has you."

Hannah put her arm around Sydney's shoulders. "You have me, too. You've always had me."

Sydney sat up abruptly, her mouth tight at the corners. "We should see if anyone's in the bar. Somebody has to know where Rory lives."

She jumped out of the car and began jamming quarters into the meter before Hannah could process what had caused Sydney's sudden shift in mood. Slowly, she unwound her legs from the passenger seat, got out of the car, and went to stand beside her daughter, whose shoulders were a rigid line. "What is it?"

Sydney spun around to glare at her. "I didn't want to get into this," she said.

"Into what?"

Her daughter's face was red, contorted. "Oh, come on, Mom. What you said, that I've always had you? Not true," Sydney hissed. "You left me, Mom, and you never came back."

"What are you talking about?" Hannah said, feeling her own anger rising. "I came back. I nearly got arrested, I came back so often!"

"What the hell are you talking about?"

"I came back, Sydney! Every week, sometimes twice a week, I drove to Ipswich, trying to convince your grandparents to let me talk to you! But they took out a restraining order. Didn't you know that?"

Sydney shook her head.

"Finally I went to court, but the Bishops had too much money and knew too many people. I didn't have the means to fight them, and I was terrified they might figure out a way to lock me up. I know that sounds silly to you now, but I didn't know anything back then, and I'd already spent enough time curled up in a little ball of misery in rehab. So I sneaked around to see you."

"Where? When?"

"I saw you any time I could. Anyplace I thought the Bishops wouldn't see me! I parked around the corner from that restaurant where you were a waitress sometimes. I used to borrow other people's cars and sit in them across from my dad's gas station whenever he let me know you were having lunch with him, just to see you with him. My dad always made sure you two ate on the picnic bench outside the station whenever he knew I could make the trip. I needed to see for myself that you were okay." Hannah took a deep, shuddering breath.

"Oh, Mom," Sydney said. "I didn't know any of that." She'd started to perspire and her hair was a bright yellow thicket around her shoulders beneath the gray sky.

The heat felt like a hammer on Hannah's neck; she moved to the shady part of the sidewalk and said, "I know, honey." She went to her then and put her arms around Sydney's shoulders.

Sydney dropped her head onto Hannah's shoulder. "I've been so wrong about everything, Mom," she said, her voice muffled.

"Not everything," Hannah said, smiling. "Nobody's ever wrong about everything. That's the good news."

Sydney pulled away. "And the bad news is that we're all wrong about some things, right?"

"Exactly." Hannah gestured at the poster on the window of the bar. "So what's our plan? Should we try the door?"

The pub was open, just a handful of patrons in the dimly lit bar, nursing their morning drinks. Sydney approached the bartender, a man with a shaved head and a tight white V-neck shirt, while Hannah hung back in the shadows.

"Excuse me," she heard Sydney say, edging up to the bar. "I was wondering if you know any of the guys in the Copperheads."

The bartender was drying beer steins; he finished twisting his towel inside one of them and hung it from the rack above the bar before answering. Even from where she stood near the entrance, Hannah could see the man appraising Sydney's shape and long blond hair. Finally he grinned. "Groupie, huh? Lucky them. And lucky you. They'll be here tonight."

"Yes, I know, I saw the poster," Sydney said. "The thing is, I was wondering if you know any of them personally."

He drew his thick brows together over his pug nose. "Like who?"

"I'm looking for Rory." Sydney arched her back a little and dropped her voice. "I met him at one of the gigs, and I'd really love to see him again." She was almost purring. "I think he'd really love to see me, too. Don't you?"

Hannah almost laughed. Her daughter should have been an actress. Maybe that was part of being a good therapist: playing a part so people would confide in you. It certainly worked with the bartender. Within seconds, they were out of the bar and blinking on the street in the bright sunshine, with Sydney waving a slip of paper and saying, "Got it."

Back in the car, Sydney programmed the address into her phone, making disgusted noises about "crappy cell service in freakin' Vermont." The phone apparently picked up enough of a signal to map out their route, though, because the robotic voice immediately directed them over the bridge.

Within two miles, they were deep enough in the hills that the signal dropped again. "Great," Sydney muttered. "Now what?"

Hannah pulled a map out of her purse. "Old-school," she said, laughing at Sydney's expression.

They found Rory's street—a dirt road, according to the broken line on the map—and drove to it without much trouble. There weren't many street signs, but there weren't that many roads, either, and the one time they got turned around, a woman on a mountain bike told them which way to go.

It was raining now, compromising their visibility. Once they were on Rory's road, they overshot his driveway and reached a Y intersection a few miles beyond before realizing it. They turned around and crept back the way they'd come, Sydney's Honda bottoming out a couple of times on the rutted road. Hannah hadn't realized she was clenching her teeth until she bit her tongue and tasted blood.

"This must be it, Mom," Sydney said, peering up a long dirt driveway tunneled over by trees. "What do you think he lives in? A tent?"

"A tent, a yurt, a tree house, a car? Who knows? With Rory, anything's possible."

Hannah felt the excitement of searching for Rory ebbing away, leaving her anxious and dry-mouthed as her daughter edged forward up the driveway, saying, "I hope to hell he doesn't have a gun."

"Rory would never have a gun," Hannah said at once.

"Because of Dad, you mean?"

"Because that's not who Rory is."

By now, they had rounded one corner and were approaching another, the rain coming down so hard that Hannah could barely see the road. "I wonder if he's with someone now," she said, raising her voice to be heard above the sound of rain on the car roof.

"Like a woman, you mean?"

"A woman. Kids. A tribe. Who knows?" Hannah winced at the thought of another woman here, sharing her life with Rory. But why not? It would be unrealistic to expect him not to have formed attachments.

Hannah swallowed past a lump in her throat and squinted through the trees. "I see a building," she said.

The building, it turned out, was a geodesic dome, a brown igloo made of wooden triangles with a deck circling the second floor and a screened porch jutting out one side. It looked as if it had sprung from the earth, fully formed, like a mushroom. A half-dozen mismatched camp chairs sat in front of a fire pit and a tractor was parked to one side of the dome. A green van, fairly new looking, was parked next to the tractor.

"Now what?" Sydney asked. "Do you want me to go to the door with you? Or do you think it's better if you go alone?"

"Alone." Hannah's heart was drumming louder than the falling rain.

She got out of the car and jumped over a series of puddles to the front door, which was thankfully protected by the deck overhang. A vegetable garden was planted to one side of the house. The door was painted teal blue; there was no bell, just a hand-forged black iron knocker shaped like a guitar. She knocked it against the door, her throat scratchy and sore because she'd been breathing through her mouth. When nobody answered, she did it again.

She had never considered how she'd feel if Rory wasn't here.

A third time she knocked, but less vigorously, knowing it was pointless. She turned away and shrugged in Sydney's direction just as the door opened behind her.

She spun around and was face-to-face with Rory. Older, yes, the creases deep around his eyes and mouth, his auburn hair still long enough to tie in a ponytail but streaked with gray, his body slightly broader but still the same, tall and strong, the legs encased, as hers were, in old blue jeans. She took all of this in as he kept his eyes on her, his hazel eyes unwavering, waiting for whatever she had come to say.

She said nothing. She couldn't. Hannah punched him as hard as she could in the chest and then wheeled away, weeping, running for the car, where Sydney was sitting and watching, openmouthed with shock.

The rain was still falling hard, streaming down her back. "Goddamn you!" Hannah shouted as she felt Rory's strong hand on her arm, preventing her from getting into the car. "Let go of me!"

"Come inside!" he shouted over the rain. "Who's in the car? Is that Sydney? My God. Sydney!"

"Let me go!" Hannah shouted, amazed by her own temptation to sink her teeth into this man's arm, to gnaw her way to freedom like some crazed fox in a trap.

"I'm not letting you leave!" Rory said. "Get inside, both of you!"

Sydney shook her head, and slowly began driving away.

"You can't leave me here!" Hannah cried out, furious at her daughter's sudden betrayal, then realized: Sydney had brought her here because Hannah needed answers from Rory even more than Sydney did.

Now Sydney stuck her head out the window as she circled around in front of the house, aiming for the driveway. "I'll be back in a few hours!" she yelled. "Don't kill each other!" Then she was gone.

"Goddamn you to hell!" Hannah shrieked, though whether she was cursing Rory, Allen, Sydney, or herself, she couldn't have said.

Rory put his arm around her waist and led her inside, Hannah keeping enough distance between them that her hip and thigh wouldn't brush against his.

The house was much larger than she'd thought it would be, the vaulted ceiling rising up over twenty feet. The enormous hexagonal windows were streaked with rain but filled the house with light. It was like being inside a tree house. Cream-colored Berber rugs, a brown leather sectional sofa, a hand-thrown pottery vase: Hannah took in these details as she silently dried herself with a towel Rory handed her that had been hanging from a hook near the door. He did the same, using the towel when she was finished.

"You bastard," she said. "How could you do this to me?"

He didn't ask what she meant by "this." She could see it in his eyes, deeper brown now with sorrow, that Rory knew everything: how she had felt when he left the farm, how she'd mourned his death, the betrayal she'd experienced when she discovered he was alive but hadn't told her.

"I would say I was sorry—and I am—but that wouldn't cover it," he said. "Inadequate."

"Yes."

"Do you want a drink? Coffee?"

"A drink in some coffee. Whiskey."

"You got it."

Rory went around to the other side of the wooden counter separating the galley kitchen from the living area. Hannah crossed the living room to the leather sofa, but was too agitated to sit down.

Instead, she paced the room, her fury keeping her upright. There were several guitars on stands, as well as a banjo and a mandolin. An electric keyboard dominated the only flat wall. The wide windowsills below each triangular window served as display shelves for objects that she at first thought were pottery, but were actually carved from stone: dishes, a vase, a statue. There was something so familiar about them. She wondered if Rory had made them and remembered a high school art class they'd taken together, where his sculptures were good enough for the teacher to send into a Boston exhibit of student work.

Rory returned a few minutes later with a tray. On it were a pot of hot coffee, a bottle of whiskey, and two cups. "I'd let you pour your own, except I'm afraid you'd throw coffee in my face," he said, setting the tray down on the pine coffee table in front of the sofa.

"You'd deserve it."

He gave her a solemn look as he handed her a cup of coffee. "I know. Say when."

She waited until he'd poured about two shots of whiskey into the coffee. "That's a start," she said, and held up a hand.

They sat at opposite ends of the sofa, the rain slamming against the enormous windows. "Did you build this house?" she asked. "I remember you always wanted one."

He nodded. "I got a kit from Montana. The guys in my band helped."

"It's a lot bigger than Thoreau's cabin."

"More heat efficient, anyway."

Their conversation stuttered along like that for several minutes as Hannah gathered her wits and felt the whiskey relax her spine, her knees.

She'd missed drinking whiskey. This was probably a mistake, drinking it with Rory. But if ever there was a time for whiskey in her life, this was it.

They each had two cups of coffee, though Hannah stopped him from pouring more than a single shot of whiskey into her second cup. By then she was almost dry, except for her hair, which she'd taken out of its braid to let dry. She started to gather it up and braid it again, but Rory shook his head.

"Leave it," he said. "I've missed your hair."

"My *hair*?" she said, furious again. "That's all you've missed? My *hair*?"

She tried to slap him, but Rory grabbed her wrist. "Easy, Gypsy Girl," he murmured.

And that was all it took. Her defenses, as impenetrable as she'd thought they were, shored up over decades of grief, collapsed the minute she heard Rory call her by the nickname he'd given her in high school. "Why?" she said past the knot in her throat. "I don't understand. Why didn't you let me know you were alive?"

"My mother made it clear you didn't want to see me."

"What are you talking about?"

"Your letters. She showed me your letters."

"Rory, I sent lots of letters to your mom's house, and not one of them ever said I didn't want to see you. I was dying without you!" Mortified, Hannah covered her mouth.

Rory was shaking his head. "Well, she showed me three of your letters. They spelled out all of the reasons you didn't want to see me after my mother told you I was in Canada. Mainly, you didn't want to see me because it would dishonor Allen's memory, and you wanted me to respect that."

"What?" Hannah finished her coffee and set it down on the table, feeling sick to her stomach, contemplating the only explanation that made sense. "Rory, those letters were fake! They had to be forgeries."

"No, I know they were yours," he said. "Your handwriting was on the envelopes, and the postmarks were—"

But Hannah shook her head so hard that her hair whipped about her shoulders. "My handwriting was on the envelopes but not the letters?"

"Yes. The letters were typed," he said, frowning. "Why?"

"Oh my God! Your mother had letters from me to you, that's true, but, Rory, she returned them to me by the shoe box full! I wrote to you every day, and she sent every one of those letters back to me! She must have kept some of the envelopes and typed up false letters to put inside them. I never typed my letters. I just wrote them out on whatever paper I had handy in the kitchen. You *know* that about me. And you know *me*!"

His face paled as he grasped what she was saying. "I thought I did. But I'd lost faith. In you. In us. In everything." Rory reached for her then. She saw his hand lift off the couch, hesitate, then take her hair between his fingers, tugging it until she slid over beside him on the couch, the rain still hammering in her head, the whiskey burning her throat and nose. Rory pressed his head against hers, hard enough that she had to close her eyes and press back, something else they used to do in high school, a signal: *I need you.*

"I'm sorry I went away, but I couldn't stay," he whispered.

"Why not?" she said, feeling every inch of Rory against her own body, their bodies still damp but warming each other now.

"Because of Allen."

"Tell me," she said, though she wondered if she'd even spoken those words aloud. Did she really want to know? It had to have been something dreadful, for Rory to leave her.

It didn't matter whether she wanted to know or not, or whether she'd spoken the words. Rory began telling her all of it, his voice soft but as insistent as the rain: the night he died, Theo had come to him, ready to fight, had stolen a knife from Rory and gone after him, until Rory pinned him with one knee to his chest and said, "It wasn't me, Theo. I was never with your mother."

Theo had run down to the lake looking for Allen. Rory thought about going after him, but he was bleeding hard, and then Valerie had come to find him, wanting a gun. Rory wouldn't tell her where the rat rifle was kept, afraid for her to use a gun with those two Israeli boys, hardly more than teenagers themselves.

Valerie argued for a few minutes, but eventually left. He thought again of going after Theo, despite feeling like he was going to pass out from the pain of the knife wounds. He started to put on his shoes anyway, but then Hannah had come to him after her fight with Allen. The next morning Theo was dead.

"That's all you know?" Hannah moved off the couch to sit cross-legged on the floor, determined to think clearly—something she couldn't do with Rory so close.

"No," Rory said, his voice still low, but urgent now. "The day he killed himself, Allen told me what happened with Theo."

"Tell me," Hannah said through lips so dry now that it felt as if the corners of them were cracked, as if she'd been stranded in the desert instead of running across Rory's muddy Vermont yard in the rain.

"After you and Allen fought that night, he went out in the boat, the way he sometimes did to think," Rory said. "He wanted to honor your marriage and ask Lucy to leave Haven Lake, but he was afraid for her, because of her husband. He didn't know what to do."

Rory waited until she nodded to continue. "Allen said he'd rowed out to the island and was just sitting in the boat when he heard something splash in the water and felt it start rocking. It was raining that night, remember? But Theo must have swum out to the boat from the dock, and Allen didn't realize what was happening because there was so much noise from the rainstorm. Allen said he got scared, having one of his waking dreams like he called them, hearing what he realized later was thunder, and thinking there was shelling going on, planes overhead, something to do with the war. And then he felt the boat rock and there was the enemy, coming up over the side of the boat to ambush him, only it wasn't the enemy, Hannah—it was Theo, poor kid, Theo coming up over the boat, that knife in his hands, going after Allen, and Allen hit him with an oar the way he would an enemy, 'that crazy-eyed gook,' he called Theo, but then he was ashamed, Hannah, because as soon as it was over, Allen knew. He knew."

"But he never told anyone," Hannah said desperately, wanting to raise her hand to stop Rory's torrent of words, but she couldn't: she had to know the truth. She thought about the fire she'd set, the incredible feeling of power as she lit the match to the kerosene she'd poured around the foundation of the small barn, how determined she was to destroy all of Allen's belongings and everything Allen was. All the hurt he'd inflicted on himself, on her, on Sydney, as well as all the pain and darkness he carried inside, from his father and the war.

But what good had her act of destruction been? Hannah had known right away that the fire was a mistake, and she'd raised her hands then, too, shielding her face from the flames, wishing she could put the fire out. But it was too late. The fire raged through the ancient structure until nothing was left of it, and of her marriage, but charred bits of timber and ash.

"He only told me," Rory said. "Allen came to me and said he'd murdered a boy, just like he'd murdered a boy in Vietnam, a little kid with a grenade, but still, he'd shot that kid to save himself and the guys with him, but even so, a little kid, Hannah. Allen said he shot a little kid and never forgave himself for that. Then Theo was dead because of him, too, and it was too much for him to handle."

"So he shot himself," Hannah said numbly, because of course Allen would have done that: every day, he'd been walking along that precipice of sanity, expecting a hand to shove him over the edge.

They sat for a few minutes in silence, the rain lessening now. Hannah uncrossed her legs slowly and stood up. She went to Rory, sat down beside him, and put her head on his shoulder. She pressed close and heard Rory's heart beating beneath his thin blue work shirt, a man's heart still beating strong in his chest despite the horror of what he'd been carrying all these years, the knowledge of what his brother had done and why he had killed himself, and the belief that the woman he loved had stopped loving him.

"Why didn't you tell me?" she said.

"I couldn't, don't you see? Allen didn't want you to ever know any of this. Because of Sydney, too. He didn't want you to know your husband, her father, was a murderer. He made me promise not to tell you. I told the police, but they said there was no way to prove any of this had happened. Too many days had gone by and of course there was no evidence of anything but Theo drowning with a gash on his head. Nothing to link Allen to Theo's death. One cop accused me of being the one to kill Theo, said I was making it up to get myself off the hook, so they investigated me all over again. But like he said, there was no evidence. They had to let me go."

"Does Lucy know?"

"Yes. I told her, too. But she felt responsible already, guilty because, however it happened, she felt she was the one who made it happen, because of what was going on in her own life, with her and Allen and her marriage," Rory said. "She didn't want to tell Valerie any of this, and I promised her I wouldn't, either. Lucy's in California now."

"I know. Sydney told me." Hannah felt as if she'd run a marathon, maybe, or swum the English Channel; she sat up, her head woozy from the whiskey, her side damp from the rain, still, and felt immediately chilled when she wasn't pressed against Rory. "But why didn't you tell *me*? I would have wanted to know."

"Allen asked me not to, Hannah," he repeated. "He thought he'd put you and Sydney through enough, the way he was. And after he died, what would have been the point? A life for a life, is what he would have said. So nobody knows but Lucy and the cops. And now you."

"Your mother?"

Rory shook his head. "I figured that when you were ready, you'd come looking for me, but you never did."

"Except that I did. I wrote to you. You have to believe me, Rory," she whispered.

"I do." He kissed her fingers. "I'm so sorry."

"Where were you, all this time? Between California and here, I mean."

He told her all of that, too, in shorthand: about the sudden decision to leave his car and hitch north from San Francisco to Vancouver, about riding the train across Canada and playing music in Toronto and Montreal and even Newfoundland. He'd married once, had another relationship for seven years, then gave up on love. He'd come home then.

"I was too far from you for too long," he said, "but I kept an eye on you. Even though my mother had given me those letters saying you wanted me to stay away, I left you messages."

"What do you mean? I never got any messages."

Rory stood up, and immediately she felt his absence as if he'd literally been ripped apart from her; she shivered and watched him cross the room as he opened the drawer of an antique pine hutch.

He came back, smiling down at her, and held out his hand. In Rory's palm lay a heart-shaped stone.

"Oh," she said, and touched the smooth granite with her fingers. "You idiot," she said, and started to cry, taking the rock from him and rubbing it between her fingers.

"Hush." Rory sat down beside her, pulling Hannah onto his lap again, this time cradling her in his strong arms, his lips to hers, securing her tightly against his body, in the world, all of it beyond them and behind them now but the love, which had been there all along, and would endure.

EPILOGUE

A stupid ritual, Sydney thought, and yet she had driven out to Haven Lake anyway, knowing she wouldn't want to miss it. Marco had wanted to come, but she wouldn't let him.

"Family only," she said, but she'd lingered in his arms this morning, letting him tangle his fingers in her hair and make love to her one more time, so that she had to rush to get dressed in the end, slipping into a skirt and T-shirt and sandals, her hair flying loose behind her as she drove with the windows open, singing to the radio, the sunset starting to stain the horizon pink.

By the time she arrived at Haven Lake, the late afternoon sun was poppy orange above them, the hills of the Berkshires a bright, hopeful summer green between the spears of dark pine trees. Dylan was sitting on the dock. He stood up and greeted Sydney with a hug; then they sat down together.

"I hope this is the right thing," he said.

"It is," she said, though she didn't know that for sure.

"I've been watching the fish," he said, "and thinking about this thing I read by Michio Kaku."

"Who the heck is that?"

"A physicist. The cofounder of string theory. Kaku's kind of like Einstein, trying to come up with some grand theory of the universe."

"Okay, if you say so." Sydney slipped off her sandals and dangled her feet in the water, laughing as a school of sunfish swam by and one pecked at her toes. "Here come your fish."

"Yeah, I feed them sometimes," he confessed. "Anyway, I was thinking that we're kind of like those fish, you know, swimming in our own tiny universe without knowing anything about the invisible dimensions beyond 3-D, just like they can't see the lily pads or anything that goes on up here above their pond universe. It was making me wonder how many dimensions there really are."

"Whatever dimension you're in is the one I want to be in, too."

It was dusk, the fireflies just beginning to wink in the fields, bullfrogs croaking in the shallows. Sydney asked if his dad had talked to him about the wedding being off, and Dylan nodded. "I think that's better for both of you," he said.

"Why?" Sydney was startled.

"My dad isn't ready to love somebody else," Dylan said. "You are."

"But you and I will stay friends, right? I hope you know that."

"Of course."

"And you're doing okay out here? Your dad said you're staying a week this time, while he does his bike race up in Vermont."

"I'm fine," Dylan said, bumping his shoulder against hers. "Happy," he amended. "I feel useful here. Your mom and I get along. And Rory's cool. He's teaching me to play guitar." He patted her hand, as if Sydney were the child who needed reassurance. "You'll be fine, too."

"Yes," she said. "I know that now."

They talked for a while longer. It was nearly dark by the time Hannah came down the hill with a cardboard box in her arms. Sydney and Dylan got up to stand with her on the beach as the red sun ducked behind the tallest mountain, leaving the valley suddenly deep in shadow. Hannah explained what they were going to do, and in a few minutes they were lining up the three boats she'd built of twigs and setting paper lanterns in each of them, red and yellow and orange. Sydney, Hannah, and Dylan each lit one of the lanterns. Hannah said a few words, then encouraged them each to say something to the people they'd loved and lost: Theo, Allen, Amanda.

Hannah had chosen this night because of the full moon, which was rising behind them as fast as the sun had fallen, casting a pearly light over the trees and the grass and their own bodies and onto the water, where the boats with their colored lights were bobbing gently on Haven Lake among the frogs and fish splashes.

Sydney squeezed Dylan's hand, feeling her own soul rise up at this moment. A dance of the soul marked by moonlight and prayers. She felt her father and Theo watching over them, and Amanda, too, present in this moment with her son, who stood next to Sydney and held her hand, the two of them watching the ripples in the pond, which might have been fish or just their imaginations.

The air was alight with souls, none of them really gone after all.

ACKNOWLEDGMENTS

People say that writing is a solitary pursuit. While it's true that writers spend many solo hours wrangling sentences into place, it's also true that no writer could ever publish books without helping hands.

I'm extremely lucky to have a home team that is noisy, supportive, and unconditionally loving. My mother taught me early on that books are essential food for the soul. My husband, Dan, keeps the home fires burning when I'm deep into writing a book and forget things like the groceries, and he cheers me on even when I am positive a book will defeat me. My children all inspire me by following their various passions and putting up with a mother who is occasionally very, very distracted.

My brother Donald and his family—Jean, Emily, and Jill—cheer me on from their home in England, while my brother Philip makes music in Ithaca and is constantly urging his friends to buy his sister's books.

My terrific in-laws, David and Christine, as well as my wonderful cousins, Barbara and John Boyle and the Shipley clan, have joined forces with my Ohio family to support my writing, enthusiastically cheering me on from all corners of the country. Whenever I have doubts, all I have to do is visit family to feel strong and brave again.

My agent, Richard Parks, a steadfast friend and adviser who has stuck with me for over two decades, is by now my family as well. He continues to buoy me up if my spirits sag, but never fails to critique and poke holes in my writing until it holds water.

At New American Library, I'm blessed to have a fantastic team supporting the production of my books. Special thanks to my wise and compassionate editor, Tracy Bernstein, who is still the smartest woman I know. I am grateful as well to New American Library publisher, Kara Welsh. I am also grateful to the publicity and marketing teams, and to copy editor Michele Alpern, who caught more chronology and grammar issues than I thought possible to make in a single book. The art department captured the essence of *Haven Lake* in a beautiful image and has my eternal thanks. *Haven Lake* is the best book it can be because of having so many brilliant, energetic people in my corner.

While researching what it's like to raise sheep, I was very lucky to connect with Wendy Ketchum, who introduced me to her Icelandic sheep at Schoolhouse Farm in Tamworth, New Hampshire. She generously showed me around her farm and shared resources both in book form and online, even reading the book in manuscript form. I am also grateful to Catherine Friend, author of one of my favorite books about being a shepherdess, *Sheepish: Two Women, Fifty Sheep & Enough Wool to Save the Planet*. Her book provided me with great factual information and the idea for one particularly hilarious scene. If you've ever thought about raising sheep, I'd highly recommend her books. There may still be errors here regarding the life of a shepherdess, but if so, they are all mine. I also want to give a heartfelt thanks to my dear friend Phoebe Adams, whose work as an educational psychologist is some of the most important service to children anyone can do. She inspired Sydney's character in *Haven Lake*.

In my writing community, I could name enough helpful people to fill another novel. To Toby Neal, Susan Straight, and Emily Ferrara: our retreats to Prince Edward Island, California, and Maine made it possible for me to write this book. Thank you for being there, always. I couldn't do this without your friendship.

Other writers and editors have also been instrumental in helping me shape my writing. A special shout-out to Elisabeth Brink, Maddie Dawson, Diane Debrovner, Elisabeth Elo, Lorraine Glennon, Terri Giuliano Long, Kate Kelly, Amy Sue Nathan, Jay Neugeboren, Carla Panciera, Sandi Kahn Shelton, Denise Silvestro, Kim Suarez, Ginnie Smith, and Melanie Wold. I have learned from each and every one of you.

Finally, I want to say a sincere thank-you to bookstore owners everywhere—especially to Sue Little, whose Jabberwocky Bookshop has been my home away from home for many years—and to all of the readers who have so generously read, reviewed, and supported my writing.

Because of all of you, I'm living my dream.

CONVERSATION GUIDE

HAVEN LAKE

HOLLY ROBINSON

This Conversation Guide is intended to enrich the individual reading experience, as well as encourage us to explore these topics together—because books, and life, are meant for sharing.

A CONVERSATION WITH HOLLY ROBINSON

Q. What gave you the original story idea for Haven Lake*?*

A. Last year, I had the honor of participating in the annual Newburyport Literary Festival, where one of the events was a conversation between the writers Ann Hood and Andre Dubus III. At one point, Ann admitted that her mind is like "that thing in the dryer that collects lint," and I had to laugh, because I know exactly what she means. My mind collects family stories, overheard gossip in restaurants, bits of novels and newspaper articles, paintings I've seen in museums, etc. Every now and then, I pluck through the brain fluff to see if there's anything valuable. *Haven Lake* was inspired by a story my mother told me about a boy drowning while her parents were running a lakeside summer camp for kids. A sudden death—especially when it involves a child—transforms lives in unexpected ways, and I wanted to write about that.

Q. Although this novel isn't about the Vietnam War, the war serves as an important backdrop. Why did you choose to write about Vietnam?

A. When I was in middle school, my father was stationed at Fort Leavenworth, Kansas, during a time when soldiers were being trained there for combat in Vietnam. I passed those soldiers doing drills on the parade grounds every day to and from school. The older brother of my best friend was killed in Vietnam. Later, when we moved to Massachusetts, I dated a young folk musician who was a Vietnam vet suffering from PTSD. Shortly after we lost touch, he committed suicide. So the war impacted me a great deal personally, as it did many people.

Q. This is your third novel. How has your approach to writing fiction changed with each book?

A. I wish I could say it gets easier over time, but it doesn't. The main difference between my first novel, *The Wishing Hill*, and the next two, *Beach Plum Island* and *Haven Lake*, is that I wrote the entire draft of *The Wishing Hill* to submit for publication, because I didn't have a publisher at that time. I was lucky enough to be taken on by New American Library, where my brilliant editor, Tracy Bernstein, pushes me to write better fiction. Once you publish your first book, most writers then sell their next books on the basis of a synopsis. This sounds like it should make writing easier, since a synopsis requires you to plot out a book in advance, but it's a tricky process. Trying to summarize an entire novel in a few pages makes the project sound both dumb and impossible to pull off. And, even with this handy blueprint, you still have to come up with voices, imagery, emotions, and settings—always a mysterious creative process. There is a point about two-thirds through every book where I'm absolutely certain that I will fail. It takes a lot of willpower and chocolate to get me through that crisis in confidence.

Q. In your novels, women almost always have careers. In this one, for instance, Hannah is raising sheep and Sydney is an educational psychologist. Have you had experience doing either of those things?

A. Absolutely not! But I think it's essential for characters in novels to do something other than be writers and professors, since that's not the sort of thing most people do. Besides, I've done those jobs, so there wouldn't be much novelty for me in writing about them. I typically give my characters jobs that I wish I could have. For instance, in *Beach Plum Island*, I made Ava a potter because I've done a lot of pottery as a hobby, and I'd love to make a living at it. In *Haven Lake*, I decided to make Hannah a shepherdess because I've always wanted to raise sheep, and I'm a knitter. I researched what it was like to raise sheep by reading and visiting a sheep farm in New Hampshire. Sydney's job is actually the job one of my best friends does, and she often tells me about her work.

Q. Your novels all feature alternative family structures, such as adopted children, stepfamilies, blended families, and gay marriages. Is this deliberate?

A. Yes and no. There are many more varied, accepted types of family structures than ever before, and I think that's a great thing. To write novels where all of the characters are in so-called nuclear families—a mom and dad plus their biological children—wouldn't truly reflect our culture. A family is created through respect, love, and caretaking, not necessarily through bloodlines. I married my second husband when our children—a boy and a girl from each side—were six, seven, eight, and nine years old. We then added another child of our own two years later, which gave us the "yours, mine, and ours" sort of blended family. It has been a happy experience for us, but not without struggles along the way; there are challenges unique to navigating two distinct family cultures. I love writing about all types of families, because I think it gives readers hope that every family has the potential to be a loving one.

QUESTIONS FOR DISCUSSION

1. Vietnam serves as an important backdrop for *Haven Lake*, affecting the lives of many of the characters. What is your understanding or experience of the war?

2. When Allen and Hannah leave college, they start an organic farm and become early members of the WWOOFing community. This is an extremely popular movement today. Had you ever heard of World Wide Opportunities on Organic Farms before reading this book? Can you imagine traveling around the world and working on farms in the way the residents of Haven Lake did?

3. Dylan is a troubled teen who has lost his mother. Many of the events in his life have led him to try to control the one thing he can: how much he eats. Have you encountered anyone in your life with anorexia or another eating disorder?

4. Gary is keen on Dylan spending less time on video games. For Dylan, video gaming is a way for him to connect socially and relax. What's your view on video games? Do you feel like they prepare young people with the computer skills they need, or are these games an unhealthy addiction?

5. Both Hannah and her daughter, Sydney, are torn between two men: Hannah between Allen and Rory, and Sydney between Gary and Marco. Why do they experience these conflicts? Do you think they followed the right paths in their personal relationships?

6. Hannah lives nearly off the grid, growing her own food and spending little time watching television or using the computer and her cell phone. Do you think it would be better if more of us spent time unplugged? Have you ever tried doing it? What was the result?

7. In some ways, the ending of *Haven Lake* is left open. What do you imagine happening to the characters as they go on with their lives from here?

Holly Robinson is a ghostwriter and journalist whose work appears regularly in national venues such as *Better Homes and Gardens*, Huffington Post, *More*, Open Salon, and *Parents*. She is the author of *The Gerbil Farmer's Daughter: A Memoir* and two other NAL Accent novels, *The Wishing Hill* and *Beach Plum Island*. She holds a BA in biology from Clark University and an MFA in creative writing from the University of Massachusetts, Amherst.

CONNECT ONLINE

---

authorhollyrobinson.com